LYRICS ON THE WIND

Lost Kings MC #17

AUTUMN JONES LAKE

COPYRIGHT

Photographer: Wander Aguiar Photography
Cover Designer: Shanoff Designs
Model: Jeff Button
Digital ISBN# 978-1-943850-61-4
Print ISBN #978-1-943950-66-9
Edited by: Creating Ink
Proof Read by: Julie B.

ABOUT LYRICS ON THE WIND

Feelings were a weakness I couldn't afford.
Until Shelby crept under my skin.
Then I fell and I fell hard.
Her touch has branded me to the bone.
She's taught me love has no boundaries.
I've always lived for danger.
But this time, the stakes are too high.
Her lyrics on the wind are calling my name.
No matter where this road takes me, my ruthless MC brothers have my back.
With their blessing, I'll seek, destroy, and ultimately deliver justice.

Lyrics on the Wind is the second part of Rooster and Shelby's story. Rhythm of the Road should be read first.

ALSO BY AUTUMN JONES LAKE

THE LOST KINGS MC™ SERIES

Slow Burn (Lost Kings MC #1)
Corrupting Cinderella (Lost Kings MC #2)
Three Kings, One Night (Lost Kings MC #2.5)
Strength From Loyalty (Lost Kings MC #3)
Tattered on My Sleeve (Lost Kings MC #4)
White Heat (Lost Kings MC #5)
Between Embers (Lost Kings MC #5.5)
More Than Miles (Lost Kings MC #6)
White Knuckles (Lost Kings MC #7)
Beyond Reckless (Lost Kings MC #8)
Beyond Reason (Lost Kings MC #9)
One Empire Night (Lost Kings MC #9.5)
After Burn (Lost Kings MC #10)
After Glow (Lost Kings MC #11)
Zero Hour (Lost Kings MC #11.5)
Zero Tolerance (Lost Kings MC #12)
Zero Regret (Lost Kings MC #13)
Zero Apologies (Lost Kings MC #14)

Swagger and Sass (Lost Kings MC #14.5)
White Lies (Lost Kings MC #15)
Rhythm of the Road (Lost Kings MC #16)
Lyrics on the Wind (Lost Kings MC #17)
Diamond in the Dust (Lost Kings MC #18)
Crown of Ghosts (Lost Kings MC #19)

Standalones in the Lost Kings MC World

The Hollywood Demons Series

Kickstart My Heart
Blow My Fuse
Wheels of Fire

Bullets & Bonfires
Warnings & Wildfires
Cards of Love: Knight of Swords

Paranormal Romance

Catnip & Cauldrons
Onyx Night
Onyx Shadows
Feral Escape

DEDICATION

Use the winds of turmoil to explore a new direction.

GLOSSARY OF CHARACTERS AND TERMINOLOGY

The Lost Kings MC™ World © Autumn Jones Lake

The series has had some shakeups in the last few books. I've updated the glossary to reflect this. *It may contain spoilers* if you are not caught up on the series or have skipped books! If you're brand new to the series—welcome! This guide might be handy. If you've been part of the LOKI family for a while—welcome back! The info might help refresh your memory.

New characters were introduced in *Rhythm of the Road* and I have tried to include them here.

Please note, this glossary only pertains to *my* romantic fictionalized motorcycle club world. It should not be construed as applicable to any other fictional club or a real-life motorcycle club.

THE LOST KINGS MC: UPSTATE, NY ("EMPIRE," NY)

President: Rochlan "Rock" North. Leader of the Upstate NY charter of the Lost Kings MC.
Sergeant-at-Arms: Wyatt "Wrath" Ramsey. Protector or enforcer for the club.

Vice President: Blake "Murphy" O'Callaghan. Murphy was the road captain up until *White Lies (Lost Kings MC #15)*
Treasurer: Marcel "Teller" Whelan. Handles the money and investments for the club.
Road Captain: Dixon "Dex" Watts (newly appointed to the position in *White Lies*)

THE LOST KINGS MC: DOWNSTATE, NY ("UNION" NY)

President: Angus "Zero" or "Z" Frazier. As of *Zero Apologies (Lost Kings MC #14),* Z is the president of the Downstate, NY charter of the Lost Kings MC.
Vice President: Logan "Rooster" Randall
Sergeant-at-Arms: Steer
Treasurer: Hustler
Road Captain: Jensen "Jigsaw" Kilgore

THE LOST KINGS MC: VIRGINIA (PORT EVERHART, VA)

President: Cypress "Ice" Caldwell
Vice President: Farmer
Sergeant-at-Arms: Pants
Treasurer: T-Bone
Road Captain: Wings

OTHER LOST KINGS MC MEMBERS

Grinder: Rock's mentor. Grinder is an older member who we met briefly in *Corrupting Cinderella* and have seen or heard about a few other times throughout the series. He's been incarcerated since right before Rock took over the Lost Kings MC.
Cronin "Sparky" Petek: Sparky is the mad genius/hippie stoner behind the Lost Kings MC's pot-growing business. He is rarely seen outside of

the basement, as he prefers the company of his plants.

Elias "Bricks" Serrano: We have seen Bricks and his girlfriend Winter throughout the series. He's one of the few members who does not live at the clubhouse.

Sam "Stash" Black: Lives in the basement with Sparky and helps with the plants.

Thomas "Ravage" Kane: We've gotten to know Rav and his snarky humor a little bit better in each book. Ravage is a general member who helps out wherever he is needed.

Sway: Former president of the downstate charter of the Lost Kings MC. We've seen Sway and his wife Tawny off and on in the series since *Strength From Loyalty,* usually annoying Rock in some fashion.

Hoot: We've seen glimpses of him since *Slow Burn* when he was a lowly prospect. He finally got his full patch, but still gets a lot of the grunt work.

Birch: We also met him as a prospect. He's been voted as a full-patch member but shares in a lot of the grunt work with Hoot.

Priest: The Lost Kings MC's national president. We first met him and his wife, Valentina, in *After Burn.*

Malik: Soon-to-be prospect for the Lost Kings MC. Helps out at Crystal Ball. Owns the Lucky Duck pawnshop in Ironworks.

THE LADIES OF THE LOST KINGS MC

Hope Kendall North, Esq.: Nicknamed *First Lady* by Murphy in *Corrupting Cinderella (Lost Kings MC #2),* Hope is the object of Rock's love and obsession. Their daughter is named Grace after Rock's mother.

Trinity Hurst Ramsey: Wrath's angel. Former caretaker of the club. She now has her own photography and graphic design business. She is married to Wrath, fiercely loyal to the club, and best friends with Hope.

Heidi "Little Hammer" O'Callaghan: Murphy's wife and Teller's little sister. Heidi just graduated from college and works at Empire Med. Murphy officially adopted her daughter, Alexa Jade.

Charlotte Clark, Esq: Teller's sunshine. Often credited with taming the brooding treasurer of the Lost Kings, Teller.

Lilly Frazier: Z's brave and devoted siren. The new queen of the Lost

Kings MC's downstate charter. One of Hope's best friends. Z and Lilly's son is named Chance.
Shelby Morgan: Rooster's sassy little chickadee. Country music singer from Texas. We first met Shelby in *Swagger and Sass.*
Swan: Lost Kings MC club girl and dancer at Crystal Ball. Swan has found a new calling as the yoga teacher for the old ladies of the Lost Kings MC and is slowly moving away from dancing at Crystal Ball.
Willow: Bartender at Crystal Ball, but once or twice we've caught her sneaking in or out of the basement with Sparky.
Serena: Former downstate club girl, still a little broken-hearted over Murphy. Abused by Shadow, the former VP of the downstate charter. We have not seen her since *Zero Regret.*
Tawny: Sway's ol' lady. The former "Queen B" of the downstate charter of the Lost Kings MC.
Stella: Pornographic film actress. The downstate charter is the sole investor in her production company. Ex-girlfriend of Z. Current...*something* of Sway. Her *Sex in Every City* series sometimes requires members of LOKI to work as bouncers on her film sets.
Anya Regal: Porn princess of the Lost Kings MC, Virginia charter.
Shonda: Club girl from the Lost Kings, MC Virginia charter.

OTHER RECURRING CHARACTERS RELEVANT TO THIS STORY

Russell "Chaser" Adams: President of the Devil Demons MC in Western NY. (*The Hollywood Demons* series contains his story.)
Mallory "Little Dove" DeLova-Adams: Chaser's wife. Daughter of mafia boss Anatoly DeLova.
Linden "Stump" Adams: Chaser's father. Former president of the Devil Demons MC.
Anatoly DeLova: Mallory's father. Leader of Russian mafia. Sometime business associate of the Lost Kings MC.
Carter Clark: Charlotte's goofy, often inappropriate, younger brother.
Remington "Ruthless" Holt: Owns "The Castle" with his best friend, Griff. It's an underground fighting ring Murphy used to participate in. We've seen him most recently in *White Lies*. Caretaker of his younger

sister, Molly. Considering forming a support club to the Lost Kings MC with Griff, Eraser, and Vapor.
Griffin "Stonewall" Royal: Remy's best friend and business partner.
Lynn Morgan: Shelby's mother.
Eraser: Owns Zips, a racetrack near the Lost Kings MC territory. Married to Ella.
Roman "Vapor" Hawkins: The book *Cards of Love: Knight of Swords* is his story. We first met him and his wife, Juliet, in *After Burn.*
Jake Wallace: One of Wrath's business partners in Furious Fitness. Jake has appeared off and on throughout the series since *Tattered on my Sleeve.* He sometimes holds self-defense classes for the ladies.
Sullivan Wallace: Jake's brother, and the owner of Strike Back Fitness. He's a significant character in *Bullets and Bonfires* and has his own book, *Warnings and Wildfires.*
Loco: Business associate of the Lost Kings MC. He covers the Ironworks area of the Lost Kings MC's territory. He has appeared throughout the series and become a strong LOKI ally.

OTHER MCS: FRIENDLY CLUBS:

Devil Demons MC: Based in Western NY. Long-time friend of the Lost Kings MC. Their clubs are intertwined and share a lot of history. More of this is explored in the *Hollywood Demons* series.
Wolf Knights MC: Mostly an ally of the Lost Kings. Runs Slater County but has had a number of shake-ups in the last few years. Whisper is their current president. Claimed to be dissolving their charter and turning Slater County over to the Lost Kings but we haven't seen them fully exit the area yet.
Iron Bulls MC (From the *Iron Bulls MC* series by Phoenyx Slaughter): Southwestern outlaw club. Meets up and does business with LOKI once in a while.
Savage Dragons MC (From the *Iron Bulls MC* series by Phoenyx Slaughter): Texas outlaw club.

ENEMY CLUBS:

Vipers MC: Used to run Ironworks until the Lost Kings took over that territory. Still active in other parts of the country.
South of Satan MC: Vermont MC who has stirred up trouble for LOKI in the past.

LOST KINGS MC TERMINOLOGY

LOKI: Short for LOst KIngs
War room: Where the Lost Kings hold "church."
Property patch: When a member takes a woman as his old lady (wife status), he gives her a vest with a property patch. In my series, the vest has a "Property of Lost Kings MC" patch and the member's road name on the back. The officers also place their patches on the ol' lady's vest as a sign that they always have her back. Her man's patch or club symbol is placed over the heart. Rock's patch is a crown. Wrath's is a star. Murphy's is a four-leaf clover. Teller's is a dollar sign. Z's is the letter Z. Rooster's is a rooster wearing a crown. As a joke, Wrath gave Rock and Hope a "product of" patch for baby Grace. Maybe it will catch on as more kids are born into the club? We'll see.

PLACES IN THE LOST KINGS MC WORLD

I use a mix of real and imaginary names to describe the places in my series. Again, I bend and shape geography to my needs as this is a *fictional world that I have created.*

Empire, NY: The territory run by the Lost Kings MC upstate charter. This is a fictional version of Albany, NY, the capital of New York State. Many of the Lost Kings MC's businesses are located in and around Empire.
Slater, NY: Loosely based on Schenectady County. Until recently it was the Wolf Knights MC's territory.

Ironworks, NY: Loosely based on Rensselaer County (Troy, NY). In the beginning of the series, it was run by the Vipers MC. It is now considered territory of the Lost Kings MC.
Union, NY: A fictional area two hours south of Empire, NY, where the "downstate" charter is located.
Crystal Ball: The strip club owned by the Lost Kings MC and one of their legitimate businesses. They often refer to it simply as "CB." Located in Empire County.
Furious Fitness: The gym Wrath owns. Often just referred to as "Furious." Located not far from Crystal Ball.
Strike Back: Owned by Sullivan Wallace but members of the Lost Kings MC have worked there in the past.
Johnson County/Johnsonville: Fictional area where Heidi grew up. About an hour west of "Empire." Where Strike Back Gym, The Castle, and Zips are located. Possibly the new home of a Lost Kings MC support club? We'll see!
Zips: Racetrack owned by Eraser where all the illegal gambling/racing in the area happens.
The Castle: Formerly a juvenile detention center. The building is now used to house the underground fighting ring run by Remy and Griff. Murphy used to fight here. Other LOKI members also blow off steam in the cage here from time to time. Located in the middle of nowhere, NY, it once-upon-a-time housed Griff, Vapor, and possibly Teller during their "troubled youth" days.
Kodack, NY: Another fictional NY area located in Western New York. Somewhere near Buffalo, perhaps. This territory is run by the Devil Demons MC.
Empire Medical Center: Local hospital where all the Kings receive medical treatment. Heidi also works there now.

OTHER MC TERMINOLOGY

Most terminology was obtained through research. However, I have also used some artistic license in applying these terms to my *romanticized, fictional version of an outlaw motorcycle club. This is not an exhaustive list.*

Cage: A car, truck, van—basically anything other than a motorcycle.

Church: Club meetings all full-patch members must attend. Led by the president of the club, but officers will update the members on the areas they oversee. (Some clubs refer to the meeting room where they hold church as the "chapel." My club refers to it as their "war room."

Citizen: Anyone not a hardcore biker or belonging to an outlaw club. "Citizen wife" would refer to a spouse kept entirely separate from the club.

Cut: Leather vest worn by outlaw bikers and adorned with patches and artwork displaying the club's unique colors. The Lost Kings' colors are blue and gray. Their logo is a skull with a crown. The *Respect Few, Fear None* patch is earned by doing time for the club without snitching. *Brother's Keeper* patches are earned by killing for the club. *Loyal Brother* is for a brother who's spent more than five years with the club.

Colors: The "uniform" of an outlaw motorcycle gang. A leather vest, with the three-piece club patch on the back, and various other patches relating to their role in the club.

Fly colors: To ride on a motorcycle wearing colors.

Muffler bunny or "bunnies": A girl who hangs around to provide sexual favors to members. Old ladies in my series will sometimes refer to them as "friends of the club," depending on the girl in question. Some clubs refer to them as club whores, patch whores, or cut sluts. These terms are not regularly used in my series. Sometimes simply referred to as a "club girl."

Nomad: A club member who does not belong to any specific charter, yet has privileges in all charters.

Old lady/ol' lady: Wife or steady girlfriend of a club member.

Patched in: When a new member is approved for full membership.

Patch holder: A member who has been vetted through performing duties for the club as a prospect or probate and has earned his three-piece patch.

Road name: Nickname. Usually given by the other members.

Run: A club-sanctioned outing, sometimes with other chapters and/or clubs. Can also refer to a club business run.

I'm sure I'm forgetting something! But that should get you started!

CHAPTER ONE

Rooster

THE DEPTH OF MY LOVE FOR SHELBY KNOWS NO BOUNDS.

Now that we're separated, that fact is abundantly clear.

I don't submit to terror. No, I'm used to doing the terrorizing.

But as I stand in Shelby's dressing room trying to process what's happened, dread slithers into my body.

My worst fear has come true.

He has Shelby.

That sick, creepy fuck who's been scaring the shit out of her for weeks with his insane letters has actually gotten his hands on her.

All because I was fucking around on the other side of the arena instead of being where I should've been—protecting my girl.

I never thought he'd try something this soon. Tonight. I was so damn confident I'd catch him before he got anywhere near Shelby.

How could I have been so fucking stupid? So arrogant?

She has to be here.

But she's not.

My mind struggles to accept the truth. My gut won't stop screaming.

The woman I love is *gone.*

Someone took her.

I race past Jigsaw, knocking him into the wall.

Outside the dressing room, I scan the near-empty hallway. "Shelby!"

My fear-clogged voice bounces off the indifferent cinderblock walls, mocking me.

I yank out my phone and study her texts. The last one said to knock three times. She sent it less than fifteen minutes ago. What the hell happened between then and now?

Sirens pierce the air around the arena.

The hairs on the back of my neck stand up.

Police? Fire? I can't tell.

Are they here for Shelby? Is she hurt?

Jigsaw's shoulder brushes mine. "Think that has something do with Shelby?"

"I don't know."

The sirens increase in volume.

I turn left, jogging toward the loading dock exit.

Bane's big ass is rushing down the hallway. Where was he when Shelby needed him? This asshole was supposed to watch Shelby for five fucking minutes and couldn't even do that.

My fist cracks his jaw, spinning him sideways.

"Logan!" he mumble-shouts. "The fuck?"

I hammer my fist into his face once more before Jigsaw bear-hugs me, yanking my body sideways. "Not now," he growls against my ear.

"Get off me." I shake out of Jigsaw's hold.

Cupping his cheek, Bane eyes me warily. "What the hell, man?"

"Where the fuck were you? She's gone—"

"There was a fire on Dawson's bus. What do you mean she's gone?" Bane's gaze darts behind me as if Shelby's tucked in my back pocket or something.

He's lucky I don't punch him again. He left my girl to go fuck around with a fire? What was he going to do? Blot it out with his hands? "You a fucking fireman now?" I growl.

"Logan!" The door leading outside slams shut behind Trent with a heavy metallic *clank.* All three of us focus on Trent's anxious face. "Did you let someone from the venue take Shelby's trunk?"

My body jerks in Trent's direction. "What? No. Why?"

"Some guy is loading her trunk into a white van outside." He tugs at his sleeve. "His shirt looked like the one all the arena guys are wearing."

I'm already moving toward him. "She's not in her dressing room."

My mind flashes back to Shelby's clothes and shoes, carelessly dumped all over her room. More than the normal mess Shelby makes.

The pieces rapidly click together in my mind.

Jesus Christ. Did this psycho load Shelby into her trunk like a piece of fucking cargo?

"*She's* in that trunk." I feel it down to my fucking bones, and I bolt toward the exit.

"Motherfucker," Jigsaw growls, jogging right behind me.

Trent doesn't question my assumption. He backs up, shoving the door open again. "I knew something was wrong. I tried to stop him," he says in a rush, following us outside. "He told me Shelby said it was okay. It didn't sound right. But I wasn't sure…" His voice falters as his footsteps quicken behind us.

The bright lights of the parking lot wash over our small group.

Outside, fire engines, an ambulance, and several cop cars are all jammed into the lot. The acrid stench of burning rubber hangs in the air.

I scan the crowded area, searching for any white vans.

"There! That one." Trent elbows me and points to an older, plain white cargo van with no windows in the back. Virginia plates. Rusty patches on the bumper. Mud-caked tires and splashes of dirt along the sides.

While my mind catalogs as many details as possible, my feet are already moving toward the vehicle.

The stairs are clogged with too many people, and I can't waste another second. I jump off the side of the loading dock and land hard on the concrete below. The impact jars my legs and rattles my teeth.

Shake it off.

My boots thunder over the pavement as I dodge firefighters with hoses, cops, and nosy assholes.

Behind me, Jigsaw's pounding the pavement just as hard. "Keep going. I'll get the plate number," he huffs out.

So fucking close.

People shout as I run past them. I knock into a few. They're nothing more than a blur.

I hit the back of the van with a thud and yank on the one door handle. The other door only has holes where the handle should be.

Locked.

I press and pull, climbing onto the bumper to jiggle or work the door open by brute force.

The engine screams to life. *Shit!* Whoever's in the driver's seat must have realized he's got company. The van lurches forward. My feet slip on the bumper. I tighten my grip on the door handle.

The van rocks up over the curb, bouncing onto the grass, sending workers scattering to get out of the way. It knocks me loose.

Legs and arms pumping hard, I trail behind the van, trying to grab on again. I can't let him get to the road. Can't let him out of my sight or Shelby's *gone.*

I throw my arm forward, reaching for the handle. My hand slaps against the door with a painful sting. Fingers slip against the metal. Once, twice.

Got it.

I curl my fingers around the slick metal.

The engine roars louder. Gravel pings off my shins.

Next step is to get my feet back on that bumper and go along for the ride.

The van picks up speed.

My grip on the handle is tenuous at best. The sharp sting of the metal from my rings pinches my flesh. I ignore it. Focus. Relentlessly, I pound over the uneven ground, trying to get the momentum to leap onto the back of the van. My brain knows it's a losing battle, but I refuse to accept reality.

Muscles straining, I swing onto the bumper and hang on tight. The van fishtails, knocking my feet to the ground again. This time, the toes of my boots drag through the grass, but still I hold on. I stare down at the bumper. Too much of a risk to let go and hope I catch it with my hands instead of my face.

The van careens wildly over the grass.

I shove my hand in my pocket and yank out my cell phone, snapping a few sure-to-be-shaky photos of the visible portion of the license plate in case Jigsaw can't get a clear shot with my big ass in the way.

Finally, the driver slows the van enough for me to pull myself upright. I shove my phone back in my pocket and pump my burning legs faster. The van brakes hard and I smack into the metal door with my forehead.

"Fuck." I shake it off and attempt to climb onto the bumper again. The van bounces wildly over the edge of the gravel road, knocking me loose for good.

My right foot rolls on the uneven stones. Pain crackles through my ankle and leg. My knee slams into the unforgiving rocks.

"Fuck!" I roll to the side and jump to my feet, then limp a few steps before continuing my chase.

The van's moving too fast.

That stumble cost me.

Jigsaw whizzes by, boots crunching over the gravel.

But it's too late.

There's no catching the guy now.

Jigsaw must realize it too. He stops, rests his hands on his thighs, and watches the van for a few beats. Breathing hard, he turns my way, points back toward the parking lot, and shouts, "Go, go, go!"

I wobble and hop on my uninjured foot until I can push through the pain and put weight on the other one. Together, we run for the truck.

People stare.

A few shout questions at us but I'm not stopping for anyone.

I slam into the side of the truck with both hands. A fire engine's parked behind me, boxing me in. "Son of a bitch."

"I got it." Jigsaw throws himself on his bike. Fuck, I'm pissed I don't have mine. It would make it a hell of a lot easier to move through this mess. His bike thunders to life as I rip open the driver's side door and fling myself into the truck.

Fuck the fire engines and everyone else in my way. I don't even hesitate to slam the truck into drive. Just like the van did earlier, I hop the curb and tear over the grass, avoiding the clogged parking lot.

The back end of the truck slides as I hit the gravel but I keep my foot on the gas. From what I remember, there's only one exit from this side of the arena. If the traffic's bad, I might be able to catch the guy at the stoplight.

Jigsaw's ahead of me and once my wheels touch the pavement, I catch up to him quickly. He weaves around cars while I jerk the steering wheel to the right and tear over more grass, careful to keep the tires on the safe side of the steep embankment running along the road.

Traffic thins out as we reach the connecting road that leads to the highway. Everyone's trying to get *into* the place. The road leading out is clearer.

No white van at the stoplight.

I slam my fists against the steering wheel.

Something thumps against my window. I click the button to slide the glass down.

Jigsaw's studying the road ahead of us and I follow his line of sight. "He had to go right." He points to the stoplight. There's a leader light to turn left and a small line of cars already backed up. "He wouldn't risk getting stuck here."

"Let's go."

We burn onto the highway. Jigsaw's able to move ahead easier than I am, weaving in and out of traffic ahead of me. My gaze searches the sea of vehicles for the white van.

Nothing.

Keeping an eye on the road, I grab my phone and send the photos of the van to Z. *Please let one of them be clear enough to make out the license plate.*

Miles and miles of highway go by in a blur. Still no sign of the van. I've even lost sight of Jigsaw.

I pass an exit. Then another one. What if the van got off on one of the earlier exits? He could be headed anywhere by now.

With Shelby trapped inside her trunk.

The sick black weight of anger and frustration slithers through my chest.

How could I fail her like this?

My phone rings through the truck's Bluetooth and I punch the button to answer the call.

"You planning to buy a van?" Z's voice rumbles through the speakers.

"He got Shelby. The motherfucker took her from the arena. Right under my nose. He has her, Z."

"What the fuck?" All humor vanishes from Z's voice. "Where are you?"

"I almost had the guy. He slipped right through my fingers." My voice breaks on the last word.

"We'll get her back," he says with calm authority. "It's gonna be okay. Where are you now?"

I explain what happened and where I am.

"Can you pull over?"

"I can't, Z." I barely choke out the words. "I gotta find her."

"Brother," he says slowly, "you can't be sure he even went that way. Or that he didn't get off the highway already. Pull over." There's a muffled noise but I still make out Z telling someone to get Jiggy on the phone.

Z returns to our call. "Where are you now?"

I flick on my blinker, carefully moving to the right until I can finally stop on the shoulder. I read the mile marker to Z. He's quiet for a few seconds.

"Okay. I'm calling Ice so he can get his guys down there. Wait for Jigsaw, then both of you go back to the arena. As much as I hate to say it, cooperate with the cops. We need every resource we can pull into this."

"Fuck." That's going to mean hours of wasted time answering stupid questions instead of searching for Shelby. But Z's right. I can't let my ego or fury get in the way of finding my girl. "He's dead, Z."

"I hear you, brother." He's silent for a few seconds. "I'm working on the photos now. Trying to make out the full plate number. Someone is running a partial in the meantime. I'll call you as soon as I have something."

"Thank you."

"We'll get her back, Rooster. I promise."

While I trust Z to do everything he can to help, I've endured enough trauma in my life to know there are no guarantees.

CHAPTER TWO

Rooster

THE ARENA PARKING LOT'S IN ABSOLUTE CHAOS WHEN WE RETURN. MOST OF the fire trucks are gone, replaced by more cop cars. A few unmarked vehicles catch my attention.

My phone's blowing up with texts from Greg asking where I am.

Me: In parking lot.

Greg: Dressing room with cops.

Jigsaw's mouth is set in a grim line and his eyes burn with fury as he watches me slide out of the truck. "I sent Z the video I got," he says quietly. "I was moving fast, so I don't know how much he'll be able to tell from it or if he can get the plate number. I'm sorry, brother."

At a loss for words, I squeeze his shoulder in thanks.

He flicks his gaze toward the crowd clustered by the loading dock entrance. "Let's deal with this. If Z gets anything, I'll distract the pigs so you can slip away."

Clearly, Jiggy's looking forward to dealing with law enforcement as much as I am.

Two Harleys thunder into the parking lot and stop in a grassy spot away from all the other vehicles. Jigsaw and I jog over to meet them.

Pants gets to me first. "I'm sorry, brother." He pulls me in and slaps my back. "Ice called in his local contact at the FBI. He should already be here. You can trust him," he says against my ear.

Shit, guess Ice has been making friends with all the alphabet agencies, not just the ATF. Don't give a fuck. Right now, I'm grateful for whatever shady business Ice has his fingers in—as long as it helps me find Shelby. "Thank you."

"We'll get your girl back." T-Bone slaps my shoulder next. "Ice is working on those photos with Z."

Guess that means the two of them are coordinating how to break into the Virginia DMV's records or whatever other databases they need. Thank fuck.

"Logan!"

I groan, recognizing Greg's voice.

"Who's the pencil neck?" Pants cracks his knuckles.

"Her manager."

He grunts in response.

"The cops are waiting in her dressing room. They want to speak to you." Greg stops short, surveying our small group. "What happened to you? Where is Shelby?"

"Bane decided to play fireman. I got held up by security. And some motherfucker stuffed Shelby in her trunk and took off." I jerk my thumb in Jigsaw's direction. "We went after him but lost sight of the van out on the highway."

"Jesus Christ." Greg stabs his fingers through his hair and yanks. "I knew something wasn't—"

"Save it. Who's here?"

"Local PD and an FBI agent. No one's called it a kidnapping yet, but the FBI showed up pretty quick."

Next to me, Pants shifts on his feet but neither of us say a word.

"Trent supplied them with the info he had, which wasn't much," Greg continues. "We were waiting for you to get back. What the hell happened?"

"Let's go." I push past him, marching toward the loading dock.

"Uh. Yeah." Greg hurries to catch up. Guess he expected me to balk at speaking to the cops. Normally, I would. But Z's right. I need every person possible searching for Shelby. Killing the fucker who took her will come later. Her safety is my first concern. Revenge can wait.

Greg wasn't quite accurate. The cops are waiting *outside* Shelby's dressing room.

A guy in a black suit and shiny loafers steps away from the uniformed officers. His gaze flicks to Pants and T-Bone briefly before settling on me. "Logan Randall?"

"Yes." I shake his hand quickly.

"Agent Adam Jackson with the FBI."

"Thank you for arriving so fast."

Even though my greeting was sincere, the corners of his mouth twitch in annoyance. Maybe he doesn't enjoy taking orders from Ice. "Before we process her dressing room, can you relay what happened?"

I blow out a breath and organize my thoughts. No point in mentioning the viewing booth I'd set up to monitor Shelby's fans. It'll just distract the cops, and I don't think any of the footage will be useful to their investigation. Then again, Greg and Trent might have already spilled that whole story.

"I was checking on something at her merchandise booth." I shift my gaze down the hallway where two security guards are talking to another set of cops. "Security guards stopped Jensen and me on our way back to Shelby's dressing room." I jerk my thumb in Jigsaw's direction. "I'm pretty sure whoever took her set that up to keep us distracted."

The agent flips to a clean page in a small notebook and scratches out a few words.

"Bane was supposed to be watching Shelby's room," I continue. "She sent me a text that the door was locked and to knock three times while we were getting hassled by security."

"Was the door locked when you got to the room?" He doesn't seem interested in our tangle with the arena's security or its possible connection to Shelby's abduction.

"No, it was ajar. Shelby never leaves it open when she's inside. She would've been changing out of her stage outfit and packing up her things."

"How long have you known Shelby?" he asks without looking up at me.

"A few months."

"And she's your…?" This time he meets my stare and raises his eyebrows.

"Girlfriend." *Old lady. Biggest fucking piece of my heart. My whole world.*

His gaze flicks to Greg. "I took a look at the letters she's been receiving. You believe she has a stalker?"

"That's why someone was supposed to be watching her at all times." I glance at the local cops behind the agent. "Local police didn't seem to think it was their problem."

One of the cops shifts and opens his mouth. Agent Jackson shoots a stern glare his way. The officer's mouth snaps shut.

"Mr. Anderson has already forwarded the letters to my office. We'll be reviewing them at length." The agent tucks his notepad away in his pocket and snaps on a pair of thin latex gloves. "Mr. Randall, follow me inside but don't touch anything. Everyone else, wait out here."

The "everyone else" apparently doesn't include the local cops because they trail us into the room. I swallow hard, surveying the mess. Shelby must've fought back. Did he hurt her? Threaten her? She had to have been knocked out or she would've been kicking and screaming the whole way.

Fear and anger drum a steady beat in my chest.

"Her bandmate says you think she was loaded *into* a trunk? What kind of trunk?"

I hold my arms out wide. "A huge old black trunk. Like something you would've seen on the Titanic." It's always amused me Shelby uses something so ancient-looking to carry all her stage stuff. "Brass locks." I point to the mess of clothes, shoes, and other stuff carelessly dumped into a heap by the couch. "Everything in that pile was inside of the trunk. She never empties it out like that and she wouldn't leave her stuff all over the place. *That's* why I think he used the trunk to smuggle her out of here."

Jackson nods slowly. "The young man said he thought something was off when he saw someone he didn't recognize with the trunk."

"Correct. He came and got me. Jensen and I went after the van but lost him."

"Heard it was quite a show, you getting dragged through the parking lot. Awfully brave."

"Not brave enough. We didn't stop him." And fuck if that's not going to haunt me for the rest of my life.

Lock it down.

Whatever anger, frustration, or inadequacy I have burning inside me will have to wait. Getting Shelby back safely is the only thing I can afford to focus on right now.

"You could've gotten killed." His keen eyes don't leave my face.

"I wasn't thinking about that."

"Trent gave us a description of the van but not the plate number." The agent flips to an earlier page in his notepad. "It's not a lot to go on."

"I've got pictures." I probably should've led this discussion with the photos—not taken this roundabout way to get to the important information. "Not sure how fuzzy they are, though." I'd barely glanced at them when I sent them to Z.

He raises an eyebrow. "You chased the van down *and* took pictures?" He holds his hand out for my phone.

"Jensen has some too, I think."

He fiddles with my cell for a few minutes. I assume he's sending the photos to himself.

After he finishes, he hands the phone back. "Thank you. That will be helpful." He jerks his head toward the bathroom. We stop just outside the door and he peers inside, pointing to the clothes on the floor. "You said she would've been changing? Can you confirm that's what she wore on stage?"

I glance at the crumpled black and blue dress. The cheerful flower pattern seems to mock me now. My throat constricts so tight, I can only nod in response.

His shrewd eyes land on the open window next. "Do you know if she opened that?"

"Doubtful." I lift my chin toward the top of the window. "No way she'd be able to reach the latch."

"Did *you* open it?"

"Hell no."

"Was it like that earlier? Before her show?"

I study the window for a minute. Shelby would've been

uncomfortable, worrying someone could spy on her. She would've said something. Asked me to close it. "No."

He carefully works his way over to the sink and squats down to examine her smashed phone without disturbing it.

"She almost always has it on her," I say. To move things along, I point to the water bottle lying on the floor. "She sent me a text saying her water tasted funny." I pull up the message and hand over my phone, not giving a shit if he scrolls through our whole exchange. I've never deleted a single one of Shelby's texts.

He hands the phone back and stares at the window, then the small shower stall. Again, he squats down, taking his cell phone out and shining the flashlight over the interior. "She use the shower?"

"Yeah, last night."

He motions me closer and holds the shower curtain back. "Boot prints."

My gaze lands on the bright circle of light. A few smudges of dirt surround two clear, muddy prints facing outward.

"Shit," I grumble.

Jackson glances at my own boots and back to the prints. "Way too small to be yours."

Something close to a snarl rumbles out of me but I don't comment.

After a few seconds, he drops the shower curtain and climbs up on the toilet, careful not to touch the window or walls. He peers outside. "Ground level," he mutters and sweeps his gaze over the space from the higher perspective.

He jumps down and barks a few orders at the local cops before ushering all of us back into the hallway.

"I need our crime scene people to go over this room. Since she received the letters, for now we'll operate on the assumption it's the same guy and not a ransom situation." His gaze snaps to Greg. "Who would someone call, just in case someone makes a demand?"

"Her mother? But they're dirt poor. She couldn't afford to come up with a lot of cash. Maybe the record company…? Me, I guess." Greg's helpless eyes land on me. "Ransom crossed my mind. We're trying to keep the situation quiet for that reason…"

"It's not a ransom," I growl. "This sick piece of shit took her."

"Stop fucking wasting time," Jigsaw adds, "and get some asses out there looking for her."

Agent Jackson narrows his eyes at Jiggy but doesn't address him. "Mr. Randall, walk with me." He jerks his head to the side, and I follow him down the hallway leading back to the loading dock. When he seems satisfied we're alone, he tucks his notepad into his pocket.

All professional pretenses seem to melt away as he laces his fingers together behind his head and stares down at the concrete floor for a few seconds. "Ice tells me you're visiting from your New York charter."

"Yeah," I answer in a bored tone. "The bottom rocker on the back of my cut can tell you that too. What's your point?"

His mouth slides into a bleak half-smile. "Before I waste a ton of resources, assure me that this has nothing to do with your club. You piss someone off? Another club got a beef with you? Maybe the Vipers decided to come after your old lady? Black Venom? South of Satan? Someone else?"

I should've seen this coming. Jackson's done his MC homework. Goody for him.

"You said you looked at those fucking letters," I answer through clenched teeth. "This has nothing to do with me or my club."

"Don't get twisted. I have to ask."

"It's *not* my club. It's some stalker fan."

"You understand I need to rule out every possibility, right?"

I stand firm and look him straight in the eyes. "Then do it quick and don't waste time."

"Is there any chance she left on her own?"

The question throws me for a second. My jaw drops. "In her *trunk?*"

"We *don't* actually know she was in the trunk."

"Are you fucking shittin' me right now?" Disbelief drips from every word. "How the fuck else did she get out of here with no one seeing her?"

"Is there a possibility the stress of the tour is too much and she skipped out? This is a lot for someone her age to handle."

"No. She's been working toward this for years. It's stressful, sure. But she loves it. It's what she was born to do."

He stares at me for a second, like maybe he didn't expect such a corny sentiment out of my crude biker mouth. "She could have hired someone to help her escape the tour—"

"You saw the same things I did in that dressing room, didn't you?" Frustration bleeds into my words. This 'Shelby escape plan' theory isn't where he needs to waste his time. There's no fucking way my girl decided to up and leave.

"It's a possibility," he suggests.

"No, it's not. Shelby's not a quitter. And she wouldn't leave without telling me. If she wanted to go AWOL, all she had to do was ask. I would've taken her anywhere she wanted. She knows that. I was planning to join her on the road. Help take some of the stress off of her."

His expression doesn't change. "Any chance she wanted to get away from *you*, then?"

"Jesus Christ, seriously?"

"I have to ask, Mr. Randall. Honestly, if I wasn't the one standing here, as the boyfriend, we'd be looking a lot more closely at *you*."

"I was on the other side of the arena when she was taken, for fuck's sake." I squeeze my eyes shut for a brief second. "Cindy. Shelby's hair-and-makeup person. She took video of the security guards hassling us."

"I'll talk to her. We'll test the water bottle too." He pulls out his notebook again and jots down a few lines. "Personally, I don't think you had anything to do with it."

"Gee, thanks."

He sighs and glances at his notepad, flipping back a few pages. "The letters are troubling."

Relief courses through me. He's moving off his Shelby-ditched-the-tour-and-her-possessive-biker-boyfriend theory. "No shit."

He ignores the sarcasm. "I had a chance to briefly read them. They did not contain any direct threats."

"Shelby sure felt threatened by them."

"I don't blame her. People who make direct threats to celebrities are *less* likely to act." He taps the notepad. "This indirect 'we belong together' crap is usually indicative that the person plans to act. Still, I'm surprised it happened this soon."

"Your point?"

He shakes his head. "Can I be honest?"

"Please do," I answer with as little sarcasm as I can manage.

"The fact that whoever it was pulled this off so neatly concerns me. He would have had to be stalking her *real* close to time the situation the way he did."

That thought's been brushing up against me since the second I realized she was missing.

"Not only that," Jackson continues, "but stalking situations usually go through stages. This guy clearly has the extreme entitlement and attachment to her, but she hasn't even had a chance to reject him."

"How was she supposed to reject anonymous letters?"

"Is it possible he was communicating with her in a different way at first? Maybe for a longer period of time?"

"She has a few creepers I've been keeping my eye on who seem to come to a lot of her shows." I pull up some of the screenshots I've taken and show him.

He raises his eyebrows again. "You're stalking her stalkers? That's…interesting."

"I was worried about her. For good reason. Obviously."

He taps his fingers against his thigh. "Indulge me for a second. All the letters were dropped off for her, correct?"

"As far as I know, yes." Thank fuck he's focusing on relevant topics.

"Who *could* have left the letters? Not why. Just *who* had the opportunity?"

"Well, I wasn't around for the first couple of letters, so I don't know about them. I'd have to assume her band, Greg, and anyone involved with the tour. From what I understand, the first one was dropped off at the venue's ticket window, and Greg brought it to Shelby's room."

"Interesting." He writes a few words in his notepad.

"The most recent one was found on the windshield of the band's van at their hotel. So that doesn't narrow the pool of candidates. Everyone involved with the tour stayed there. Shelby and I stayed somewhere else."

"How close is she to her band?"

"Not that close. I think they were hired just for the tour. Except for Trent. They go way back."

"Romantic relationship?"

"Not that I know of."

"How does he feel about you muscling your way into her life?"

Clearly, he's trying to taunt me, but I'm not falling for it. I shrug. Since I haven't spared a single fuck about Trent's thoughts on my relationship with Shelby, there isn't much to say. "You'd have to ask him."

Jackson stares at me, as if waiting for a more complete answer.

"We get along but mostly stay out of each other's way." I let out an irritated sigh. "Like I said, I don't know him that well."

"What about the manager?"

"Except for not taking the letters seriously from the beginning, he's all right. For real, *Shelby* didn't take the letters seriously until recently either. She just told me about them *yesterday*."

"Manager seems to have it in his head that this can be kept quiet for now." He gestures to the walls around us. "But word will spread fast. I would like our investigation to remain under wraps for as long as possible. Otherwise, people will call with bullshit 'tips' and slow us down."

"Okay…and your point?"

"Stay away from any press."

I snort. "You don't have to worry about that with me."

"What about the other band on the tour?"

"Shelby hasn't had much interaction with them that I know of. She says they keep to themselves."

"What about Dawson Roads? How does he feel about a hot, new young thing stealing his thunder?"

If Dawson played any part in this, he's a dead man walking. "I haven't gotten that impression from him at all. She's the opening act. Seats weren't even filled when she was on stage a few weeks ago. If anything, he's helped her out by having her perform with him during his set. One of the nights, he came out to do a song with her during her time slot. It helped." I swallow hard, my gaze flicking in the direction of the stage. "Tonight was the most packed it's been during her set."

I should've been waiting for her when she got offstage. Not fucking around with my stupid surveillance experiment.

His disinterested expression says he doesn't give a shit about Shelby's audience size. "Is it possible Mr. Roads has a romantic interest in Shelby?"

"I wondered that at first," I answer honestly. "Shelby kind of probed him about why he wanted her to perform with him one night. He admitted it was mostly business but a little personal."

His shrewd eyes narrow. "Explain."

"Guess there's a woman he broke up with recently. Another country singer. The song he and Shelby performed a few times was one he recorded with his ex."

"So, singing it with another woman was his 'fuck you' to this ex-girlfriend?"

"He didn't put it that way, but yeah, probably. You'll have to ask him for details."

"Oh, I will. What's her name?"

"Shit." I run my hands through my hair. "Glenna something. Once Dawson admitted that was one of the reasons, Shelby felt bad. She's new to the business and was worried she was making an enemy of a woman she's never even met."

Under his breath, the agent lets out a distracted "hmmm" noise as he writes all that down.

"Dawson's the one who assigned Bane to watch her when the record company wouldn't hire security," I point out.

"You seem to have a positive comment about everyone, Mr. Randall."

There's something I've never been accused of before. "That wasn't really positive or negative."

"You realize it's possible one of these people was involved, right?"

"No shit," I growl. "I'm trying to give you whatever information I have so you're not wasting time chasing your tail."

"All right, moving along. This guy—Bane—has been watching her. What did Shelby think of him?"

"She thought he was nice. He seemed to keep an eye on her." My expression turns sour. "Until tonight, when it really mattered."

"What was his excuse for leaving?"

"He said something about a fire on Dawson's bus."

"Convenient how that happened," he mutters.

Isn't it, though?

"Made for a nice distraction," he adds. "I still need to talk to the fire department and obtain more details."

"Yeah, don't waste too much time on that. Focus on finding Shelby."

He glares at me. “What’s her family situation?”

Lynn may be an overbearing mom trying her hardest to push me out of Shelby’s life, but I doubt that information is relevant, so there’s no point painting her in a bad light. “Her mom’s in Texas. Works as a waitress. Shelby’s dad walked out on ’em years ago. She and her mom are pretty close.”

“Greg doesn’t want to inform the mother yet, but we’ll have to.”

“I’ll do it.” I’m not looking forward to that conversation. But the news has to be better coming from me rather than a stranger.

He scribbles in the notebook again. “She have any contact with her dad?”

“No.”

“No? Not even with her getting famous?”

I snort out a sad laugh. “No. She assumes he’ll pop up eventually, wanting some cash, and is looking forward to telling him to fuck off.”

“Spirited girl.”

“Yes, she is.”

“That’s good,” he says quietly.

I swallow hard, considering what he’s implying.

Neither of us say it out loud.

But we both know that if the guy who took her is as unhinged as we think he is, Shelby’s gonna need every ounce of strength she has to survive.

CHAPTER THREE

Rooster

An even larger crowd is clustered around Shelby's dressing room when Agent Jackson and I return. Yellow crime scene tape has marked off her doorway and a portion of the hallway.

He stops me halfway down the hall. "Listen, I understand what's going to happen to this guy if you get your hands on him before we—"

"My only concern is getting Shelby back safe."

"And I'll help you do that." His gaze shifts to two new plainclothesmen who reek of FBI, and another wearing a jacket identifying him as ATF. "Try not to make my job harder, and keep me in the loop."

I don't know Jackson. Sure as fuck don't trust him. He doesn't trust me either. Which is fine. He shouldn't. But right now, I need his help, so I'll pretty much say anything to reassure him. "I want her back as soon as possible. That's all." I swallow hard. "We both know the longer he has her, the more…" I can't say the words. We both know the longer he has Shelby, the more likely it is he'll hurt her, or worse.

Jackson's lips twist, and he rocks back on his heels for a second. "I have worked a few cases similar to this one. It's not a guarantee but from the letters, he seems infatuated with her. She hasn't officially ever 'rejected' him, which is usually the trigger for something...violent. So, hold onto that."

Hold onto what? Hope? Do I look like a kid he can placate with a bedtime story about friendly monsters?

"Where are you staying?" he asks when I don't respond to his "hang in there" pep talk.

I won't be able to sleep until I have Shelby back, so where I park my ass tonight is irrelevant. "At the clubhouse. But I might grab a hotel room closer to downtown."

We exchange information, and I promise to call him if I hear anything.

Apparently, I'm free to go.

"I might have more questions after I speak to a few other people. Don't disappear on me," he says before turning away.

Or not.

The other agents scowl as I'm dismissed. Maybe they expected Jackson to handcuff me to a railing or something. One agent steps toward me, but Jackson shakes his head as he approaches them. He seems to be the one in charge.

Jigsaw, Pants, and T-Bone slowly form a wall around me. "Any word from Z?" I ask quietly.

"They're working on it," Jigsaw says.

I send Z a quick text to let him know I'm done talking to law enforcement for now.

As I finish sending the text, my phone buzzes.

Z.

I answer and turn the corner away from the cops. Jigsaw follows.

"What's up?" I answer.

"You clear?"

"For now. You got something for me?"

"I'm close, brother."

Damn, I want better news. I squeeze my eyes shut and pinch the bridge of my nose. "Fuck."

"I know. Listen, Wrath, Murphy, and Dex are on their way down. Steer and Hustler are joining them. Griff and Remy are riding along too. They're all meeting here and heading to Virginia."

"What? Rock can't spare anyone right now. You can't either."

"Fuck that. I'd be there too, brother, but I want to keep digging up whatever info I can on my end. I don't want to leave the searching to Ice. I trust him, but…"

But Z's a hands-on control freak, and I couldn't be more grateful for it. "No, I appreciate what you're doing. Thank you." I consider who he said was on the way. "Griff and Remy?"

"From what I was told, Murphy was at Remy's bar when he heard what happened. They volunteered to come. Flex those support club muscles, I guess." The laughter fades from his voice. "Ice's crew has your back too from everything I'm hearing…?" The question in his voice is clear.

"Pants and T-Bone are at the arena with us now."

"Good. We'll send more brothers—"

"There's no point. Nothing for them to do. No clue where to start searching until I have a name and address."

"You staying at their clubhouse?" he asks.

"Thinking I'm better off at a hotel. I don't know yet."

"Do what you need to do. I'll call as soon as I have something."

I hang up, frustrated but also comforted that Z's working on the search and brothers are on their way down.

Jigsaw cracks his knuckles. "Please tell me he's got a name or a lead. Anything to go on?"

"Not yet. Wrath, Murphy, Steer, Hustler, Remy, and Griff will be here in a few hours, though."

He lets out a somber laugh. "Good. I hope Pants gets a chance to show off his hog farm while they're around."

I hadn't even thought that far ahead.

No, my thoughts revolve around the letters Shelby received. The ominous rabbit-in-a-cage threat. Where the fuck are they? He can't have taken her far. Traveling is too risky. What if she suffocates in her trunk? Did he tie her up on top of drugging her? She's going to be so scared when she wakes up alone with this monster.

The more fear consumes me, the quieter and stiller I become. Jiggy's the exact opposite. He's vibrating menace—eager to punish someone in the most brutal way.

Right now, I need to rescue my girl.

I'll shift into punishment mode later.

CHAPTER FOUR

Shelby

A MAN, SINGING OR HUMMING.

Mouth so dry. *Mine.*

Skull throbs.

Limbs ache.

Drifting for a while...

Again, the singing. Bad singing. Off-key. Unpleasant.

Sleeping sounds better.

I slip under again.

Bright lights flare and I moan in pain.

The quality of the singing doesn't improve, but the words become clearer.

Little rabbit. Little rabbit. I finally caught my little rabbit.

It all comes back in a painful burst of images firing through my sloggy brain.

Mr. Creepy Letters.

He stuffed me in my own trunk!

Not wanting to alert him that I'm awake, I shift my body a millimeter at a time, trying to figure out if I'm still in my trunk or not. Pain sizzles through my skull, and I vaguely remember banging my head at some point. My arms drag, like I'm swimming through mud.

He drugged me.

Ice-cold fear slides through my stomach. A tear slips down my cheek, lands in my hair.

Rooster will find me. I know he will. He'll tear apart the whole state of Virginia if he has to.

Oh, shit! What if we're not in Virginia anymore?

How long have I been out?

Panic overwhelms me as I consider all the awful options. I could be in another state or even another country. There's no way to know. How will anyone be able to look for me?

Quiet.

I focus on inhaling a long, deep breath and try to use my senses to figure out my surroundings.

We're not moving. There are no tires bumping over the highway, and no gentle rocking of a boat or thrum of an airplane. That's a good sign.

A crackling sound.

I sniff the air but can't smell anything. Nothing at all.

Again, I attempt to move my fingers, brushing them along the surface I'm curled up on. It's smooth. Fabric lining—my trunk. I think. It should smell like lavender. But I've been in here so long, maybe I've gone nose-blind.

The singing moves closer and I still my body. Better to delay any interaction with my kidnapper for as long as I can stand it. Maybe Rooster will find me before anything bad happens.

Well, before anything *worse* happens.

There's a creaking above me. Cool air floats around my body—both a relief and a new source of terror.

"Little rabbit," someone whispers in a singsong voice.

I work hard not to cringe or signal that I'm awake. I'm in deeper waters than I can swim here, which isn't saying much, since I can't swim at all. What's the right course of action? Play possum? Try to reason with him to let me go? Befriend him until I can make a run for it?

Something whispers over my cheek. My nose twitches. That would be a normal reaction, even if I was asleep, right?

"Time to wake, my little sleeping beauty, before you end up with more aches and pains."

Now he's worried about my aches and pains.

Clearly, he's not fooled by my sleepy act. I groan and press my cheek to the bottom of the trunk—like a little kid resistant to getting out of bed for school. Dryness forces my mouth to remain glued shut. My cracked lips sting as I peel my tongue from the roof of my mouth.

Another pathetic groan bubbles out of me. Not even a fake one this time.

There's a sweep of light, and I cringe. After the deep blackness, even the dimly lit room hurts. I blink and turn my head. A man starts to take shape above me.

With the light at his back, he's not much more than a vaguely human-shaped shadow looming into my space. That's fine. My brain can't handle detailing the features of my captor yet.

I curl my toes, feeling the familiar confines of my cowgirl boots.

I am so kicking this asshole the first chance I get.

"Momma?" I whisper, trying to sound as pathetic and confused as possible.

"Sweet little rabbit." Something brushes my cheek again. His fingers. *Eww.* "When I'm sure you'll behave, you can call your mother. I know how close you two are."

Well, aren't you a magnanimous asshole.

"Where are we, Momma?" I whisper.

"You're home, little rabbit." Something strokes over my hair. "Far away from all the badness you were getting tangled up with. Your new life will be quite safe."

Safe my round, rosy butt.

And we're far away? As in, a rustic cabin in the woods—like the clubhouse Rooster took me to? Or far away, like a remote island surrounded by shark-infested waters?

Better not kick him until I get a better understanding of my surroundings. I'd hate to flee just to end up as shark food.

The completely absurd image pulls a chuckle out of me.

"Shelby?"

Huh. A little unhinged laughter spooks him. Go figure. I file that tidbit away for later and try to push my body into an upright position.

"That's it, little rabbit. You had me worried."

Oh, were you worried drugging someone and stuffing them in a trunk might have side effects, moron?

I barely hang onto the sarcastic retort. Sass won't save me here. He isn't a bar patron I can whirl away from. Or Rooster, who enjoys my little zingers. No, this is a sicko with a poor grasp of reality who drugged and kidnapped me.

Zipped lips might save this ship.

Groaning, I sit up and peer into the dim room, carefully avoiding direct eye contact with my captor.

My gaze lands on a large four-poster bed.

Of course it's a bedroom. Why else would I be here?

Ignoring that stabbing jab of reality, my gaze skips to the heavy wood furniture, slick hardwood floors, and homey braided throw rugs. A window straight across from me appears to have shutters closed and locked over it. No daylight seeps in around the edges.

Painfully, I turn and peer out of the bedroom doorway into a portion of the hallway and living space beyond. Not a hotel room. Details, arbitrary and disjointed, register in my foggy brain. A home or cabin maybe? Dim lighting bounces off glossy hardwood floors. More locked and shuttered windows. Another couple throw rugs. No other decoration that I can see.

"Let me help you." He wraps his doughy fingers around my upper arms and jerks me upright. Pain explodes through my skull and I bite my lip to stop myself from screaming.

"Give me a second," I whisper.

My legs wobble but I refuse to lean on him. Bracing my hand on the open trunk lid, I slowly lift one leg over the side, then the other. My boots softly clunk against the wood floor.

"Come into the kitchen so I can feed you," he says.

He's gotta be joking. As if I'd accept food or drink from him.

"Where's the bathroom?" I rasp.

He studies me for a second before walking me to a door and pushing it open. "Behave, little rabbit. I'll be waiting right here. Don't take too long."

I stumble into the room and try to shut the door behind me. He stops it with one booted foot. "Hurry."

I glare at him before remembering to appear weak and pathetic.

A second later, he removes his foot and turns his back. Thankfully, he doesn't seem to be interested in watching me pee. I hurry over to the toilet and shove my jeans down. My scared bladder doesn't want to empty. I have to close my eyes and take a few deep breaths to coax myself into relaxing.

Only when I'm finished and my jeans are all zipped into place do I take inventory of the bathroom.

Not one damn thing to use as a weapon. Not even a crummy plunger. This isn't the movies. There's no time to smash the mirror and fashion a knife out of the shards of glass without him stopping me.

The window has a shutter that's latched shut and I study it, searching for signs of an alarm system or hidden locks. With him lingering right outside the door, I don't dare test the latch.

I wash my hands and try not to cry at my reflection in the mirror. Wild, tangled hair. Remnants of smeared stage-makeup. Redness on my cheek that will probably turn into a bruise. My vision blurs and I rock on my feet. Gingerly, I touch the back of my head. My fingers come away smeared with blood. *Dammit.*

"Come on. You need food." He pushes the door wider and holds out his hand.

Ignoring him, I finish washing up before stepping away from the sink.

Pathetic and meek routine or not, I can't willingly force myself to touch him. I slide out of the bathroom, careful not to touch him.

"Come." Irritation colors his command. He marches out of the bedroom, expecting me to obey.

Relief flows through me. I want to get as far away from this room as possible.

Of course, who knows what horrors await me on the other side.

CHAPTER FIVE

Rooster

THE NIGHT DRAGS ON. THE COPS QUESTION DAWSON FOR SO LONG, HE ENDS up taking the stage an hour late. Can't muster up an ounce of give-a-fuck for his predicament.

Wanting to keep tabs on law enforcement, I stick around the arena. My brothers stay with me. Pants talks to the ATF agent a few times.

The forensics crew seems to be finished with Shelby's room. After they leave, I slide up to Agent Jackson. "I need to get my computer. That gonna be a problem?"

I jerk my chin toward the table where I'd been set up earlier. Pants and Jigsaw had located the photo booth and cameras and packed them in the truck earlier.

Agent Jackson scans the hallway and shrugs. "Yeah, go ahead."

I pack quickly, trying not to let my mind linger on the stillness. Piles of Shelby's colorful clothing lay scattered around, taunting me for failing her. She's too bright and vibrant to be caught up in the dark fantasy of a madman.

Is she awake by now? Scared? Wondering how I let this happen to her?

Fingerprint powder covers almost every surface. "You pull any prints yet?" I call out to Agent Jackson.

From the doorway, he eyes me wearily. "Nothing yet. He might not be in the system."

No, I bet he's not. Probably flies under the radar of life, fooling everyone into believing he's a nice, normal, if not somewhat weird, guy.

When I've collected the computer equipment I borrowed from Ice, I sling the backpack over my shoulder and step into the hallway. "What's your plan?" I ask Agent Jackson.

"We've got an APB for a white van. Just says we're looking for a white female, early twenties, possibly inside a box or trunk in the cargo area."

"Yeah? Any hits yet?"

He cocks his head, projecting a would-I-still-be-standing-here-if-I-had face at me. "No."

My phone buzzes and I pull it out. Jackson watches my every move like a hawk.

Z.

"Hey," I answer, stepping away, putting a few feet between me and the nosy FBI agent.

"Where you at, brother?" Z asks.

The excited rush of his voice sets me on edge. "Still at the arena. With the Fed working Shelby's case."

"Good. I pulled a name. Guy matches our profile. White van with the same last couple numbers we were able to get off the plate. Residence is not too far from the arena."

I'm already moving toward the exit.

Behind me, there's a quick whistle—Jigsaw, signaling to the others it's time to move.

"I'm sending you the info, but bro, I don't want you going there."

I stop in my tracks. "What? Are you—"

"Rooster. Chill. Give the agent the info I'm sending. Play nice. Be cooperative. Trust me."

Brotherhood. Loyalty. The club works because we trust each other with our lives. Do I trust Z with Shelby's life?

Yeah, I do. He's put his faith in me to protect his wife, Lilly, before. There's no way in hell Z would do anything to jeopardize Shelby.

Still, I can't help the urge to hunt down the piece of shit who grabbed my girl. Pushing against my nature, I pull the phone away from my ear and look at the picture and address Z sent.

Martin Suggs. Fifty-three. Virginia address. Looks awfully similar to one of Shelby's over-enthusiastic Instagram followers.

"Jackson!" I call, because I can't force my feet to move away from the door leading outside. He scowls and walks over.

"I promised to be straight with you, right?" I wait until he confirms with a quick nod before continuing. "My guy has a name."

He scowls at me. "Do I even want to know—"

"Probably not." I cut him off and send him the info. He rushes to confer with some of the other cops and I return to Z.

"Tell me why I just did that?" I growl into my phone.

"Stop and think. If this is our guy and he used his own vehicle, he's not bringing her back to his place. After the way you chased down the van, he knows you probably got the plate number. It's too easy. Besides that, I'm looking at an aerial shot of his house right now. He's in the city." He pauses and adds, "No privacy."

The painful understanding of what Z's implying penetrates deep into my soul. *No privacy*...too many people around who might overhear Shelby's screams. "It's the only lead we have." My stomach clenches. "I can't *not* check it out, Z."

"Ice is running down another angle right this second," he promises. "Guy was left some property a few years back by an uncle. It's in a trust, under another name, so the court records have been hard to access. We're trying to pull the address now. Let the cops check out his house." He lowers his voice. "You want to get to him first, brother. It'll buy you some time if they're wasting their efforts somewhere else."

"I don't even care about that."

"You will," he assures me. "And if she *is* at his house, they'll find her."

A strangled noise pulls from my throat. My logical brain agrees with Z's reasoning. My heart's ripped in half, desperate to get to Shelby.

"It'll probably take the cops a while to even track down the name of the trust. Hope's the one who had me search for it," Z says. "I'm also tracking down any family members in the area you can pay a visit to if we can't get the address. So far, it looks like the uncle was his only relative."

Fucking great. And this stalker thinks he's going to populate a new family with Shelby.

A second later, the decision is made for me. Agent Jackson and his buddies race past us. Guess my info panned out. Jigsaw and Pants follow, flinging questions at Jackson.

"Cops are on the move," I say to Z.

"Head up to the clubhouse. Ice is getting everyone ready to roll out as soon as we have the address. You're gonna need the van..." His voice falters. "Just in case."

No need to question Z. The implication is clear. I'll need the van in case I have to rush Shelby to the hospital.

Or in case I need to drag the body of Martin Suggs to the hog farm.

CHAPTER SIX

Shelby

I HATE SOUP.

It's hotter than Hades most of the year in Texas. When you walk outside in summer, it gets so humid, it feels like you're swimming in soup. No need to eat it.

My captor seems to be a big fan. One look in his cupboards as he's preparing supper reveals a whole lot of canned soup.

A stockpile of soup.

Like he plans to be holed up here for a long, long time.

Time for us to...be *together*.

A bunch of wasps buzz in my belly, stinging me with fear from the inside out.

I study the kitchen. Dated marigold-yellow appliances. A door that I assume leads to outside with rusty-red and tan gingham curtains covering the window at the top. The window over the sink has the same interior latched shutters I've noticed covering the rest of the windows, blocking any outside view. This one has matching gingham window treatments.

It doesn't give the place a homey feel. At all.

Either this guy just moved in or he hostage-proofed the place before bringing me here. I haven't spotted a phone, a knife, or anything I could use as a weapon. Even the chair I'm currently perched on is shackled to the table with only enough room to pull it out and sit. No way to pick it up and smash it over his head.

Better the chair be chained down than me, I guess.

The pan he's warming the soup in is a decent size. I fantasize about picking it up by the short handles and flinging the hot liquid in his face.

Of course, if I miss, I risk burning myself as well as pissing him off.

While he's been cordial so far, the threat of violence looms in the air.

Weakness permeates my limbs. I haven't fully shaken off the drugging, and my extended nap in the trunk, yet. Every part of my body aches. My mind won't stop screaming about my grotesque predicament. In an instant, I've gone from Shelby, a woman who gave the best performance of her tour and couldn't wait to hug her boyfriend, to the prisoner of a crazy person.

It's a huge adjustment.

"What's your name?" My voice barely comes out above a whisper. I can't force it any louder.

"It *is* about time we get to know each other better, isn't it, darling?" He smiles at me over his shoulder.

I can't decide which endearment I hate more—*little rabbit* or *darling.*

When I don't answer, he scowls, and returns to stirring the pot on the stove. Round and round. I'm dizzy from watching him.

"What would you like to drink?" he asks.

"Sprite?"

"Coming right up."

Well, ain't that sweet. A glimpse inside the fridge reveals he's also stocked up on my favorite soda. He pulls a can from one of several six-packs in the fridge, grabs a plastic cup off the counter, and sets both on the table in front of me. After a quick pat on my head that makes my vision blur, he returns to the stove.

I pop the tab on the soda and suck half of it down, not bothering with the cup. The cool, crisp bubbles soothe my raw throat but the sugary drink leaves me thirstier. "Could I have some water too?"

This time he frowns. *Gee, so sorry if I'm asking for too much.*

He sets a glass of tap water in front of me and I whisper a "thank you" before taking a few long swallows.

His stare lingers and my gaze roams the kitchen. Anywhere to avoid him. No knife block, rolling pin, glassware—not even a heavy cutting board. Nothing useful.

While I've been happily on tour singing my heart out every night on stage, this person's been planning my abduction and imprisonment. How could I not know this cosmic shift in my life was coming for me?

"I'm so happy you're here." He clasps his hands under his chin and flashes an angelic smile.

The dead-eyed look I give him in return wipes it clean off his face.

I'm too mad and scared to play along like I'd planned. Time to work on keeping my attitude in check.

"This will make you feel better." He sets a heavy bowl of what looks like pink mush in front of me.

I pick up the plastic soup spoon and poke at the steaming goo. "I'm allergic to tomatoes," I say quietly.

"What? No, you're not."

I push the bowl away. "Yes. I am. My tongue swells up and I break out in hives. My doctor has warned me that I could go into anaphylactic shock if I consume them one too many times." I slowly glance around the kitchen. "And since I'm guessing you don't have an EpiPen around here, I'd rather not take the risk." I sit back in my chair and cross my arms over my chest.

Anger blazes in his droopy brown eyes. Carefully, he removes the bowl and sets it on the counter. "You need to watch your attitude," he says without turning around.

I say nothing.

He returns to the stove and pulls out a fresh pot, and another can of soup from the cabinet. "Are you allergic to chicken noodle?" His tone can't be called anything other than snide.

"Read me the ingredients."

He grits his teeth and lists them one by one.

"It should be okay."

I use the extra time to examine the hallway. A few closed doors. Bedrooms, probably. A long stretch into darkness. I'm guessing the front door lies somewhere that way.

Finally, he sets the bowl of soup in front of me and hands me another plastic spoon.

"All this plastic is bad for the environment, you know." I dip the spoon in my bowl.

"I can't risk you trying to fashion a weapon out of metal utensils."

"Ahhh." I blow on the soup and take a tentative taste. "So you're not a complete nutter. You know what you're doing is wrong."

He sets his bowl of tomato soup across from me and plops into his chair. "We belong together." His matter-of-fact statement seems to be the only response I'll get to calling him a nutter.

"That right?" I sip my chicken broth slowly, grateful for the warm liquid. "I've finally come face-to-face with Mr. Creepy Letters, I take it?"

If I gave a damn about his feelings, I'd worry I'd hurt them. His pinched expression doesn't pull on my pity strings one lick.

"My letters were *not* creepy," he insists.

"Sure, okay." I flick my gaze up at him. "You're the guy who gave me the fan at one of the shows, right?"

He lifts his chin, almost preening that I remembered his kind gesture. Hate to break it to him, but I only remember because he gave me the willies.

"I almost had you that day." His mouth screws into a frustrated wrinkle. "If Trent hadn't interrupted us."

"Really?" I adopt the same tone I'd use with a toddler who'd just told me he'd learned to pee in the potty. But inside, I'm shaking.

I take another sip of my soup to hide my shock. If I survive this ordeal, I need to re-evaluate my desire to talk to any and every one of my fans. There's a fine line between being polite and being downright stupid, apparently.

"Then you had that...brutish beast in our way," he continues.

I assume he's talking about Rooster.

"My source said my next best chance to rescue you would be at the Virginia shows. Which worked out well for me since I know the area."

Coldness cracks through my chest. "What *source*? Who told you that?"

"Never mind. If the stars had not aligned on this venture, I was going to try again in North Carolina or Georgia. Although those wouldn't have been ideal since I'd have to travel longer."

Does that mean we're still in Virginia? It must. Not that it matters.

His cold features screw into something more terrifying. "And if that filthy, unkempt dog who'd been trotting after you had gotten in my way, I would've taken care of him."

A firestorm of anger lights up my chest. How dare he talk about Rooster that way.

A cold smile spreads over his face. "But the security at that arena was comically easy to distract, and they kept your guard dogs busy."

So *that's* why Rooster didn't make it back to my dressing room in time.

"Although. . ." He laughs, the sound more creepy than humorous. "He came this close to catching up to us outside." He holds his hands a few millimeters apart. "He held on to the back of my van for quite a while. Too bad I didn't back up over him when I finally shook him loose."

Oh. My. God.

Tears prick my eyes. Rooster came close to saving me. I can't even imagine how furious he must be right now. But if he got that close, he must have seen the license plate? Or gained some other helpful details?

Maybe he'll be able to track me down before this psycho sticks me back in my trunk. Or worse.

Would Rooster give the information to the police? Is he out there trying to find me on his own? Or did he ask the club to help him?

For the first time since waking in this nightmare, I have a sliver of hope to cling to.

Mr. Creepy glances at my soup. "Eat up."

Too stunned to say anything, I dutifully take another spoonful, forcing my brain to come up with some neutral conversational topic. Anything to keep him talking and avoid the inevitable return to the bedroom. Maybe even figure out where the hell I am. Who he's working with.

"So, we're still in Virginia?" I ask as casually as possible.

"You'll be happy here," he says, sidestepping my question.

"Ya think so, huh?"

He screws his face into a disapproving scowl.

Ignoring him, I go back to the soup, every now and then darting a quick look around the room, searching for anything to use to my advantage.

"Once you're more...settled," he says, "we'll have a nice ceremony."

Ignoring that, I keep slurping my soup.

A scraping noise draws my attention. He's sliding his phone across the table. When I reach for it, he clucks his tongue, and taps the screen. A photo of me tucked in between Rooster and Jigsaw backstage appears.

Where did he take that photo? I frantically scramble through the tour dates in my head. How long has he been following me?

"That's my boyfriend and his friend. What's your point?"

He flips to a picture of me on stage with Dawson. My skin crawls. I mean, obviously I knew he'd been stalking me, but it's a whole different feeling to be confronted with the evidence of said stalking.

"You're too intimate with too many men," he says. "No more."

My blood simmers but I bite my tongue. I want to get out of this alive. Not trigger him into…doing Lord only knows what. My mouth stretches into my sweet, southern, charming smile. "Who I may or may not be *intimate* with ain't really yer business."

He scoffs. "Of course it is."

"For your information, I'm not *intimate* with Dawson. I barely know him outside of the tour. Those performances were for *the show*."

"It's not appropriate. And you're on that van with all those men from your band. You should have your own private vehicle."

Unhinged laughter bursts out of me. "That's not how the music business works, pal. It's a tour bus. A way to get from point A to point B. A business decision. Not orgy time."

His nose wrinkles. "Well, what are people supposed to think?"

"I dunno, maybe if someone has a problem with it, they can foot the bill for a private bus. 'Cause my label sure ain't gonna do it until I bring in more money."

His face screws into a confused expression. Maybe there's some other aspect of a business he knows nothing about that he'd like to mansplain to me. *Asshole.* "And, by the way, I don't give a damn what anyone thinks of my travel arrangements."

Whoops. There goes my temper again.

But, really, no amount of me bein' nice is gonna cure this crazy.

His eyes gleam, like he's thinking he's about to score a conversational point. "You were intimate with men on that television show too."

"Thought you said you *fell in luuuv* with me on the show?" I can't help the mocking tone that creeps into my voice.

His expression settles into the kind of calm condescension I'd like to slap right off his flaccid cheeks. "I saw something good and pure worth saving in you. And I will. You won't need any other man but me."

My spoon falls from my fingers and floats over the top of the soup. As if this creature can really be considered a man. "Who appointed you judge and jury over my life?"

"Someone has to be. Otherwise what would happen?"

"Well." I sneer at him. "I reckon when my boyfriend finds me, he's gonna kill you slow."

He purses his lips in a startling imitation of a cat's butthole. "Don't do that."

"Speak truth?"

"Don't do that 'I reckon' thing."

"Why exactly do ya think we belong together again?" My inner southern bitch is coming out loud and proud, now.

He winces. "Your accent is horrible."

"Are you joking me? You drugged me. Kidnapped me. Stuffed me in my trunk. Took me Lord only knows where. You're insinuating I'm a slut. Now you're insultin' my speech, on top of *all* that?"

So much for the meek act.

I'm absolutely boiling at the absurdity of the situation. Words are the only way I know how to deal with this overwhelming, powerless sensation.

"Shelby," he says in a tone a normal person might use to calm a snarling dog. "We'll work on your speech. I can't have you passing that dialect to our children."

"You're barkin' up the wrong tree there, mister."

"Martin," he corrects. "Martin Suggs."

"I don't give a good goddamn!" I slap my palm against the table. "I ain't making babies with *you* or anyone else."

An expressionless mask slides over his face, terrifying in its absence of any emotion. I'd almost welcome anger over this blank demeanor. But I'm too pissed off to stop myself.

"How do you even know I can have kids, huh? Did ya ever think of that? Never mind the fact that I don't *want* 'em. And I sure as shit would never have any with some crazy asshole who kidnapped me."

"You're meant to fulfill your female duties."

Outrage constricts my throat. So many retorts land on my tongue but I can't force out a single one.

He stands and walks over to a drawer by the sink. "You're obviously... upset. When you're not so hysterical, we'll discuss our future."

"Hysterical? You haven't seen hysterical. *We* don't have a future. My future is singing and being with the man I love. Ain't none of that got anything to do with you and whatever hell spawn you think you're forcing on me."

Ignoring my outburst, he slowly slides open the drawer and pulls out a small black case and a clear vial of liquid.

Fear slams against my ribcage.

He uncaps a huge needle.

"Oh, hell no." I stand and back away from the table. "You're not a doctor. You're gonna end up killin' me." Tears sting my eyes but I refuse to let them fall.

"Hush, rabbit. I know what I'm doing. This is what's best for you."

I turn and *run*.

My boots pound over the hardwood floors. Down the dark hallway, praying like hell my guess about a door at the end is correct.

"Get back here!" he thunders.

"Fuck you!"

Panic surges over me in waves as I navigate the unfamiliar house. My head spins. Blood thunders through my ears. Fuzzies swim in front of my eyes. I blink hard to clear my vision and keep hauling ass away from my captor.

Aha. I slam into a door, yanking and twisting the metal knob. It doesn't budge.

Damn.

Deadbolt.

I twist the lock but it still won't open.

My terrified eyes scan the darkened area. Make a run for one of the shuttered windows? No. They could have bars or something.

I glance up.

Another lock. It's above my reach but I jump up and slap the slide once, twice.

Finally the door opens.

To another damn door.

This one's a screen door and I easily click the latch and fling it wide.

Not sweet freedom. A screened-in porch. With another door.

What is this? Some nightmare maze of doors to nowhere?

I stare into the inky darkness beyond the screen. A cool breeze tickles my cheek. This is it. Outside. I flick that lock and shove the flimsy metal so wide it bangs off the side of the house with a sharp metal clack.

Terrified and knowing he's coming, I leap without looking, missing the short set of stairs and landing hard in the grass.

Run! Run! Run!

My gaze swings wildly around the unfamiliar terrain.

Dirt driveway.

White van.

I'll be way too visible running down the driveway.

It's dark but I think we're surrounded by trees. I make a mad dash for the tall, looming shadows at the perimeter of the property. My legs wobble and tremble, stiff from so many hours stuffed in my trunk, but I push past the awkward sensations and haul ass.

Rooster, where are you?

A tiny spark of hope prompts me to imagine he's close by.

"Help!" I scream.

What'd my momma tell me one time? If you're in trouble, scream "fire!" People don't want to get involved if a woman's in trouble. They're more likely to help fight damage to property than a person.

"Fire!" I yell. "Fire!"

Something heavy pounds behind me. Hard breathing. Boots slapping against the ground.

No. No. No. How could that fat bastard catch up to me already?

I push harder. Pump my legs faster. So close to the trees. What I'm going to do when I reach them, I have no idea. Gut instinct says I'll have a better chance when I can hide.

I don't waste any more breath screaming. No lights are visible in the inky blackness. I'm utterly alone, wherever the hell I am.

Despair washes over me. I might as well be on another planet.

Don't give up. Keep running!

Something slams into my back, knocking me to the ground. I tumble and roll through the wet grass, scrambling to get away.

An arm bands around my chest. My feet slip, and my knee bangs painfully against hard earth.

"No! Let me go!" I slam my elbow backwards, hitting something solid but squishy. He grunts out a harsh breath.

"Stop fighting me. No one can hear you anyway."

Sweet freedom was so close.

Or maybe I never even had a chance.

I buck, kick, and jab with every ounce of strength I have left. He squeezes tighter, pinning my arms to my sides. Something pricks my neck and a ragged scream tears out of my throat. "No!"

Burning fire rushes through my veins. Scorching flames sear my skin.

The burning sensation recedes to nothing.

My body goes limp.

He pushes me off him and I roll into the grass without feeling a thing.

This is worse than before.

So much worse.

He hoists me in the air, throwing me over his shoulder like a lumpy sack of potatoes. I can't see where we're going but I'm sure it's back inside the quaint little cabin of terror.

Why couldn't I keep my dang temper in check? Pretend to be docile for a little while until I figured out a better plan?

Each step he takes snuffs out any hope of escape.

He grunts as he lifts me up the steps. "For such a small woman, you're heavier than I expected."

Great. Now he's insultin' my weight on top of everything else.

The bedroom I was in before is on the right and he carries me inside, kicking the door closed.

Sounds like a nail poundin' inta my coffin.

I don't wanna go back in my trunk.

Tears leak from my eyes into my hair. I can't feel them but I watch their glistening trail down my dirty, messy tarnished-gold waves.

I focus all my energy on sending a signal to my legs or hands but it's like being caught in a nightmare where I see the monster coming but can't so much as twitch a muscle to defend myself.

He sets me on the floor next to the bed with a thud. My head smacks against the hardwood, rattling my teeth.

My vision swims.

If my body wasn't fighting whatever drugs he pumped into me, my heart would be jumping in terror.

Bending over, he grunts and struggles to pull something out from underneath the bed.

Finally, he rolls out a long box. The same color as the bed. Same length. Reminds me of one of those platform beds with the trundle underneath like Hayley and I had once begged our parents to buy us.

Hayley. At least if I don't make it out of this, I'll get to hug my baby sister again.

Oh, Lord. My poor momma. She's already suffered losing one daughter.

A metal clacking noise draws my attention back to the box.

Nope. Not a box.

The top is made out of a thick, black metal lattice with two heavy-duty sliding barrel locks—one at the top and one at the bottom. The top hinges open, like a fancy cat carrier.

Realization slams into me.

It's a *human cage*. He plans to lock me inside it.

My brain renews the effort to force my limbs to move.

He scoops me up and arranges me inside. "You'll stay in here until you learn to be a good girl."

My sleepy gaze sweeps over the interior of my new prison. It's not tall enough for me to turn over or sleep on my side. Worse, it's hidden so well, integrated into the bed seamlessly. How will anyone ever find me?

Drowsiness creeps over me from the injection, but somehow my arm finally receives the signals my brain has been sending. My hand jerks to life. My fingers slowly curl into a fist and I loosely raise it. As my last act of defiance, I sweep my fist into a wide, lazy arc, connecting with his cheek. It barely glances off the side of his face.

He *tsks* at me, slowly shaking his head.

Can't do another thing. My brain's too fuzzy. Soft. Barely able to concentrate on anything except for the fear of being sealed away in a box under the bed.

One last thought remains as the blackness pulls me under.

At least I went out fightin'.

CHAPTER SEVEN

Rooster

PITCH BLACKNESS ENGULFS THE ENTIRE AREA. NO STREETLIGHTS. HAVEN'T seen another house for miles.

I pull the truck off the road, rolling it underneath the shadow of trees before stopping.

Behind me, a black van quietly crawls to a stop. The door opens. One after another, brothers dressed in black jump out, landing in the overgrown grass with nothing more than a dry rustle. In the darkness, they appear as little more than blurry movements in the night air.

More brothers on their bikes are waiting farther down the hill in case we need backup. But having them thunder all the way up here would be as good as announcing our arrival over a bullhorn.

"Ready?" Jigsaw asks.

I nod once, too focused on what's ahead to bother with words.

Pants had suggested we wait until morning. To my relief, Ice had shut that idea down fast.

We go in now and we go in *hard.*

Once Shelby's safe in my arms, I'll decide what to do about Martin Suggs.

In addition to his gun and knife, Jigsaw's carrying a set of bolt cutters in his gloved hands.

Just in case.

I pat the Glock in my side holster under my cut and briefly touch the hunting knife strapped to my leg. Not that I plan to use the weapons. No, I'm looking forward to getting up close and personal with my kill.

Ice, Pants, and T-Bone meet us at the bottom of the driveway.

The mailbox says "Stannard," which is apparently the name of Martin Suggs' uncle.

Please let Z's hunch be right.

This has to be the place. Otherwise, we're out of leads.

The five of us slowly creep up the driveway, sticking to the grassy edge. The barest hint of moonlight illuminates our path.

White van.

Jackpot.

"That's it," I whisper. The urge to storm up to the house blazes in my veins but I remain calm and focused.

"Thank fuck," Jiggy mutters.

"Don't get too excited yet," Ice cautions.

He's right—I still want to punch him for saying it out loud.

Slowly, we approach the house, careful not to trigger any possible motion lights or alarms that might be on the property.

But Suggs doesn't seem concerned about security.

That should be a red flag.

Jigsaw, Pants and I go around the right side of the house. Ice and T-Bone take the left.

Windows appear to be shuttered over. No light spills from behind them.

I count four windows on this side.

No sound.

What if he's not here? Maybe he dumped the van, grabbed another vehicle, and took off for somewhere else?

What if I'm too late?

At the back of the house we meet up with Ice and T-Bone.

"Nothing," Ice whispers. He holds up three fingers. "Windows."

I hold up four fingers and jerk my thumb back in the direction we just came.

Here, there's a door with a smaller window.

"Kitchen?" Jigsaw asks.

"Maybe."

Ice takes the crowbar in his hand and points to the lock. "We'll go in the back. You three go in the front."

Pants lifts his own crowbar and Jiggy wiggles the bolt cutters.

The three of us creep back to the front of the house.

Jigsaw and I crouch on either side of the door while Pants tests it.

It opens with a soft screech. Pants stops and waits.

Nothing.

He pulls it wider. I slip in first, Jigsaw after me, and Pants last. For such a big guy, he moves with stealth, quietly closing the door behind him.

It's darker than dark and I hold my arms out in front of me, carefully shuffling my feet, praying I don't bang into anything that alerts Martin to our arrival.

Another door.

Screen door.

Locked.

I unsheathe my knife and neatly slice the screen, slip my hand through the hole, and flick the latch. Slowly, I thumb the handle and open the door, praying the old metal hinges don't screech.

From the back of the house, there's a crash.

"Subtle time is over," Jigsaw whispers.

I shake my head. "We may need to grab him if he comes running this way."

Inside, a man screams. Ice's deep, lethal voice shouts, "Where is she?"

"Fuck." I twist the knob on the door but it won't open.

I slam into it with my shoulder while Pants works his crowbar along the seam.

Heavy boots echo over the floor inside and a minute later someone flings the door open.

"We got him." T-Bone flicks his gaze to the side. "No sign of Shelby, yet."

She *has* to be here.

I muscle past T-Bone, turning toward the light, and march down a long hallway. Ice has the doughy guy in a chair at a table with two bowls, two cups, and a can of Sprite on it. A puddle of soup slowly drips from the tabletop to the floor.

My gaze follows the puddle of soup to a glint of silver under the table.

The chairs are secured to the table by a thick silver chain.

All my fury and fear rush through me. I rear back and slam my fist into Martin's face, sending him sideways. "Where the fuck is she?"

"Who?" Martin screams. "Who are you?"

T-Bone pushes him upright while Ice unrolls some duct tape. The two of them work together to wrap long strips around the guy's chest, affixing him to the chair for a long, painful night of questioning.

Blood trickles from the corner of Martin's mouth. The whites of his eyes show as he stares in horror at a bright red drop landing on his shirt.

"Look at me, motherfucker." I grab his chin and force his head back. "Where is Shelby?"

His gaze fixes somewhere over my shoulder. "I don't know what you're talking about."

"Like fuck you don't." I grab a fistful of the heavy chain and kick the table on its side. T-Bone jumps to the side as the heavy wood batters the floor. "What's this? Some shitty decorating choice?"

Martin wriggles under the tape while I unwind the chains from the table legs.

Ice cuffs him on the back of the head. "Settle the fuck down, asshole."

Cobra fast, I strike again. This time wrapping the metal links around the psycho's throat. Tight until he's choking. Using all my weight, I use the chain to shove him and the chair he's in over the kitchen floor until I slam it into the counter. The move leaves two deep grooves in the flooring.

The man gasps and struggles, desperately trying to dig his fingers between the metal links crushing his windpipe. "No—"

I pull the chain away, noting without satisfaction the deep, red pattern blazing over his throat. "What?"

"I didn't do anything." He coughs.

Jigsaw steps up next to me and backhands the guy. "Who were ya eatin' dinner with then?"

"No one!"

I'm snorting fire as I wrap my hand around his neck. Much better than using the chain. His pulse drums over my fingers and I squeeze harder. So tight he chokes and wheezes. His Adam's apple jumps against my palm. A little more pressure and I'll crush his windpipe.

Frantic, he jerks his secured body from side to side.

His face turns purple.

"Rooster!" Jigsaw shouts. "Easy, brother. We still need him."

"Where. Is. She?" I release him and he slumps forward—as far as his binding allows—coughing and sputtering.

After a few gasping breaths, Martin flashes a demented smile at me. "She's *mine*."

His claim jacks my rage to nuclear-blast levels.

"Fuck no you didn't," Jigsaw growls. He turns to me. "Search the house. I'll work on him."

Martin's big, round eyes dance between Jigsaw and me, clearly trying to decide which one of us will inflict the most pain.

"No, he's mine." I barely recognize the savagery in my own voice.

"He hurt my brother's girl," Jigsaw says against my ear. "Let *me* handle this for you. You need to focus on finding Shelby. First thing she's gonna wanna see is *your* face. Not my ugly mug."

I nod quickly, taking a step back to give Jiggy's vicious side some room to work.

Jigsaw holds the bolt cutters in front of Martin's face and makes a *snip, snip* motion. "Hope you know your ABCs, motherfucker."

The veins in Martin's neck bulge as he strains and jerks his head from side-to-side. The effort of trying to free himself leaves him panting and sweat rolling down his forehead.

"That's right," Jigsaw says in a hollow voice, "I'm about to break your bones in alphabetical order and floss my teeth with your tendons."

Behind us, Pants chuckles. "Yeah, brother."

I pat Jigsaw's shoulder before leaving the kitchen.

I'd been so focused on Martin, I hadn't noticed Ice and T-Bone leaving the kitchen. They must be searching the rest of the house. I meet them in the darkened hallway.

"Nothing." Frustration bleeds into Ice's voice.

"Another bedroom's over here." T-Bone points to an open door. "I think her trunk—"

He doesn't even finish his sentence before I rush past him.

Inside the room, I stop dead.

It's Shelby's trunk all right but it's empty. Lid open. Nothing inside. I stare into it as if I have the power to will it into giving up its secrets.

"Fuck." I jab my hands through my hair, yanking on the ends, while my gaze frantically bounces over every surface. Bed, neatly made up. Rug. Nothing out of place. No signs of a struggle.

Where is she?

I run to the kitchen, muscling Jiggy out of my way. Lifting my foot, I slam it into Martin's thigh, sending the chair sliding sideways. "Her trunk's here. Where is she?"

In the short time I was gone, Jigsaw's worked him over pretty good. Not with the bolt cutters—yet. But Jiggy's fists are plenty lethal. Especially when he's on a rampage.

Martin smiles at me, his split lip bleeding onto his tan pants. "You'll *never* find her."

"Playtime is over." Jigsaw lifts the bolt cutters. "Pants, grab his hand."

"No!" Martin screams.

"Start with his pinkies." I slap Jigsaw on the back and return to the bedroom.

She's gotta be here somewhere.

"Shelby!" I close my eyes and listen.

Nothing but Martin's screams.

"Shut him up for a second!" I shout.

The screaming cuts off with gurgling yelp.

Ice's shoulder brushes mine. "Did you see a basement?" I ask him.

"Yo!" he shouts. "This place got a basement?"

"No!" Jigsaw shouts a few seconds later. Guess the loss of a pinky finger motivated Martin to start answering some questions.

I stomp into the bathroom and rip the shower curtain aside.

Nothing.

She's too big to fit in the cabinets but I check them anyway. Linen closet too.

The screaming from the kitchen resumes—although a bit muffled now. Combined with the harsh questions from Pants, and Jigsaw's crazed laughter, it's one hell of a psychotic symphony.

Coming out of the bathroom, my eyes zero in on the bed. The wooden frame extends all the way to the floor. No way to hide a person underneath.

Ice flings open a slim door. A shallow closet—barely the depth of a normal-sized hanger. With ruthless focus, Ice tears clothes out of his way and tosses them on the bedroom floor. Next, he sweeps his arm across the shelf and dumps several shoe boxes on top of the clothes.

Together, we search for any sort of hidden space or doorway—tapping on the walls, brushing our hands over the shelf and above the door.

Just an ordinary closet.

My gaze drops to the shiny hardwood floor of the bedroom, then shifts to the carpeted closet floor.

Odd choice of flooring.

I pull my knife out and rip up the carpet.

Well, fuck me.

There's a small square in the floor with a pull ring that fits flat against a recess in the surface so it's easily concealed under the carpet. "Motherfucker."

Bracing myself for whatever's inside, I pry the door open and drop to my belly. As I shove my face into the hidey-hole, my vision's immediately swallowed by the darkness. "Shelby?"

No answer.

Ice hands me a small flashlight and I use it to illuminate the dark space. All four sides are carpeted. A small stack of books, a pillow, a scratchy-looking blanket, and a bottle of water are arranged neatly in the corner. Waiting to welcome a new prisoner or left from a previous captive?

"What the…?" I whisper. I pull my head out of the space and sit on my heels. "He's kept someone in there. Or he was planning to. It's empty now."

"Who *is* this sick fucker?" Ice takes my place and checks out the hiding spot.

I press my hands against the dresser next to me. It groans as I shove it sideways. I search the dusty floor and the wall the dresser had been leaning against. No hidden panels or doors.

Together, Ice and I move almost every piece of furniture, toss each throw rug, and scour every available inch of the hardwood floor for hidden latches or panels.

No more hidey-holes.

My gaze lands on the bed again. It looks solid. Heavy. Thick wood with broad, black iron accents.

"Help me flip this thing." I nod to the bed.

"Bro," Pants says from the doorway. "He swears she's not here. Says he left her somewhere else and we're not gonna find her."

"What do you want to do?" Ice asks me.

"She's in this house. Somewhere. She has to be. He didn't have time to stash her somewhere else and make it all the way out here." Actually, I have no idea if that's true or not. "I'm not leaving until I've turned this place inside out. Why leave her somewhere else and hide here by himself?" I gesture toward the kitchen. "Who was he eating dinner with? It doesn't make sense."

"Good points." Ice gestures to the hallway. "Let's keep searching."

Pants wanders over to the closet and peers inside. "What the fuck's that?"

Ignoring him, I press my palms to the bed's wooden frame and start shoving. At first, it won't budge. Ice scrambles over to help me push. Then I realize, the top of the bed *is* moving. The underneath isn't.

"Shit!" I drop my hands from the bed and fall to my knees, tugging on the two black O-rings on the side of the bottom part of the bed. It's a separate piece that easily rolls out on two steel tracks.

...You remind me of a soft, tiny rabbit. Cautious, yet unaware of the dangers that surround vulnerable creatures in need of the safety of a cage.

The final letter he sent Shelby.

He wasn't joking or waxing poetic about putting her in a cage.

Through the thick, black metal lattice I make out Shelby's still form.

Sweet fucking relief flows through me. Followed by stone-cold fear.

"She's here! I got her!"

I work the latches and throw the top open.

"Shelby!"

She's on her back. Hands folded over her stomach. So still.

Devastation ravages my soul. My entire world turns black.

"Baby, no," I keep repeating in a ragged whisper. Carefully, I slip my arms under her limp body and lift her out of the shallow box, cradling her body against my chest.

"Jesus Christ." Jigsaw drops down next to me. "Shelby?" He brushes her hair out of her face.

She's breathing.

Low and shallow. Her chest is barely rising and falling. But she's breathing.

"Fuck," Ice mutters. "We need to call an ambulance." He turns, barking orders to Pants and T-Bone to load Martin into the van.

Ignoring everything else around us, I kiss Shelby's forehead.

"Baby, wake up." I stroke my hand over her cheek. A red gash on her forehead brings my rage to the surface.

Wetness trickles over my arm.

Another bump on the back of her head has blood coming from it. Angry red patches and bumps line her arms, chest, and cheeks.

"What the fuck did you do to her?" I roar over my shoulder, torn between ripping Suggs to pieces and not wanting to release Shelby.

Pants and T-Bone drag Martin into the bedroom. His pathetic gaze latches onto Shelby immediately.

Ice slaps Martin across the face to get his attention. "What did you give her?"

Martin's eyes settle on something across the room for a brief second. "I won't tell." He flashes an evil grin at me. "You can't take my little rabbit. I caught her fair and square."

Ice stares at a black leather case on top of the nightstand. He picks it up, unzips it and studies the contents.

"What is it?" I ask.

"No label." Ice zips it shut and holds onto it. "We'll give it to the doctors." He focuses on Pants again. "Take him out to the farm. Don't fuckin' finish him yet. He's Rooster's kill."

"Got it."

"W—what are you talking about?" Martin stammers. "No. You can't make me leave. I'm not going with you."

Ice punches him this time. His fist making a sickening crack against Martin's cheek. "Now you know how Shelby felt, asshole." He lifts his chin at Pants. "Get him out of here."

A few seconds later, the van starts up and drives away.

"Rooster, we gotta go," Ice says. "Call me."

I tear my gaze away from Shelby. "Thank you, brother."

His gaze falls on Shelby and his jaw works from side-to-side. "Thank fuck we found her." He shakes his head and walks out of the bedroom.

"Shelby, baby," I whisper. "Come on. You're safe. We've got you. Wake up."

Nothing.

"It's all right. She's breathing. She's gonna be okay," Jigsaw keeps repeating. Whether he's trying to reassure me or himself, I can't tell.

Sometime later—minutes or hours, I have no idea—sirens fill the night air, slowly growing louder.

Jigsaw slaps my shoulder and stands. "I'll get someone for her."

Careful not to jostle her too much, I stand with Shelby limp in my arms and walk into the hallway. Every light in the place is blazing now. Paramedics rush into the house with Jigsaw shouting directions at them.

Agent Jackson follows, scowling at me. When his gaze lands on Shelby, he closes his eyes briefly.

"She's breathing. We don't know what he gave her," I explain to the paramedics, ignoring Jackson.

"Where is he?" Jackson shouts.

"Don't know. He was gone when we got here," Jigsaw answers smoothly.

The paramedics don't seem to understand the situation. They fire off question after question at me.

Has she been drinking?

Does she do drugs?

Is she diabetic?

"No! None of that. The guy kidnapped and drugged her, or he knocked her out with a sedative. She's got a head wound."

They lay her out on a stretcher, supporting her airway and administering oxygen. She's so limp, like a fragile doll.

"Puncture wound," one of the paramedics says, studying her neck.

"We found this on the nightstand." Jigsaw hands over the black case. Thank fuck. I'd been worried Ice left with it.

"Ambulance is out front. Let's get her to the hospital."

I move to follow and Jackson stops me with a hand against my chest. "Wait a minute. I need information from you."

I brush his hand off. "Not now. I'll be at the hospital. You can catch me there."

Jigsaw blocks Jackson's path. I edge around them and run to catch up with Shelby, wincing every time the stretcher bounces and shakes down the stairs and over the grass.

"How long has she been out?" one of the paramedics barks at me.

"I don't know." I jump into the back of the ambulance, not waiting for an invitation. "We just found her."

"Sir, move into the corner." He jerks his chin.

I fold my big ass into the spot he indicated and brace myself. Sirens pierce the air. The ambulance rolls out at a quick and bouncy clip.

"I think he drugged her water when he took her. Not sure if he injected her with something else here." Words keep rambling out of my mouth. I'm so fucking afraid of whatever he did to Shelby in the few hours that he had her.

The paramedic grunts in acknowledgment and keeps working on Shelby.

The ride to the hospital is excruciating. I keep my gaze focused on Shelby, watching for any sign she's waking up.

Every minute she remains unresponsive murders a piece of my heart.

CHAPTER EIGHT

Rooster

FRIEND OF THE CLUB OR NOT, AGENT JACKSON IS RELENTLESS.

The doctors took Shelby away immediately and started working on her. The paramedics handed over the stuff we found at the house. The doctors questioned me, but I didn't have a lot of information to share. They finally sent me to the waiting room with a promise someone would keep me updated. Jackson tried corner me the second Shelby disappeared behind the swinging doors, but I'd dodged him easily.

I haven't had a chance to confer with Ice yet to know what he wants me to say to his FBI buddy.

Greg and Trent arrive at the hospital, both grim-faced and tense. Confident Greg can answer at least a few of Jackson's questions, I slip away to phone Ice.

"What's going on?" he answers, his tone casual.

"Got her to the hospital. Jackson's on my ass, though."

"We got everything you need. Just tell it like it is. Suggs and the van were gone when we located the house. We searched the cabin and found her under the bed. That's it. You can say we're hunting for him now if you want."

"All right."

I hang up and push through the side door into the hospital.

Agent Jackson's waiting for me in the hallway. "Get your story straight with your prez?" he asks in a dry tone.

"No *story* to get straight." I relay the barest 'facts' to him.

He grunts in response. "I suppose your brothers are out there trying to track him down so you can get a piece of the guy."

I force my mouth to twist down, like I'm so terribly conflicted about the situation. "You saw what he did to my girl. What would you do?"

"Let the justice system handle it."

I don't buy that for a second. "Bullshit. You wouldn't be so friendly with Ice if that was true."

His lips twitch into a smirk. "Probably." The humor in his expression fades. "This is turning into a high-profile case. I need something solid to close it out."

"If they find Suggs, I'll have them turn him over to you, okay? I have Shelby back. All I care about right now is making sure she's okay." I choke on the last word, and this time I'm not faking. "I gotta get back inside. I still need to call her mother."

"First, tell me something." He holds up his hand in a stop gesture. "How'd you know where to find her?"

"We searched the house. Saw the hidey-hole he had in the closet, so I just started moving furniture to see what other hidden spaces he might have."

"That's not what I mean and you know it."

I shrug and back into the elevator, jabbing the 'close' button before Agent Jackson decides to join me. "Had a hunch and it paid off."

The door shuts as he's opening his mouth to respond.

Later, Jackson.

Upstairs, I find Greg in the waiting room, fretting and staring at his cell phone. "It's out. The story's out. Shit! This isn't good, Logan."

As if I give a single flying fuck about his PR problems. "Did anyone call her mom yet?"

He shakes his head miserably. "I didn't know what to say to her."

Yeah, neither do I. "It's all right. I'll call her now."

"Thank you. Someone needs to let her know before she reads it online. It's going to be everywhere in a couple hours." He's obviously too much of a coward to be that someone.

"Are they reporting where she is now?" People trying to get information or sneak a photo is the last damn thing we need.

"I don't think so. Not yet, anyway. But the story about her being kidnapped from the arena is big news."

"Shit." I yank out my phone and search for a quiet place to make my phone calls and arrange some travel. The sun's barely peeking above the horizon. Exhaustion settles over me but I push it away. I locate an empty room and make some arrangements before settling in to call Lynn.

"Rooster?" she answers with a yawn. "You know I work the late shift. Why the hell are you callin' me at this hour?"

Can't say I feel good about fucking up her morning. But better she hear it from me than someone else.

"Lynn." I grit my teeth and decide to get straight to the point. "Shelby's in the hospital."

"What?" she shrieks so loud I pull the phone away from my ear. "What happened?"

Shit, how the fuck do I explain the kidnapping over the phone?

"She's had this obsessed fan following her." Bare details. Just give her the few pertinent facts. "He got to her last night. Gave her something that knocked her out. We don't know what yet. The doctors are working on her now."

"Can I talk to her? What do you mean an obsessed fan? Who?"

"She's unconscious." I swallow hard. This has to be the worst phone call I've ever made. "I'm waiting for an update from the doctors."

"Rooster." She sobs and I feel like fucking shit for doing this to her over the phone. "Is my baby going to be okay?"

"Shelby's a fighter." I choke on the last word. "You know that."

"I…I need to be there…I—"

"I know." Finally, I can be useful. "You got a pen nearby? I have you booked on a flight this afternoon. It was the first one I could get you on. You're going to need to give them your I.D. and check in as early as possible. I'll have someone at the airport here to pick you up when you land and drive you to the hospital."

She's silent for a few seconds. It's hard to tell if she's writing something down or absorbing the information. "You have me booked…*what?*"

"Can you get ready and leave soon?"

"Y-yes," she stammers.

"All right. When we hang up, I'm going to arrange a car service to take you to the airport. I'll text you the information." I read her the flight info. "Call me if they give you any trouble."

Another long pause. "Thank you."

"No problem. I'll see you soon."

I hang up and make the arrangements for the car service. As I finish texting Lynn the details, a shadow passes the doorway then returns.

I glance up and Jigsaw smirks at me. "Want me to pick up Mom?"

"If you promise not to be a creep to her."

He shakes his head, all humor melting out of his expression. "I don't have it in me today, brother."

"Thanks. Any word from the doctors yet?"

"Nothing. Greg was gettin' on my nerves and that FBI jackoff keeps eyeballin' me in a way I don't particularly care for."

I drop my gaze to his bloodstained knuckles. "Might want to wash your hands." No doubt that's the blood of Martin Suggs, and the last thing we need is Jackson getting ideas to examine Jiggy or something.

He huffs a laugh. "Good point."

I copy Lynn's flight information and hand it to him. Next on my list is a phone call to Z.

"You all right, brother?" he answers right away.

"Yeah. At the hospital, waiting for news about Shelby now." I share a brief outline of what happened, leaving out the extra-incriminating details.

"Give me the address of the hospital. I'll send it to Dex. Last time they checked in with me, they weren't far from you guys."

I have to find the nurse's station to locate something with an address and recite it to Z.

"Got it," he says.

We talk for a few more minutes, but there's not a lot I can say with so many people around. I think Z understands that.

Finally, we hang up and I return to where Greg and Trent are waiting. "Any news?"

"They're running tests. Trying to eliminate different things," Greg answers. He cocks his head and stares up at me. "How did you find her?"

I take the chair next to him, leaning back and stretching my legs out, resting one ankle over the other. "You really don't want to know."

I close my eyes and immediately drift into an uncomfortable sleep state. Aware of the sounds and activity around me but since none of it has to do with Shelby, I'm unable to open my eyes or give a shit.

At some point, I pick up Agent Jackson's voice, speaking in low tones to Greg.

I crack open one eye and listen to Greg whine about the bad publicity for a few seconds before Jackson realizes I'm awake.

"We need to speak." He jerks his head toward the hallway.

"Do we?" I ask in a lazy tone, adding in a yawn.

He scowls and glares at me. I follow him into the hallway, and together we trudge over to a window overlooking the parking lot.

"Did Shelby say anything when you found her?" he asks.

"No." My fists clench and my throat tightens. "She was unconscious. We almost *didn't* find her." I haven't stopped thinking about what would've happened if we hadn't looked under the bed. If I'd believed Martin's story about her not being at the cabin.

"I got a look at the cage under the bed. Fucking sick."

Unable to form any words, I nod.

"How did you know where to look for her? And don't fucking get cute with me this time."

"What's wrong? You mad your guys didn't figure it out faster?"

He swoops in, getting way too up close and personal for my taste. "You realize it could look like *you* orchestrated the whole thing, right? Maybe Shelby needed some extra publicity—"

"Fuck you." I shove him out of my face. "That's bullshit. She's in the hospital. No one can figure out—" My voice breaks. "I'd never do anything to hurt her," I finish in a quieter tone.

"Maybe you hired someone and he got carried away."

"No wonder the Feds are so fucking useless. This the caliber of your investigation skills? Or are you just bottom of the barrel?" I lean down in his face. "That why Ice has you dancing on his hook?"

He ignores the taunt. "Then tell me."

I glare at him for a few seconds. "Club has…lawyer friends. I don't know the details but one suggested we look for other assets that he might have access to. Found a trust that led us to the property."

"Why didn't you call me?"

"There wasn't time. You were checking out the other address." I pin him with a stare. "Not like you bothered to keep me updated on how *that* was going."

"I don't answer to you."

"And I don't answer to you."

We continue glaring at each other for a few seconds before he finally backs down. "Has anyone contacted her family yet?"

"I just talked to her mom. Booked her on a flight. She should be here this evening."

He raises his eyebrows. "She's okay with you dating her daughter?"

I snort. "No, but not for the reasons you're thinking."

He doesn't ask for details.

"Where you at, Jackson?" I ask since he seems to have calmed down. "You think Suggs was acting alone or you think he had help?"

He rocks back on his heels for a second while his face smooths into place. "I can't discuss that with you."

"Like hell."

"You don't want me to jeopardize the investigation, do you?"

Threatening to call Ice and tell him Jackson isn't playing nice feels too drastic. Besides, one way or another, I'll find out whatever Jackson thinks he's hiding. If Suggs was working with someone else, it'll come out eventually.

When I don't bother with threats or plead for more information, Jackson bobs his head in an approving manner.

"I don't think Suggs acted completely alone," he finally says in a low voice. "But *obsessed* isn't a strong enough word for how he felt about Shelby."

"Meaning what?"

He sighs and quickly glances around. "He's been tracking her since she was on some television show." He coughs and looks away. "Not sure if your buddies came across it or not, but Suggs has a history of being *inappropriate* with young women. For years now. But these days, his house is dedicated to all things Shelby Morgan."

Sounds like that house and his shrine to Shelby need to be burned to the ground. "That's just great. So glad he's been running around loose, unchecked."

"Nothing we could nail him on until now."

I cock my head. "Why are you sharing this with *me*?"

"I *shouldn't,* since you withheld information from me and made me look like an asshole, but I thought you should know. Since he's *on the run.* Technically, Shelby's still in *danger.*" He glares at me. "I figure you'll want to add some extra protection here at the hospital. In case he comes looking for her."

While I'm puzzling out what seems to be an invitation to add more Lost Kings to the hospital waiting area, he checks his phone.

"You think someone on the tour was working with Suggs?" I ask.

"I didn't say that," he answers quickly.

"Logan!" Dawson's voice echoes down the hallway, his heavy boots thundering over the tile. "Any word about her yet?"

He stops when he recognizes Agent Jackson. "Jesus Fuck. Not you again."

I duck my head and laugh. "Popular guy."

"Fuck off," Jackson mutters, which only makes me laugh harder. He turns and flashes a wide shit-eating grin at Dawson. "How are you, Mr. Roads?"

"Fine." Dawson's gaze slides to me. "Everything okay here?"

A prickle of unease slides down my spine. Did Dawson have something to do with Shelby's kidnapping? To my knowledge, he cooperated with the police. His concern seems genuine, but it could be an act. Or maybe he knows Bane was involved and he's covering for him to avoid the bad press.

My jaw clenches as I work through the possibilities.

Jackson's hand lands on my shoulder. "Easy. It's not him."

Dawson's troubled gaze pings between Jackson and me. "What's going on, Logan?"

I'm not sure if I trust Jackson's judgment, but I try to calm myself before answering Dawson. "We're still waiting for news about Shelby. Doctors are working on her."

"Thank God. Thank God you found her before…" Anguish tears through his voice. "Never had somethin' like this happen before…crazy fans, yeah. But this…this is a whole new level. Poor Shelby."

Something about his *poor Shelby* comment rubs me wrong. Shelby's tough as nails. Once she makes it through this, she'll be kicking ass in no time. I'm sure of it. She doesn't need Dawson's pity. Or anyone else's.

Dawson's phone buzzes, and he digs it out of his pocket. "Shoot." He holds it up. "Made the mistake of talking to my ex a couple of days ago, and now she won't leave me alone. Give me a minute." He holds up one finger and shoves the door to the stairwell open. It clangs behind him, and his muffled voice comes through loud enough for me to tell he's irritated, but I can't make out the words.

Jackson stares at the door, watching Dawson through the sliver of glass.

"What's on your mind?" I frown at Jackson. "You think Dawson's involved?" Five seconds ago, he seemed certain Dawson had nothing to do with it.

"No," he answers slowly.

"Logan!" Greg shouts. "Get down here."

My feet start moving immediately, jogging down the hall faster than the hospital folks probably care for. "What?"

A doctor's in the waiting room with Greg. I skid to a stop inside and she backs up a step. "I, uh, privacy reasons, I can't share a lot of details, but Miss Morgan has woken up."

"Thank God." I squeeze my eyes shut.

"She's asking for Rooster…?"

"That's me." I raise my hand like the most eager kid in class.

"Oh, well. Follow me."

Instead of taking me to see Shelby, she leads me into a smaller room—a doctor's lounge with a coffee machine and a few scattered chairs. She remains standing.

"What's going on?" I glance at the door and back to the doctor. "Can I see her?"

"In a minute. She's in and out of it. Not quite lucid yet. Besides being sedated, she had some sort of allergic reaction, as well as several bumps, bruises, cuts, and a mild concussion. Her body's been through a lot. She needs rest."

"But she's okay?"

She glances down at her chart. "A kidnapping. I don't see a lot of those. Anyway, she's going to need to talk to someone. I'll have a counselor stop by when Shelby's more with it."

"Whatever she needs." I jab my fingers through my hair. "Thank God. I'm just so glad she's awake. She's going to be okay?" I ask again. The doctor hasn't exactly given me a definitive answer yet.

"We'll continue to monitor her. I want to keep her on oxygen a little longer. I think she'll recover fine. Like I said, she needs to rest, and she'll probably need to talk to someone." She glances at her chart again. "She's… a singer? In the middle of a tour, someone said?"

"She is."

"Well, I don't think she'll be able to go back on the road right away. Don't let anyone talk her into it before she's ready." She pauses and peers up at me, her lips thin, as if she regrets the last comment.

"Shelby's not easily talked into stuff but I'll make sure no one pressures her."

Relief softens her professional-doctor expression. Maybe she thought I was an overbearing manager-boyfriend or something. "Good. That's good. Does she have any other family?"

"Her mom's on her way from Texas. She should be here later this evening."

"I'm pleased to hear that. It will help her to have some familiar faces around that she trusts."

"Some of my brothers are coming down from New York as well." Might as well warn the doctor that in a few hours, her waiting room will be full of even more Lost Kings.

Instead of the dirty look I expected, her gaze drops to my VP patch and she smiles. "Well, that should certainly help her feel safe. I understand the police haven't caught the person who abducted her yet."

"Not yet." I adopt a more serious expression. "No one knows where he is."

CHAPTER NINE

Shelby

Ow.

Old socks line the inside of my head. Empty socks. Flapping in the breeze on a clothesline. Like my head's no longer attached to my body.

Cool, fresh air floods my nose. The rhythmic inhale and exhale of my breathing centers and grounds me.

My body aches.

Where am I?

I reach into my memory, trying to pull something loose.

The box.

That man put me in a damn *cage*.

Anger burns somewhere distant in my mind. I'm too exhausted to expend a lot of energy on any emotion.

Painfully slowly, my fingers curl against something scratchy but yielding. Not the hard, unforgiving bottom of my trunk or the cage. I wiggle my toes and something loose flaps against my feet.

Where'd my boots go?

Rooster. Rooster. Rooster.

I remember a dream of him holding me. Speaking to me. Freeing me from the box.

Was it a dream? Hallucination? Wishful thinking?

Shoot, I hope I'm not dead.

"Miss Morgan," a gentle female voice says. "I'm Doctor Landry. You're safe now. You're in the hospital."

Something gentle brushes against my hand. I hook my fingers around it and squeeze. At least, I think I'm squeezing. I feel weaker than a kitten abandoned by her momma cat.

"That's good. Can you squeeze my hand again?"

It takes some effort, but I grasp her cool fingers even tighter.

"Excellent."

Hot itchiness inches over my chest and down my arms. I'm too weak to scratch at it and end up moaning instead.

"Thank God." That's Greg. Is he here too?

My mouth is so dry, my lips so cracked, I barely whisper, "Logan?"

Something brushes against my arm. "Right here, chickadee. Don't worry about anything. Just rest."

How long have I been out of it? How many shows have I missed? Is the tour over? Did I miss the whole thing? Did they go on without me? Replace me?

Each question drifts through my mind but I can't latch onto any one long enough to voice it out loud.

"I'll let Trent know she's coming around," Greg says.

Peeling my eyes open is a slow, painful process.

White.

White walls. Green privacy curtains. White tile.

A hospital.

I close my eyes again.

Did I imagine the cabin? Running for the trees? The cage?

No. It happened. All of it.

I struggle to open my eyes again and focus. "How did you find me?"

The oxygen mask muffles my words. Rooster squeezes my fingers gently. "We can talk later. The doctor wants you to rest. You're safe now."

Safe.

That's nice.

I drift for a while.

Someone pokes and prods at me. Rudely lifts my eyelids.

"Cut that out." I try to swat the hand away but I'm too tired.

Feminine laughter. "She's doing better than I expected."

Gee, thanks.

More poking.

I cough and try to sit up so I can show this person I'm fine and they should leave me alone. But I'm too tired.

"Your body needs rest, Ms. Morgan." This voice doesn't sound as nice as the earlier one. Where'd the nice lady doctor go?

"Stop poking me then," I mutter.

Another soft chuckle. "I'll be back to check on her later."

"Thank you," Rooster says.

Time passes. I can't tell how much. Some noises filter into the room. Other times I'm drifting on a soft wave for long stretches of time.

My arms itch, but when I try to scratch them I get tangled in tubes and wires. Someone stills my hands. Firm fingers rub something soothing on my itchy skin. The uncomfortable prickling fades.

Sometime later, I peel my eyes open and realize Rooster's still in the chair next to my bed. He's quietly watching over me and when our eyes meet, a faint smile ghosts over his lips.

"How do you feel?" he asks.

Groggy, dirty, fuzzy…"Bleh," I mumble.

"You're safe here," he reassures me. "Your mom's on her way. She should be here in a few hours."

"Really?" Who told her what happened to me? How'd she make it here? My mother hates to fly, and we sure don't have the extra money for plane tickets.

Sudden despair hollows me out and my vision blurs. "Please?" I whisper. I attempt to extend my hand toward Rooster. Sweat rolls down my forehead from the effort.

He shoots up and reaches for the buzzer. "What do you need?"

"You."

His expression softens as he sweeps his gaze over me. Gently, he slides his arms under my body, shifting me just enough to give him room to stretch out by my side. My aching joints protest the movement but the satisfaction of Rooster's warm, solid protection is worth the pain. He holds me to him as tightly as possible with all the wires and tubes in his way. He nuzzles my neck, the familiar tickle of his beard further grounding me. In his arms, I feel cherished, safe, and—most importantly—alive.

CHAPTER TEN

Rooster

"Psst, Rooster." Ice's hushed tone pulls me out of sleep.

Shelby finally seems to be resting comfortably and I hate to disturb her. Slowly, I extract myself from the bed without waking her and step into the hallway, quietly closing the door behind me.

"What's up?" I stretch, wincing as my spine snaps and crackles into place with the movement.

"New York's here," Ice says. He lowers his voice and moves closer. "And Pants has some info you're going to want to hear. In person."

"Shoot." I glance at the door. I really don't want to leave Shelby, but she knows I was here and I wouldn't leave unless it was important.

Ice lifts his chin at something behind me. I turn and find Murphy and Heidi walking toward us.

"Holy shit, you came too, Little Hammer?" I pull her in for a quick hug and mouth a *"thank you"* to Murphy over her head. While Shelby knows my brothers are here to protect her, I bet she'll appreciate a bit of female companionship.

"Is she okay?" Heidi pulls away, staring up at me with worry dancing in her dark brown eyes.

"I think so. She woke up for a bit. Doctor says she needs to rest."

"Wrath and everyone else are down in the waiting room." Murphy jerks his thumb over his shoulder. “Staff was a little squirrelly about having so many bikers here.” He and Ice share a laugh. “Ice said you might need to run out. Heidi and I can sit with her until you get back.”

Maybe I’m tired but the offer chokes me up. Murphy somehow *knows*. Sure, Ice is a brother—I can trust him. Hell, every brother in Virginia has helped me out in one way or another over the last few days. But I’ll be a hell of a lot more comfortable with a NY brother watching over Shelby while I’m gone. That way if she wakes up again, at least she’ll be greeted by familiar faces.

“Thank you, brother.” I pull him in and slap his back. “Really appreciate you coming all the way down here.”

“Not a problem.” He searches the corridor. “Where’s Jiggy?”

“Probably on his way to the airport. He’s picking Shelby’s mom up for me.”

Murphy raises an eyebrow.

“He promised to behave.”

“Yeah, okay. First time for everything, I guess.”

After all the tension and misery of the last couple days, I laugh a little. “You sure you don’t mind...being here?” I ask.

Murphy spent a fair amount of time in the hospital not that long ago. Can’t imagine he’s eager to hang around one now.

He snorts. “Thanks for the concern, but as long as I’m not the one in the gown getting my hair and beard shaved off, I’m fine.”

“Now that you mention it.” I squint and rub my hand over my own beard. “That ol’ chin curtain of yours sure grew back awfully fast.”

His mouth twitches. “Heidi says it’s because I have an overabundance of testosterone.”

I roll my eyes Heidi’s way. “Of course she did.”

She grins at me. “It’s true.”

“There *is* another possibility.” I scratch the side of my head, like I’m deep in thought. “He’s part Sasquatch?”

“Anything’s possible.” Murphy shrugs.

I open the door, checking that Shelby’s still asleep. Murphy claps me on the shoulder. “Fill me in on all your adventures when you get back. I won’t let anyone near her.”

“Thanks, brother.”

He and Heidi quietly tiptoe into the room and I close the door.

Ice nudges me down the hall toward the waiting room.

He wasn't kidding. The room's bursting with Lost Kings and friends of the club.

Anya leans up and quickly hugs me. "If Shelby needs anything, let me know, okay?"

It's a kind offer considering Anya and Shelby have only met one or two times. "Thanks, sweetheart."

"Rooster!" Wrath picks me up in a big bear hug—possibly cracking a rib or two in the process—before setting me down. "How's she doing?"

"Better. She woke up a bit." My lips twitch as I remember Shelby telling off one of the nurses who came in to check on her.

"Sorry we couldn't get down here faster."

I glance at the clock on the wall. "You made good time, brother." My gaze lands on Trinity, standing slightly behind Wrath. "You came too?" I can't help but be a little choked up that my brothers *and* their old ladies dropped everything to be here. "Thank you."

Trinity squeezes me in a quick embrace. "No problem."

Dex steps forward to hug me as well.

"Shit, brother, you have a lot on your plate at home. Thank you for coming down," I say.

"You got it." He slams his fist into his open palm. "Wish we'd gotten here sooner to help you find this guy."

I glance around the room. Jackson has a way of blending in, and I don't want to say anything he'll overhear. "He's on the loose right now. But Feds are on it."

Dex's face remains impassive. "Good to know."

Griff shakes my hand next. "Whatever you need. We're here for you, Rooster."

"Jumping right into the support club gig?" I pull him in and slap his back.

"Nah, man. When we heard what happened…" He glances over his shoulder at Remy. "We just wanted to help out if we could. That's really fucked up."

It's bullshit—Griff and Remy definitely want to know how far the club will go to protect what's ours. Probably want to get a feel for being on the road with the club and visit one of our other charters, too, before they commit to forming a support club. It's what I'd do in their position, so I'm not offended.

I flick a quick glance at Dex, who nods. Yeah, this might be a sign they're moving closer to forming the support club. "Appreciate it." I slap Griff's shoulder, then Remy's. "Thank you. Glad you're here."

Steer and Hustler try to crack my ribs next with their enthusiastic embraces. Guess I'm missed in New York. I rough my hand over Steer's big, bald head and plant a loud, sloppy kiss on Hustler's cheek. "Thanks for coming."

"Z was frothing mad he couldn't ride down with us," Steer says carefully.

"I understand." Without Z's help, we wouldn't have found Shelby so fast, so I'm sure as fuck not complaining about his absence.

"What a lovely family reunion." Jackson's sarcastic comment silences the room.

In a brave, bold move, he pushes his way into the middle of our group while slow-clapping his hands together. "Why *exactly* are so many of you needed down here?"

Wrath scowls and tosses a who-the-fuck-is-this-joker look my way.

Jackson scans us again. "Two different charters from New York, huh?" He tilts his head in my direction. "You must be awfully important to your club."

Ice grips my shoulder. "Fuck with one of us, you fuck with all of us." It sounds more like he's warning Jackson than explaining the basics of club life.

"Still, I don't see any of your Mississippi brothers here?" Jackson makes a big show of checking out the room. "Florida?"

"Congrats, you've done your homework," I say in a dry tone. "You in charge of the National MC Threat Assessment report this year or something?"

Wrath smothers a smirk and wraps his arm around his wife's shoulders. "This is purely a social call," he says to Jackson.

Jackson eyes Wrath, then Trinity. His gaze skips to Steer. "*Both* of New York's enforcers here." He fake bites his nails. "Whoever will protect the club in your absence?" He finishes the dramatic performance in a high voice.

Jackson's either a brave motherfucker or he has a death wish.

None of my brothers take the bait.

"Another New York brother and his wife are sitting with Shelby now." I jerk my thumb over my shoulder. "If you want to go harass them too."

"I wouldn't," Remy warns with a big, cocky grin. "Murphy's an ex-fighter. He might fuck you up if you bother his wife."

"I'll keep that in mind," Jackson sneers. He scans our group again. "Where'd the other one go—Jensen? What's he doing?"

"He left to meet Shelby's mom at the airport." I cock my head. "We need a hall pass from you or something? I'm plannin' to stop by the men's room next. You wanna come hold my dick?"

Everyone except Jackson laughs.

Ice nudges me and inclines his head toward the exit. I turn and follow him out of the room. We pass a few local cops who scowl our way but don't say anything. Guess they're the reason Jackson was laying on the asshole performance extra thick.

"Whoa!" Jackson calls out behind us. "Where are you two going?"

"Told ya." I point toward the men's room door. "I was only joking about holding my dick, Jackson. Didn't think you'd take me so seriously. But, I mean, if you really wanna come watch…"

"Don't get cute."

Ice slaps his palm against Jackson's chest and leans in close. "I understand you need to put on a show for the locals, but remember who you're dealing with."

Jackson backs away. "You need to tell me where you're going."

"I don't answer to you," Ice says. With that, he slaps Jackson's chest with another crisp thump and heads toward the exit.

I FOLLOW ICE TO THE HOG FARM PANTS OWNS, OR PARTIALLY OWNS. I'M NOT clear on all the details—only that it's safe and often used as an interrogation or holding space for enemies of the Virginia Lost Kings.

Apparently, hogs will eat any evidence you toss them.

They also smell. At a certain point, a wall of stench slaps me in the face. There's no amount of breathing through my mouth or holding my breath that makes it tolerable.

We pass an old house that's seen better days. Ice keeps moving toward a smattering of barns at the back of the property. He slows and stops his bike in front of the last building, an aging, cavernous red timber number that would look more at home on Leatherface's farm than Old McDonald's.

"That's quite a repellent you've got there," I say as I walk up to Ice.

He laughs. "Man up, brother. That's the smell of money."

"Smells remarkably like shit." I shake off the stench. "What was up Jackson's ass back there?"

"Just flexing his muscles so the locals don't think he's on our payroll." He shrugs. "Probably the most excitement he's had in a while, so he likes to play it up."

As long as their power struggle doesn't impact Shelby, I really don't give a shit.

He slaps my shoulder and steers me toward the large, wide doors. There's a gap between them and Ice slides the right side open.

Daylight illuminates the inside. I'd say it's been a while since the barn's been used for its original purpose.

Cement floors and strategically placed drains would make the floor easy to bleach and hose down. Lots of iron hardware is bolted into the wood beams at a height more suited to restraining humans than animals.

Downstate has its own murder room beneath our clubhouse, so I recognize the purpose this building serves right away.

Martin Suggs is way in the back—a shadowy corner where Pants has Shelby's kidnapper strung from the ceiling, his hands stretched over his head, his feet barely grazing the floor.

"Please let me down. My hands hurt," he whines. Whether he's addressing Pants or he hears our footsteps approaching, I can't tell. More like he's begging anyone within hearing range to set him free.

Pants ignores him and lifts his chin at me.

Martin dances on his toes, trying to turn his body around to see who's coming.

"Were you worried about Shelby's comfort when you stuffed her in her trunk?" I ask quietly, stopping directly behind him.

He smacks his lips a few times but doesn't seem to have an answer.

"No, that's right. You drugged her." My fury explodes. I land one fist somewhere near his right kidney. My knuckles sink into his flesh and bounce free. He squeals and curls away.

He coughs and wheezes, fighting to catch his breath. "Your psycho friend cut off my finger!" he yelps as if that's going to stop me.

"It's just the tip." Pants yawns and rolls his eyes. "Quit whining about it."

"Did you bother to make sure she could breathe in that cage under your bed?" I slam my other fist into Martin's left side.

He screams, frantically tiptoeing to the right where he's stopped by Ice's big, solid frame. "No escape for you," Ice says in a cold, detached manner.

Martin gasps and scoots back a few inches, bumping into Pants.

"You weren't concerned about doping her up." I punctuate the sentence with another punch to Martin's side. If he lives to see tomorrow, at least he'll be pissing blood. "Making sure she wasn't allergic to whatever you gave her." *Punch. Punch.*

He screams and wails with each hit. "What are you talking about? She was safe in the box! I made it special for her."

This time, I punch him in the gut. His knees sag and the ropes pull at his wrists, exposing his raw, abraded skin.

"She's in the hospital, you fucking moron."

Martin doesn't have an answer this time. He's too busy wheezing and trying to catch his breath.

Finally, the stupid motherfucker raises his eyes to mine. "But I love her. We're meant to be together."

I lunge for him but Pants and his tree-trunk arms catch me around the middle, barely holding me in place.

"Easy, brother," he warns me. "The slug has info you might want."

"Suggs," Martin corrects.

Ice backhands him.

I glare at Pants. "What's this piece of shit got to say that I give a fuck about?"

"You have to let me go," Martin begs. "If I tell you. Promise."

"I'm not promising you shit." Calmer now, I grip a fistful of his hair and yank his head back. "You scared my girl for weeks with your psychotic letters. Then you dared to *touch* her. Take her. Hurt her. There isn't a single reason I should let you live."

I cock my fist back and he squeezes his eyes shut, straining to duck his head as if he thinks he can avoid the blow. "Someone helped me!"

"Who?" I release him and stagger backwards. My brain runs through the possibilities. *Greg? Trent?* I'll gut them both and dump them on the side of the highway.

Shit, I left Greg at the hospital. What if he *was* involved?

No, Murphy won't let anything happen to Shelby. She's safe.

"If I tell you," Martin begs, "will you let me go?"

"You don't get to bargain here."

He shakes his head, sweat pouring down his round face. "Don't hit me anymore."

I grab him by the throat and yank him closer. "If you *don't* tell me, a few punches will be the least of your worries. I'll torture you with every piece of rusty equipment I find in this barn until you're begging for death. Something tells me you'll break before I get to the castration tools."

He flinches, then licks his lips. His gaze darts between Pants and Ice, as if pleading with them to save him.

Since that'll never happen, I guess Martin needs some motivation to start talking. I unsnap the hunting knife at my side and hold it up to his face, letting him have a good look at the long, shiny blade. His eyes widen and his body twitches as he struggles to get away.

But death is his only chance of escape.

I drop my knife hand and poke the sharp tip of the steel blade into his groin. "I read *every* letter you sent my girl. You're sick and need to be put down," I whisper in his ear.

It's taking every ounce of my control not to jam the knife into his flesh.

"Please," he begs.

I dig the tip of the knife into his chin and push his head back until he meets my eyes. "Start talking or I start cutting."

CHAPTER ELEVEN

Rooster

"How do you want to handle Jackson?" I ask Ice once we're alone outside.

"Don't worry about him, bro." He cocks his head. "You really want to turn him over just to get this bitch?"

I run my hands through my hair. "I don't know. I can't exactly ask Shelby what she wants to do. There's a good chance the publicity it'll bring will make her life difficult."

"Ninety-five percent of this is on Martin. He didn't have *that* much help," Ice points out.

"I know."

Ice shrugs. "Then again, we can always get to him later. You might not be able to do the deed yourself if he's inside. We'll have to contract it out. You cool with that?"

"We'll see."

He slaps my shoulder. "Let's load him up. If you change your mind, we can always come right back."

"Thanks." I stop Ice with a hand to his chest. "I mean it, brother. Everything you've done to help me get her back. I was supposed to be down here to help *you* out, not calling in your favors with the Feds and dragging you into something—"

"Please don't get weepy on me, Rooster." He pats my chest. "I'm glad we got her back. Z was a relentless motherfucker." His lips twitch into a smirk. "Guess I won't get to poach his VP after all."

I snort at the suggestion. "You got a solid team here." I jerk my thumb over my shoulder in Pants' direction.

"I have a good crew," he agrees. "You'd be an excellent addition."

It's nice to be wanted, but if I ever leave downstate it'll be to go Nomad, not move to Virginia.

T-Bone rides up, his engine drowning out any more conversation. He shuts down his bike and saunters over. "What're we doing with this fool?"

"Handing him over to Jackson," Ice answers.

T-Bone raises his eyebrows. "Yeah? You're all right with that, Rooster?"

"He didn't act alone."

"Well, fuck. How you plannin' to explain his injuries?"

Ice shrugs, like he couldn't give a fuck less. "Car accident? That's Jackson's problem, not ours."

"THEY BEAT ME UP," MARTIN WHINES AND HOLDS UP HIS RAW WRISTS. "ONE of those psychos cut off my finger." He wiggles what's left of his bloody pinky.

We're in the parking lot behind the hospital. No one's close enough to overhear our conversation, but that could change at any moment.

Now that I've returned to the hospital, I'm eager to get this over with so I can see Shelby.

Jackson sweeps a dismissive glance over Martin's injuries. "You stole a biker's girl. You're lucky that's all they did to you." He leans in closer. "You'd done that to a member of *my* family, no one would ever find your body."

Martin's jaw drops.

Another officer joins us, snapping handcuffs on Martin and tossing him in the back of a police car.

"What exactly am I supposed to do with him?" Jackson seethes once the other officer is out of hearing range. "It would've been better for everyone if you'd disposed of his body."

Guess Jackson's over his earlier snit.

"That might still happen," I assure him. "But he needs to tell you who was involved, first."

"Well, fuck." Jackson rocks back on his heels. "The manager?"

"Nope. Dawson's ex."

He stares at me for a long moment. Long enough that I start to wonder if he already suspected Glenna Wilson. "Shit. Was Dawson in on it too?"

"I don't think so. Sounds more like she was pumping Dawson for information under the guise of a reunion, then fed that info to Suggs."

"Jesus Christ." Jackson cocks his head and stares at the sky for a few seconds. "I looked into her. Something didn't smell right, but she's a high-profile gal. Been in the business for a *long* time. Lot of people around her."

"What are you trying to say? She's untouchable?"

"More or less." He pins me with the hard eyes of a cop who's seen justice perverted one too many times. "It could get ugly for Shelby."

Unfortunately, that thought has already occurred to me.

"How sure are you that she *hasn't* had a fling with Dawson?" Jackson asks.

"Hundred percent," I growl. Shelby wouldn't have kept something like that from me. "Even if she did—which she absolutely did not—it's irrelevant."

"Won't matter. Press will paint her as the Jezebel of country music."

"You an expert on the music scene now too?" Ice asks.

"Let me talk to Dawson and Greg," I say, cutting them off before they start a new round of trying to out-piss each other. "I'm not going to stress Shelby out with this stuff right now."

"I'm booking him with kidnapping, arson, assault and battery, and whatever else I can come up with. He won't see daylight anytime soon," Jackson assures me.

"Good."

Ice glances over at the cop car. "You should've worked him over a little more, Rooster. A weakling like him won't last long inside."

Regret squeezes the air from my lungs. I should've ended Suggs.Who knows when I'll have the chance again.

CHAPTER TWELVE

Rooster

UNCERTAIN ABOUT TURNING SUGGS OVER TO THE COPS AND UNSURE WHO'S the best person to ask for advice, I stalk into the hospital.

On Shelby's floor, I run into Greg. Somehow he's even more disheveled than he was when I left.

"It's breaking. The story's all over the place now. Even made it to cable news." He points at the small television in the waiting room. "They haven't released the name of the hospital, so at least she won't get mobbed here, but it's only a matter of time."

"My brothers won't let anyone near Shelby."

Greg doesn't exactly seem thrilled by that plan. Too bad. He better get used to lots more Lost Kings providing Shelby's security for the rest of the tour.

My phone buzzes. Shit, I hope Shelby's mom isn't having any problems at the airport.

But it's an unknown number with a 716 area code. Western New York. "Give me a minute, Greg." I step into the stairwell and answer the call. "Yeah?"

"Rooster?"

"Who's this?" I have my suspicions but I want to be sure.

"Chaser."

I blow out a breath. "Hey."

"I heard about Shelby. She all right?"

"I think so. I'm still at the hospital with her."

"They catch the guy?"

"Something like that."

He chuckles. "Not gonna ask."

"Feds have him now."

"That's too bad."

"Yeah."

"You need anything? Anything we can do to help?"

Although I'm not really sure what assistance Chaser's club can give me, I appreciate the offer. "Thanks."

"No sweat. Don't ever hesitate to call me." He waits a beat or two before continuing. "So, was this a random stalker?"

"Yeah, he's a fucking loon. Started out sending her these crazy letters and it escalated from there." I don't have it in me to get into the whole story over the phone.

"Fuck, brother. Been there. Nothing quite this awful," he hurries to add.

I almost forgot about his and Mallory's Hollywood ties for a second. Maybe *he'll* have some useful advice. "Can I ask you something?"

"Anything."

I lean over the railing, checking no one's in the stairwell. "You know how she's out on tour with Dawson Roads?"

"Tell me he wasn't involved." The rumbling menace in his voice comes through loud and clear.

"No. Not him. I don't think so, anyway. But his ex-girlfriend."

"Glenna Wilson?" He whistles low and long. "Shit. Seriously? They had an ugly breakup or something recently. And before you ask, it was all over some blog my daughter reads. She told me *all* about it after we ran into you guys."

I smother a laugh. "I don't know much about it, other than what Shelby said. But somehow Dawson's ex contacted this crackpot when she noticed him commenting on all of Shelby's Instagram posts or some shit."

"Christ, that's fucking weird."

"It's totally fucked."

"What's your question?"

"The agent in charge seems to think if they go after her, it could blow back on Shelby. Somehow make *her* look bad. Fuck with her career since she's so new and this woman is more established. Honestly, I was concerned about that before he even said it."

Chaser blows out a long breath and doesn't speak for a minute. "I stepped away from all that years ago to help my dad run the club, so I don't know all the key players these days."

While running the Devil Demons MC must take up the majority of Chaser's attention, I can't picture him staying completely away from the entertainment industry. Dawson said as much when he let it slip that he'd spoken to Chaser's "people" about writing some new material together.

"But I know who Dawson is and I know about Glenna," Chaser continues, confirming my suspicions. In the background, it sounds like he's clicking a pen or typing on a keyboard. "The press on Glenna isn't great right now. Rumor is she got caught cheating. Public opinion isn't really in her favor."

"That should be good for Shelby, then."

"Key words—*should be*. The business is totally fucked, so it could always go the other way. But Shelby's young, well-liked for the most part. Worked her way up from nothing. People love the underdog. She's been through something scary and scandalous—a kidnapping. Everyone likes to jack off to some juicy trauma porn," he adds in a dry way that makes it clear how he feels about people who get their kicks out of others' misery. "My guess would be sympathy's gonna land on Shelby's side. Especially if you play it right. She got a PR person?"

"I don't think so."

"Let me find you a name. It might take me a minute to track down the right person but I'll ask around."

"Thank you."

"No problem. I'm sorry she's going through this. Glad she's got you looking out for her."

Yeah, because I'm doing such a bang-up job.

"I'd watch out for anyone in the business telling Shelby not to press charges or sweep it under the rug. They might be more worried about Glenna's interests than Shelby's."

"Thought of that too."

"Or they're just straight-up spineless."

That describes a few people I can think of. "Hate to ask for another favor..."

"Ask away, Rooster. I wouldn't have called if I didn't want to help."

Part of me can't stop wondering what favors Chaser will want in return. Another part of me doesn't care. "I'm gonna have a few brothers traveling with us for the rest of the tour—"

"You looking for extra protection?"

"Possibly. If not this tour, then the next one."

"Yeah. Anytime you're gonna be rolling through our territory, let me know. You still coming to our anniversary party?"

"You send us an invite?"

"I'll ask Mallory." He laughs. "But we'll have brothers from all over in for the party, so I'll introduce you around. Make sure everyone knows you're a friend of the club."

That's one hell of a generous offer. "Thanks, brother."

"Anytime. Let Shelby know Mallory and I hope she's okay."

"Will do."

We hang up and I contemplate calling Z to let him know about my conversation with Chaser. Even though it had to do with Shelby, eventually it'll bleed into club business, so I should give Z a heads-up.

Below me, the *scuff-thump* of someone hoofing it up the stairs grabs my attention. Sounds like cowboy boots maybe?

I press my back to the wall so I'm facing the staircase and casually cross my arms over my chest.

A few seconds later, Dawson appears on the landing below.

His eyes widen when he notices me waiting by the door to the hallway. Can't exactly avoid me.

"Logan. What's up?" He glances back the way he came. "I'm trying to avoid any reporters."

When I don't answer, he frowns and jogs up the final few stairs.

I back him into the corner. "We need to chat."

Misery seems to wash over him and he glances down at his boots. "Shit. Glenna was involved, wasn't she?"

He sure arrived at *that* conclusion fast. "You knew?"

"I *suspected* her involvement. *After* Shelby was already here. When Glenna called me earlier." He pauses and stares straight ahead. "Something she said didn't sit right. Story hadn't fully broken yet, but she somehow had details even *I* didn't have."

"You motherfucker. Why didn't you say something?"

"What was I going to say?" He waves his hands in the air. "You were gone. I didn't want to tell Greg my suspicions. How was that gonna help anyone?"

"You talk to Jackson?"

"That FBI prick? Fuck no."

"So what were you planning to do? Keep quiet and let your girl get away with it?"

"I didn't know for sure." He presses his fist to his stomach. "It was a gut feeling. I wanted to talk it over with you."

"Right." My tone conveys how much I believe that story. "Not like you have my number or anything."

Some of the rugged country boy persona he's known for seeps into his hard expression. "Didn't think you'd want to discuss it over the phone with the FBI monitoring your every move. Come on, now. I know you MC boys better than that."

Even when I was a boy, I never cared for anyone calling me one. "Careful, Dawson. Me and my *MC boys* don't give a fuck who you are."

Dawson doesn't flinch. I don't elaborate on my threat. Don't have to.

"I have friends in a few clubs," he says, testing the waters.

"That right?" He's smart enough not to go dropping names, so maybe he does have a few club connections. Doesn't really make a difference to me.

"Ah, fuck." He waves his hand between us. "You know I respect Shelby a hell of a lot. I'm fucking furious about what happened to her."

He *did* cooperate with the cops. Fuck knows, he could've told Jackson to stuff it, hopped on his tour bus and headed out of Virginia without Shelby. Instead, he's canceled a bunch of dates, which has to be costing him a fortune.

"Knowing I'm somehow responsible?" he continues. "That's not sitting well with me, Logan. Shit, you have any idea how many women I've been through? None of them ever pulled a stunt like this."

"Guess you're a real heartbreaker."

He huffs out an annoyed breath. "If anyone's heart was broken it was *mine*. First, when she fucked my best friend. And again, discovering she had a hand in Shelby's kidnapping."

"Your heart really isn't my concern, Dawson."

"We were together a long damn time. I never…thought she was capable of something like this. I don't know what the hell was going through her mind. Whether she thought he'd really nab Shelby or it was some sick game."

His phone buzzes and he checks the screen. "Speak of the she-devil."

Now we're getting somewhere. "Answer it."

"I—" He opens his mouth as if to argue with me, then shakes his head and accepts the call. "What do you want?" he snaps.

Dawson holds it up between us so I can hear their conversation. Something I didn't ask him to do. The action alleviates any lingering suspicions of his involvement.

"Why so testy?" a soft, seductive voice purrs out of the phone. "What's the—"

"Glenna." His gruff tone cuts her off. "I'm gonna ask you somethin' and I need you to be straight with me."

"What's that, baby?"

He rolls his eyes. "You have something to do with Shelby's kidnapping?"

Nothing like going straight for it, Dawson.

"Now, why would you ask me such a question?" Her outraged voice has a tinny fakeness to it. "I don't even know your new plaything."

"Jesus Christ, how many times do I need to explain this? I'm not beddin' her. Never was. She's my opening act. That's it. I would've been on tour with *you* this summer—just like the last two years—if you hadn't been screwin' Tucker behind my back."

"I told you that was a lapse in judgment."

"And I told *you*, I don't give a fuck. You're both dead to me. Time to let go and move on, darlin'."

He uses the word *darlin'* just about as sarcastically as any biker's ever used it. I smother a laugh.

"Now, answer me," Dawson continues in a cold, business-like tone, "were you involved?"

"How could I be involved?" she answers coyly. "I don't know Martin Suggs."

My eyes widen. As far as I know, no one's reported Martin's name yet. He's still an "unknown suspect."

Dawson meets my eyes and raises an eyebrow. I nod.

"Right," Dawson says slowly. "I notice you haven't even asked if Shelby's okay."

"Why should I care? She's nothing to me."

Dawson winces. Yeah, I'd be embarrassed too if I'd been in love with such a cold-hearted bitch. I've never hurt a woman, but I hope to fuck I never run into this one. It'd be awfully tempting to rip out her fucking throat.

She blows out a long, dramatic breath. "Fine, how is the little girl? I hope nothing bad happened to her," she says with all the sincerity of a B-list actress.

Dawson glances at me again and I shake my head.

"Don't know yet," he answers.

"What's wrong?" A little more concern creeps into Glenna's tone.

"Doctors won't tell me. I'll talk to her boyfriend later and find out."

"She has a boyfriend?"

"Yeah, darlin'. Big biker guy. Pretty sure his club has a charter not too far from Nashville."

"Don't you threaten me, Dawson." Her shrill tone echoes in the stairwell.

"Who's threatening?" Dawson's response is smooth as butter. "Just making a lil' conversation."

"You tell anyone I was involved, I'll bury you *and* Shelby in the press. Every last seat on your pathetic tour will be empty."

"My, my," he drawls. "Seems like an overreaction for someone who claims to be innocent."

"I took the blame for the Tucker incident because I felt bad. But I could just as easily share the 'real' scoop—that you and Shelby were screwing around behind *my* back first."

"That's gonna be a little hard to prove since I hadn't even *met* Shelby when we split, Glenna."

"Does the truth matter? People believe what they want to believe. I can be convincing."

"Yeah, don't I know it," Dawson mutters.

"I'm not kidding." Glenna's tone sharpens. "I'll talk to Bud and get your ass booted from the label. We both know I'm the better earner."

"*Suuure.*" Dawson draws out the word in a low, mocking tone. "Be my guest, darlin'. Been thinking of going in a different direction for a while now, anyway."

"Shelby will never get signed."

"That girl's got more talent in her pinky fingers than you'll ever have, so good luck with that."

"Talent is irrelevant. *You* oughtta know that better than anyone, Mr. Beers and Blue Jeans."

I choke on a laugh while looping my finger through the air in a "wrap it up" sort of gesture. Dawson glares at me. "I gotta go, Glenna. Looks like there's news about Shelby."

Silence from the other end.

"I hope she's okay." It almost sounds sincere.

"For your sake, I hope you're telling the truth, Glenna. What you did to me was bad enough, but to drag that innocent girl into it... It's like I never knew you at all."

Poor bastard looks so miserable, I'd rather be standing anywhere else, listening to any other conversation, than one so personal.

"I never wanted to hurt anyone. Especially you," she says so softly, I almost miss the words.

Dawson's face takes on that hard expression again. "Yeah, well. When you play dangerous games, someone's bound to get hurt."

He ends the call and stuffs his phone in his back pocket. "Figured I'd never get her to outright admit it. We need to warn Jackson to build his case before he goes at her hard. I don't doubt for a minute she'll follow through on every threat."

"Worried?"

"I couldn't give a fuck." He snorts. "Rumors that I had a fling with a hot twenty-two-year-old ain't gonna hurt my reputation."

A low growl rumbles out of me and he holds up his hands.

"It'll hurt Shelby more than it'll hurt me. It ain't fair but that's how it is."

"You publicly refuting any rumors would be helpful."

"Of course I will. But keep in mind, if I deny it *too* much, people will assume it's true. Glenna will try to smear Shelby as much as possible. Even with the truth on Shelby's side, it'll taint her reputation."

What fucked up world are we living in? Shelby works so damn hard. She hasn't done a thing to deserve any of this.

"I never thought when I asked Shelby on the tour that something like this would happen. I wanted to help out a new artist. Lift someone up. The way folks did for me early in my career. If I'd known it would make her a target…" Dawson sounds more broken up than I'd expect. Maybe I should put a lid on my cynical side and take him at his word. "I'll make it up to her."

"How exactly are you gonna do that?"

He stares at me. "Let me think on it a bit."

CHAPTER THIRTEEN

Shelby

After a few hours of actual restorative sleep, I feel almost human again.

Rooster's no longer in bed with me when I wake up.

I startle when my gaze lands on a bulky figure in a chair. His back is to the bed, so he's facing the door. After a few seconds of study, I recognize Murphy and breathe a sigh of relief.

"Murphy?" I croak out.

He jumps up. "You all right? Need something?"

"Water?"

"You got it." He pours from a pitcher near the bed and hands me a small plastic cup.

With shaking fingers, I manage to take a few sips and hand the cup back to him.

"Where's Rooster?" I force a smile that probably looks more deranged than humorous. "Not that I'm not happy to see you." Then it hits me. We're in Virginia still, I think. "You drove here from New York?"

"Couple of us rode down. Heidi's here too. She went into the hall to make a phone call."

My eyes water. "Really?"

"Hell, yeah." He gently squeezes my hand. "We were all worried about you."

"Thank you." I lick my cracked lips, and Murphy motions to the water. I shake my head. "Is Rooster okay?"

"He needed to run out and take care of something," he says with the evasiveness I've come to expect from Rooster's club brothers. "He'll be back."

My eyes are already closing and Murphy's last words take a few seconds to sink in.

Nightmares of suffocating chase me. I'm buried in a shallow grave while someone tosses heaps of dirt on top of me. Too powerless and weak to dig my way out of the hole…

"Rooster! Oh my gawd!" my mother's shrill voice pierces through my terror-struck unconscious. Is that really my mother? Or have I shifted to a different dream?

"What happened? Shelby? Baby, are you okay?"

With monumental effort, I open my eyes. Nope. She's here. Great relief washes through me. I'm not being buried alive, and my mother's here by my side.

Her warm fingers wrap around mine and she gently kisses my forehead.

"I'm okay," I mumble, squeezing her fingers and closing my eyes again.

At some point, Rooster must have returned to my bedside. Where'd Murphy go? Did he say Heidi came with him or did I imagine that whole conversation?

"My poor baby. Is she okay? Why isn't she awake?"

"She's been in and out of it. Doctor says she's going to be okay," Rooster explains in hushed tones. "She needs to rest, though."

Huh. Almost sounds like he's warnin' Momma to keep the drama to a minimum. Good luck with that, Rooster.

"Did you catch him? Where is—" Her question cuts off so fast, I can picture Rooster making a slashing gesture with his hand. At least, that's how my mind fills in the blanks. I'm too tired to open my eyes again.

"Let's talk outside and then you can sit with Shelby," Rooster offers. "I'll try to track down the doctor so you can ask your questions."

"Well, I, uh..."

"Come on, Lynn," Greg says.

How about that. Greg's here too.

Still can't muster up enough interest to open my eyes.

"How could you—" My mom's accusatory tone scratches my nerves.

"Outside," Rooster says in a harsher tone. "Please."

My lips twitch. Although I hate having the responsibility fall on Rooster's shoulders, it's nice to have someone with a spine dealing with my mother for a change.

Their conversation fades, and I'm free to return to floating on air. Is it too much to ask for a dreamless sleep?

"The tour's on hold while you recover, Shelby," Greg says in a low voice. "Don't you fret about a thing. Everyone's worried about you and just wants to see you get better."

"Thank you," I mutter. His words actually ease some of my gathering anxiety.

"You're awake?" He sounds genuinely surprised.

"More or less," I mutter.

"Need anything?"

Nope.

I'm so tired, I'm not sure if I say the word or not. Everything's quiet for a while. Or maybe I go back to sleep.

"I've never been so scared in my life. When we realized you were missing..." Greg says. "I'm so sorry I didn't take the letters seriously sooner."

His pitiful voice tugs at me. Whatever happened isn't his fault. At least, I don't think so. I can't round up any anger anyway. Only relief that I'm safe.

"The CMA nominations were announced," Greg continues.

Wow. Just a few days ago, that seemed like the biggest thing in the whole universe. Now, I feel...nothing. Oddly detached from my old aspirations.

"Really?" I ask, more to be polite than anything else.

"You're up for Best Female Vocalist of the Year and Best New Artist of the Year. Best Single of the Year for 'White Knight,' and 'Big Lies' for Song of the Year. That nomination includes Trent. He's pretty stoked." Greg's tired voice is tinged with excitement.

Wow. My fuzzy brain tries to count up the nominations. Four? Dang. That's more than I ever hoped for. Too bad my current predicament puts a damper on any mounting celebration. "They probably felt sorry for me." I sweep my hand over the hospital bed.

Greg sits up, leaning closer. "No. Don't do that, Shelby. They were announced *before* the story about your kidnapping broke. Those nominations were sealed. Done deals. This is all *you*. Not pity nods, Shelby. Your hard work this year paid off. Huge."

Maybe in a few days it'll hit me and I'll be more enthusiastic. But inside, I'm too hollow to celebrate a damn thing. It all seems so insignificant after…everything.

I fall back against the pillows and close my eyes. "That's good."

Greg blows out a frustrated breath. "Shelby. Your dedication. Your talent. It's finally being recognized in a big way. I know what happened was awful, but please try to focus on something positive. This will do amazing things for your future."

Future? What's my future going to look like? Being terrified every time I go someplace new? Scared of every fan I meet? Wondering which one is the next nutjob who thinks he's in love with me? Fearing that the guy who shook my hand and asked for an autograph is secretly plotting to drag me off to his cabin in the woods?

"You can take a break, Greg." Jigsaw's rumbly voice is more of an order than a suggestion. "She awake?"

Metal scrapes against the tile and Greg clucks his tongue. "She seems to be in and out of it."

Sure, if that's how he wants to explain my lack of enthusiasm about the nominations, I ain't gonna stop him.

They talk quietly for a minute. I flick my eyes open and watch them at the door. Greg finally nods and disappears into the hallway.

"Jiggy," I whisper.

He eyes widen, and he slowly prowls closer to the bed. "Songbird, we had quite a scare," he rasps.

I blink. My eyes well up.

"Shhh." He brushes his rough fingers over my arm. "How you feeling?"

I try to nod, but it hurts too much, and end up wincing instead.

Jigsaw's chiseled jaw turns to stone but he gently curls his fingers around mine. "We got to him, Shelby. He hasn't suffered nearly enough yet. But he will," he says, so low I almost can't hear him.

Does it make me a horrible person to enjoy the idea of my kidnapper being tortured by Rooster and his brothers? If so, I guess I'm goin' to hell.

"I tried to get away. I tried. I ran. But he—" My voice breaks. I can't stand Jigsaw thinking I'm weak. Too weak to be Rooster's girlfriend.

"Shh. Take it easy." Still holding my hand, he drops into the chair next to my bed. "Go back to sleep if you want. I'll be right here watching over you until Rooster gets back, okay?"

"Thank you," I whisper.

Knowing Jigsaw's by my side, I slide back into sleep.

CHAPTER FOURTEEN

Shelby

AT SOME POINT, MY MOTHER RETURNS. HER FAMILIAR CRISP, SPARKLING scent wraps around me, comforting and anxiety-provoking in equal doses.

"Here. Take my chair," Jigsaw says.

"Thanks, Jensen."

Jensen. Did I know that was Jiggy's given name?

I can't seem to dig the information out of my head.

"I talked to her a little before. But I bet having her mom right here will help her get better even sooner." Jiggy sounds sincere instead of the sarcasm I've grown to know and love about him.

Their hushed voices lull me back to sleep.

The door clicks closed.

My mother brushes her fingers through my hair. "Oh, Shelby. I never saw somethin' like this coming, baby."

You and me both.

After a few minutes, her warm, soft fingers curl around mine. "This is one more good reason to be single right now. Can't let those nutters who are obsessed with you get jealous, you know?"

Has she lost her mind?

Slowly, I peel my eyes open. "Are you kiddin' me right now?"

Her eyes widen. Maybe she thought I was asleep and wouldn't hear that tidbit of advice. "Shh. Don't get all flustered. I want what's best for you. This is career advice. Not personal."

Bullshit. I snatch my hand back and struggle to pull myself upright.

"Greg told me about the nominations. I'm over-the-moon excited for you." She leans in and lowers her voice. "Dawson's up for Male Vocalist of the Year. Wouldn't it be perfect if you two attended together?"

Yeah, perfectly awful. "If you're so hot for Dawson, maybe *you* should date him."

"Hell, Shelby." She dismisses the idea with a wave of her hand. "I'm too old for a man like that."

Brave. Be brave. I'm a big girl. I can buck up and explain myself. I've done it before.

Not that she ever listens.

Rooster *rescued* me for goodness' sake. Shouldn't that be enough to stop this foolishness? "Listen to me good, Momma. I'm *in love* with Rooster. Big time. I'm not pretending to be single or pretending to date someone else for you, my career, or any other reason."

"Oh, Shelby," she moans, like I've just confessed I flunked out of college. "Love's a damn disease. It comes on strong and dies slow. Painfully. Don't do this to yourself. Especially after such a horrible event. It's the trauma bonding y'all together."

Ignoring that bit of psychobabble, I push as much force as I can behind what I want to say. "I was in love with him *before* this happened." I take a deep breath. "I'm not looking for your advice or opinion when it comes to my relationship, Momma."

"I'll always want what's best for you. Whether you want to hear it or not."

Nope. None of my words are penetrating her thick wall of crazy. "I think you should go."

She pulls her hand away and sits back in the chair. "That's how you thank me for everything I've done? Kicking me out? A handsome face and big dick make you turn your back on your mother?"

"You're being vile." I wince as I struggle to sit up. Stupid hospital bed. "What's the matter with you? This isn't me turning my back."

"Shelby, this isn't like you."

That's probably true. I've never stood up to her when she interfered in my relationships before. I didn't feel a fraction of what I feel for Rooster for any of my exes, so they weren't worth arguing about. "I'm explaining that Logan's part of my life and you're not listening. I want you to be happy for me, not lecture me."

"Thank the Lord I talked you into getting that IUD," she mutters. "Since you're being so unreasonable."

Utterly confused, I frown at the change in conversation. "What are you talking about?"

"So he can't tamper with your pills or something. Men do that sort of thing, you know—knock you up so then you're tied to them forever. Especially if you're more successful."

"You have too much to drink on the plane?" Maybe it's because I'm out in the world and away from my mother now, but I never realized how weird her obsession with this topic was. I'm painfully aware she gave up her singing career when she got pregnant with me. While I understand how much it must have hurt her when my father left, living in the past isn't healthy for either of us.

I'm desperately trying to create a future for myself, yet my mother has a backlog of bitterness to clear up. I sure as heck can't do it for her. And I refuse to allow all that bitterness to taint *my* relationship.

"Logan is *not* like that." My voice comes out a whole lot more steady and calm than I'm feeling.

"Maybe not now. But men like that can't handle a woman who's in the spotlight—"

"Oh, cut the bullshit!"

"That's enough, Lynn." Rooster's voice rumbles from the doorway.

I shift and tuck the flimsy hospital sheet around me. Shame heats my skin from cheeks to toes. How much of our insane conversation did he overhear? Does this hospital have a psych ward? Maybe I can check Momma in while we're here.

"Can I speak to you privately." Rooster's tone makes it clear he's not *asking*.

"I, uh." My mother's head swivels between Rooster and me. "I don't want to leave Shelby alone."

She reaches for me but I cross my arms over my chest and stare at the wall. Right about now, Rooster could kick her ass back to Texas and I wouldn't bat an eyelash.

Rooster steps out of the room and returns with Heidi a few seconds later.

"Hi, Shelby. Hi, Mrs. Morgan." Heidi smiles brightly at both of us, and dang, is she a welcome sight.

"Heidi will sit with Shelby so we can talk." Again, Rooster's not exactly *asking* to speak to my mother.

I'm too tired and irritated to introduce Heidi to my mother, but Heidi doesn't seem concerned about my lack of manners. The tension in the room rises to an unbearable degree.

God bless her, Heidi keeps smiling like nothing's wrong. Like Rooster's not boiling with anger and my mother's not being an overbearing pain in my ass.

"Oh, okay." My mother brushes past Heidi.

The door clicks closed behind them and Heidi turns to face me.

"I'm so sorry about that," I whisper.

She waves off the apology. "Oh, I'm no stranger to screwy family dynamics," she assures me. "I've got stories that would make your hair *and* toes curl."

I would've thought it was impossible, but somehow, Heidi's upbeat chatter washes the bitterness of my mother's visit away. The knot of tension in my chest loosens, and I actually laugh.

"Murphy and I were sitting with you earlier," Heidi says.

"Oh, good. I thought I imagined talking to him before."

She chuckles. "Nope."

"I can't believe you came all the way down here."

"Hell, yeah." She squeezes my shoulder and smiles warmly. "You have a whole new big family, Shelby."

Well, thank heavens for that since my blood family seems determined to drive me nuts.

CHAPTER FIFTEEN

Rooster

NOT THAT I GET OFF ON INTIMIDATING WOMEN, BUT LYNN HAS ME SO fucking furious, it's hard not to tower over her, snorting like a bull.

Shelby's mother is a proud woman. Brave too. Maybe that crazy shit I overheard is an overreaction to the horrible situation. Jackson had given her an outline of what happened to Shelby. Then, she'd listened to what the doctors had to say. Maybe all the information pushed her over the edge.

Nah, fuck that. She's been beating this subject to death since before the kidnapping. Using what happened to Shelby to get her way is the last straw.

I stroll down the hallway searching for an empty room and some extra patience. The visitors' lounge is full of my brothers and not really where I want to have this conversation. Finally, a darkened room catches my attention. I shove the door open and peer inside. A stripped-down hospital bed and not much else. Perfect.

I flick the lights on and open the door wider, ushering Lynn inside first.

"What do you want?" Lynn crosses her arms over her chest and lifts her chin. It's a proud, defiant expression, so similar to one I've seen on Shelby that it melts a portion of my anger.

Since I don't trust Lynn right now, I leave the door open.

"You need to stop this shit, Lynn. Even before"—I wave my hand toward the hallway—"this happened, your meddling was stressing Shelby out. It needs to end. She really doesn't need it now."

"Don't tell me what my daughter needs. I'm her mother." She wiggles her fingers at me. "You've been in her life for five minutes."

My mouth quirks. I get it. We haven't been serious for long. Lynn knows that better than anyone. But by now, she should've accepted this is more than a hookup. "Listen, I get why you worry about her so much—"

"You're not a parent, so I don't think you do."

"No, I'm not. And I'm not eager to become one anytime soon, either." Maybe *that* will finally shut her up. "Since you seem so concerned about *that* topic."

"Big surprise." She snorts. "No man *wants* kids. They just don't like anything in the way of gettin' their dick wet."

I blink and stare. Not how I envisioned our conversation going. At all. "I get that your ex was a piece of shit, Lynn."

She recoils as if I'd slapped her. Maybe later I'll feel bad about that. Right now, I'm glad she's so stunned she keeps her mouth shut.

"I'm not saying there aren't a lot of assholes out there," I continue, "but *I'm* not one of them. I love your daughter."

She drops her gaze and kicks the toe of her boot against the metal bedframe. "She's enamored of you. I'm sure it seems exciting to be with an experienced older man. But she has to focus on her career. She won't have a second chance."

"You don't give her enough credit. Shelby's got no problem expressing herself around me."

"She's too young to know what she's doing."

Wait a second. Is *that* Lynn's problem? "You realize I'm only six years older than her, right?"

She squints up at me. "I assumed you were older."

"Yeah, you assume a lot of things about me that aren't true." I stroke my hand over my beard. "Is it the beard? Does it give me a dirty old man vibe, or something?"

My attempt at a joke doesn't penetrate her attitude of steel. "No, it's your VP patch. Figured you had to be a *lot* older to earn one of those."

I glance down, taking in the patch that still looks pretty clean even though I stitched it on a few months ago. She might have a point. Some clubs probably have age requirements for officeholders. Mine isn't one of them. Merit and the vote of our fellow brothers are all we need.

Now I'm curious. "How many bikers have you known, Lynn?"

She glares at me. "Enough."

"Was Shelby's dad a biker?"

"Lordy, no."

"So what's your problem with me?"

"It's not *you,* specifically." She tilts her head to the side. "I like you fine, Rooster. Now just isn't the right time for her. If you two still feel this way in a few years when Shelby's more established, then give it a shot." She raises her eyebrows hopefully, as if she thinks she's come up with a perfect solution. "You know…if ya love her, set her free. And if she comes back…"

My entire body recoils at the suggestion.

Miss out on years with Shelby for some imaginary reason Lynn's concocted in her warped mind? *Hell fucking no.*

"That's not gonna happen."

"You don't understand. She's wanted this since she was a little girl—"

"I know that."

She plows ahead as if I hadn't spoken. "I don't want her giving it all up for a man."

The suggestion that I'm disposable or interchangeable with any random guy who might pop into Shelby's life at some point pisses me off, but I keep my tone level. "I don't want her to give anything up."

"That right? You'll be okay with her on the road all the time? Won't find someone else to warm your bed while she's gone?"

Somehow, I don't think informing Lynn that I plan to travel with Shelby is going to ease her mind.

"What about those award shows?" she presses. "That's a big deal for Shelby. She needs a man on her arm who enhances her career."

Well, *that's* something I can't do for her. Fuck, if anything, my club ties could fuck up Shelby's career. Strange how that's not Lynn's go-to argument.

She flashes a triumphant smile when I hesitate.

No. Fuck that. "Stop worrying about shit that's none of your business. And stop making her miserable, Lynn."

The hurt on her face almost makes me wish I'd chosen my words more carefully. Almost.

"She said I make her miserable?" she asks in a small voice.

"Shelby doesn't *have* to say it. I can see it with my own two eyes every time she talks to you. Stop harassing her. And while you're at it, stop calling Greg. He's not going to toss me off the tour. Especially now."

She swallows hard and averts her eyes. "He told you that?"

"Yes."

"He told you I wanted you off the tour..." She stumbles over the words. "But you *still* paid for me to fly out here?"

I didn't want to rub that in Lynn's face but it's nice to have her finally acknowledge it.

"Whatever beef you think you have with me"—I tap my chest—"doesn't change the fact that Shelby needed her mom here."

"Thank you," she whispers.

I think that's as close to a truce as I'm going to get with Lynn.

Still, I can't help being a bit of an asshole about the situation. "And trust me, your daughter's not so *twitterpated* over me she forgets about birth control."

Her cheeks turn red.

I probably enjoy the shock on her face a little too much. Good. I hope I made her as uncomfortable as she makes Shelby.

This better be the last time Lynn and I need to have this conversation.

But somehow, I doubt it.

CHAPTER SIXTEEN

Shelby

HEIDI'S STORIES ABOUT THE RIDE DOWN HERE DO THE TRICK AND PULL ME out of my funk.

"Thank you for coming all that way. I can't believe...you must have enough to do at home."

Heidi shrugs. "I was worried about you. We all were."

"Where's Alexa?" I can't imagine it's easy for a young mom to just take off at a moment's notice.

"With Rock and Hope." Her lips curl into a softer, warmer smile. "We lived with them for a while, so she's comfortable there. Still has her own room at their house. And she loves them to pieces. My brother will look after her if they need a break."

"Oh."

"Yeah, the little ones get spoiled rotten in the LOKI family." She raises her eyebrows as if that's a perk I should be excited about.

Someone knocks softly on the door and pushes it open. Trinity's pretty face appears in the crack. "Hey, Shelby. Mind if I join you?"

I scoot up a little. "You came too?"

"Sure did. How are you feeling?" She closes the door behind her, long blonde and blue ponytail swishing over her back.

"Almost human again." I still haven't sorted through all of my feelings but I feel safe for the moment, and that's a start.

Trinity approaches the bed and my gaze drops to the bag in her hand.

"I brought you something. I, uh…" She hesitates and glances down. "I was going to send it to you for your birthday but with everything, I thought maybe you should have it now. I hope you don't mind."

Now I'm curious and don't understand why Trinity seems so nervous and hesitant. "Thank you. That was sweet."

She sets the bag on my lap. I peel it open and pull out a mint-green T-shirt. The faint scent of vinegar wafts up as I unfold the soft cotton.

"Oh my God!" An excited squeal bursts out of me. "My flocking fabulous flamingo!" A sassy pink flamingo with a teal guitar and teal cowgirl boots is front and center on the shirt. I couldn't have come up with something more perfect if I'd tried.

"You like it?" Trinity asks.

"I love it," I whisper, too shocked to look away from the gift. "Did you…did you make it?"

"Well, I created the design but had it printed up. There's a blanket and tote bag too." She flashes a quick smile. "But I didn't have a lot of room or time to pack."

"I can't believe it."

"Don't feel like you have to use it or I'm stealing your idea or anything…" Trinity hesitates like she's waiting for me to yell at her or something.

"Are you kidding? I *love* it! I can't believe you remembered and designed it for me. It's perfect. Thank you." I reach for her and pull her down for a hug.

"Oh!" She hugs me back gently. "You're welcome."

She gives me an easier smile and holds up her right hand. "I promise I won't be one of those people giving you flamingo knick-knacks every holiday for the rest of your life. I just…wanted you to have this."

"I love it. Really."

"Rooster said you're into yoga." Heidi pats Trinity's shoulder. "Trin drew up this super-cute, like, totally Zen flamingo meditating too." She closes her eyes, tips her head back and holds up her hands, touching her middle finger and thumb together to demonstrate.

"Zero flocks given." Trinity winks at me.

I squeal and clap my hands together. "I love it!"

Heidi grins at us. "It's *so* cute."

The door opens and Rooster pokes his head inside. "Everything all right?"

I hold up the shirt. "Look what Trinity made me!"

He smiles and lifts his chin at Trinity. "It came out nice."

"Thanks."

They share a look that resembles conspiring siblings.

"Where's my mom?" I ask.

"Talking to Greg." He glances down the hallway. "You want me to grab her?"

"That depends. Is she in a more sane and reasonable mood?"

He shrugs and bites his lip like he doesn't want to say anything bad so it's wiser to say nothing.

"Murphy's looking for you, Heidi." Rooster lifts his chin at me. "I'll be right back."

"Everything okay?" Trinity asks once we're alone.

"My mom…she thinks she's looking out for me but…she doesn't approve of Rooster…of our relationship."

"Because of the club?" she asks gently. "I understand why that might make some mothers uncomfortable."

"No. Well, at least she hasn't used that as a reason yet." I sigh and fiddle with my chipped nail polish. "She's worried I'm going to repeat her history. Get knocked up, quit singing. I don't know what she's thinking."

"I realize we don't know each other that well yet." Trinity gives me a hesitant smile. "But you seem pretty smart and determined to me."

"Thanks. I keep trying to explain, you can't help when you fall in love."

"Nope. For what it's worth, Rooster's a pretty smart and determined guy himself. You're a good match for each other."

A brief smile flickers over my lips. "I think so too."

"Maybe she just misses you because now you're out on the road?"

"Maybe." Although I don't think that explains all Momma's crazy.

Trinity's quiet for a few minutes, watching me. Not in a creepy way. More thoughtful or maybe protective. "I don't know everything that happened to you, Shelby. But if you need or…want to talk about it, I'm here."

Tears prick my eyes, and I swallow hard. "Thank you."

"You're safe and won't have to worry about him again." Her grave tone leaves me with no doubt as to what she's implying.

"Jigsaw mentioned something…similar."

"Oh, I bet he did." Her expression remains serious. "Being a biker's ol' lady means if someone hurts you, the whole club hits 'em back. Hard."

"I've gotten that impression." I try to force a smile. "Truthfully, I'd rather not get hurt in the first place."

"Well, truthfully, only someone stupid or suicidal goes after a Lost Kings girl." She winks at me.

"You and Heidi make it seem so…normal. But I've never had anyone look out for me that way before."

"I understand," she says softly. "After my dad died, no one looked out for me either until…Well, the club will protect you."

"I haven't seen Wrath in action, but I've noticed Jigsaw's just as ferocious as Rooster."

"Yup, they're all like that."

"But to leave everything and run down here. That means a lot. Everyone has jobs and—"

"The club always comes first. Wrath and Murphy own a gym together. And trust me, my husband loves bossing their other partner around, so I'm sure he left Jake a lengthy list of instructions." She chuckles. "I have my own business and a lot of it can be done remotely. Heidi's part-time at her job so I think she just switched some days around." Her mouth quirks. "Besides, they probably wanted some alone time to make a Baby O'Callaghan."

I cringe at the idea of a baby *anything.*

Trinity bursts out laughing, curling her arms over her stomach and falling forward. "Oh, shit. That's the same face I make every time someone asks *me* when Wyatt and I are having a baby."

"Ugh. People are so rude."

She straightens but laughter still sparkles in her eyes. "They have no boundaries for sure."

"I can't…Lots of girls I went to high school with already have kids and stuff. I can't even imagine...It sounds like so much *work*," I finish on a whisper.

"Being a mom is rough," she agrees. "A hundred-and-sixty-eight-hour-a-week job. I adore my little nieces and nephews. And I'd straight-up murder anyone who tried to hurt them," she says with a savage smile. "But babysitting them has never given me the urge to have my own. Like, *never*."

"Good to know." What a relief to find someone to talk about this stuff with. "People keep telling me I'll get baby fever eventually. Why? Because I'm female? I knew when I was little, I didn't want 'em." A happy memory curves my lips. "Now, my little sister Hayley wanted babies. Lots of 'em. She was the sweetest, most patient kid. She would've been a great momma." My voice falters on the last word. I miss her so much.

"I didn't realize you had a sister," Trinity says gently.

"She died when she was eight," I whisper.

"Oh shit, Shelby. I'm sorry." Trinity bites her lip and sits forward, resting her hand on my arm. "I didn't know."

"That's okay." I pick at the blanket. "Watching my parents go through that kind of pain...I couldn't ever take the risk."

She doesn't offer any weak platitudes or sentimental words. None of the callous "God has a plan" bullshit people told me after Hayley died. Instead, she just quietly holds my hand for a few minutes.

"Thank you," I finally say.

"No problem."

Someone taps on the door and pushes it open. "Hi, Ms. Morgan. Doctor Landry asked me to stop by. Can we chat for a minute?"

Trinity stands and pats my hand. "We're all down in the waiting room if you need anything."

"Thanks."

I watch her leave, wishing I could follow. The new doctor closes the door behind Trinity and approaches the bed with sure steps.

I've been poked and prodded by a lot of different people since waking up. But this doctor seems different. I can't pinpoint why. Maybe it's her slower manner. The way she carefully checks her charts and doesn't seem to be in a rush like everyone else who has breezed through my room.

She holds out a business card. "Doctor Lola McDavis. I'm a consulting clinical psychologist with the hospital."

"Oh." I accept the card and briefly shake her hand. "Hi."

"How are you feeling?" She smooths her skirt over her legs and perches on the edge of the chair closest to my bed.

"Hurting. Tired."

"That's understandable." She nods to the door. "You seem to have a lot of friends and family here for support."

My lips twitch into a sad smile. It's been just my mother and me for so long, it feels strange to think of having "friends and family."

"Mostly my boyfriend's family but my mother is here too," I explain.

"That's good." She makes a quick note on her chart. "I understand this was a stranger abduction? You're a singer…and this was an obsessed fan?"

I shudder. A vision of the man's ugly face, the acidic scent of tomato soup, and the relentless fear while he chased me through the dark, all press down on me like a thousand pounds of nightmares. "Yes," I whisper.

"That sounds really scary." She pierces me with her steady gaze. "Do you want to talk about it?"

"Not really."

She doesn't seem put off by my abrupt answer. Instead, she nods slowly. "I understand it's tempting to bury this in an attempt to move on with your life. But I want to caution you—that can present problems later on. If you're not comfortable speaking with me, I can recommend someone else."

And give these people more reason to keep me here when I should be out on the road? Nope. "What's there to talk about? It's over."

"Yes. And I know it's too soon to assess any lingering issues, but I want you to be aware that some survivors have nightmares, flashbacks, and/or depression. Certain events could trigger any of those adverse symptoms. It could happen now or months from now. And it's completely normal."

I close my eyes briefly, recalling some of my earlier nightmare. "I suspect I'll have nightmares for a while," I admit.

Her expression doesn't change. No triumphant gotcha-to-open-up smile. Just calm reassurance. "Do you want to talk about that a little?"

Before I realize it, I'm spilling the whole awful story. The kidnapping, my fear, my escape attempt, my anger, and how certain I was that I was going to die.

She listens to every word, hardly taking down any notes.

When I've purged it all, I finally feel lighter.

"That is a lot, Shelby. You're very brave. And none of it is your fault."

I'm really not sure how to respond. I don't feel brave. Or blameless. "Thank you."

"Do you meditate?"

"Yes. Usually before I go onstage. Sometimes after, if I'm really keyed up."

"Good. That's good. If you have a nightmare, try to ground yourself with your breathing. Remind yourself that you're safe."

"I'll try."

"I'll be honest, I don't recommend going right back out on tour."

"I have to. This is…this tour is a huge break for me. Everything was going so well before…"

"I understand." She holds up her hand and smiles. "Actually, I don't. I can't carry a tune in a bucket."

Finally, something worth chuckling about. "Well, I can't counsel anyone, so we're good."

"Do you have people on tour who are supportive? Is your mother on the road with you?"

"Lord, no. She'd make me even more nervous." I glance down at the scratchy blanket and pick at a loose thread. "My boyfriend, Logan. He was planning to join me on the rest of the tour…before this happened."

"You think he won't want to now?"

"Oh, no. I think he'll be on me like wet on rain after this."

"How do you feel about that?"

"Honestly? Good and bad."

"What's the good?"

"I love being around him. We have a lot of fun together. He has a way of making things so much…easier. Less stressful. I definitely feel safe with him."

"That is good. What's the bad?"

"I hate for him to feel…I don't know, obligated? To upend everything to watch over me now? I don't know if I'm explaining it right."

"How long have you been together?"

"Not long."

"So the relationship is newer. Is he your first serious boyfriend?"

I don't have to ponder my answer. Any other relationship I've ever been in was a dress rehearsal compared to what I feel for Rooster. "Yes."

"Is it hard for you to depend on others? Accept help?"

"Oh, yeah. Big time."

"So, can you try to accept his word at face value?"

"I can *try*."

She smiles. "That's a start."

There's a gentle knock at the door. Rooster pushes it open, smiling until his gaze lands on the doctor. "Your mom went down to the cafeteria. Do you want anything?"

I wave him inside, not sure if Doctor McDavis will approve. But she stands and introduces herself, offering her hand for a quick shake.

"Can he join us?" I ask. "I don't mind if he hears any of this."

She turns back to me. "Actually, we're all finished for now. I'll let you get some rest. You have my number if you need to reach me."

"Thanks." I won't need more counseling. Martin won't get near me again. Rooster tamed my mother. Life should be smooth sailing as soon as I get out of this damn hospital.

But I should know better. Whenever I least expect it, troubled waters have always threatened to drown me.

CHAPTER SEVENTEEN

Rooster

I CATCH UP TO THE YOUNG DOCTOR AS SHE'S LEAVING SHELBY'S ROOM.

"Can I talk to you for a second?"

She flashes me a tired smile. "Sure."

She leads me to the elevator and down a few floors to a small, cluttered office. "What's on your mind?"

"Is she…is Shelby okay?" I'm not sure how to phrase my question but that seems like a good place to start.

"Just so we're clear, Shelby stated she was okay with discussing this in front of you, Mr. Randall. Otherwise, I wouldn't."

"Okay." I jam my hands in my pockets, not sure what to do or say. "I just want to do what's right for her."

"It seems heartless to say this, but she's lucky. She wasn't with her abductor for long and from what she describes, she was unconscious for most of it. So they didn't have a lot of interaction."

That has been my impression, too, from the bits and pieces I've gathered.

"While she seems to be stable right now, once she processes the events…there could be flashbacks, nightmares, panic attacks, or depression. It might not happen right away or it might never happen. Everyone is different."

That fucker hasn't suffered enough yet for what he did to Shelby. I'm having serious second thoughts about turning Suggs over to the FBI.

"Even so, an abduction—the callous, violent nature of it," the doctor continues, "the stripping of her identity and treating her as less than human—it's traumatic. The trauma could manifest itself in several areas for her—safety, trust, control, her self-esteem." She raises an eyebrow. "Intimacy."

"Okay, so what can I do to help her?"

"Let her make decisions for herself. The kidnapping…took away her control. Give that back to her as much as possible. From what she said, you've already helped her feel safer. That's important." She shakes her head as if she wants to say something more.

"Anything else, doc?" I prompt.

"I understand she's under a lot of pressure. But I don't recommend she goes back to touring right away. Shelby indicated taking time off wasn't an option for her, but she really should take at least a few days to rest and process everything before jumping right into a stressful schedule again."

Shit, Shelby's career stuff isn't something I've ever wanted to stick my nose into. But this is different. "I'll talk to her manager. From what I've heard, the tour's on hold right now."

"Good. She has my number and I can give her other referrals if she prefers. If she seems especially withdrawn or not like herself, have her call and talk to someone. Even if she's on the road. She can make appointments online around her schedule."

"Thank you." I shake her hand and head back toward Shelby's room.

Jackson and another goof-in-a-suit are sneaking in the door as I turn the corner.

"Motherfucker," I grumble under my breath, hurrying my steps. Somehow, I knew this jerkoff wasn't finished annoying the shit out of me yet.

Although, to be fair, he'd held off on questioning Shelby a hell of a lot longer than I expected. Too bad for Jackson, I'm not in the mood to be fair.

I push open the door. Shelby's relieved expression cements my decision not to leave no matter what Jackson has to say. I probably should've held off on chasing down the doctor.

"Logan." She holds out her hand to me and I cross the room to take it.

Jackson lets out a long, drawn-out sigh, and scowls at me. "If you're staying, keep your mouth shut. I need to collect information from Ms. Morgan without your interference."

I point to the chair over in the corner. "I'll be right there, blending into the wallpaper." I brush my knuckles over Shelby's cheek and she leans into me for a second. "That okay with you?" I ask in a low voice.

She nods.

On my way to the chair, I lean over and whisper in Jackson's ear, "You upset her, we'll have a problem."

"Duly noted," he grumbles. "This is my partner—"

I wonder if he's dirty too. Other than that, I tune out the introductions. Jackson's pal barely acknowledges me. He seems to be here merely as decoration.

"Can you tell me what you remember, Shelby?" Jackson uses a kind, "concerned father" tone I haven't seen him employ before. *Good start.*

I still don't trust him.

"Where do you want me to begin?" she rasps.

"How about the arena?"

With slow, methodical steps, she talks him through the attack in the dressing room. It's close to what Jackson and I figured went down. Suggs stepping out of the shower. The water making her feel fuzzy. Thank fuck Shelby didn't drink more of the tainted stuff. Her terror when she realized Suggs planned to carry her out inside her trunk is hard to listen to.

An inferno of rage spins in my chest as I absorb every detail of what my girl went through.

She's brave and gives as many details as possible without shedding a single tear.

"What do you remember next?" Jackson prods.

"Waking in the trunk. The guy…singing." She scrunches her face up as if the memory brings a wave of physical pain. "I tried to pretend I was still asleep. But he wasn't buyin' that."

"So, he let you out of the trunk?"

"Yes. Helped me to the bathroom. Wouldn't go away so I could use it in private." Her cheeks turn pink and she crosses her arms over her chest, dragging her blanket almost to her chin. "Then he took me to the kitchen. Which was fine with me. I wanted to get the hell away from that bedroom."

A smile of genuine respect flickers over Jackson's lips but he doesn't interrupt.

"His pantry was stocked for Armageddon or something. He had, like, a million cans of soup." She shudders. "I hate soup. Then he got mad when he gave me some creamy tomato glop and I told him I'm allergic to tomatoes."

I raise an eyebrow. Seems like something I should know about my girlfriend so I don't…oh, I don't know, accidentally *poison* her one day. With this new information, what I always thought was her being picky or doing that female watch-your-weight thing takes on a different light. I make a mental note to ask her about it later.

"Did you eat the soup?" Jackson asks.

"Heck no. He got a burr in his saddle over it, but made me chicken noodle instead."

Jackson frowns. Aw, does the big, smartass agent need help interpreting Shelby's little southernism? "So he fed you. Gave you something to drink."

Shelby pins him with a hard stare. "I didn't feel like I could leave. You know, after he *drugged* me and *abducted* me. So don't go acting like this was a lunch date, sir."

Jackson holds up his hand. "Not at all, Ms. Morgan."

Obviously, Shelby doesn't trust him. She waits, watching the agent carefully but not saying a word.

I couldn't be prouder of my girl.

SHELBY

How many more times am I going to have to go through this story? Reliving all the details isn't helping at all.

Finally, after what feels like days, Agent Jackson seems satisfied.

"Thank you, Ms. Morgan. We have Mr. Suggs in custody and I'm doing what I can to make sure he doesn't post bail. If for some reason he does, I'll be in touch."

I'm not sure if that's ordinary procedure or not, but I thank him. Nothing in my life has been *ordinary* lately.

After the agents leave, I fall back against my pillows. "That's it. I can't tell this story to one more flippin' person."

Rooster pulls his chair closer and takes my hand. "I hope that's it for now."

"I want him…punished…but good God, I can*not* keep reliving it constantly." Even as I say it, I know how unlikely it is. There will be a trial and who knows what else in the future. Suggs is still influencing and controlling my life, even from afar.

Rooster shifts. An unreadable expression darkens his face.

"What?"

"Nothing." He forces a smile. "Your mom's been downstairs for a while. With Jigsaw. God only know what's going on there."

The very idea unleashes a wild torrent of laughter. "He better buckle up."

"Hey." A more serious expression settles over him. "Why didn't you ever tell me you're allergic to tomatoes?"

I blink. "I don't know. I guess I don't like talking about it."

"Yeah, but I don't want to end up making you sick or something one day."

"Rooster, I know how to look out for myself."

"I know you do."

Expectation stretches through the air between us. Damn, I don't feel like talking about this now. "It's not like a nut allergy," I begin, picking my words carefully. "I won't *die*…well, I guess I could. It's been a while. I hate talking about it because some asshole always thinks I'm making it up or being dramatic, then tries to 'prove' I'm not really allergic by slipping one in my food."

"What? That's sick." Shock widens his eyes. "Who the fuck does something like that?"

"Well, my grandma, for one. She was a crazy old biddy, though." My throat itches just remembering the couple times she'd tricked me into eating something I shouldn't. "Almost killed Hayley when she was little by feeding her peanuts too." I adopt my grandma's haughty Texan twang. "In my day, we didn't coddle youngins. The kids ate what they were given and were thankful."

"That's fucked up."

I shrug. "Momma refused to leave us alone with her after the incident with Hayley. She and my dad fought about it a lot. He had a hard time telling his momma 'no' and *my* momma was pretty relentless when it came to protecting her kids."

He snorts and sort of nods.

"Anyway, Grandma Morgan died not long after. Problem solved." Maybe I should feel worse talking about my grandmother's death so casually, but the woman tried to kill me twice, so I can't get too worked up about her demise.

"Still wish you'd told me. I'd never do anything to hurt you." He runs his hand over his chin and down his beard. "None of my brothers would ever pull a stunt like that and if they tried, I'd fuckin' gut 'em."

"I trust you." I shrug. "It hadn't really come up yet or I would've mentioned it."

One corner of his mouth hikes up. "How the heck do you avoid tomatoes in Texas with all that salsa floatin' around?"

"It's not easy." I let out a yawn.

"Why don't you get some rest." He pats the bed. "People have been at you all day."

Unable to stop myself, I yawn again. "I really want to get out of here."

"Soon, hopefully." He glances at the clock over the doorway, then leans in to kiss my forehead. "Close your eyes."

CHAPTER EIGHTEEN

Shelby

TODAY'S NURSE IS BRISK AND BUSINESSLIKE. "ALL RIGHT, MS. MORGAN, ARE you ready to go home?"

Thank you, Lord! "Home or back on the road?"

"Wherever you want." She flashes a quick smile. "But you can't stay here."

Aren't you hilarious.

Bless my boyfriend's kind heart and never-ending patience. He was here again first thing this morning waiting for my eyes to pop open. "Is the doctor going to stop by and see her before she leaves?" he asks from his perch on the chair next to my bed.

"Uh, sure, I can let her know you want to talk to her first."

She pivots and leaves my room.

"I don't need to talk to the doctor," I protest.

Rooster shrugs. "The other day, they were all 'you need to rest, your body's been through a lot.' Now they're saying, 'get out.' Doesn't hurt to ask a few questions."

I stretch and take a cautious inventory of my aches and pains. "I feel better. Still a little fuzzy in the head, but overall, better."

He curls his fingers around mine and squeezes gently. "Good."

My mother bustles through the door with a paper cup of coffee in each hand. Without a word, she hands one to Rooster. Thank the Lord, she seems to have accepted Rooster's here for good. Or rather, she's placed the you-should-be-single campaign on hold.

"I ran into the doctor and she said you're being discharged." She sips her coffee and sets it on the table next to my bed.

"So I hear."

"That's good." She casts a disgusted look around the *spanky*-clean room. "Hospitals are full of germs. We don't need you catching something while you're here."

"So cheerful, Mom."

Rooster chuckles. "She has a point. Even Heidi said it's best to get you out as soon as possible so you don't catch some superbug."

I slowly turn my head and bare my teeth at him. Gettin' along with my mother is one thing; ganging up on *me* is another.

As if he knows exactly what I'm thinking, he pats my leg in a reassuring way. "Just worried about you," he says quietly.

"I need to get home, baby. But I don't want to leave while you're still in here," my mother adds. "Greg said they secured a rehearsal space at the hotel. I'd love to see y'all run through a few songs before I go."

I blink and stare, trying to work out my feelings about singing right now. It feels about as familiar as climbing on a spaceship and being flung at the moon.

"Let's worry about getting her checked out and set up somewhere comfortable first," Rooster says.

Momma shoots a glare at him but wisely keeps her mouth shut.

My eyes prickle. I know she loves me and means well, but Momma's always been a show-must-go-on-no-matter-what kinda person. Rooster's purely concerned about what's best for *me*, no matter what. It strikes me for the first time—he's the only one who has no vested interest in my singing career. Sure, there's a one-in-a-million chance I'll hit it Dawson Roads big and be rolling in hundred-dollar bills one day, but that's a long shot. For better or worse, Momma's pinned her hopes on me becoming a super-star or at the very least earning enough to be comfortable. Greg only makes money if I do. Same for Trent.

Whatever Rooster does for the club provides him with enough income that he's not banking on my career.

It's a weird slap-in-the-face sort of revelation while I'm sitting in a hospital bed after being kidnapped and almost killed, listening to my momma talk about me getting back out on stage right away.

Not that she doesn't love me—I know she does—but the nagging sensation that I just stumbled upon something profound won't leave.

"You all right, honey?" my mother asks.

"Tired."

"Another reason you need to get out of here. Hospitals suck all the life outta ya."

"Probably." I yawn and stretch again.

Someone knocks on the door and slowly pushes it open. Trinity peers inside. "Mind if we come in?"

"No, please do." I wave my hand at her.

Trinity pushes the door wider and joins us, Heidi following. "We weren't sure what you had access to, so we stopped and got you a few things in case you get discharged soon." Trinity sets a large blue and pink travel cosmetic bag on my lap.

"Oh, wow. You didn't have to do that."

"Well..." Trinity winks at Rooster. "We figured he wouldn't know all the right girly stuff to get."

"True." Rooster grins back at her. "I'd just buy you some three-in-one shampoo-conditioner-body-wash combo and call it good."

I shudder at the thought.

Trinity wraps an arm around my mother's shoulders. "Your mom gave us some pointers on what you might like."

My mom gives her a warm smile.

I hadn't been aware Trinity and my mother had gotten to be buddies while I'd been in and out of consciousness. "Thank you."

"No problem," Trinity says.

"Just trying to be useful while we're here," Heidi adds.

I cast a helpless look at Rooster. How will I ever repay the girls? They took time out of their busy lives to sit around the hospital even though they barely know me. Suddenly, I'm overwhelmed with gratitude and also a little embarrassed.

Finally, the doctor pops in. She flips through pages in her chart, hands my mother a bunch of paperwork, and declares me ready to leave.

Of course, I still have to wait for someone to bring me forms to sign.

"Good grief," I mutter. "Think they'll hunt me down if I just run away?" I shove the blanket and sheet off me and swing my legs over the side of the bed.

"Shoot, what am I gonna wear?" I never thought to ask what happened to my clothes or where my cowgirl boots went. If I lost them, I'm going to be *so* mad.

"There's stuff in there for you," Rooster says, pointing to the closet.

"We'll give you privacy." Trinity hooks her arm through Heidi's and hustles toward the door. "Lynn, do you want to grab lunch with us?" she asks over her shoulder.

"Oh." My mother's gaze shifts between Trinity and me. "Sure. Are you sure you don't need me, Shelby?"

"If I forgot how to dress myself, we've got problems." I flap my hand toward the door in a shooing motion. "Go eat. Lord knows how long it'll be until they release me."

After they leave, I shuffle over to the slim closet door. Rooster jumps up, shadowing but letting me get there on my own. "Thanks for staying," I say.

"Of course." He reaches past me and pulls the long, narrow closet door open. It's more like a locker than an actual closet.

Inside, my boots are waiting for me. Someone must've cleaned the mud off and shined them for me. "Phew. I was worried someone tossed 'em." I grab them first.

"We'll need to get you another pair," Rooster says quietly.

There's a white plastic bag from a mall store I recognize. I pull it out and peer inside. Plain, simple black yoga pants and a long, blue tunic inside. Simple and comfy.

"Your mom brought that stuff by yesterday," Rooster explains.

"Ah, she knows me well." I pull out the bundles, finding a soft, stretchy bra and a pair of plain cotton underwear at the bottom. "I feel so gross but I don't want to shower here."

"When we get to the hotel, you can do whatever you want."

"Shoot, where's my mom staying?"

"Uh…" He runs his hands through his hair. "I booked her a room at the same place Dawson and everyone else are staying."

Tears prick my eyes. I reach up on tiptoes and gently kiss his cheek. "Thank you."

"Not a problem. Figured she'd wanna be close to you. And a room at the clubhouse wasn't gonna impress her too much." One corner of his mouth hitches up.

"Probably not." I wobble into the bathroom, leaving the door slightly open in case Rooster needs to fish me out of the toilet, and clean up. By the time I slip into the new clothes, I'm exhausted.

"Need help?" Rooster asks from outside the door.

"All done." My gaze strays to the bed. "Now I need a nap."

"Go ahead. I'll get your stuff together so you're ready when they say you can go."

ROOSTER

After hours of waiting around, Shelby's finally released from the hospital. Lynn fusses over her the whole way to the truck.

"Just stick me in the back. I'm ready for a snooze," Shelby says.

Lynn seems to be dragging too. They're both quiet on the short drive to the hotel.

"We're here, chickadee." I open the door and run my hand over Shelby's arm. "A shower and comfy bed are minutes away."

She slowly peels her eyes open. "You're speakin' my language now."

"Need me to carry you?"

"Nope."

I lift her out of the truck anyway and set her down on the sidewalk, not really caring that Lynn's watching every move I make with her daughter.

Inside, we run into Greg and Trent, who hug Shelby. "We're all getting together in one of the banquet rooms downstairs to celebrate you being out," Trent says.

"Oh, sure." Shelby glances down at her outfit, then at her mom. "That all right with you?"

Lynn flashes a nervous smile at Greg. "Sure."

Shelby raises her eyebrow at me.

I'm not about to stop her from hanging out with her band. "If you think you're up to it."

"I *would* like to eat some normal food."

"Let's do it."

Confident she's safe with her mom, Greg, and Trent, I leave them and run upstairs to our room to drop off her stuff before heading downstairs and following the directions Greg gave me for the room they've taken over.

The plush hotel carpet absorbs my steps as I move from one narrow escalator to another before finally landing on the right floor. Outside the room, I run into Dawson.

"Logan! Lots to celebrate tonight." He holds out his hand and I shake it quickly, eager to find Shelby. "Your buddy's watching over Shelby and her mom."

I shoot a questioning eyebrow at him.

"The scary one who looks like he's thinking about slicing and dicing my nuts off any time I get too close to Shelby," he adds.

I snort. "That's Jigsaw."

He turns his head from side to side, searching the surrounding area. "Can we talk for a minute?"

"Nothing would make me happier, Dawson."

He ignores the sarcasm and pulls me into a quieter corner of the wide corridor running between the different meeting rooms. "I don't want to bother Shelby with any of this stuff. I talked to Greg and he wanted me to address it with you."

Interesting. "What is it?"

"Well, I had to let Bane go. I know he thought he was doing the right thing, but Shelby got taken on his watch and I—"

"No complaints from me. If he hadn't been off playing fireman, he might have stopped Suggs from getting her out of the arena."

"Exactly. He understood."

As if I give a shit about Bane's feelings on the matter.

"I gotta hire someone else. I'm having an expert come in to do a risk assessment. The fire was started by the guy who nabbed Shelby, from what I've gathered."

My, Martin Suggs was busy.

"But he never shoulda been able to get that close to my bus. This whole thing's costing me a fortune. We're losing money every damn day we're stuck here." He holds up his hands. "I ain't complaining or blaming Shelby. Had to get my bus repaired and two of my guys were in the hospital. Got injured in the fire."

"Shit. I didn't realize it had been so bad."

"I didn't want to make a big deal with everything Shelby went through. Don't bother telling her, either. It's not something she needs to worry about."

Well, at least halting the tour makes more sense now. And my respect for him grows.

"I've got a guy from California who handles security. He and his team come highly recommended. He's, like, written the book on celebrity safety or something."

"Okay." I'm still waiting for him to get to the point.

"He's going to do a complete risk assessment for me. But he also offers security training. I'm having all my guys take it. I thought you and"—he waves his hand toward the conference room— "the scary one might want to join in."

The biker in me wants to scoff and ask if he really thinks I need to learn how to kick someone's ass. The man who wants to protect his girlfriend at all costs is the one who answers. "Yeah. We'll do that. Thanks."

"All right." He slaps my shoulder. "Whoever else you got coming on the road with you can join too. We can talk more about it later. Let's go eat."

Apparently, Dawson has been busy. The hotel has a buffet set up for our party. I recognize members of his band and road crew. A few nod to me or stop and shake my hand.

I spot Jigsaw sitting at a round table way in the back of the room. He's keeping his eye on Shelby and her mom but stands as I approach. "Startin' to wonder what happened to you, brother." He slaps my hand and pulls me in quick, thumping my back.

"Stopped to talk to Dawson." My gaze shifts to Shelby. "You all right?"

She barely glances up from the slab of prime rib she's demolishing. "Happier than a possum eatin' a sweet potato pie."

"Do possums *like* sweet potato pie?" Jigsaw asks.

Shelby side-eyes him but doesn't bother answering.

Lynn pats her daughter's back.

Laughing, I nudge Jigsaw. "Why aren't you eating?"

"Made sure the girls were content first." He glances at Lynn and the two of them share a smile that's unsettling as hell.

"All right then." I point myself in the direction of the buffet and pick up a plate.

By the time I return to the table, Greg's planted himself in the chair next to Shelby's mother. I take the one next to Shelby, and Jiggy drops into the one next to me.

Greg leans over the table to focus on Shelby while I eat. "Are you ready to talk about the CMAs a little?"

She flicks a glance at her mother and sets her fork down. "Yeah."

He rubs his hands together. "A few designers have expressed interest in dressing you for the awards."

Shelby lifts an eyebrow. "You don't say?"

"Nothing crazy, Greg." Lynn's worried gaze lands on the haggard manager. "She should look like a princess not an experiment. And some of the designers these days…"

"Shelby has a good sense of what she likes and doesn't," Greg answers in a neutral tone.

By her blank expression and the way she's stirring her spoon through her coffee, I think Shelby's checked out of the conversation. Under the table, I rest my hand on her leg.

"This should be fun stuff, no?" I ask quietly.

She lifts one shoulder. "I guess."

"You want to go upstairs?"

Her red-rimmed eyes meet mine and she nods once. "I'm beat." She pats her stomach. "And stuffed like a Thanksgiving bird."

I shove my chair back and stand, dropping my napkin on the table. "We're heading upstairs."

Greg glances at Shelby. "We have rehearsal—"

I spear him with a pointed look, and his mouth snaps shut. "Unless something is physically on fire, don't call us in the morning. I'll let you know when Shelby's up and ready."

Jigsaw cough-laughs into his fist.

Greg opens his mouth, probably to object.

Trent places his hand on Greg's arm. "We've got plenty to work with. Ain't like Shelby forgot the words to her own songs."

Ignoring Trent's perfectly reasonable tone, Greg glares at me. "All right."

I nod a quick thanks at Trent.

"Lynn, do you need anything?" I ask.

She glances at her coffee cup. "I'll stay down here. I'm not tired yet."

I flick my gaze at Jigsaw, silently asking him to look out for Lynn, and he responds with a quick nod.

Lynn walks out of the room with us, stopping at the elevators to hug Shelby tight. "Get some rest. My flight isn't until late afternoon. We'll talk before I go, okay?"

"Night, Momma."

Lynn stares up at me for a few seconds, then leans up and kisses my cheek. "Thanks, Logan."

"Sure."

The elevator dings. Inside, Shelby rests her body against mine while I punch the button for our floor. I wrap my arm around her, keeping her close. "Tired?"

The only answer she gives is a gentle nod against my chest. An overwhelming urge to pick her up and carry her to our room barrels down on me. When the elevator chimes and opens, I sweep her up.

She sighs and settles against me, wrapping her arms around my neck. At our door, I fumble to slide my hand in my pocket while bracing her body against the wall so I don't drop her. It takes a few seconds.

"I can walk." She wriggles for me to put her down just as I finally press the card to the door sensor.

"I got you." I kick open the door, turning us sideways to slide into the room, then tap it shut with my boot. "See?"

"Hmm."

"Want to go right to bed?"

"No." She picks up her head and yawns. "I need a shower in the worst way."

"All right." I carry her into the bathroom and set her down in front of the sink. "I'll grab your stuff."

I hesitate to leave. All she does is stand there sort of swaying, not really looking at anything. But she bobs her head once and I hurry to grab her bath stuff and something for her to sleep in.

When I return, she's checking out the bathtub and shower combo, adjusting the water.

"You want help?" Shit, why do things feel so awkward all of a sudden?

She blinks up at me almost as if she feels it too. "Can I have a few minutes by myself?"

Remembering what the doctor said, I'm not offended by Shelby's request. "Yeah, sure. Of course." I set her stuff down.

"I promise not to drown or anything." She forces a small smile.

"Yell if you need me." I close the door with a soft *click* and enter the bedroom. Edgy and restless, I pace the thick tan carpet for a few seconds before pulling a few things I need for the night out of my bags. I don't risk turning on the television or radio, worried any extra noise could mask a cry for help from Shelby.

The running water switches to the shower spray. None of the familiar little singing or humming noises Shelby usually makes accompany the pitter-patter. I stretch out in an oversized armchair by the window and reluctantly switch on my phone. The stories about Shelby's kidnapping are on every major news site and every celebrity blog.

"Shit," I mutter, scrolling through article after article. Just what she needs. None of the pieces have anything new or exciting to add. They're all various regurgitations of the same few bits of information. Some dug deep with background about her time on *Redneck Roadhouse*. One interviewed people she went to high school with. Not one has anything relevant to contribute. I'd bet my bike none of these people ever really knew Shelby.

Greg managed to get Shelby's cell phone replaced while she was in the hospital. It's in my backpack and unless Shelby specifically asks for it, that's where it's staying. No reason for her to see any of this garbage right now.

After a while, the shower sounds filter into my brain and I glance at the bathroom door, then the clock.

Damn, she's been in there a long time.

Unease thrums through my chest. I set my phone on the nightstand

and move to the bathroom door. Rock still, I listen for any sounds of movement or noise other than the steady drumming of the shower.

Nothing.

Shit, I know she wanted to be alone but this is way too long. What if she slipped and hurt herself?

I knock once but she doesn't answer.

Fuck this. I shove the door open. Steam billows around me and I turn, seeking a switch for the overhead fan. I close the door so she doesn't catch a chill. "Shelby?"

No answer.

"Hey." I pull the shower curtain aside.

She's sitting on the tub floor, arms wrapped around her shins, cheek resting on her knees. Exhaustion and misery cling to her as she lets the water pour over her body.

I shove my fingers under the stream. At least it's still warm. "You okay?"

She tilts her head and peers up at me, looking so damn forlorn my heart jumps. Never should've left her alone. "I wanted to shave my legs but now I'm too tired to get up," she explains in a small voice.

My gaze drops to the razor and tube of aloe gel sitting by her hip. Kneeling next to the tub, I run my hand over one of her shins, then the other. "Feels smooth to me."

No reaction.

"You want me to help you out?" I ask gently.

It's hard to tell if it's tears or water streaming down her cheeks but she finally nods.

"Okay." I twist the taps off.

She holds out her hands and I help her up, carefully lifting her over the edge of the tub and setting her down on a towel. I grab one of the white terrycloth bath sheets and wrap it around her. My big, clumsy fingers can't seem to knot it right, though.

A hint of a smile flickers at her lips—*big relief*—and she takes over, tucking the towel tight above her breasts. I hand her another towel and she flips her hair, wrapping it all up in a neat little beehive.

"Feel better?"

"A little," she whispers. "Thank you."

"What else do you need?"

Her tired gaze skitters around the steamy bathroom, finally settling on the travel case the girls gave her. "Is there any baby oil in there?"

"Maybe. Seemed like they bought one of everything in the drug store."

Another brief smile. "That was real sweet of them."

I unzip the bag and after a few seconds of searching, Shelby joins me.

She pulls a clear plastic squeeze bottle out.

"Where do you want it?" I ask.

"My legs." She glances down. "I can do it. I'm fine."

"Come here." I curl my hands around her waist and boost her onto the edge of the sink. "Have a seat."

I lower one knee to the floor and place her foot on my thigh. Holding out my palm, I motion for her to give me the gel. She squirts a small amount into my hand and I work the slippery stuff into her skin, from ankles to knees. "Good?"

"Mm-hmm."

"Slick stuff," I mutter as I smear it over her other leg. Can't deny getting her all slippery is giving me certain *other* ideas. But I'm able to take care of her without being a big fuckin' pervert. At least, I think I can.

I press a quick kiss to her knee before finishing up. "What's next?"

She's busy lazily rubbing lotion on her arms and slowly slides off the counter without looking at me or answering my question. I take the tube and work some lotion into her shoulders and back, trying not to lose my shit over all the black and blue marks painting her skin.

"Here," she whispers, passing a different tube over her shoulder. "Can you rub some of this on the bruised parts?"

"I don't want to hurt you." I take the orange bottle and flip open the cap.

"It's arnica. Trinity said it would help the bruising."

She winces a few times even though I'm as gentle as my big, rough hands allow.

"I look battle-worn," she says, staring listlessly into the mirror.

"You are." I set the tube on the counter when I'm finished. "Next?"

She lets out a jaw-cracking yawn and unwinds the towel on her head. "I'm going to work this through my hair." She holds up a small bottle of gold oil labeled *hair serum*.

"You're gonna be lubed from head to toes."

She laughs softly. *Improvement.* "Bet you never wanted to know so much about girly routines before."

"Wrong. I want to know *all* your routines."

She rubs the oil into her damp hair in sections, then runs a wide-tooth comb through from scalp to ends.

"You want me to help you dry it?" I ask.

"Do you mind?"

"No, Shelby." I don't mean to be harsh, but I wish she'd stop assuming she's annoying me and just let me help her. I locate the hotel's dryer and plug it in. "Tell me where to aim it," I shout over the noise of the little motor.

"Follow the comb!" She waves the copper-colored, wide tooth comb and a large round brush at me.

I'm not good enough that it's time to consider a career-switch, but together, we manage to dry most of her long, thick waves. Shelby twists it into two loose braids before finally setting her comb down. Her legs wobble and I slip an arm around her waist. "Time for bed."

"That sounds good."

She squints as the bright light from the bedroom hits her eyes. I flick off the overhead bulbs, leaving only the lamps next to the bed on.

Her blank gaze searches the room for a second before settling on the bed.

"Here." I hold up one of my shirts. "Let's get you under the covers before you catch a chill."

She nods slowly and moves closer, tossing the towel on a nearby chair. I slip the shirt over her head and pull the fluffy white comforter back.

Once she's between the sheets, curled on her side, I cover her up. But damn, she still looks so miserable and I have no idea how to relieve her.

Time. She needs rest and time.

"You're safe, Shelby." How can she believe me after she was stolen on my watch once before? "Sleep as long as you need. Don't worry about a thing."

She shifts, patting the pillows behind her. "Are you coming to bed?"

"Yup. I'll be right next to you all night."

"Okay." She yawns and tucks her hand under her chin, closing her eyes.

I switch off the lamp, watch her for a few more seconds, then quickly hurry through my own nightly routine.

She's still curled on her side when I return. I flick off the rest of the lights, plunging the room into total darkness. Helpless little noises pass her lips. Her body jerks, arms and legs twitching. Every tortured cry twists the thorns of guilt in my chest even tighter.

"Shhh." I slip into bed and pull her body against mine. Gradually she relaxes, her breathing turning deep. "I'm right here, Shelby."

I hope it's enough to help her feel safe.

CHAPTER NINETEEN

Shelby

ANXIETY TINGLES THROUGH MY CHEST.

I blink open my eyes and stare into the shadowy room.

Long curtains come into focus. Weak sunlight peeks around the edges.

A heavy presence behind me shifts.

My heart jumps, then settles when I recognize Rooster's breathing. Something tickles over my shoulder. His heavy arm curls around my waist. I roll to my back, wincing as all my aches and pains wake with me. I must've slept in the same position all night and my body's announcing its extreme displeasure.

"Morning." Rooster's gruff rumble greets me.

"You're awake?"

"Mostly. It's early, though. Get some more sleep."

I stare up at the ceiling. How'd everything go from great to horrible so fast? My thoughts are too jumbled to sort and my eyelids slowly close.

The room's brighter the next time I wake.

I roll to the side, coming face-to-face with Rooster's warm chest and I burrow against it. He slides his arm around me, gently rubbing my back. His presence is such a sweet, stunning relief, and I snuggle closer.

"How do you feel?" he asks.

"Hurt."

His hand stops moving and he rolls to his back.

"No, I—"

"Shelby, I'm so sorry." The pain in Rooster's voice cuts straight through me.

I pull away. "Don't." My voice quivers. "Please don't apologize. You *rescued* me—"

"He never should've gotten his hands on you in the first place." Regret clings to his words, filling the space between us. "That's on me. It'll haunt me until the day I die."

I shift and sit up, resting my hand on his chest and staring into his troubled eyes. The hurt and remorse etched on his face releases the sorrow that's stuck with me since waking in the hospital.

Logan's always so stoic. Steady. Rock solid. Admitting any sort of weakness isn't in his nature. But being honest and expressing his grief to me is more important than his pride. His admission heals some of the brokenness inside me.

And I need him to understand none of what happened is his fault.

"Logan, I never once blamed you."

He opens his mouth—probably to argue with me—but I silence him with a finger against his lips. "Please, listen."

When he nods, I move my hand from his mouth to his cheek. "You heard what I told Jackson. He…the guy…" I refuse to say my kidnapper's name. "He told me he'd been stalking me for a while. Longer than we suspected. He originally planned to grab me earlier at a different show. You weren't with me then."

I blow out a long, shuddering breath. Between the numb moments, I've thought about this a lot. Considered all the possible scenarios. "The truth is, I don't know what would've happened if you hadn't been there the night he took me. If you hadn't reacted as fast as you did—chasing down the van, getting the plate number—"

"Shelby." His raw voice slices into my heart. "I was supposed to be protecting you. He never should've gotten so close. Never. That's on me."

"No. It's *not*." I put enough force in my voice to knock down his stubborn wall.

"It shouldn't have happened at all. I let you down. I'm going to be furious about it for a long damn time."

How do I get through to him? "What would've happened if he'd grabbed me the first time I ran into him? You think Greg or Trent would've gone to the lengths you did? They might have been upset but they wouldn't have searched for me."

He grunts in a noncommittal way.

"No one would've known where I was or who to look for. I would've been trapped in that…" my body shudders at the memory, "…*cage* for God only knows how long. No one would've known how to find me. I would've been lost. At the mercy of the police deciding *if* something had happened to me or if I'd skipped off the tour. If your club hadn't conducted their own search, who knows how long it would've taken before anyone found me?"

Oh yes, I've thought long and hard about all the possible ways it could have turned out. Rooster's the only person both relentless and capable enough to pursue me no matter what. "You're the one who saved me."

"I'm no savior, Shelby. Believe me." His haunted voice ties me in knots.

"To me, you are." I cup his cheek, forcing him to meet my eyes. "My white knight who's always rescuing me."

He tilts his head, kissing my inner wrist. "I don't want to *rescue* you. I want to love you. I want you safe."

"I'm safe with you."

His jaw sets in a stubborn line. He wants to deny it. Blame himself more. But Logan's an honorable man. He won't pout and keep harping on it once I've said my piece. No, I'm worried he'll store up his guilt and take it out on himself.

"Please, don't do this," I plead. "I love you. I'm so grateful to be here with you right now. You have no idea."

"Come here." He pulls me closer, gently wrapping his arms around me, and touches his forehead to mine. "I love you too. You don't need to worry about me. I'm not gonna flip out and do something stupid because I'm mad at myself."

Geez, maybe we know each other a little too well.

A hint of a smile ghosts his lips. "Is that what you were thinking?"

"Not exactly. But close."

His big hand cups my cheek, brushing loose strands of hair that escaped my braids out of his way. "This scared the hell out of me, Shelby.

He won't be the last. The more people who fall in love with your music, who think they're in love with *you*, the greater the odds of another psycho thinking you're destined to be together. I need to learn from this and do better for you. I won't fuck up again."

"*You* didn't fuck up." I press my finger to his lips to silence any response. "I hate hearing you say it, but I know you're right—he won't be the last. And Lord only knows what kind of kook it'll be next time."

"That's my fear."

"We'll learn from this *together*. I'll take every letter seriously. I won't go off on my own without letting someone know. I'll be more careful about my social media—"

"Stop. This wasn't your fault."

"I'm not saying it was. Trust me. *Martin Suggs,"* I spit out the name. "He's the *only* one I hold responsible. But, I'm trying to be practical and honest here. If I want to keep growing my music career—and I do—then I need to take every threat seriously. What can I do to lower my risk without ruining my life?" I turn my head and brush my lips against his wrist. "It's not all on you."

"I'm never letting anyone near you again."

"Good."

He turns his head and blows out a long breath. "Dawson's revamping his security team. Calling in some heavy-hitting experts. They do a training class and he offered it to me last night. I told him Jiggy and I would sign up."

"Wow. Really?" Somehow I don't picture the two of them in a classroom letting a stranger tell them how to provide protection. Rooster already has a bossy, vigilant protector personality in spades.

His lips twitch as if he senses my surprise. "If it were simple bar fights I was protecting you from, I could handle it fine. But this is so much more. Your career is only going to get bigger and more complicated. Until you can afford to hire professionals—"

I cut him off with a kiss. "I love you so dang much."

His mouth curves up and his hand absently rubs the top of my scalp. "Dawson's gonna help me set up a small team for you."

"Wait, why's he getting so involved?"

"I think he feels bad about all this."

"Why? It's not his fault."

His mouth twists as if he disagrees but doesn't want to say it out loud. "It happened on his tour."

"Yeah, but that creep had been following me since my *Redneck Roadhouse* days."

"The tour gave him the opportunity," Rooster says carefully.

I wrinkle my nose, thinking that through. What if Martin tried tracking me down in Texas? That could've been worse. But maybe he wouldn't have bothered if I hadn't come so close to him. "I guess so."

"He fired Bane."

"Shoot, really? Poor Bane."

"Poor Bane my ass," he growls. "That fucker should've been doing what he was told to do—watch your door. Not running off to live out his fireman fantasies."

I chuckle at that last part but Rooster doesn't so much as crack a hint of a smile.

"Great, now there's someone *else* out there who probably hates me."

"Fuck him." Even though his words are harsh, Rooster gently strokes his hand over my cheek. "I need to tell you something else."

My heart rate kicks up at his serious tone. "What?"

"We strongly think Glenna Wilson was involved. Actually, we know she was."

I shoot straight up, my head spinning so I hard, I wince in pain. "What? Why? How?"

"Shh." He pulls me back down next to him. "She denies it of course. But when I had my little interrogation session with Suggs, he named her."

"Wait, you did what?" My harsh voice bounces off the walls. How did Rooster accomplish so much *and* manage to be there when I needed him in the hospital? Good Lord, how long was I out? Flipping through my thoughts, I realize I don't even know what day it is.

"I shouldn't have turned him over to Jackson. But I wanted it on record she was involved."

"Why would she do that?"

"Sounds like she was jealous." He shrugs. "Thought you were having an affair with Dawson. Poor bastard. She really screwed him every which way," he says in a flat tone that suggests he doesn't give a fuck one way or another about Dawson's feelings.

"So *that's* why he's trying to fix things?"

"It's the least he can do," he grumbles. "Chaser got me the name of a PR person. She's supposed to call and—"

"What? You called Chaser? He knows now too?"

"He called me," Rooster says gently. "Your kidnapping has been all over the news."

"Oh my God." I squeeze my eyes shut. *Country music's bimbo Barbie* is going to feel like a delightful compliment compared to all the *poor victim* stories people will write.

"It's gonna be fine. I just want to prepare you for what's coming."

"Yeah. Guess no one else was gonna bother to tell me," I grumble.

"I asked Greg not to say anything. I wanted you to rest before being bombarded with all this stuff."

Waves of other people's deceit and jealousy continue to toss *me* around, spinning *my* world out of control.

But Rooster's my steady constant, anchoring me to sanity.

"What's gonna happen to Glenna now?" I ask.

"Don't know. Probably not much. She fed Suggs some info about the tour, venues, schedules, stuff like that. Not very hands on, but enough to give Suggs the insight to put things in motion."

"He said something about a 'source.' I wondered who he was talking about." I peer up at Rooster. "Do you think Dawson was involved too?" It would kill me if the man I'd been touring with for months participated in this madness.

He considers my question for a few seconds before answering. "I wondered that too. But he let me listen in when he called Glenna. I don't think he would've done that if there was a chance she'd rat him out. He was pretty shaken up." He strokes his hand down my arm. "She… threatened to smear you in the press if he made any allegations that she was involved in the kidnapping."

"What the—are you joking me? Smear *me*? She's the one who helped get me captured by some crazy psycho who stored me in a fucking box under his bed!"

"I don't think she had details of Suggs' plans."

"What'd she think he was gonna do with me? Play dress-up and hold tea parties for my dollies? I never did nothing to her, and she helped set me up to be some crazy man's baby-making machine!"

He winces. "Shh. I know. I agree. That's why we're going to talk to the PR woman. She's supposedly the best at this sort of thing."

"Psycho exes and kidnappings?" I snort. "Seems like a niche market."

He rumbles with laughter. "Yeah."

"I don't have money for *the best*." No, what I have now, courtesy of Martin Suggs, and apparently Glenna Wilson, is a mountain of hospital bills and a lifetime of fear to sort through.

"We're...working it out. I don't need you to worry about that right now. You're going to meet with her and see what she has to say, then we'll go from there."

"Jesus, Rooster. This isn't what you signed up for. At all." I snort out a sad laugh and cover my face with my hands. "This isn't the ride-the-wind, open-road adventure you thought it would be. I might as well fire Greg and have *you* be my manager."

"I know dick about the management and entertainment stuff. And even less about country music," he says, his voice hoarse with emotion. "My *only* concern is the keeping-Shelby-safe side of the business."

What did I do to deserve this man?

He rolls over and checks his phone, growling before tossing it back on the nightstand.

"Is Greg looking for me?" I ask.

"Are you up to rehearsal?" he counters, indirectly answering my suspicion. "Be honest."

"I don't know." I shrug, feeling prickly all over. "Normally, I wake up with music or notes floating around in my head. Ideas I can't wait to write down or try out...Even when I'm tired or nervous, I'm usually excited to go to practice."

"And?"

"It's been so...quiet. Inside." I tap my chest. "I feel a whole lot of nothing. Whatever magic propels me to create has vanished. I'm scared it's gone for good." I finish on a whisper, terrified to confess my growing fear. "And it'll never come back."

"Come here." He hugs me against his body. "A lot has happened in a short amount of time. You need to recover. It'll return when you're ready."

"But I don't have *time* to wallow. Dawson's gotta be losing a fortune canceling those dates."

"He didn't just cancel because of you. The fire on the bus was worse than I realized. Two of his people got injured too, so—"

"Jeepers." I frown at him. "Anything else I don't know?"

"I found that out myself last night." He holds up his hands. "Don't feel pressured to get back to it if you're not ready."

"Yeah, but his bus got ruined because of *me*. His crew got hurt because of *me*. I wouldn't be surprised if he kicks me off the dang tour for bringing so much trouble."

"Uh, I blame Martin Suggs, Glenna Wilson, and the lack of proper security at the venue for the fire. And I'm pretty sure Dawson feels the same way." His expression turns feral. "And if he doesn't, I'm happy to persuade him."

"Easy, killer."

He grins at me.

A little laughter bubbles up.

"That's better." He leans in and kisses the tip of my nose.

"You know what?" I slap the comforter with my open palm. "I *would* like to go to rehearsal. Even if I just sit there like a stump."

"That's my girl."

I throw back the covers and roll out of bed, then waddle my way to the bathroom. "Be right back."

Everything hurts but I take care of my morning business and almost feel human after brushing my teeth.

Rooster's sitting on the edge of the bed when I return.

"My mom's planning to fly back to Texas this afternoon, right?"

He sets his phone down and glances at me. "That's what she said. You want to have some mother-daughter bonding time?" he asks. "Just the two of you?"

"Uh, no." I rest my hands on my hips. "She needs to accept you in my life. End of story."

He stands, closes the distance between us, and cups my cheeks with his big hands. "I love you for saying that. I do. But she's coming around."

His mouth twitches into a smile. "Slowly. I'm gonna see you every day for the next few weeks. You two should spend some time together without me in the way."

"You're not *in the way*. Don't say that."

His lips twitch. "I need to take care of a few things. But I'll be back in time to go to the airport with you. How's that?"

"Better." I wrap my arms around him, hugging tight and not letting go.

Things *will* get better, right? I survived something awful but this bad mood has its teeth in me. I can't stop thinking if it hadn't been for Rooster's relentless determination to find me, I might still be at the mercy of Suggs. Gratitude should color my every thought—and it does, to an extent.

Fear, anger, and anxiety won't quit crawling around inside me though either.

CHAPTER TWENTY

Shelby

Once we're both dressed, Rooster leads me a few doors down from our room and knocks.

My mom opens the door wide and wraps me in a big, warm hug. "How you feelin' this morning, baby?"

"A lot better." At least that's mostly true.

She grabs her purse and follows me to the elevator.

"You know where we're going?" I ask Rooster as he punches the 'down' button.

"Rehearsal's the same room we had dinner in last night," my mom says.

"Glad someone has a clue." I laugh and shake my head. *Get it together, Shelby.*

The hotel's quiet at this hour. We don't pass many people, but the few we see offer warm greetings.

Now that Rooster's told me my story's been all over the news, I'm twitchy if anyone looks at me for longer than two seconds.

I blow out a sigh of relief when we arrive downstairs.

"Dawson said the hotel was in between events this week, and that's how he was able to get the conference rooms on this floor reserved," my mother says. "Otherwise, y'all woulda been SOL."

"That's...good." *I guess.*

Some of Rooster's club brothers are waiting outside the conference room and nod hello.

Jigsaw saunters over to my mother, a primal smile fixed on his face. "Morning, Ms. Morgan. You're looking lovely today."

"Oh, Jesus," Rooster mutters at the ceiling.

"Good morning, Jensen. Nice to see ya again." My mother seems… flustered? I don't know. Whatever's happening here ain't right.

Before I have time to ponder it, Jigsaw's hand lands on my shoulder. "How ya feeling, little songbird? Glad you're out of the hospital?"

"Oh, yeah. I slept much better last night." Didn't even have any nightmares. I'll need to jot that down in the 'improvements' column of today's checklist.

He flicks a sly glance at Rooster. "I'm sure you did."

My cheeks heat. *That* hadn't crossed my mind at all last night or this morning. Guess I'll have to mark *that* down in my 'still broken' column.

"Shut up." Rooster shoves Jigsaw. "You coming with me or not?"

"Sure," he answers smoothly.

Rooster takes my arm, pulling me aside. "I won't be gone long. Wrath and Murphy will be here—"

"That's really not necessary."

He stares down at me. Obviously, this isn't optional. "Trinity and Heidi wanted to watch the rehearsal if that's okay."

Sure, make it seem like a social call. "Yeah. Not sure how much rehearsing they're gonna see." I wiggle my stiff fingers. No magic. Nothing.

He takes my hand, bringing it to his lips to brush a kiss over my knuckles. "You'll get there. Give it time," he assures me in a low voice not meant for anyone else to hear.

He jerks his head and Jigsaw says goodbye. The two of them wait for us to go into the room before pressing the button for the elevator.

Greg's the only one here so far and he's vibrating with excitement when his gaze lands on me. He rushes over, hands out in front of him, an excited manager personified.

"I have the most amazing news," he says in a rush, not wasting time with greetings. "All sorts of offers are coming in, Shelby. The silver lining of this whole mess is starting to sparkle."

Starting to sparkle? "Maybe you should dial down the coffee consumption, Greg."

"Shelby." My mother elbows me, then shines a sunny smile on Greg. "What kind of offers?"

"Interviews, endorsements, and a lot of other things we'll sort through."

"Wow." I press my hand to my chest. "I assume some of those interviews are people who want ugly details?"

Greg gnaws on his bottom lip for a second. Too bad if he doesn't appreciate the question. I have no intention of allowing anyone to exploit every creepy and grotesque moment of my ordeal so the general public can get their jollies at my expense. No way. I won't relive the most terrifying moments of my life over and over to boost my career.

"We'll vet the offers carefully, Shelby. I won't advise you to accept any if we don't think they'll be respectful."

Yeah, sure. I've heard that before. "I'll tell you right now, any shock jocks can go take a suck."

He flashes a tight smile. "Noted."

"Morning, Shelby." Even though I recognize Trent's voice, I jump about a mile when his hand lands on my shoulder.

"Jesus," I yelp.

"Nope, just me," he teases, not questioning my overreaction.

"You guys have the space until eleven," Greg says. "You sure you're ready for this, Shelby?"

"Do I have a choice?"

His mouth works, like he's trying to form an answer that won't piss me off. I *am* being pretty awful this morning. I can't seem to help it, though.

"Come on." Trent takes my arm. "I have something I want to play for you."

"All right." I follow him to the small, raised platform. Kenny and Abram meet us, dishing out hugs and kind words. My bass player and drummer aren't usually so touchy-feely and their effusive greetings further unbalance me.

Abram has his sticks but no one bothered to bring his drum kit inside. Interesting rehearsal this will be.

Trent strums three chords in D minor.

"Kinda melancholy." It's not the most popular chord to write songs in. Definitely not in country music. It matches my mood, though.

"Something I was playing with…while you were…gone." His earnest emotion tugs at me. We've known each other a *long* time.

I reach over and press my hand to his. "You know you'll never get rid of me."

He lifts his gaze, staring at me long enough that I twitch, regretting the attempt at a joke. "Your man knew what to do right away. I hesitated. He didn't. Went after that van like wildfire."

I'm not exactly sure what he's trying to tell me but I sense guilt of some sort. "I'm glad you didn't. I'd be upset if you got hurt."

He cringes and looks down.

Maybe that was the wrong thing to say.

Maybe I'm not ready to hear what he's trying to tell me.

He strums the same three chords, then moves on to a chord progression in C major. After a few notes, I recognize one of my favorite Carly Simon songs. I've sung *You're So Vain* a million times. Know the words by heart. Normally, I'd jump right in.

But I've got nothing today.

"I know it's been covered a bunch of times, but you could really do this justice," Trent says as the last note fades.

"Nothing will ever top Faster Pussycat's version."

He snort-laughs. This has been a frequent argument of ours for years. The bit of normalcy feels like an inside-out sweater today.

I reach out and flick his hair. "What's with the baby manbun?"

He cups the back of his head. "What're you talking about? This is in. The chicks have been digging it."

"Yeah? You get lucky in Virginia?"

"A gentleman doesn't tell."

I glance around. "I don't see any here."

"We rehearsing or not?" Kenny shouts.

I cough and rub my throat. "I'm still…my voice is pretty raw. You guys go ahead. I'll listen in."

It's only a tiny white lie. My voice isn't raw—it's gone. Along with my muse. All I can picture is opening my mouth and nothing coming out. Not sure how I'm supposed to go back on the road like this.

My mom brings me a cup of tea and a packet of honey. "See if that helps, baby."

"Thanks." My eyes well up and I will away the tears before anyone notices.

Damn, this sucks. My mood's all over the place this morning. One horrible event seems to have turned me into different people trying to co-exist inside the same skin. I hate it. Hate this timid girl who jumps at her shadow. Hate the emptiness inside me.

Most of all, I hate the missing music.

CHAPTER TWENTY-ONE

Shelby

"WELL, THAT WAS POINTLESS." I SIGH AND DROP INTO A CHAIR OUTSIDE THE hotel's coffee shop upstairs.

"The band sounds good. Trent's grown up an awful lot. He looks so professional now." My mother sips her coffee and wrinkles her nose, reaching for another packet of sugar. "How do *you* feel?"

Scared. Out of body. Like I've aged ten years in the last few days. "Okay."

She stretches over the table and brushes my hair from my shoulder. "Your hair's getting so long. I wish you had more people attending to you on the road."

I tug at the ends of my hair, still wavy from braiding it last night. "I like it. Besides, it's all mine. I'd hate having to stick extensions and stuff in every night."

"Well, I hope you're using a good heat-protecting spray or something on it," she says, still studying me.

"I use whatever Cindy has and try avoid heat on my days off."

"Good."

"Is my *hair* really what you want to talk about before you go home?"

She shifts her gaze from my hair to my face. "I'm just disappointed. I always thought things would be more, I don't know...*glamorous* for you out on the road. That you'd be traveling with rolling racks of fabulous wardrobes, have a large entourage, a bus with your face—"

My whole world tilts on its axis. This is the last damn conversation I want to have after my bust of a rehearsal. Momma chose the wrong day to unravel this particular ball of yarn. "Nothing I do will ever be good enough for you, will it?"

"That's not what I meant at all, honey."

The hell it isn't. "Not many artists tour that way these days. I'm still so new to the business. But I'm doing what I love. Can't that be enough?"

"I want the best of everything for you."

I'm sure she believes that, so I let it go.

"I like Trinity. I think it'll be good for you to have a female friend of sorts on the road with you."

"Yeah, and her husband's hella scary, so hopefully his presence keeps the wackos at bay."

Her mouth twists with worry. Shoot, maybe I shouldn't have brought that up right before she leaves. But hell, the whole reason we're even sitting here is because of the kidnapping…abduction? I'm hardly a kid, so kidnapping feels weird. God*damn,* I wish I'd kicked that bastard in the balls while I had the chance.

"I *am* glad Rooster and some of his brothers will be protecting you the rest of the tour," she says.

I have to pick my jaw up off the table.

"Don't look at me like that." She huffs and fixes her blouse. "I still think you're too young to settle down."

"I'm hardly 'settling down.'" I've thought long and hard about how to approach what I want to say. *Now or never*. I reach over and rest my hand against hers. "I know how much Dad hurt you when he left—"

"Oh, screw that man to hell and back." Her eyes are practically spitting sparks. "I don't care about him walking out on *me*."

The table jiggles and I tilt my head to the side. My mother's bouncing her leg so fast she's about to launch herself into the sky.

"Maybe I should've told you this when you were younger." Her words are soft and hesitant now, but that leg of hers is still jumping a mile a minute.

"Told me what?"

Her throat works as she struggles for words and breath. That can only mean she's about to mention my sister. Which makes sense. Hayley and my father's departure are so deeply and painfully intertwined in our family history.

"Your father and I…even if Hayley hadn't…we would've split up."

I piece together her fragmented sentences. "Really?"

"His reaction…the way he handled Hayley's diagnosis…shredded me. Some couples, a tragedy reveals who each person is at their core. Their strengths complement one another and bond them together. Or it exposes their weaknesses and breaks them apart."

"I remember you fighting a lot," I whisper. "Now I can see it was a tremendous amount of pressure for both of you to be under."

"Our finances made it worse, but that wasn't all of it. Instead of being stronger together, we turned on each other. He wanted me to work more so we weren't so broke but I couldn't *not* take care of Hayley. Be with her. It was an impossible choice." Her eyes shimmer with tears. "Well, not impossible. I would've moved into our car rather than leave my baby girl alone in the hospital."

My throat tightens and tears blur my vision.

"We still had you, so maybe that was irresponsible on my part," she says. "Neither of us were wrong, I guess…"

I sure think one of them had it backwards. "I wasn't neglected," I whisper. "And I never resented the time spent with Hayley. I wanted—" My voice breaks. "I *wanted* to be with her as much as possible. I would've hated it if you were working instead of at the hospital with her."

"Thank you, Shelby. It means a lot to hear that," she says softly, as if my simple admission lifted a weight off her shoulders.

"Anyway, I don't hate your father for leaving *me*. I hate him for leaving *you*. You'd already lost your sister. Losing your father too…I can never forgive him for that."

"Do you…do you think something happened to him?" The little girl in me always wonders if maybe my father died and that's why he never contacted me again.

"No." She kills that theory with one word. "I tracked him down once. Begged him to see you. At least spend time with you. But he refused. I never told you because…"

"I understand." It doesn't feel good to hear that *now*; I can't imagine how a younger, more vulnerable me would've swallowed the rejection.

"I'm sorry. I never wanted to tell you that."

"I'd rather know." As much as it hurts, I prefer living with the truth than constantly wondering.

"You were such a joy, Shelby. In the darkest part of my life, you kept me going. I'm sorry if that put a burden on you. It broke my heart that he left. I couldn't understand how he chose to miss out on your life. Maybe that's why I worked extra hard to be so involved in everything you did. To make up for what you'd lost." She reaches over and cups my cheek. "I'm proud to be your momma. Watching you grow up and become the woman you are is the best thing I've ever done. He's a fool for missin' out on it."

My throat's so tight, I barely choke out a "thank you."

She sighs and delicately wipes a finger under her lashes. "That's enough emotional talk. I don't want a stuffed-up head on the plane."

I force a smile and a bit of a laugh. "I'm surprised you're gettin' on a plane at all."

She narrows her eyes. "Don't remind me. I was so worried about you on the way here, I didn't have time to fret about it."

"You'll be okay."

"God bless Rooster for organizing everything for me."

"Wait, what?"

Pink spreads over her cheeks. "He's certainly a man of action. Had all the arrangements made before he called me." She drops her gaze. "I don't know how I'm gonna repay him. I'm sure that last-minute ticket cost a bunch."

"Wait. He did that?"

"Yes. How else do you think I was able to get here?"

Jeez, and she still had the nerve to give me grief.

As if she read my thoughts, she says, "I *do* like Rooster, honey. If you were more…settled in this new phase of your life, maybe I wouldn't worry so much."

I snort. "At least I know he's not after me for my money."

She bites her lip. "Eventually, you might be making a lot more, honey."

"Big *might*. I might also be waitressing again."

"You need to believe in yourself."

"I do."

"Afternoon, ladies." Rooster's warm greeting lights a fire in me.

Before I even know what I'm doing, I jump out of my chair, knocking it backwards. I slip my arms around him, dragging him down for a long hello kiss. "I missed you," I whisper against his lips.

"Missed you too." He presses a quicker kiss to my lips. "I'll go away more often if you always greet me that way."

Next to us, Jigsaw clears his throat—loudly. "Do you need a refill, Lynn?" he asks my mother.

While they chat, Rooster leans down, touching his forehead to mine. "How was rehearsal?"

"I don't want to talk about it."

His mouth turns down but he rights my chair, and holds it out for me to sit, then drags a chair over for himself.

"She'll get there," my momma says. "Just listening to them play was good for her."

Rooster nods but the tight line of his mouth seems to say he disagrees.

"Greg says there are a lot of interview offers and other stuff he needs to discuss with me," I say to take the attention away from rehearsal.

His eyebrows shoot up. "Good."

"I didn't tell him about the PR woman, because I wasn't sure..." my voice trails off.

"That's fine."

"One of the interview offers was from *People*," my mother says.

"Really?" That's news to me.

Momma's eyes glitter with excitement. *People* has been one of her favorite rags for as long as I can remember. She takes a long dramatic pause, her gaze pinging between us to make sure she has our full attention. "They want an *exclusive* and they're willing to pay."

"An exclusive with *me*? I thought they only paid for celebrity babies and super-secret superstar weddings."

She straightens her spine, looking like a proud momma kangaroo. "Talk it over with Greg but I think you should consider it. Wouldn't that be something? Your face at every checkout counter back home?"

"Oh. Yay." I lift my fist in the air with an obvious lack of enthusiasm. Momma rolls her eyes at me and sips her coffee.

Rooster's phone chimes, and he quickly shuts it off. "Ready to head to the airport, Lynn?"

"Oh, thank the Lord you were paying attention." She glances at her phone. "I totally forgot what time it was."

"I'll ride with you," Jigsaw says casually.

Rooster side-eyes him. "You hate being in the truck."

"But I love your big, ugly face," Jiggy says, while slapping Rooster's cheeks and making kissy lips at him.

"Jensen, will you help me grab my bags from the front desk?" my mother asks, ignoring their display of brotherly affection.

"Yes, ma'am."

Rooster shakes his head as they walk off together. "He promised he'd behave."

"My momma can handle him. Don't worry."

He glances down at me. "I'd rather not end up with him as my step-father-in-law one day."

I snort at the absurdity of that idea. "I'm like ninety-nine percent certain she has no plans to remarry. Ever. And I don't feel like Jiggy's a big proponent of marriage either."

The implications of what he *actually* said don't hit me until later.

CHAPTER TWENTY-TWO

Rooster

At least Lynn's departure is more pleasant than her arrival. No more complaints about me—or at least none that I overhear.

"I made sure I talked you up every chance I got," Jigsaw assures me with a smug expression as we watch Shelby and her mom tearfully hugging goodbye at the airport security gate.

"Thanks. Exactly what I need."

"She's a feisty one." Jigsaw rubs his chin, still focused on Shelby's mom.

"Can you please *not* eyeball my girlfriend's mother?"

"Why? She's a fine woman. Meant to be appreciated. Like wine."

"You're a beer drinker. Appreciate her from a distance."

"A man's taste develops, you know."

"For fuck's sake," I grumble.

"Bye!" Lynn waves to us one final time before heading through the metal detectors.

Shelby turns our way, sniffling and wiping her eyes. When she's close enough, I pull her into my arms. She presses her face against my chest and lets me hold her for a few minutes.

"Aww," Jigsaw mouths, forming a heart with his thumbs and index fingers.

"Asshole," I mouth back over Shelby's head.

"I'm surprised your mom doesn't want to be on the road with you, Shelby," Jigsaw says.

She pulls away. "Bite yer tongue. I love my momma but I'd never go onstage again if I had her nitpicking at me every dang night." She scowls. "'Your hair's too long. Why don't you have more costume changes? More makeup. Less makeup.' No effing thank you."

Jigsaw's mouth opens, then closes. "I thought she made your dresses?"

"Some of 'em, yup. And I'm damn proud to wear 'em onstage too. Then send her pictures."

Chuckling, I wrap my arm around her shoulders and steer her toward the exit. Jigsaw falls into step beside me. "So, what's our plan today?"

I throw a glance at him after the word "our." "I wasn't aware *we* had plans."

"That's why I was asking, dickface. Unless you need me, I'm gonna check out of the hotel and stay at Ice's until we're ready to hit the road."

"Good idea. I still need to finish some stuff for him."

"I can do that for you, brother."

"Thanks."

Shelby seems lost in thought, not adding anything to our discussion. I wait until we're back at the hotel to ask her what she wants to do.

"Whatever you need." She gestures toward the door to our room. "I'm sure all this stuff has put you behind."

"Don't worry about that." I drop down on the edge of the bed, running my hands over my jeans, carefully considering my next question. "You want to go look for some luggage maybe?"

She taps her fingers against her thigh. "I didn't think of that. Where'd all the rest of my stuff end up?"

"I think Greg and Trent shoved everything in some plastic bags and tossed it in the van."

"Shoot. All my clothes are gonna be wrecked." She moves closer and drops down onto the bed next to me, staring straight ahead. "I can't…I'll miss my trunk. I've had it forever, but I don't think I'll ever look at it the same way again. Although I'm sure the FBI don't plan to give it back any time soon." She flashes a pained smile. "You're right. I need a suitcase or something. But no luggage I can fit inside of."

It's too early for me, but I'm glad she's able to joke about it a little. I reach over and take her hand. "Sounds like a plan."

"Think we can find a Walmart or something around here?"

"We can do better than that. You need something sturdy for all the traveling you're doing."

"I can't afford *sturdy*."

For now, I let it go. Shelby's proud and I respect that. But she's dating the wrong man if she thinks I'm not going to take care of her needs.

"Let me fix my hair and then I want to track Greg down to find out where my stuff is."

"All right." While she's in the bathroom, I pull out my phone and google *luggage for touring musicians.* I search through a few suggestions, finally deciding a hard-side case with spinning wheels will probably work best for her. The one that's rated the highest even comes in Caribbean Blue. Looks close enough to Shelby's favorite color—electric teal.

Done.

Next, I search for any locations near us that actually has the set. One of the malls has it, so while Shelby's still occupied, I give the store a quick call to confirm they have each piece and ask the salesperson to set them aside for me.

Luggage issue solved.

"All ready." Shelby drifts over, brushing her leg against mine. "Who were you talking to?"

I click my phone off. "No one. Ready to go?"

Suspicion glitters in her eyes but she nods.

"How do you feel about staying at the clubhouse tonight?" I ask. "Ice said they're having a party and strongly hinted he'd like to see my face."

"Sure. Of course."

I pack the few things I brought with me. Shelby gathers her stuff and meets me at the door.

Greg lets us onto the van to grab Shelby's stuff. I drag the garbage and tote bags over to the truck.

"My dresses are a wreck." Shelby paws through one of the giant plastic bags, sighing and frowning at the jumble of clothes.

The other bag must have all her shoes in it. It's lumpy and already has heels and toes poking through the sides. Now that I have a better idea of how much stuff she has, I consider calling the store back to see if they have *two* sets of the Caribbean Blue hard-side cases.

"We can have the hotel dry-clean your dresses and pick them up tomorrow if you're doing rehearsal here again."

"Shoot, you know how much a hotel's gonna charge for that?"

"It's kind of a business expense, isn't it?"

She scowls at me. "I guess. Maybe we'll stick it on Greg's tab, since he made this mess."

"Works for me."

"I'm kidding. I wouldn't do that."

I shrug. "We'll work it out later. Grab the stuff you need cleaned."

Inside the hotel, while Shelby's talking to someone in guest services about her laundry, I text Greg to give him the heads-up about the massive fee that's about to be tacked onto his bill and to let him know we're staying at the clubhouse tonight. He responds with a time for her to be here for rehearsal in the morning.

"You're awfully intense." Murphy's rumbling voice pulls me away from my phone and I set it down.

I stand and slap his outstretched hand in hello. "Where you been hiding, fucker?"

One corner of his mouth lifts, and he strokes a hand over his beard. "Just enjoying kid-free time with the wife."

"Where is she?"

"In our room."

"Poor Heidi. Can she even walk?"

He lifts his hand, wobbling it from side to side. "I came down to find some Gatorade."

"Jesus Christ." I laugh and shake my head. "Too much info."

"You need to get back to that?" He nods at my phone that's now blinking and buzzing across the table.

I check the message from Greg, send a quick response, and set it down again. "Her manager."

"You're like her go-between now."

"I guess." I glance over his shoulder, watching Shelby still chatting about her dresses. "Someone needs to be. After everything she just went through, I don't want her to feel pressured, you know?"

"I hear you." His expression flattens into something more serious. "I was only kidding. You're right. No one else is gonna look out for," he taps his chest, "her well-being."

"Since when do you say things like well-being?"

"Don't be a dick. She's got Greg to look out for her *business* stuff. But no one's looking out for *her.*" He throws his arms wide. "Enter, Rooster. Cock-a-doodle-motherfuckin'-do."

I roll my eyes but can't help laughing. "I can't sit by and watch when she needs something and not fix it, you know?"

"Trust me, I get it."

"We're heading over to the mall to find her some luggage. You two want to join us?"

He shrugs. "Sure. Wrath and Trin will probably want to go too. She said she needs something for her camera."

"Hey, Murphy." Shelby walks up alongside him.

"How you doing today, Shelby?"

"Meh. Rehearsal sucked. My momma went home. And I just handed over half my wardrobe to this hotel. Hoping they can clean it without wrecking or losing it." She returns his smile. "How are *you* doing?"

He shakes his head. "Better than that. You mind if Heidi and I tag along on your shopping trip?"

Shelby's gaze slides my way. "Shopping trip?"

"The luggage?" I remind her.

"Oh, right. No, of course not. The more the merrier."

SHELBY

Rooster pulls the truck into a parking spot and I glance at the mall entrance. "You know where we are?"

He checks his phone, swiping through a few screens before nodding. "Yup. Should be right inside."

"What should?"

"Don't worry about it."

We're supposed to meet up with his brothers in the food court and the flat brick wall with the big white department store sign on the side doesn't look like it's serving up pizza and hamburgers. But I follow him anyway.

He stops in front of some fancy-ass luggage store and pulls me inside.

"I can't afford anything in here," I whisper.

A saleswoman approaches us with a blank expression. Maybe we don't look like her usual customers. "Can I help you?" Her eyes widen as she gives me a second glance. Shit, I hope she doesn't recognize me or something.

I fidget and squeeze Rooster's hand. He squeezes back but doesn't take the hint that I want to leave.

"Yeah, I called a little while ago about the expandable hard-side set in blue?"

My jaw drops and I cock my head, peering up at him.

"Sure!" Now the saleslady has a pep in her step. She waves her hand in the air, inviting us to follow her to the register. "I have three pieces. Large traveler. Medium traveler. And carry-on size."

She wheels all three pieces in front of the counter for us to inspect. Rooster takes a step back, studying them intently. "Do you have another large one?"

"Sure. I'll be right back." She disappears into a door behind the register.

I grab Rooster's arm, yanking him toward me. "What are you doing?"

"Do you like the color?" His lips curve up. "Online it looked kinda close to electric teal."

Oh. My. God.

My heart absolutely melts. When we first met, I told him electric teal was my favorite color. I was sort of being silly, wanting him to understand I wasn't a pink, frilly girly-girl type. But he took it to heart. First, buying me a pair of boots in that color, and now…

"Shelby?"

"When did you…How'd you even?" I'm too overcome to spit out the right question.

He holds his hands in the air, tapping his fingers as if he were on his phone. "I told you, my google-fu is strong. I looked up what would be appropriate for touring musicians. This set had good reviews. Found a place not far from the hotel that had it…and here we are."

Maybe it's a mundane thing to get all love-buzzed over, but that he did all that to solve my rather banal problem is so sweet, I'm not sure what to say. Not that I can't google stuff myself, but I probably would've gone to the closest Walmart and picked out whatever looked big enough. "Thank you."

"Do you like the color?"

"I love it."

"Good. Open 'em up and see if you think the compartments will work for how you like to organize your stuff."

"You're acting like I organize at all." I nudge him with my elbow. "You saw what my trunk looked like."

He huffs a quick laugh. "Yeah, I remember."

I crouch down, turn the biggest suitcase on its side, and unzip it. It's full of pockets, hidden compartments, and straps to keep everything secure. "It's great."

The saleswoman returns with a second large roller. Rooster eyes all four pieces together.

"I don't think all that's gonna fit in the van or on your bike," I whisper.

He slides his gaze my way but doesn't say anything, then lifts his chin at the clerk. "Can we break up a set? The two large bags and the carry-on?"

"Sure. Whatever you want. They might be heavy when they're fully packed."

Rooster flexes his arm. "Not a problem. That's what she has me for."

I lean into him. "Stop. You're not my butler."

"You think that's enough to fit everything?" he asks me.

"Gosh, I hope so."

The woman ends up talking him into packing cubes and helps him pick out a case for himself. At least this isn't *all* about me. When she rings up everything, I squirm.

"Rooster," I whisper. "I can't—"

The stern expression he turns my way snaps my mouth shut.

There's no elegant way to carry giant ol' suitcases out of a store like this. At least Walmart would've had a shopping cart. The clerk helps us tuck our purchases inside the two large suitcases and sends us on our merry way.

Well, Rooster seems merry as he clutches both handles in one hand and rolls the cases out of the store. I'm still gagging over the price.

"Logan." I hurry to keep up with him and he captures my hand with his free one.

"Figure we'll put everything in the truck and drive around to meet the others at the food court. That okay?"

"You…I…I don't know what to say." I rush ahead to open one of the doors, which earns me a scowl, but for God's sake, he's already wheeling around my luggage. I can at least open the dang door for him.

He loads the two suitcases into the back seat. They take up almost the entire space.

Inside the truck, he hands me his phone, open to a map of the mall. "Are there any shops you want to visit while we're here?" He fires up the truck and guides it around the massive, sprawling building to the far side, and slides into another spot.

"Are you volunteering to do *more* shopping with me?"

"Yes. You've been on the road for a while. Is there anything you need or you're running out of? Something you want?"

I glance at the map again. "I'd actually like to look for a new pair of yoga pants."

A positively feral grin lights up his whole face. "Can I watch you try them on?"

Laughing, I hand the phone back to him. "There's a store near the food court." I pin him with a stern look. "I'm buying them, though."

"Agreed. You're buying your own pair of yoga pants."

I squint at him. "Why do I feel like we're agreeing to two different things?"

"We're not. You're buying a pair of pants. I heard you."

"Okay." Still keeping an eye on him, I unbuckle my seatbelt. "You got a hat or something in here? Now that you told me the story's been all over the place, I'm nervous. That saleslady looked at me funny and I was scared she recognized me."

"Ah, shit. I'm sorry I didn't think of that." He curses under his breath as he twists in the seat, searching the back of the truck. "Not my vehicle, or I'd have something," he mutters.

"It's fine. I have my sunglasses." I search through my purse for a ponytail holder. "I'll stick my hair up. I usually get photographed with it down."

"You'll be with three bikers and two ol' ladies. Anyone who bothers you is going to wish they hadn't."

I laugh, remembering how fierce Heidi can be. "Shoot, you think Heidi's packing her ballpeen hammer?"

"Probably. Trinity's pretty lethal too."

"I'm not exactly a melting snowflake, you know."

He leans over and kisses my cheek. "You're right. You're not a snowflake. You're a motherfuckin' blizzard."

"I like that." I search my purse again, pulling out a small notebook. "I want to stick that in a song or something."

"Will I get credit?"

I scoot closer and brush my hand against his cheek. "Absolutely."

"You snookered me."

Rooster's eyes widen with phony indignation. "I *what?*"

I point to the bag in his hand. "I said I was buying my stuff. You've done enough for me already."

"We agreed you were buying a pair of pants." He nods to the bag in my hand. With the *one pair* of pants I purchased. "And you did."

Next to me, Trinity covers her mouth and laughs. "He's got you, Shelby."

"If it makes you feel better, I don't think that stuff is even for you, Shelby," Murphy adds. "Rooster likes the way yoga pants feel on his balls." Murphy shapes his hands into a V in front of his crotch. "He thinks they present his package in an appealing way."

"Did you just say *balls* to my girlfriend?" Rooster shoves Murphy. By the way the two of them keep trying to wipe the smiles off their lips, they're both close to bursting with laughter.

"I was talking about *your* balls, so I figured that was okay." He pokes at Rooster's bag.

"Is there something you need to share?" Wrath squints at Murphy. "Why are you so concerned with a brother's balls all of a sudden?"

"Good grief." Heidi takes my bag and hands it to Rooster. "You guys have fun discussing your *balls*. We're going on ahead."

"Again, it was Rooster's balls, not mine," Murphy shouts.

The girls walk faster, giggling so hard they both bump into me. "Whatever," Heidi says over her shoulder.

"As if they're going to let us out of their sight." Trinity slows to a more normal pace. "Especially you, Shelby."

"No kidding. Rooster said the story's all over the place. I've been afraid to look."

"Don't worry," Heidi says. "We won't let anyone bother you."

Trinity pats her own cheeks and grins at me. "My fuck-off face is cocked and loaded."

"Ooo!" Heidi stops dead and pivots to the right. "Can we stop here? I want to look for a pair of boots for Alexa. She's already growing out of her last pair."

"If you two have another girl, she's going to have a fabulous wardrobe from day one," Trinity says.

"I know, right?" Heidi nudges Trinity's shoulder. "Since certain aunts spoil my kid rotten."

Thankfully, the store has adult sizes too. I'm browsing through rows of shoes when an inky-blue western boot embroidered with gray stars and flowers is thrust in front of my face.

"Those are pretty." I tip my head back to look at Rooster. "A little girly for ya, though."

"Cute." He shakes the boot, drawing my attention to them. "Do you like them?"

I do very much. They'd caught my eye when we walked in but I'd been afraid to look at the tag. "If I say yes, are you going to buy them?"

"Sir, here's the size seven." One of the salesgirls sets down a box on a bench behind us.

"How about that?" Rooster tips his head toward the bench. "If you like them, will you try them on for me?"

"Do you need help?" the salesgirl asks.

"No, I'm fine," I sigh.

"Those are so pretty," Heidi squeals. "They're LOKI blue too." She plops down on the bench next to my box and strips off her shoes.

"I thought you were looking for boots for your daughter?" I ask.

"Momma needs new shoes too," she says without looking up from the pair of hunter-green ankle boots she's about to try on.

Murphy's watching her with laughter on his lips, shaking his head. "She really doesn't."

"See? Like Heidi said. They're club colors." Rooster nudges me toward the bench. "I didn't see any boots in this color down in Texas."

I drop down next to Heidi and open the box. Inhaling the fresh, leather scent, I unwrap the boots. Damn, they're pretty.

Rooster drops down on one knee and holds a boot out to me.

"Look at you," I tease to calm the fluttery sensation in my belly. "My own Prince Charming. But with a cowgirl boot instead of a glass slipper."

"I'm a King, baby, not a prince." He lifts his chin in a *hurry up* sort of way. "Come on, slide that pretty little foot in here."

The boots are nice and snug. Rooster helps me with both and I stand, pacing a few steps back and forth. They're perfect, really.

"They'd match that silver dress you have, wouldn't they?" Rooster asks.

"Such good fashion sense." Murphy slaps Rooster's chest.

Rooster ignores him, still focused on me. *Yup.* These would look and feel a hell of a lot better on stage than the black heels I've been wearing with that dress. But I hate having Rooster drop even *more* money on me today.

I drop onto the bench and tug at the left boot.

"They kinda rub my heel a little," I say in a low voice.

Rooster squats in front of me, helping me pull the boot all the way off. "Want to go up half a size?"

"No, that's okay."

He leans in close. "It would really make me happy to see you wear these on stage. If they honestly don't fit or you don't like 'em, say so. But if you're just worried about me buying them for you, don't."

Why is this so hard for me to accept?

He brushes his knuckles under my chin, forcing me to meet his questioning eyes. "Tell me what's going on. I bought you boots down in Texas and you were okay with it."

"That was different."

"Why?"

I blow out a breath and stare at the ceiling, thinking of a way to put it into words without sounding awful. "Back then, what we had was a hookup. I wasn't sure I'd actually see you again. So, it felt more like a memento of a hot fling."

He doesn't so much as chuckle at my completely lame explanation. "And now?"

I shrug, uncomfortable exposing myself like this in the middle of a damn shoe store. "Now, you're my…partner. I love you. I don't want to take advantage of you."

His eyes widen. He swallows hard, then swoops in and brushes a soft kiss over my lips. He sets the box down with a muted thump and grasps both my hands in his. "You don't know how much I love hearing you say that." He squeezes my hands gently. "But here's the thing. I'm your man." He pauses, waiting for an acknowledgment, I suppose, so I nod. "And I really like spoiling my woman."

My gaze lands on the box again. "They *would* be pretty with that dress."

"Good. Done." He presses a quick kiss to my cheek.

Heidi returns and slips off the shoes she'd been trying on, murmuring a few words to Murphy. He grabs her box and heads to the register.

Rooster raises his eyebrows in a see-no-big-deal expression.

"Yeah, but they're married," I whisper.

He shrugs and holds out his hands for the boots.

The six of us regroup outside the store. Trinity links one of her arms through mine and one through Heidi's, pulling us ahead of the guys. "Can we *please* find the electronics store now?"

"Sorry," Heidi says. "It's just nice to shop in person instead of online for a change."

Trinity chuckles. "You make me feel old." She turns to me. "What's wrong? Those boots are so pretty. I thought about trying them on too," her lips curl into a playful smile, "but I wasn't sure we were at that matching outfits level of our friendship yet."

I burst out laughing. "I think I could handle it."

"No, seriously. Everything all right?"

I still haven't been able to wrap my mind around Rooster's *spoiling his woman* comment. "He's already done a lot for me. I don't want Rooster to think I'm some gold-digger."

Trinity winces. "That term needs to die already." She slows her relentless walking pace and pulls me to the side against the railing overlooking the first floor of the mall. "Shelby, you're a lot younger than me, and I don't know what kind of men you've dated before."

"A lot of selfish jerks. Immature—"

"Right," Trinity continues. "Well, let me tell you this—real men, *good* men—aren't keeping score. They're not resentful. They provide for the people they care about no matter what." She flicks her gaze over my shoulder where I assume the guys are close to catching up with us. "Rooster's a provider and a protector."

"All of our guys are," Heidi adds.

"He's also smart. If you were trying to fleece him, he'd sense it. He seems to really care about you." The honesty in Trinity's eyes and voice stuns me right before she delivers her final knock-out. "Let him."

CHAPTER TWENTY-THREE

Rooster

"Well, fuck, brother. I had no idea your ol' lady was famous." Ice flaps a glossy tabloid in my face. "One of the girls brought it in."

This is my punishment for deciding to spend our last couple days in Virginia at the clubhouse? Really?

"What a relief you're not a subscriber to *Gossip Club* magazine, Prez." I roll my eyes. "I said she was on tour. We were at the arena when it all went down."

The clubhouse is quiet now, but the atmosphere is festive. Girls move around, straightening up the place. Brothers stock the bar while heckling each other and eyeing the club girls.

"I don't pay attention to country music," Ice says.

Sure. He has way too many porn stars to look after. "Yeah, I didn't either."

Shonda brought our stuff up to our room with Shelby, and as the girls bounce down the stairs together, Ice studies Shelby a little too closely for my liking. "You're really taking an ol' lady at your age?"

I hadn't realized Ice and I were at the sharing-our-hopes-and-dreams-for-the-future stage of our relationship. "I've plowed through enough bunnies to know she's a keeper. *The one*. Thanks for the concern, though."

"The *one*." He scoffs. "Well, news says she's about to be a *huge* star."

Can't say I care for what he's implying there. "It's not like that. We met before she started blowing up."

"She seems nice. A real stunner too." He slaps my back. "Happy for you, brother."

"Thanks." I hope that's the end of the conversation. Part of me remains tense, worried next he'll ask if she'd like to star in a celebrity sex tape or something.

He's quiet, watching the girls stop to talk to Trinity and Heidi with more interest than I'd expect. Doesn't he have more important things to do elsewhere? Bunnies to fuck? A club to run? Porn to upload?

Oh, wait—that last one was supposed to be *my* job.

"I'm sorry all this shit took me away from finishing up Anya's project. I have a couple days before we—"

"Nah, I think she's all set. Don't worry about it." He pauses and rubs his hand over his chin. "On second thought, maybe take a look before you go. Make sure it's all right."

"You got it."

"Have you ever considered how much attention your relationship might bring the MC?" he asks, eyes *still* on my girlfriend.

"It's crossed my mind a few times," I answer carefully.

"If her tour's going through Mississippi, I'd stop to visit Priest and introduce Shelby around. Let him get to know her so he's feeling more protective of her than resentful if a spotlight lands on the organization."

Well, fuck. Now I can't even be mad about him eyeing Shelby. It's solid advice. Insightful. Since Ice has years in the club and acting as president under his belt, he's in a position to be more knowledgeable than I am about our national president's quirks.

"Thanks. I was planning to stop by and talk to him. Pay my respects. I wasn't sure if I was going to bring Shelby or not."

"Definitely bring her. Valentina will probably love her, and that always goes a long way with Priest."

Another helpful bit of advice. "Thanks, brother."

"I'm sure Z would've told you the same thing. Priest's sweet on *his* ol' lady." His lips twist in an amused or irritated smirk—hard to tell with Ice. But it's true. Lilly's one of the few ol' ladies outside of the Mississippi charter to have Priest's patch on her 'property of' vest—something some of the old ladies in *my* charter haven't taken well.

"He's always happy when his officers settle down," Ice mutters.

This conversation gives Ice's single status new meaning. "He give you a dad speech about taking an ol' lady of your own?"

He blows out an annoyed breath. "Only every time I see the old goat."

How the fuck does Priest have time to keep tabs on the financials and arrest records of all the charters around the country *and* worry about his officers' love lives? "You and Anya seemed pretty close the other night." I must be feeling cocky from my impending departure, otherwise I'm not sure I'd poke around in that particular hornet's nest.

He gives me a heaping dose of side-eye. "You've noticed there's a bit of an age gap there, haven't you?"

Well, fuck. Ice might be the first one-percenter I've ever known to voice *that* concern. "Yeah, because no biker's ever dated a younger woman before."

Not so much as a chuckle out of him. "He won't welcome a porn star as an ol' lady."

"Why the fuck not?" More than half the clubs earn their money from running strip clubs. Well, that might be an exaggeration. Most of them use the strip clubs as a way to launder dirty money from other ventures. But we're earning good money producing porn. I scratch the side of my head. "Isn't it Lost Kings legend that Priest shot a brother for disrespecting Valentina when they were dating?"

He bursts out laughing. "You advocating I shoot our national prez?"

"Fuck no. I'm just saying, no one should question you. Besides, she brings more money into the organization than some patch holders do. Priest should respect *that,* if nothing else."

"Solid point. Money definitely changes his perspective." He taps my shoulder. "Thanks, brother."

"Doctor Rooster, at your service." I salute him.

SHELBY

I really don't think I'm a prude. I mean, I love sex. Especially sex with Rooster. But I'm not used to seeing *other* people having sex. Right in front of me.

Unfortunately, that seems to be the theme at the clubhouse tonight.

And I'd thought the upstate New York clubhouse was wild.

In the chair to Rooster's left, the big guy I'd met earlier—Pants—has a mostly naked redhead grinding on his lap like her life depends on it. His face is buried in the crook of her neck and he appears to be whispering stuff to her. One hand's cupping her extremely generous bare breast and the other one's tucked up somewhere under her tiny pleated skirt.

Not that I'm staring. But it's kind of hard *not* to look. They're so close, Rooster could shift his leg a few inches to the left and easily turn their party into a threesome.

I cough and huddle closer to Rooster, who doesn't seem to notice the free show. "Are you guys filming tonight?"

He glances down, confusion clouding his eyes. "No. Why?"

I discreetly lift my chin in the grinding couple's direction. "Beauty and the beast over there. Seems like a waste not to get that on film."

He turns his gaze their way. A quick smirk curves his lips. "Yo, Pants! You auditioning for a part in one of Anya's movies?"

Pants releases the girl's breast long enough to flip Rooster off, but otherwise ignores the taunt.

To my right, Jigsaw's shaking with laughter and watching the couple like someone's going to ask him to write a detailed report on it later. He leans toward me without looking away. "You have any special piercings, Shelby?"

"What? No. Why?"

His lips twist in a playful way. "No reason."

Rooster leans down, pressing his lips against my ear. "What'd he ask you?"

I turn to answer, "Noth—" but my words get cut off by a glint of metal from under the girl's skirt. *Ewww,* I didn't need to know how this stranger bedazzles her labia.

I whip around and smack Jigsaw's arm. He bursts into more loud laughter.

"You want to go outside?" Rooster asks me.

Instead of answering, I shift my body. I throw one leg over his thighs and perch my butt on his lap, resting my hands on his shoulders. He immediately runs his hands up my jeans-covered legs, stopping to squeeze my butt. "What're you doing, chickadee?"

I tip my head to the side. "Well, not *that*." I lean in and brush my lips over his. "That's not what you expect of me, I hope."

He squeezes me tighter. "No. Why would you ask that?"

"It seems to be a general theme." I twirl one finger in the air, indicating the rest of the room. Pants' performance is the least risqué of what's happening around us.

"Never." He glances over my shoulder. "In fact, I'm considering gouging out T-Bone's eyeballs right this second if he doesn't stop staring at your ass."

I twist to peek over my shoulder, but he stops me with a hand on my cheek. "Thanks for staying here tonight. I didn't realize it'd be this raunchy, but I wanted to spend time here before we leave since they helped—"

"As long as I'm with you, I'm happy."

"I shouldn't take you away from hanging out with the band and—"

I stop him again, this time with a finger on his lips. "I'll see plenty of them on the road. It's fine." I lean in and give him a quick kiss. "Thank you. For everything."

He brushes his knuckles against my cheek for a brief second before gripping my hips and sliding to the edge of the couch. In one smooth movement, he stands, lifting me in the air. Startled, I squeal and wrap my arms around his neck and my legs around his waist. He rumbles with laughter and palms my butt.

Jiggy flashes an angelic smile—or demonic, considering what's probably about to come out of his mouth. "Pool table?"

"No, fuckhead," Rooster growls, lashing out with his booted foot, kicking Jiggy's shin as we pass.

"Where *are* we going?" I ask, resting my head on his shoulder.

My question's answered a few seconds later when something hard presses into the back of my legs. I untangle myself from Rooster and discover he's perched me on top of the bar. He rests one hand on either side of my hips and leans in. "You want something to drink before we leave the party?"

"Rooster, you bring us a new bar decoration?" a biker I don't recognize asks.

"No. This is my ol' lady." The warning in Rooster's voice can't be missed.

"Well, fuck. Sorry, brother." The man nods to me and returns to flirting with one of the girls behind the bar.

"We're leaving?" I ask, curling my fingers in the back of Rooster's hair.

"You seem uncomfortable."

"I was…am…I guess. I'm not used to having glittery va-jay-jays shoved in my face."

He blinks, then bursts into laughter. "Okay."

Something awful occurs to me. Why haven't I thought of this sooner? "Do you…Is that what *you* did before me?"

He glances over his shoulder briefly. Another brother has joined Pants and the redhead. It's quite a show, and they're attracting a crowd.

"No," he finally answers.

It took an awfully long time for him to answer what should've been a simple question.

Jigsaw sneaks up behind Rooster and slaps his shoulder, shouting, "I did *not* need to know that Pants shaves his balls."

"Then why'd you shove your face up there?" Rooster asks.

"Good grooming is just the polite thing to do, Jigsaw," I say sweetly.

His jaw drops, and his eyes widen for a brief second before his mouth curls into a smirk. "Such a funny little songbird." He slaps his hand on Rooster's shoulder. "You planning to lay her out for body shots?"

"Fuck no." Rooster shrugs off Jiggy's hand.

"Then get her off the bar before someone assumes she's a fuckin' party favor."

"Aw, such a sweetheart." I curl a finger, inviting him closer. "Quick question. Is this the kind of thing you two got up to before I came along?" I jerk my chin toward Pants, the redhead, and the new guys who've joined their party.

His gaze shifts to Rooster, who shoots him a death glare.

"You see," I say in a teasing, singsong voice. "I asked Rooster, but he took an awfully long time to answer."

Jigsaw scratches his hand over the back of his head. "Of course not. In fact, I think he was a virgin until he met you. Yup. Almost positive I heard that somewhere. Choirboy."

I break into giggles. "So you two never…?"

Jiggy makes an *X* with his index fingers. "Crossed swords? Hell no."

"Crossed…*ewww*." I groan as the meaning sinks in. "No, I meant have a threesome."

Rooster closes his eyes and rubs his temple. "What exactly did I do to deserve *this*?"

"Aww." I loop my arms around his neck again. "I'm just teasing."

"You know what? I'm so happy to see you smiling that I don't even care that you're busting my nuts over something that probably didn't even happen before I met you."

That's probably the kindest 'yes' anyone's ever received to such an invasive question.

He leans in closer. "I don't want anyone but you." His dark gaze shifts to the side, his voice a deep growl. "Alone. Where I can focus all of my attention on the only person who matters."

"Aww," I breathe out.

"However…" He leans down, pressing his forehead to mine, forcing me to maintain eye contact. "If you're feeling curious or adventurous. If *you* need something else…" The determination burning in his eyes steals my breath. "…I'm not built that way. Not when it comes to you."

"I don't want anyone else."

"Good." He flashes a tight smile. "We've been around this sort of party before and it didn't bother you so much."

I shift my gaze to my lap. "Yeah, but my feelings are way, way bigger for you now. And—"

He cuts me off with a kiss.

Loud, orgasmic shrieks pierce through the noise of the clubhouse. Shouts of approval follow.

Laughing, I pull away from his embrace. "And this is way more, uh, in-your-face."

"I can't even tell anymore." He shrugs.

Jigsaw elbows him in the ribs.

Rooster throws him a glare and signals one of the bartenders over. "You got a few bottles or cans of Sprite back there?"

"Sure thing," she drawls. "Coming right up."

A few seconds later, four cans of ice-cold soda *thunk* onto the bar next to me. I glance down as a short stack of plastic cups lands on top of one of the cans like a party hat.

My vision narrows as I stare at a bead of water rolling down the side of one shiny, green aluminum can.

The noises around me fade in a sucking rush. My heart slams against my ribcage. Sweat dots my forehead. Suddenly, I'm right back in the log cabin kitchen with no hope of escape.

Breathe. I can't get any air.

"Shelby?" Rooster's voice sounds so far away. "What's wrong?"

I squeeze my eyes shut but that only intensifies the helpless feeling. Air—I can't draw in any air.

My hands flap uselessly around my face while I gasp and wheeze.

"Shelby." Rooster cups my cheeks. My eyes pop open. He's close. So close, staring into my eyes like the calm inside a hurricane. "Breathe, baby. It's okay." He takes a long, deep, exaggerated breath, encouraging me to do the same.

Tears roll down my cheeks.

Someone squeezes my hand. "Relax, little songbird. We got you."

The frantic drumming in my chest won't settle down.

"*Shhh*. Breathe with me. Come on," Rooster encourages. "You're okay, Shelby."

I suck in a long, ragged breath. My lungs burn in relief.

"There ya go," he praises. "In and out. Nice and easy."

I take another breath.

And another.

All the sounds and scenery come rushing back with a wallop.

Squeezing my eyes shut, I lean over and rest my elbows on my knees. God, I hope no one else noticed my freak-out.

Rooster runs a soothing hand up and down my back. "You're okay."

I sit up, blinking at my surroundings. No one's paying attention to our trio. Rooster's studying me intently. Jigsaw's watching me with a serious expression I haven't seen on his face often. They're arranged around me in a way that provides a pocket of privacy.

My mouth twitches into a shaky smile. "Phew. Sorry."

"Don't apologize." Rooster runs his hands over my arms. "Can you tell me what brought that on?"

For a second, my mind's completely blank.

"The Sprite." Shivers run all over my body. "That asshole ruined my favorite soda."

ROOSTER

So much for a night of relaxation and letting go. First, the sex show from my brothers. Then Shelby's panic attack.

Although, if she was going to have one, here was probably the safest place to do it. No one noticed. And even if they did, no one would dare say anything and make her uncomfortable.

"She okay?" Jigsaw asks as I step into the hallway.

I leave our bedroom door open so I can keep an eye on Shelby in case she needs me. For now, she's a small, still bundle under the heavy comforter.

"I think she'll be all right." I close the door until it's only open a crack, hoping our conversation won't disturb her.

Jigsaw's antsy, rubbing his hands together, curling them into fists, shifting from foot to foot. "I should've cut more fingers off that son of a bitch."

"I'm really regretting turning him over to Jackson now."

"I know why you did it, but yeah. It sucks. What if that happens to her while she's on tour? Thank fuck she was here. With us. With you, I mean."

I fight to keep the smile off my face. This is why Jiggy's been my best friend for so long. He's ready to dismember anyone who hurts his family one second, worried about my girl's feelings the next. Under all his scary indifference, he's a sensitive soul. Way, way down.

"Her doctor said something like this might happen. I'll see how it goes. If she has another episode, I'll call one of the doctors she recommended."

"You two are so couple-y now."

I wait for him to add some detail to the observation. "Your point?"

"Nothing. It's good. You still planning to go get the thing tomorrow?"

"Yeah, if you'll give me a ride."

"What are you going to tell Shelby?"

"That I have an errand to run. She'll be safe here."

"She doesn't know?"

"Nope."

"All right." He slaps my shoulder. "Text me in the morning."

"You gonna go downstairs and check out Pants' sack again?"

"No, dick." He waves his hand at the bedroom door. "You want me to sit by the bed and watch you two sleep?"

"Only if you read us a bedtime story." I grin at him.

"See you in the morning, fucker."

CHAPTER TWENTY-FOUR

Shelby

THE UTTER JOY OF BEING ALIVE AND FREE COURSES THROUGH ME, PULLING me awake.

It takes a second to remember where I am.

And what's happened.

Today, I feel lighter. Optimistic.

I peel my cheek off Rooster's arm and slowly sit up. His eyes are closed, but he reaches for me as I slip out of bed. "I'll be right back," I whisper.

The thick, soft carpet silences my steps as I tiptoe into the bathroom. I take care of business and splash some water on my face, but don't bother looking in the mirror.

I'm alive. That's all that matters.

In the bedroom, light spills around the edges of curtains covering the high, rectangular windows. The air-conditioner kicks on. Cool air drifts over my shoulders.

Rooster's still sprawled on his back. The thin white sheet covers him from the waist down, except for one big foot and part of his leg poking out. A smile tugs at the corners of my mouth. A surge of love and a whole lot of lust speed through me. This big, beautiful, sexy man *rescued* me. Risked everything to find me.

Last night, when panic nearly consumed me, he patiently helped me breathe through it, then tucked me into bed.

I'm bursting with the need to be close to his body. Enjoy every inch of him.

At the side of the bed, I run my fingers over his leg.

A sexy hum rumbles from his chest but he doesn't open his eyes.

I want to wake him in a special way. Lavish attention on him. He won't mind, right? What guy would be upset about that?

Carefully, I shift the sheet to the side. Black camo boxer-briefs block the path to what I'm after.

Softly, so I don't disturb his slumber, I press my knee to the mattress on my side of the bed and crawl over. Kneeling next to him, I take a moment to absorb his perfect rugged beauty. Thick hair, all tousled from sleep. Beard. Broad, sturdy shoulders. Hard chest. Chiseled abdominal muscles. So, so carefully, I place a knee between his thighs and bend to kiss his stomach.

"Hmm." He shifts. His fingers brush over his abs briefly. I lift my gaze, watching him for a few seconds.

Still asleep.

Backing up a few inches, I hook my fingers in his briefs and tug them down just enough to free—*perfect*.

Consider me *lumberjill,* here to take care of this case of morning wood. I grip his cock—rock hard, hot, and silky smooth. Desire pools low and insistent in my body. But I really want to take my time. I stroke him once, enjoying the feel of him under my fingers. My center aches for him, reminding me how long it's been—nope, I'm staying right here in this moment.

I lower my head and trace my tongue against the underside of his cock.

He wakes with a sharp inhale that fades to a low, rumbling groan. "Oh, fuck. What are you doing?" he rasps, reaching to push my hair off my face.

I feel like it should be self-explanatory. But maybe he needs a better demonstration. My hands tremble as I caress his velvety, soft flesh. "I wanted to wake you up in a special way."

"You did."

I kiss the tip of him, my tongue darting out for another taste. He groans a second time and falls back against the pillows. I shift closer, curling over to take him deep in my mouth. My tongue flattens against him. His hips jerk, and for a second I choke. He eases down and I continue.

His hands ball into fists at his sides. More curses spill from his lips. I glance up, admiring the way his stomach muscles clench and quiver. He plants his elbows in the mattress, lifting himself so he can watch me better. I'm a performer, after all, so I put on a good show.

He groans, his head falling back. "Shelby, baby. Fuck." After several minutes of me savoring the taste and feel of him, he reaches for me. "Please. Come here."

But I'm having too much fun. I suck harder, working my hand and mouth in a rhythmic motion that leaves him shaking. There's something so satisfying about having my big, powerful man under my spell that I can't stop.

"Oh, fuck," he groans, tangling his fingers in my hair. "That's it. Right there. That's so good." He groans again, throwing his head back and lifting his hips. More appreciative noises rumble out of him. "Best way I've ever woken up."

Breathing hard, I pop my mouth off him but keep sliding my fist over his flesh at a lazy pace. "I couldn't resist. You looked so sexy all sprawled out."

"Mmm." He grazes my cheek with his fingertips. "Come 'ere."

The sleepy-happy-sexy smirk is too inviting to ignore. I kneel, straddling his legs, but keep my hand moving up and down.

He sucks air between his teeth and curls his finger, beckoning me closer.

With my legs tight to his body, I shuffle my way forward, resting my hand on his chest for balance. When I'm close enough, he pulls me down for a kiss.

I twitch my hips, brushing my center against him, and another sexy humming noise rumbles from his chest. He clutches my ass and rocks me back and forth. Desperately hungry for every inch of him, I trail my lips over his cheek and along his jaw, burying my face in the crook of his neck, kissing and sucking. A little lower, I graze my teeth over his nipple. His whole body shudders.

"Please." His voice is a hoarse, urgent whisper. "Make my morning complete. Ride my dick."

"It's like you read my mind." I grip him tight and lower myself, humming with pleasure as his cock grazes my sensitive skin.

"Hang on." He flings his arm toward the nightstand, desperately reaching for the drawer. "Wait a sec."

"It's okay."

He freezes and slowly slides his gaze over my body. "Are you sure? I'm really not in a position to talk this out with you."

Laughing, I bend down and kiss him again. "I'm sure. I want you. All bare and hot. Inside me."

"*Fuck*." He squeezes his eyes shut and groans.

"Is that a yes?" I tease, leaning forward and bracing my hands on either side of his head. "Hmm? Is it?" I roll my hips.

He squeezes my thighs. "Fuck me, woman. Stop teasing."

Slow enough to drive us both insane, I lower myself, closing my eyes to relish the delicious, stretching sensation. "Oh my God. You feel so good." I wiggle and brace my palm against his chest, whispering a string of curses to rival his own.

"Yes." He squeezes his eyes shut. "Do that again."

He slides his hands up my ribs, gently cupping my breasts, rolling my nipples between his fingers.

Tingles of pleasure shiver down my spine. Hugging my knees to his sides, I sit up and ride him faster.

"Fuck yes." He grabs my hips, urging on my movements. "Harder."

Hot. I'm so hot all over. Sweat mists my skin. Tension expands into a deep ache. I'm so close to gratification. "So close. So close," I chant.

"Yes," he groans.

I glance down and his eyes are closed, head thrown back, jaw tight. My movements slow.

His eyes pop open. "Why'd you stop?"

"Am I hurting you?"

"What? No." His hands slip into the curve of my waist. "Your pussy feels so fucking exquisite on my bare dick that I'm trying not to come like a virgin on prom night."

Laughter bubbles out of me. "Exquisite is the *last* word I ever expected to come out of your mouth."

He shoots a sexy glare at me.

I squeeze him with my inner muscles and he groans.

Gently, I shift back, slowly finding my rhythm again.

He curls his fingers around mine. "I always want you to come first, baby. But you're making it *really* hard."

I duck my head and laugh.

"Oh fuck," he groans. "Don't do that."

I move faster, encouraged by his urgent noises. He slips his hand between my legs, his thumb circling my clit in a steady motion. "Oh!" I gasp. My hips jerk. I'm torn between seeking release and wanting to stretch out this feeling forever. I ignite, pleasure shooting a scorching path through my body.

"Love watching you come on my cock," he says through clenched teeth.

"Don't interrupt. Not done yet," I whisper, working even harder.

His hips roll, punching up, giving me an extra boost. The second my movements slow and I catch my breath, he flips us without breaking our connection. He hikes my legs up, hooking his elbows under my knees and spreading me wide.

He pistons into me, hard and frantic, searching for his own release, grinding into me so hard he triggers another orgasm for me.

"Ah, fuck." He lets out more of those sexy, humming, growly noises as he explodes into me, slowing his movements with erratic jerky thrusts.

Finally, he gathers me in his arms and presses his cheek against my sweaty chest. "Your heart's racing," he murmurs, kissing my breast.

"I wonder why," I tease, gently running my fingers through his hair.

Still panting, I shift underneath him.

He pushes off me. "Didn't mean to crush you."

I hook my arm around his neck, dragging him back down. "I like the weight of you on top of me."

ROOSTER

I can't stop kissing Shelby.

Even though she said she was fine, I'm worried about my big ass crushing her small body into the mattress. I roll to the side, taking her with me so I can keep on kissing her.

"Umm." She nuzzles against my chest.

"I don't think I can move."

She picks her head up. "Are you saying I screwed you into exhaustion?"

"Pretty much." I slide my hand over her hip and pinch her ass.

Her soft laughter jiggles her body against mine. I bring my hand up, cupping her breast. "I didn't worship you enough. You caught me by surprise."

"You complainin'?"

"Hell no." Now that I'm thinking with my head instead of my dick, I stroke my finger over her cheek. "Are we…are you okay?"

Her gaze drops to the mess we've made and she wrinkles her nose. "I'm fine."

"Are you sure?"

"You don't have to worry."

"I'm not worried about *me*. You made it clear before *you* had strong feelings about this." Fuck, I really should've gone for the damn condom instead of being a selfish dick.

She sighs and rubs her forehead over my pec, hiding her face. "I have an IUD."

"Oh."

She peeks up but avoids my gaze. "They're supposed to be super effective, but I worry anyway. Never can be too careful or whatever." She still won't meet my eyes.

There goes my chest squeezing again. Her trust in me is a gift I want to tuck into a box for safekeeping. "Hey." I place my finger under her chin, tipping her head back. "I've always worn a condom and always tested negative for stuff. Just so you know."

"Okay." She blinks as if that had never occurred to her. That's a good sign, I guess, since last night she was questioning how often I took part in clubhouse orgies. "I did too. The hospital, I mean. They ran all those tests."

I lean in and kiss her forehead. "Come on. Let's clean up. Then go find food. I'm starving."

"Aww, did I use up all your energy?"

"Yes." I roll out of bed and turn, holding out my hand to her. "Damn, you're pretty all after-sex-y."

Her lips twitch into a smile glowing with happiness that I'm damn glad to see after her panic attack last night. Not that I'm planning to bring it up but it's still on my mind.

What will trigger her next time?

CHAPTER TWENTY-FIVE

Rooster

I'VE NEVER BEEN RELIGIOUS BUT TODAY I'M CONVINCED HEAVEN CONSISTS of watching your woman get dressed. Wearing nothing more than a steel-blue satin and lace bra with a pair of jeans, Shelby's bent over, jamming her feet into her new boots. I'd offer to help, but I'm enjoying the view way too much for my tongue to function properly.

"What do you think?" Shelby stands and slaps her hands on her thighs, drawing my attention to her legs encased in tight blue denim. She turns from side to side, showing off the blue and gray boots.

"Sexy as fuck." I'm really glad she got over whatever was bothering her yesterday and let me buy them for her.

She shakes out a steel-blue tank top and holds it to her chest, obscuring my view. "Shonda gave me one of these. Is it okay for me to wear it around?"

"Hell, yeah." My charter has a similar shirt—our skull and crown with a simple LOKI spelled out underneath in big block letters. A way for brothers to identify her as important to the club without scaring civilians with large, obvious MC symbols. "You're supporting your man's club, but it's tame enough to wear around non-affiliated folks."

"Ooo, I feel special now."

"You are."

She slips the stretchy tank on and stares down. "Hmm, it's a little tight." She winks at me. "I'm sure that's deliberate."

"Looks good to me." I reach into my backpack and pull out a blue-checked flannel. "Wear this over it if it makes you more comfortable."

"It's kinda hot for flannel. Does it bother you? I can change."

I stalk closer and curl my finger in one of her belt loops, yanking her to me. "Already said I like how it looks on you. I'm not the guy who'll tell you what you can and can't wear, Shelby."

"I meant because we're here, with your club. I don't want to do the wrong thing."

"If anyone has an issue keeping their eyes off you"—I raise my fists in the air, fighter-style—"I'll be happy to give them a free therapy session."

"I'm sure you will." She rests her hand on my shoulder, then tugs the collar of my shirt aside. "Oh, shoot."

"What?" I tip my head at an awkward angle, trying to see what she's so interested in.

"I think I left hickeys on your neck."

I rumble with laughter. As if I'd ever be mad about *that*. "Feel free to mark me as yours whenever you want, chickadee."

"Is that right?" Her eyes gleam with mischief. She opens wide and playfully bites my side through my shirt.

"Shit!" I jump, laughing at the same time. "That fucking tickles."

She does it even harder, moving around, locating all the ticklish spots I never knew I had. She even adds in some *nom-nom* noises until we're both laughing uncontrollably.

"Stop. Stop."

Instead of stopping, she loops her arms around my neck and leans up to kiss my cheek. "I like when you laugh. You're so serious most of the time."

"No one else has the nerve to try and tickle me." I tease my fingers over her ribs. She flinches and giggles.

My damn phone buzzes on the nightstand and Shelby pulls away. "I hope it's nothing bad."

"Nah, it's probably Jiggy."

She glances around the room, pats her pockets, and almost seems confused for a few seconds. "Shoot, I don't even know where *my* phone is.

CHAPTER TWENTY-SIX

Rooster

AFTER A MORNING OF ENDLESS IRRITATION, I FINALLY RETURN TO THE clubhouse. It takes me a few seconds to line up and park the way I want. Jigsaw waits patiently before pulling Ice's truck in next to me.

"Think she's back from rehearsal yet?" Jiggy asks.

"I hope so."

This afternoon, the clubhouse is quiet. No one setting up for any wild parties. Yet.

Inside, Shelby's in the main room, talking to Anya and Trinity.

"Hey!" She jumps up and rushes over. "I was wondering when you'd be back from your top-secret mission."

Next to me, Jigsaw snort-laughs. "You still didn't tell her?"

"It's a surprise," I growl, elbowing him to shut him up. I lean down and kiss Shelby. "Come out to the parking lot with me for a minute."

"Am I gonna like this surprise?" she asks Jiggy.

He throws his hands in the air and jerks his shoulders in an exaggerated shrug.

Ignoring his antics, I reach for Shelby's hand and tug her toward the door. My blood boils at the fading bruises on her arm as she slips her fingers through mine. "How'd rehearsal go?" I tuck her close and kiss the top of her head.

"Better than I expected, honestly." She rubs her free hand over her throat. "Feels less raw today. And the music came easier."

"The few days of rest probably did you good."

She hums an affirmative noise.

We stroll outside and into the parking lot.

"Now *that's* cool." She stops and points to the camper and truck. "When I was a kid, I used to sing at fairs and stuff sometimes. I always envied the families that pulled up in their RVs and stayed for the week."

"You guys didn't stay?"

She shrugs. "Best we could do was sleep in the cab of my dad's truck. Four of us tucked in tight wasn't a whole lotta fun."

Her story wraps around my heart and squeezes in the best possible way.

It's a fight to keep the smile off my face. I keeping walking, circling around to the back of the camper. "I'm glad you told me that story today."

"Why?" She blinks up at me.

"This is *ours*." I pull the keys out of my pocket and unlock the door, rolling it up to show off the small space where I'm planning to load my bike.

Her eyes widen and she stumbles backwards. "What are you talking about?"

"I can't ride in the van with you guys. It's too small. Plus, I think you'll feel better if you have your own space to decorate how you want. Stock it with the food you like. It'll be more comfortable and give you some privacy."

"But…but…I thought you said you were going to ride along? On your bike." She slaps her hand over her mouth, slowly shaking her head. "This is…this is…"

I hadn't expected her to freak out so much. "The extra space will be useful when a brother's traveling with us." I tap the side of the camper. "Two bikes will fit back here." I point to the bed currently folded into the roof. "In a pinch, that folds down into an extra bed and a couch if we move the bikes."

"Logan," she whispers.

I reach for her hand, tugging it away from her mouth.

She shakes her head, still staring at the camper. "This is…we looked at something similar before the tour." Her gaze slides to the GMC 2500 Sierra that'll be towing our little home on the road. "I *know* how expensive a setup like this had to be. You really…I can't."

"I can and I did."

"But it must have cost a fortune."

I shrug. "I have good credit."

"I can't ask you to do this."

"You *didn't* ask me. I honestly think this is the best solution for us. When the tour's over, I'll park it in your mom's driveway." I wink at her. "Give us a little privacy while we're in Texas."

Finally, it seems to sink in that this is real. She jumps and wraps her arms around my neck, squealing and hugging me tight. "You're serious, aren't you?"

"I told you I'm all in, Shelby."

She pulls back, staring into my eyes for a few seconds before peppering my face with kisses. "Thank you."

Not wanting to lose contact, I encourage her to wrap her legs around me and carry her to the door. "You want to see the inside?"

"Heck yes."

I set her down and open the door, motioning for her to step inside first. She's quiet while she walks through the small space, checking out every little cabinet, drawer, and nook she encounters.

"How did you…I know it's not my business." She casts another quick look around the interior. "Does porn really pay this much?"

Rumbling laughter pours out of me. "I do fine." I shrug. "I'd been saving for a down payment on a house. But what's the point putting down roots in New York when my girl's gonna be out on the road?"

"But what about when I'm *not* on tour? You'll want to go home. To New York. Now you'll be stuck driving a big ol' truck instead of riding your bike."

I shrug again. She's really worrying about this way more than she needs to. "I can always hire someone to drive it home. Sell it. Rent a storage place. I'm not worried, Shelby." A worse thought occurs to me. "Are you afraid of us spending too much time together?"

"I'm afraid you're making a lot of expensive sacrifices and you'll end up hating me later."

"Shelby," I say as gently as possible. "At some point, you have to trust me. I love you. I want you to be safe and happy. I want to be *with* you."

"I wish I was a bigger deal so I already had this stuff sorted." Pink spreads over her cheeks. "I can't reciprocate at all. It's not fair."

"Fair? This isn't some fifty-fifty, tit-for-tat thing. I *love* you and want what's best for you." I cock my head. "Do you like singing? Being on stage? Touring?"

"Yes."

"Are you comfortable in the van?"

"Not really."

I push her hair off her forehead and stare into her eyes. "You're my girl. I want you to feel safe and I'll do whatever needs to be done to take care of you. End of story. There's no tab at the end of the day. Just my love for you."

She eyes the camper again. "But this is such a huge…investment for you. With the possibility of no payoff. I may never be—"

"I'm not here for any future payoff. I'm here for *you*. You're worth taking the risk on. *Our love* is worth the risk. I've never been good at playing it safe. It's just not who I am. When I'm in, I'm *all* in."

The doctor's warning at the hospital about letting Shelby make decisions to help her regain a sense of control sends a splinter of doubt slicing through my plan. "I know I did all this without asking you, but I promise all the other decisions are yours. Decorate it inside and out however you want." My lips quirk. "I even know a guy in Mississippi who can wrap the camper in your flocking fabulous flamingos if you want."

"You don't want to be seen driving a vehicle with pink flamingos all over it."

"Do I look like someone who gives a shit what anyone thinks?" I hold my arms out to the sides.

She cocks her head. "I dunno. You look like a man who's aware of all the panties he melts."

I snort at the absurdity, even though she's just being cute.

She lets out a long sigh. "It's not *just* this. I know you paid for my momma to come here too. Why didn't you tell me?"

"It's not like I hid it." I shrug. "At what point was it relevant to bring up who paid for her plane ticket?"

"And her hotel room." Her gaze strays to the floor.

"Shelby, I didn't lie to you."

"I wasn't in my right mind or I would've asked."

"Why does it matter?"

"It's bad enough if *I'm* a burden on you, but my mother...especially when she hasn't been nice—"

"Stop right there. You're not a *burden* on me. Please stop saying that. You needed your mom with you in the hospital, and I got her there in the easiest, most efficient way." I stop and study her while I carefully consider my next words. Shit, I can't believe I'm about to ask this. She's so skittish as it is. How the fuck do I phrase it without scaring her away? "Answer something for me."

She raises an eyebrow. "What?"

"If we were married, would you have this much trouble accepting things from me?"

Her hand flies up, landing on her chest, and she stumbles back a step, bumping into the counter. "What?"

I take a step closer. "You heard me."

"I...uh, I don't know how to answer that."

"I'm not trying to claim anything that isn't mine. Your music business stuff was yours long before I showed up. But I also can't sit by and say, 'sucks for you if you can't afford it' when it's easier for me to give you what you need. That's not the kind of man I am."

"What if I'm a huge failure and you end up drowning in debt because of me?"

"You're only a failure if you stop chasing your dreams."

"What if..." She glances down at her boots. "...if *we* don't work out?"

A blast of cold gusts through my chest. Us not working out isn't an option.

I gently squeeze her shoulders and she lifts her gaze. "If you want me to leave, just say so. I'll take my toys and go home like a big boy. Promise."

"I don't want you to go anywhere," she whispers.

Good, because I'm probably lying anyway. I'd never leave her stranded. More like, I'd hire someone to drive her around until the tour was over so she didn't have to go back to living in the van with the rest of the guys.

Then I'd take my sorry ass home and figure out how to live in a world without the only woman I've ever loved.

SHELBY

"You're sure this isn't too soon?" No matter how much Rooster reassures me, I can't wrap my head around this enormous sacrifice he's made. For me. Because of me.

He frowns and cocks his head. "Too soon for what?"

I glance around the space, still so overwhelmed. "For us to...well, it's like we'll be living together."

He continues staring at me. "That's the point."

Shoot, I'm not trying to hurt his feelings. "I'm not always sunshine and sweet tea, you know."

A smile teases the corners of his mouth. "Is that right?"

"Well, yeah. I get crabby when I'm tired. Moody." I flick my gaze toward the small bathroom door. "Once a month, I go through an intense steak and Ben and Jerry's binge. Hell help the person who gets between me and my Cherry Garcia."

He crosses his arms over his chest and ducks his head. His big body shakes with laughter.

"I'm serious." I've never lived with a boyfriend before. I have no idea what to expect or what *he* expects.

"Are you dipping the steak *in* the ice cream?" He tips his head and pins me with a half-serious stare. "Because *that's* a deal-breaker for me."

"No." I shoot him a half-hearted glare. "They're separate meals."

"Phew." He wipes a sarcastic hand over his forehead. "Close one."

"All right, smart ass."

His face settles into a more serious expression. "What are you really worried about?"

"I just told you. Living together. Out on the road. It's stressful." I glance down at my feet and pick at a thread on my jeans. "I don't want us to end up hating each other."

"Shelby." He sighs and rests his hands on my shoulders. "I could never hate you."

"Don't be so sure."

"I'm not always Mr. Charm, either, you know." He squeezes my shoulder gently. "We'll make it work."

"I don't think I'm a diva but I can be particular about things."

"You think I haven't noticed?" He steps closer. "I enjoy *all* the little things that make you who you are."

I slide my arms around his waist, leaning against him. "I'm still in a bit of shock. I really do love it," I mumble against his shirt.

"Good." He wraps one arm around my shoulders and turns us to face the kitchenette. "I'm going to use the next day or so to make a few modifications before we get on the road. If you think of anything that would make your life easier, let me know."

I study the compact space around us. Everything looks so perfect. Clearly it was designed to get the maximum use out of every square inch. I can't imagine messing with it. "What kind of modifications?"

He points to the wall next to the dining table and benches. "I want to install a secret compartment there."

"Ooo, sounds very James Bond."

"Not really. Just a place to store our valuables. The dealer does customizations but they couldn't get it done before we have to leave."

"Oh." I step away from him, investigating the space with purpose. "I really don't know what I might need."

"Don't stress about it. We can always stop at a home improvement store along the way."

Across from the dinette, a television's mounted to the wall. "Think I can make this a yoga space in the mornings?"

"We'll find the room for whatever you need."

Smiling up at him, I bump my shoulder against his arm. "Think you'll do morning yoga with me?"

His lips curl up. "Let's not get crazy."

He's already done so much, I probably shouldn't push him. "Sorry."

"I'm teasing." He squeezes me tight.

The warm sensation flooding through my body cools. Worry digs its claws into my heart.

This has to be the best moment of my life.

But I can't seem to squelch the terrified voice inside me that says this could be the ruin of our relationship.

CHAPTER TWENTY-SEVEN

Rooster

THAT WENT BETTER THAN I EXPECTED.

Should I be insulted or happy Shelby's worried about us living together?

Honestly, until she put it that way, I hadn't considered it as *living together*. I just want to be with her as much as possible while making sure she's safe.

"So, you're good?" I brush my knuckles over her cheek.

She swallows hard and slowly meets my eyes. "Overwhelmed. Excited too."

Someone bangs on the door. Shelby jumps.

"Let's see it!" Murphy shouts.

Shelby's lips quirk with amusement. "Your brothers all knew, huh?"

"Well, I needed Jiggy to go with me and naturally he blabbed to everyone."

She laughs softly and shakes her head.

I reach over and push open the door. "Heidi can come in. You stay outside, Ginger Yeti."

Shelby playfully swats my side. "Be nice."

Murphy snorts with laughter and follows Heidi up the steps.

Heidi's gaze slowly slides over the space. "This is the coolest thing ever." She pats my arm. "You're a brilliant man."

I flash a smile at Shelby. "I didn't even ask her to say that."

"You *are* brilliant." She leans up and kisses my cheek. "And thoughtful. And—"

"Yeah, yeah. Rooster's a peach," Murphy grumbles. "Are we getting a tour or not?"

I walk them through the place, chuckling as Heidi oohs and ahhs over every detail. Until the shower.

"Ooof. That's tiny. No shower sex for you two."

"We'll improvise." Shelby winks at me.

I love this woman.

"There's an extra bed back there if someone needs to crash." I point out the smaller guest space. While it's not spacious by any means, it'll be better than sleeping outside in a pinch.

Heidi eyes the distance between the guest bed and our bed up front. "That won't provide you with much, ahem, *privacy*."

Murphy peers down at her. "Something on your mind?"

"What? No." Heidi's cheeks turn pink. "Never mind."

Shelby chuckles and takes Heidi's hand, dragging her over to one of the built-in closets.

"This is something else, brother." Murphy cocks his head and stares at me.

What does he expect me to say?

"It's wildly romantic!" Heidi calls over her shoulder.

"Z know you're gonna be on the road this long?" Murphy asks in a low voice.

"We talked about it before I left." I'm not annoyed by the question. Not too much, anyway. "If anything, he encouraged me."

He holds his hands in the air. "Cool. Not really my business."

"Nah, of course it's your business. We're all each other's keeper, right?" I poke him in the *brother's keeper* patch stitched onto his cut. The patch we earn by killing for our club. I get his concern. He grew up around the club with Z as his vice president for years. Murphy's one of the most loyal brothers, especially to Z. "He has a few things he wants me to check on while I'm on the road." My explanation's vague but enough to ease Murphy's concern.

"I don't think we're going to get as far as Mississippi with you." Murphy rubs his hand over the back of his neck.

"No worries, brother. I appreciate you coming at all." I slap his back and steer him toward the door. "What do you think Ice has going on here tonight?"

"Hell only knows."

Something pounds against the door. I swing it open and find Wrath filling the entire space.

"You can't come in," Murphy says. "There's a weight limit."

"Well, then you should definitely get out." Wrath ducks his head and climbs into the RV, pushing Murphy away with a hand to his chest.

"Easy, big guy," I warn, pointing up.

My head's already flirting with the ceiling, so Wrath's will definitely hit it if he tries to stand straight.

"Nice tuna can." He nods, his gaze scanning the space quickly. "Trin and I talked about getting something similar. Good to know I'll need the jumbo edition." He clomps down the stairs back out into the parking lot. "See you went with a big boy truck," he bellows in my direction. "Nice."

Murphy chuckles. "He's thrilled someone joined his GMC tribe."

"He has a point." I slap Murphy's shoulder. "You can join too, if you ditch that F250."

"Never."

"Ahh, your love of motorized vehicles extends to those with more than two wheels, huh?" Shelby teases.

Heidi rolls her eyes. "My brother's even worse. I'm convinced that's why he bought Charlotte's truck, so he'd have something new to play with."

"Slick words from someone who got a Hellcat for graduation," I remind Heidi.

She snuggles up to Murphy's side. "I didn't say *I* wasn't spoiled. Or that I don't love my car."

Murphy leans down, kissing Heidi's temple.

"What is that?" Shelby asks.

Heidi's more than happy to show off pictures. "Next time you visit, we'll have to take you out to Zips and you can take it for a few spins around the track."

Murphy shakes with laughter and mouths "sorry" at me.

I shrug. As if I'd ever complain. If anything, I want to hug Heidi for making future plans that include Shelby spending time in New York.

CHAPTER TWENTY-EIGHT

Shelby

AFTER SHOWING OFF THE RV TO ALMOST EVERYONE, THE GUYS ARE CALLED into "church."

Rooster takes my hand, pulling me aside. "I'm not sure how long we'll be."

"That's okay." I glance over at Trinity, who's engaged in what seems to be a similar discussion with her husband. "We'll entertain each other."

"Thanks." He leans down and slowly slides his lips against mine. For a few seconds, everything else melts away.

"Cock-a-doodle-do later, brother!" someone yells.

Rooster groans and pulls back. "Assholes," he growls, glaring at the space behind me. I'm not sure who's responsible for the taunt.

I reach up and pat Rooster's cheek. "Have a good meeting."

"I'll try."

The majority of the men have already disappeared behind the mysterious sliding doors that look like reclaimed barn wood. Before following the herd, Rooster and Murphy take Griff and Remy aside for what seems to be a serious talk.

"Probably giving them a list of instructions," Trinity says, walking up to me. "Come on." She motions toward some furniture scattered in the main room.

Trinity tucks herself into a corner of the couch with a magazine and Heidi takes the space next to her. I pull a comfy-looking, overstuffed chair closer to their end of the couch and sink into it. Griff confiscates a similar chair, placing it closer to the other end of the couch where Remy has taken up residence.

A girl who'd introduced herself as Rumer earlier drops into Remy's lap and immediately runs her fingers through his hair. Heidi rolls her eyes and angles herself away from them.

I lean in closer to Heidi, hoping the guys can't overhear me. "So, if we weren't here, is that what—"

"Don't date him if you can't trust him." Heidi flicks her gaze at Trinity who shrugs.

Not helpful, girls.

But I understand what Heidi's saying. I guess the same goes for me. Rooster knows guys are all around me on tour. Either he trusts me, or he doesn't.

Remy cocks his head and seems to be more interested in our conversation than in the girl whispering in his ear. No need for him to overhear my insecurity so he can joke about it later.

"You two don't get an invite?" I ask, tilting my head toward Griff and nodding at Remy. I'm still not even sure why they came or how they fit into the club's pecking order.

Remy shakes his head, ice-blue eyes glittering with mirth. "Nah, we're here for moral support." He flicks his gaze toward Griff. "Right, bro?"

"Huh?" Griff doesn't look away from his phone. "Support, yes."

Heidi drops her gaze to Griff's phone. A slight flicker of amusement plays over her lips. "How's Molly doing?"

Griff slowly tears his gaze away from his phone. "She's good. Keeps asking me when you're coming back to Zips."

"Tell her I said hi," Heidi says.

Griff nods and returns to his phone.

Remy scowls in his friend's direction. "Why is my baby sister texting *you* instead of me?"

Unruffled by Remy's sharp tone, Griff turns his screen toward him and wags the phone. "Probably because she knows *I'll* actually answer her."

Remy sits forward so fast, poor Rumer is thrown off his lap, landing on the floor in a heap, her short, silver skirt ending up around her hips. "What's wrong?" Remy asks.

"Nothing's wrong." Griff eyes his friend with caution. "She's at Zips with Ella."

"Seriously?" Remy snaps the phone out of his friend's hand and studies the screen before returning it. "I told Eraser to keep an eye on her, not let his wife give her racing lessons."

"Ella *is* a good teacher." Heidi grins.

Remy smirks in her direction. "Not the point, Little Hammer."

"Little Hammer?" I ask. "Is that new, Heidi?"

Her gaze slips to Griff, then Trinity. Finally she shrugs. "Something the guys started calling me." She taps a small patch on her vest and I squint to get a better look at the clover, crown, and hammer. "Rooster gave me this one. *Murphy's queen wields a hammer.*"

"A mean hammer too," Griff says, grinning at her.

While I've witnessed Heidi carry a hammer for protection, I've never seen her actually *use* it on anyone. A shudder works down my spine. Probably a good thing. She may look sweet and innocent but I've definitely caught a ferocious vibe from her once or twice.

Trinity wraps her arms around Heidi's waist, squeezing her tight. "I'll still call you 'little sister' if you want."

"Always," Heidi says, resting her head on Trinity's shoulder. I can't deny I'm a little jealous at how close they seem to be. Focusing on my singing career hasn't exactly left room in my life for making *or* keeping friends. And the time I spent on *Redneck Roadhouse* made it almost impossible for me to trust anyone who gets close to me.

Until Rooster.

"Why don't *you* have one of those yet?" Remy's voice pulls me out of my thoughts. I glance up and he points at Trinity and Heidi's vests that have their *property of* patches on the back.

I blink and shift my gaze between Remy and the girls. "I...uh..." I stammer, not sure how to answer. Rooster once explained that property patches were similar to an engagement ring in his world. While Rooster mentioned the M word when he was showing me the RV, I don't think we're quite there yet.

It's impossible to ignore the way my heart flutters at the thought, though.

Trinity throws a stern scowl at Remy. "That falls under *club business,* Remy. But feel free to ask Rooster when he plans to patch his ol' lady."

Damn, Trinity's a protective lioness. And I'm feeling like her lil' cub.

The smirk slides off Remy's face.

"Does every club have them?" Griff asks, taking the attention off his buddy's gaffe.

Trinity seems less annoyed by the more general question. "No. It's something every club decides on their own."

Griff flicks his gaze toward Remy. "I think it'll be a deal-breaker for Vapor."

Remy shrugs.

"You should really talk it over with Dex and Murphy," Trinity suggests, the 'leave me out of it' clear in her tone.

So many questions pop in my head. But I'm not comfortable asking in front of the guys.

While I'm mentally sorting out the short discussion, Anya squeezes between my chair and Griff's. "Mind if I join you guys?" she asks Trinity.

While Trinity assesses the newcomer, Heidi's more welcoming, patting the couch cushion next to her.

"Hey, Anya," I say.

She scoots forward and gives me a quick hug. "I'm so happy you're okay," she gushes. "Rooster was a mess while—" her jaw drops and shakes her head. "Sorry."

"It's okay." Shoot, I'd rather people just openly say whatever's on their mind than tiptoe around me like I'm made of glass. "I'm lucky Rooster was on the road with me and the club was nearby." I glance at Trinity and Heidi. "And New York was willing to come all this way."

"Hell yeah." Griff bumps my elbow. "We volunteered as soon as we heard Rooster needed the extra muscle."

My gaze skips over Griff's granite-hard arms. An inappropriate, but welcome, fantasy of all the guys taking turns beating Martin Suggs to a bloody heap dances in my head for a few seconds.

I hate that he's turned me into such a vindictive person.

CHAPTER TWENTY-NINE

Rooster

CHURCH IS MORE OR LESS THE SAME AT EACH CHARTER. SOMETIMES IT'S only open to members if there's sensitive business to discuss. Other times, anyone wearing a Lost Kings patch is invited inside.

This morning, Ice made it clear he expected me to attend. Shelby's safe. She's hanging out with Trinity and Heidi. Remy and Griff were told to keep their eyes on the girls and not let them out of their sight.

As visiting brothers, Ice asked us to take spaces up front. I would've been happy blending into the background, but I'm not about to disrespect Ice in his own house. Jiggy took the seat to my right and Murphy's on my left. Wrath's holding up the wall across from me with Dex and Steer on either side of him. Not sure where Hustler ended up.

I'm silent—and bored to death—while they go through business that only concerns their charter. Although, I do make a few mental notes of things to discuss with Z. About an hour into the meeting, Jiggy squirms in his seat and I bump his elbow as a reminder to settle the fuck down.

"And finally, we owe thanks to Rooster for spending his time helping get Anya's site running." He holds up a sheet of paper. "Money's already looking good."

Brothers clap and offer thanks.

I hold up my hand and sit forward. "I'm the one who needs to thank

Virginia. Thank you for having my back." I turn toward Ice. "I don't know what would've happened if you hadn't been so quick to help us search for Shelby." I swallow hard, trying not to get choked up in front of everyone. "And calling in your favor with Jackson—"

"I'm not so sure how useful he actually was," Pants jokes.

I kind of agree, but since Jackson's basically a club asset, I'm not about to insult him. He didn't get in my way, and that alone was a huge help. "No, brother. He made it look good for his people but he didn't interfere. Didn't hassle us about the condition Suggs was in when we turned him over, either." I smirk at Jigsaw who gives everyone an 'aw-shucks' shrug.

Ice taps the table. "We'll keep tabs on the worm as he works his way through the system. You want him gone, all you have to do is say the word."

"They're lettin' Shelby go back on the road, right?" Pants asks. "Does she need to return if there's a trial?"

"Probably. Jackson knows how to reach her if he needs something."

"Anytime you need it, you've got a place to stay here," Ice says.

"Thanks, brother." I drum my fingers over the table, not sure how to phrase my next offer. "I'm not clear on your arrangement with Jackson." I hold up my hands. "Not prying for information. But I'd like to make a donation to help with any costs."

"Not necessary. But I appreciate the offer," Ice says.

I'd feel better if Ice would take some cash to cover whatever bribe he pays Jackson, but I offered and he rejected. End of discussion. It's disrespectful if I keep pushing in front of everyone. And I run the risk of offending Ice.

"Rooster, you think you can pull your tongue out of your girl's pussy long enough to party with us tonight?" T-Bone shakes with laughter.

My upper lip curls into a snarl.

"He ain't wrong." Jigsaw wiggles his tongue at me and adds some disgusting sloppy noises to draw the attention away from me gettin' ready to pop T-Bone in the jaw for talkin' about my girl that way.

Brothers around the table laugh and lob some insults at Jiggy. He grins and takes it in stride.

"Pussy patch!" a brother everyone calls Boots shouts. He slams his fist against the wood plank table. "That should be our next challenge patch."

I roll my eyes Jigsaw's way. "Look what you started."

"Technically, it was T-Bone."

Guys start banging their fists on the table while chanting "Pussy patch!"

Ice glances down and chuckles under his breath. "Jesus Christ." He flicks a look at his VP. "That what you wanna spend your time doing?"

Farmer sits forward and slowly rubs his palms together. "Yeah. We can have a little cat face patch made up."

"You wanna wear a fuckin' kitty cat on your cut?" someone shouts.

"Fuckin' A." Pants punches his fist in the air. "Great fucking story when someone finds the balls to ask one of us."

I don't think their definition of 'great story' is the same as mine, but whatever. Not my club. Not my problem.

While the organization as a whole has its rules for certain patches, other decorative—or frivolous—patches are up to individual charters to decide. Each still needs to be earned or given to a brother. Can't just decide you feel like stitching something cute on your cut for shits and giggles. It's gotta mean something.

Even if it's something filthy. Hell, especially if it's filthy. The dirtier the story behind the patch, the better. Hence the old MC urban legends about "red wing" patches. Bikers are notoriously fond of sharing stories to mindfuck civilians.

"Listen up!" T-Bone slaps his palm against the table to get everyone's attention. "These are the rules. Every day for thirty days, you gotta eat some cat."

"Not a few token licks," Boots adds. "You need to get the lucky lady off for it to count."

"Thirty days?" Wings asks.

"What's wrong, bro?" Boots taunts. "Weak tongue?"

"Fuck off." Wings reaches below the table, I'm guessing to grab his dick. Thankfully I'm not close enough to verify. "Where's my patch for gettin' my dick sucked thirty days straight?"

"In your dreams," Pants zings back.

"Question." Wings punches his fist in the air like that eager kid in class you always wanted to punch in the face. "Does it have to be thirty days in a *row*? Or can we like double-up on days?"

I drop my head and rub my temples. *Do I really need to be here for this?*

The guys argue the merits of thirty days or thirty acts of oral culminating in an actual orgasm. Someone else asks about thirty times in *one* day, which Boots determines should be its own separate patch.

Once that discussion is finished—thirty days in a row is determined to be the harder challenge—T-Bone raises his hand in the air. "Dibs on Shonda."

Brothers around the room groan.

"No way!" Boots pulls himself out of his chair and leans over the table so he can glare daggers at T-Bone.

"They take their pussy seriously here," Jigsaw whispers to me.

"Apparently."

"You can't call dibs," Boots argues. "There ain't enough girls to go around as it is."

Someone at the end of the table lifts a hand in the air. "Prez, is Anya—"

"No," Ice snarls before the question's even out. The brother who asked puts his hand down fast. After a second or two, Ice wipes the vicious expression off his face and adds in a milder tone, "Not unless you wanna film it for her site."

At least six guys raise their grubby paws. "Fuck yeah, I don't mind having the whole world watch me—"

"Settle the fuck down. Anya's off-limits." Pants glances at Ice who doesn't respond one way or another. "She's not free ass. End of story." As SAA Pants' word is law and no one else so much as breathes Anya's name again.

"We should do *two* patches," Raze says. "Black cat if it's a different girl every night. White cat if it's the same chick."

"Don't feel like explaining to the Mrs. where your tongue's been?" T-Bone asks.

"Eat my ass."

"That's good. Maybe black cats with different color eyes." Boots is fully immersed in this idea now. He rubs his hands together and reaches for a notepad and pencil from the center of the table. "We'll pass out punch cards." He lifts his hand in the air, opening and closing it a few times. "I'll hand out heart-shaped hole punchers to the girls." He glances up and sweeps his stern stare over everyone in the room. "No fucking cheating. No honorable brother wears a patch he didn't *earn*."

That's it. I can't take it anymore. I cover my face with my hands and fucking lose it. "Virginia is for lovers, all right," I spit out through my laughter.

"Anyone planning to warn the local ladies what's about to go down?" Murphy snickers at his little pun.

I hold out my fist for a bump. "Nice one."

Wrath's squinting at the ceiling like he's trying to do some quick calculations. "Make me up a lion patch." He holds his hands out a few feet apart. "Got at least fourteen hundred days stacked up."

"Yeahhhhh." Wings draws out the word slowly, adding in a dirty eyebrow wiggle. "If my girl looked like yours, I'd never let her out of bed."

Wrath's glacial stare lands on the Virginia charter's road captain. "Careful." His low, rumbling voice holds a world of threat.

Wings swallows hard and drops his pervy attitude. "Just payin' your ol' lady a compliment."

I lean over and whisper in Murphy's ear. "You *have* to earn that patch, bro. Teller's head'll explode every time he sees it."

Nodding at my suggestion, Murphy covers his mouth with his hand and chuckles.

Should I be stirring the shit? Probably not. Can't seem to help myself, though. I love Teller, but his brotherly-love-hate-rivalry thing with his little sister's husband is one of my favorite things about hanging out with the upstate charter.

"Wives shouldn't count," T-Bone says. "They'll punch those cards no matter what."

Raze leans forward. "Have you *met* Allison? She'll hold my feet to the fire on this."

"Or your tongue on her clit," Hustler adds from somewhere way at the end of the table.

"That too." Raze lifts a middle finger at Hustler.

T-Bone holds out his arms like the gracious host he is. "New York, you're all obviously invited to participate. You can mail your cards in when the thirty days are up."

"Hard pass," Dex says. "But thanks."

Pants lifts his chin my way. "I'll be on the road with you guys for a lil' while. Shelby got lots of female fans hanging around?"

"Yeah," I growl, pissed he's asking. "Most of 'em are little kids."

Pants curls his lip in disgust.

"The headliner—Dawson—has tons of chicks hanging around. Don't worry, bro," Jigsaw assures him.

"Jesus Christ," I mumble. "Really?"

"What?" Jigsaw shrugs. "Dawson can't handle that much tail. There's bound to be spillover."

Murphy's laughing so hard, his arm knocks into mine. He swipes his cheeks. "This is gonna be so much fun. I'm sorry we can't stay for the whole tour."

Ice hasn't uttered a single word since his enforcer laid down the law about Anya. I glance over at him and he's rubbing his forehead like he's ready for an aspirin—or a shooting spree. Hard to tell which.

A fucking pussy patch.

I can't wait to call Z and let him know what our charter's been missing out on.

CHAPTER THIRTY

Shelby

"Hey, there's a Fed Ex truck in the parking lot. Guy says he has a package for you, Heidi." Griff scowls at the front door. "Are you expecting something?"

Heidi jumps off the couch and eagerly rubs her hands together. "I sure am!"

Trinity watches her for a minute, then shakes her head and returns to her magazine.

"I wonder if it's the stuff I asked Heidi to order for me." Anya watches the front door. "I should probably help them out."

Before she has a chance to move off the couch, the door swings open again. Griff follows Heidi inside carrying a large, square cardboard box.

"It's all the goodies we ordered." Heidi rubs her hands together and hurries over to us.

Well, now I'm curious.

As Heidi pulls out a small pocketknife, flips it open, and neatly slices through the tape sealing the box shut, I remember Rooster telling me Heidi has a side hustle. Selling sex toys.

"Let me see what's in here." Heidi carefully checks each package inside against the invoice. "I ordered a few extra things."

"Thank you so much for this, Heidi." Anya dives in, pulling out various boxes after Heidi's checked them off her list. "Especially for getting it all delivered on short notice."

"Anytime you need something, let me know. I'm your girl." And in an extra cheery tone she adds, "I work on commission."

"Am I looking at a giant box of…sex toys?" I ask, leaning over to peer inside.

Anya waves an elegant pink and gold vibrator in my direction. "Rooster sort of sparked this idea for me—"

"My boyfriend suggested you order a bunch of vibrators?" I ask slowly, dreading her response.

A quick flash of guilt ripples over her face. "No, no. Sorry. I should've phrased that better."

Ya think?

"He just asked me if I'm sure I want to be doing films forever, you know? Like it might hurt my chances of finding another job one day." She shrugs. "He was really nice about it."

Well, shoot. That's actually kinda sweet. And I can totally picture Rooster giving that advice. But can he get in trouble for talking her out of making movies for the club?

"Anyway," she continues, "it got me thinking of hiring some other girls and just sitting back to produce the content."

Trinity's protective lioness instincts must've caught that last part. She lifts her head from the magazine and side-eyes Anya as if she's worried Heidi and I are the ones Anya wants to hire.

"I might return to solo stuff." Anya taps the box again and hesitates. "Maybe. We'll see. Or keep going with the more romantic, catering to the female gaze stuff. I need to track some stats on my site first."

Decisions, decisions.

Since I actually like Anya, I'm trying hard not to judge. But I'm also finding it hard to come up with anything to add to the conversation that won't sound snarky.

"Do you honestly think you have a lot of female viewers?" Heidi asks, with what seems like genuine curiosity.

"Some. They're not like the guys who send me creepy emails and messages, but they're out there."

A cold sliver of fear slices through me at the mention of creepy emails from male "admirers." Have any of her fans ever tried to stuff *her* in a box? It doesn't take a genius to realize adult films probably draw crazier fans than country music. No wonder Anya needs the support of the club to keep her safe.

"You all right, Shelby?" Trinity asks.

My tongue won't loosen, so I nod quickly.

Heidi continues pawing through the box and when she reaches the bottom, she hums a happy noise and pulls out a long, blue rectangular package and thrusts it in my direction. "This one's for *you.*"

"I…uh, what?" I stare at the box for a few seconds.

Heidi undoes the side flap and slides a long, metal cylinder out.

"Is it a science experiment?" I joke.

"Nope." She unscrews the cap and pulls out a thick, iridescent blue wand with a black silicone head. A few other pieces slide into Heidi's lap when she tips the container. "It's rechargeable. And," she flicks her gaze around the room and leans toward me to whisper, "it delivers orgasms in like twenty seconds." A bit louder she adds. "Not the fireworks on the Fourth of July kind. More like the sparklers on your birthday cake. Still fantastic."

My oh my. Look at Heidi all knowledgeable about different kinds of orgasms. Heat sears my face from forehead to chin. "I didn't even realize there *were* different kinds until, well… recently."

Anya chuckles and says in a low voice, "Go Rooster."

Heidi's gaze strays to the side. Her lips curl up and I don't need to turn my head to know she's thinking of Murphy. "My husband's *extremely* dedicated to this subject. He missed his calling as a researcher." She giggles and waves the wand in the air between us. "Anyway. The company sent me an extra and it's all yours." She thrusts it into my hands.

"What?" I take the wand, impressed by its weight. "Wow. This is serious equipment."

"Nice extra," Anya says. "Those are expensive."

"There's a red one in there for you." Heidi gestures to the box at Anya's feet. "But it's a plug-in, so it's a monster size-wise." Heidi returns her attention to me. "Figured space might be an issue for you on the road."

"How…thoughtful."

"Ooo!" Anya squeals and yanks a large rectangular red box out, clapping her hands like a little girl unwrapping a gift from an extra-dirty Santa.

This has to be the strangest event of my life.

Okay, that's not true. Being stuffed in my trunk and kidnapped was way stranger.

My whole body shivers with the memory.

Something warm and solid lands on my shoulder. "Everything all right?" Rooster asks.

His presence chases the unwanted memories and fear away.

Pink spreads over Heidi's cheeks. She grabs the wand out of my hand and stuffs it back into its packaging.

"What's that?" Rooster asks. The question comes out innocent enough but by the tilt of his lips, it's clear he knows *exactly* what he's looking at.

"Heidi's handing out presents like she's appointed herself the naughty elf of our little group," I explain.

Rooster's gaze narrows on the colorful boxes scattered on the couch and floor around us. "*Really*?"

Heidi hands over my gift and I hold it up for Rooster to inspect.

"Very nice." He runs his hand over his beard a few times. "We'll put that to good use. Thanks, Heidi."

"You're not bothered or threatened by toys in the bedroom?" Anya asks.

Rooster snorts. "No." Thankfully, he doesn't elaborate. I'm ready to melt into the floor as it is.

Anya bundles everything together into the larger box and thanks Heidi again.

"Wait, no gifts for Trinity?" I ask.

One corner of Trinity's mouth lifts and she nods to where her husband's standing across the room talking to Ice and Murphy. "My husband keeps my toy chest well-stocked, don't worry."

Rooster reaches for the box in my lap. "Do you want me to put that away?"

"Do you really want to be seen carrying it around the clubhouse?"

He rolls his eyes. "Do I look like I'm worried?" He wiggles his fingers in a hurry-up-and-hand-it-over sort of gesture.

I pass him the box.

"I'm going to put it in the RV." He raises an eyebrow. "Unless you feel like trying it later."

"How loud is it, Heidi?" I ask.

"Not that bad." She glances around the clubhouse. "I don't really think you need to worry about it here, though. Not like anyone will notice. Or care."

"If you're heading out to the parking lot, will you help me load this in my car?" Anya kicks the box by her feet.

"Sure." Rooster leans over and kisses my cheek. "You good?" he whispers.

I nod quickly.

"I'm going to plug this in while I'm out there." He presses another kiss to my lips. "So it's charged and ready to go." His eyes meet mine. A bolt of desire electrifies me. *Why exactly was I being so uptight about this again?*

"Sounds good."

He grabs Anya's box and hefts it into his arms as if it weighs nothing. "Be right back."

"You two are so adorable together." Heidi claps her hands. "Rooster's such a good guy. I'm so happy you two met."

"Technically, he fished me out of the water," I joke.

"So romantic." Heidi sighs.

"Who's romantic?" Murphy's voice rumbles from behind us.

Heidi nods to the clubhouse door. "Rooster."

Murphy throws himself down onto the couch next to Heidi and wraps his arm around her. "Not much romance happening in *this* clubhouse for a while."

"Lies," Jigsaw says. He rests his hip on the arm of my chair and peers down at me. "Where'd my boy go?"

"Parking lot. Helping Anya load her car with some stuff."

He tilts his head. "You're okay with that? Why didn't he ask *me* to do it?"

"I don't know. You weren't here. He wanted to run out to the RV anyway." I shrug. "If I'm gonna worry about my boyfriend banging someone every time he's out of sight, we probably shouldn't be together. That *is* what you were implying I might be worried about, yes?"

He taps his forehead, then mine. "Ah, songbird. We're like one mind sometimes."

I slap his hand away. "I highly doubt that."

"Why are you annoying my girl?" Rooster's voice hovers between amused and annoyed.

"Why'd you leave her alone?" Jigsaw responds, jumping away from my chair.

Rooster glances at me and I shrug. "Jiggy's just looking out for me."

Murphy points at Rooster, then me. "Did you have the decency to warn your girl about what's going down here?"

Rooster shoots him a cool look. "Not yet."

"Ooo, what's going down?" I ask Rooster.

"Everyone," Jigsaw quips.

"Later." Rooster touches my shoulder. "The PR woman got back to me. She has an opening in her schedule. Ice said we could use his office."

"Now?"

He slaps Jigsaw's back. "Don't worry. This fuckwit will still be around causing trouble when we're done."

"All right." I glance at Heidi and Trinity. "Guess I'll be back later."

CHAPTER THIRTY-ONE

Shelby

MIRANDA, WHO IS APPARENTLY MY NEW PUBLIC RELATIONS SPECIALIST TO help me ward off any bad press from my abduction, is full of ideas.

I'm exhausted just listening to her.

On the computer screen, she comes across as tiny but feisty. Maybe a little older than my momma, with black hair slicked into a bun so tight it gives her eyes a catlike appearance. By her confident, cut-throat tone, I don't doubt she knows her business.

"Congratulations on your nominations, Shelby. This is a huge thing and could really help bury this whole nasty kidnapping, Glenna Wilson fiasco."

She makes it sound like a trivial event instead of the most terrifying thing that's ever happened to me.

"Now, hear me out," she continues in her bubbly voice. "I'd really like to see you attend the *Small Screen Music Awards* that are coming up. It'll be a nice dress rehearsal for you before the big show."

Sounds like she's worried I don't know how to behave on a red carpet or something. "But I only have one video. For Big Lies."

"That doesn't matter. The SSMAs don't hold the same prestige they did back in the Eighties. Today, getting nominated is more of a who-you-know situation. But it's a fun event where you'll be photographed a lot."

"Okay," I answer slowly. "I'm on tour now."

"I know." She blows out an exasperated breath. "Let me see what I can do. Dawson's probably up for a few nods himself. So maybe you both can work it into the schedule."

I don't think I like where she's going with this, but I don't want to piss her off yet. I'll have to reserve judgment for later.

"Now," she says, briskly transitioning to the next item on her list. "The *Glow* magazine interview is scheduled. They're going to meet with you the day after the Atlanta show."

"I thought that show got canceled?"

"Well, Dawson says it's on or it's been rescheduled." She waves her hands in the air as if it doesn't matter, which I suppose it doesn't. I don't wanna bring another lick of negative attention to myself on this tour. No matter how understanding Dawson's been, if people start to think I'm a magnet for trouble, I'll never be invited onto a major tour again. And Lord knows, I'm not big enough to headline my own shows yet.

Unless I want to be kicked back to my roots of headlining bars and honky-tonks, *shut up and deal* is my new motto.

A flush of fear ripples over my skin. How can I be so excited to get back on the road *and* terrified at the same time?

Next, Miranda relays an obscene amount of money *Glow* wants to pay me for the interview and reminds me that interviews aren't usually paid but they're willing because this is a "special circumstance."

I take that to mean they expect the goriest of details no matter how uncomfortable it makes me to relive the kidnapping.

"You made it clear to them that they need to be respectful, right?" Rooster says as if he'd read my mind.

"Yes, of course," Miranda huffs. "But they will pose serious questions. It's probably better if you're not there to alter the vibe of the—"

Rooster laughs, low and threatening. "Yeah, not happening."

"Mr. Randall—"

"I won't open my mouth and say a word, unless I have to. But Shelby's not doing *any* interviews alone."

Under the desk, I slide my hand over his leg to let him know how much I appreciate that. He reaches down and squeezes my hand.

"Shelby," she protests.

"Nope." I lift my chin. "That's non-negotiable."

"Fine." She tips her head down, furiously scribbling over her notepad, adding what looks like a dozen exclamation points. "All right. Dream Makers. I'd like to set something up and—"

"Not gonna happen. I don't use those visits for publicity. Never have. Never will."

"Jesus," she grumbles. More strokes of fury with her pen. "All right. I think I saved the best for last." Under her breath she mutters something I can't make out. "Diamond Tough Denim—you heard of them?"

"I don't know. Maybe." Since I couldn't afford many—or any—brand name stuff growing up, I've never paid much attention to labels. Even now, it's not something I care about. Why waste time wanting stuff I can't afford?

"They're an old company. All American-made, so they're on the pricier side. Quality stuff. They used to lean more toward work clothes for, you know, rich people who wanted to play dress up and pretend they were stable workers or whatever."

I can't really make sense of what she's yammering about, but I nod along, waiting for her to get to the point.

"Well, they'd like to break into a more youthful, fashionable market and they're looking for someone to help them influence that transition by targeting their ideal demographic."

"Okay..."

"They want you to wear their pants in public, on your social media, on stage, and take some photos in them for money, Shelby," she spits out in an exasperated rush.

"Well, why didn't you just say *that*?"

"They think you'd be perfect. You're very down-to-earth and have that graceful, Southern belle vibe."

No one's ever confused me for a Southern belle. This lady sure has some strange ideas about the South.

"And of course, country music is very popular. So you hit all their sweet spots."

"Great."

"You're open to it?" she asks with two delicately penciled, hopefully raised eyebrows.

"Yes. Absolutely."

"Fantastic."

"No nudity or anything gross, though, right?" I mean, from her description, it doesn't sound like it will be a problem, but I feel compelled to throw that out there.

"No, honey. That is absolutely not what we want for your image. We'll need to find you some people to go over these contracts. But I'll get working on this now. I don't want them to offer it to anyone else."

This sounds great and all but before we go any further, I need to clear something up. "We haven't discussed your fee yet, Miranda—"

"You and I can discuss that later," Rooster says to the screen.

I choke and turn his way but before I open my mouth, Miranda whistles for our attention. "My fees have been covered for now."

What? "By who?" I sputter.

"Dawson," she answers matter-of-factly.

"What?" I half-jump out of my chair. Except, where exactly do I plan to go? I sink back down in my seat. "Why would he do that?"

"We had a long discussion. I understand he feels guilty about all of this. Glenna being his ex and all." Miranda shrugs. "Does it matter?"

I guess it doesn't. I side-eye Rooster and he nods.

"Thank you, Miranda." Even though the situation is weird, my momma raised me with manners after all.

"The agent and lawyers will probably want a percentage but you'll work that out," she says.

Great. More people taking a cut of what I work my ass off for.

Why is this so complicated? I don't want to prance around in jeans. I want to sing songs.

And buy my momma a house one day.

"What do you think?" Rooster asks after we log off the call with Miranda.

"That was...exciting and a little weird." I'm still staring at the computer monitor which is just a screen saver of a Harley now. "She's intense."

"Chaser says she has a good reputation and a long list of A-list clients."

"Thank you for setting that up." I slap my hands on my thighs. "Damn, you've been busy. Buying vehicles and sorting my career—"

"It's not my intention to interfere with anything. I wanted to help."

I grab his hand between mine and hold his gaze. "I know that. I'm trying to thank you. Sorry if it didn't come out that way."

He rubs his thumb over the back of my hand. "It scared me and pissed me the fuck off that Glenna had a part in this but somehow she could make *you* look bad. Ruin all of your hard work. I don't want to take any chances." He clenches his jaw tight. "After what you went through. What that psycho did. No one's taking your career away from you or fucking with it, Shelby. The security stuff, I can handle. I *will* handle it. But this—" he waves his hand at the screen. "I can't do a damn thing for you on that end."

There's a whole lotta love and faith running through all his words. I'm so close to tears, I bite my lip to hold them back. "Thank you." After a few seconds, I'm calm enough to ask my next question. "Did you ask Dawson to cover her fees?"

"Hell no. I got her name from Chaser. But since he's not really in the country music 'scene,' I asked Dawson for his opinion. He knows her and must've spoken to her. I was going to cover whatever she charged until you get rollin'."

"I can't ask you to do that."

"You didn't." He cups my cheek and rubs his thumb over my bottom lip. "I don't like letting another man take care of anything for my girl. But I also feel like he owes you. So for now, it's fine. The second you feel there might be a conflict of interest, though, you fire her and we'll find you someone else. Okay?"

I'm impressed with Rooster's mercenary attitude.

There's a knock at the door, drawing our attention away from our moment. I rip off the few pages of notes I'd taken during the call and stuff them in my back pocket.

The door opens and Anya's gaze pings between the two of us. "Is now okay, Rooster?"

"Yeah, we just wrapped up." He waves her inside. "Sorry," he says to me in a low voice. "I promised Ice I'd finish up here and Anya needs me to help her with something."

"Oh. Of course. No problem." I stand, feeling sort of awkward.

Anya flashes a quick, warm smile. "You don't have to leave, Shelby. It shouldn't take too long."

"No, I, uh, that's okay."

Rooster works his jaw from side to side. I can't tell if he's annoyed with *me* or the situation. His fingers fly over the keyboard, tapping hard enough to bend plastic. Within a few seconds a log-in page pops up on the screen.

A few more clicks of the keyboard and we're all staring at what must be Anya's porn site. It's a lot slicker and more professional-looking than mine, I'll give her that. A lot more skin on display too.

I move behind the chair I'd been sitting in, offering it to her. "Maybe you should sit here." I motion toward the small love seat against the wall closest to the desk. "I'll be there."

"Thanks, Shelby."

Rooster clicks through a few pages, enters some more info. He's so focused and intent on each action. Finally, he arrives at a screen with nothing but rows of numbers and charts.

"Yes!" Anya bounces in her seat. "*This* is what I didn't know how to access."

Rooster walks her through the process slowly. She grabs the notepad I'd used earlier and diligently writes down everything Rooster explains. He's a patient teacher. Doesn't get annoyed or act superior when she asks him to repeat a few points like a lotta techy guys would. He glances at me over her head and raises an eyebrow, checking in to make sure I'm okay with all of this.

Can I be any more head over boots for this man?

I blow him a quick kiss.

"Okay." Anya reaches forward and taps the screen. "How do I get the details for a specific scene? I want to look at the most recent one I posted."

"You want analytics, here." Rooster slowly clicks through a series of links until we're staring at a still shot of two guys and Anya. Correction, two naked guys and a naked Anya. Color me not shocked—Anya's even more flawless with her clothes *off*.

Fabulous.

Rooster skims his finger along a line chart underneath the video. "This is what you want, right?"

"Yes! Can you click on that giant peak, right there?" She vigorously taps the screen with one long, red fingernail. "I have a hunch."

Rooster flashes an apologetic look my way. A few seconds later moaning, groaning, and slapping noises accompanied by wild female shrieks of pleasure fill the room. All the naked flesh on the screen is misty with sweat. Everyone's working hard.

The tall, thin, heavily tattooed guy on the screen rhythmically thumps into Anya from behind while the shorter, heavily muscled and tattooed guy standing in front of her leans down, one hand on her chin, tilting her face up while kissing and talking to her softly.

"See? *That's* the peak. I knew it." Anya all but pumps her fists in the air.

She half-turns in her seat toward me. "When they switched places, Aaron accidentally bumped my chin with his knee. He felt bad, so he stopped to check in with me. Normally, you'd edit that stuff out but I left it in because it was a sort of sweet genuine moment—"

I'm not sure if sweet and genuine are the words I'd use, but okay.

"That I left it in. And I was right. *That's* the most-watched part." She taps the screen triumphantly. "I used to work with this producer who told me stuff like that was stupid and no one wanted to see it. But I was *right.*"

Yay for trusting your instincts?

Rooster traces the whole raised portion of the bar graph. "This entire section has the most activity."

She takes the mouse from him and replays that portion of the scene. I guess it's cute in a hardcore, pornographic way. She and the guy share a genuine laugh over the incident. Even the guy pounding her from behind stops to kiss Anya's shoulder and make sure she's okay.

I mean, I could've gone my whole entire life without seeing these people in their most intimate moments with each other, but here I am.

"See. Look." She points to a few more spikes and stops to watch those sections. "The eye-contact is always *huge* with my audience. Women want to see more of that romantic, emotional connection. No woman finds twelve minutes of jackhammering penetration sexy in real life *or* porn."

I snort-laugh. She's not exactly wrong there. It's still weird as hell that I'm watching a clip of her screwing two other guys while she's sitting right in front of me, talking about the aesthetics of it all like it's no big deal.

I flick my gaze to Rooster. His expression remains neutral.

"Okay, I think I got it," Anya says finally. "I can access this from my computer too, right?"

"Yup. I sent you all the instructions." His gaze slips toward me for a second. "If you have questions, just shoot me an email and I'll help you out. We can schedule a chat if you need me to walk you through it again."

The jealous girlfriend in me is working real hard to keep her mouth shut.

It's only business. It's for the club. He's going to be on the road with me for flock's sake. Settle down.

"I should be okay," Anya says. "But thank you." She jumps out of her chair and spins around, hugging me quickly. "Thank you so much, Shelby. I'll see you guys out there." She breezes out the door.

"Sorry about that," Rooster says as soon as we're alone.

"It was…surreal. Those images might be permanently seared into my…I need brain bleach or something."

He stares at me for a few seconds. "You've never…?"

"What?"

"Watched stuff? Like that?" he gestures toward the screen.

"*That*? On my own?" I ask, trying to dial down the shock in my tone. "Lordy, no. I mean, I had a boyfriend once who kept trying to talk me into a threesome. He'd show me stuff with two girls and…it wasn't my thing. It just made me really uncomfortable thinking of him jacking off to those videos while comparing me to those girls."

There goes his jaw ticking again.

I cock my head. "You really hate it when I mention an ex, huh?"

He nods once. "I can't help it."

"It was just for context."

"I know." He sighs and glances at the screen. "I'm sorry. I guess I've been immersed in this crap for so long, I'm immune to it."

"I'm not a choirgirl or anything but yeah, it was a little shocking." I stand and close the short distance between us, brushing my knee against his leg. "You're not immune to *me,* are you?"

His gaze travels down my body so slow, heat follows the trail. He grabs my hips and pulls me closer. "Definitely not."

"Good." I perch on the edge of the desk. "So, the emotional connection of it all didn't get to you?" I say lightly.

He sighs. "I understand what she was getting at. But that's not a true emotional anything and you and I both know it."

"I get what she was saying too. And she's right. If I wanted to watch people screwin', that's the part I'd be more interested in too, I guess. She's a smart cookie. Got good instincts for the business she's in." I pause, considering if I should say this next part. "Speaking of, Anya mentioned how you talked to her about alternate careers."

He pinches the bridge of his nose. "Yeah, I probably overstepped there. I don't know—"

I touch his arm to draw his attention to me. "No, I think that was sweet of you."

"Sweet, huh?"

I stare at the ceiling for a second, trying to figure out the best words to convey my feelings. "You treat me like gold. No question. But I've always thought it's the way a man treats the other women in his life—even the ones he *doesn't* want to bang—that reveal his true character. And you tellin' her something like that, even though your club probably wouldn't appreciate it…well, not many men would probably bother."

"I didn't say it because I want to bang her," he confirms.

"That was kinda my whole point." I lift one shoulder. "I can't lie and say I'm super excited you watch beautiful, naked women gettin' plowed on a regular basis…"

"Honestly, I've told you this before, I upload the files and look at the back end numbers more than anything."

I snicker at *back end* and Rooster shakes his head.

"Anyway." He holds my gaze for a few seconds before continuing. "Anya wants control over the uploading and all of that stuff. I'll be more like tech support."

I run my fingers through his hair and he rolls the chair closer to me, resting his hands on my thighs.

"Watching that really did nothing for you?" I ask, tilting my head toward the computer.

"*That*? No."

"What does?"

He squeezes my hips. "Right now? I can't stop thinking about peeling these jeans off, spreading you out on this desk and licking your pussy until my beard's dripping—"

A knock at the door stops Rooster's hypnotizing words. Probably a good thing since I was about five seconds away from letting him do exactly what he described. Which would be kinda rude to do on another man's desk.

Whoever it is, doesn't wait for an invitation. The door swings open and I turn my head. Ice steps in, amusement flickering over his intense face. "Sorry, thought you were done when I saw Anya out there."

"We are." Rooster stands smoothly, completely confident, while I'm off-balance from almost getting caught with my jeans around my ankles.

Shoot. *Ice.* Rooster said this was the president's office.

I scoot my butt off his desk so fast my boots hit the floor with a hard clackety-thump.

"Shelby, hon, you mind giving us a few minutes?" While Ice phrases it as a question, the way he's standing by the door doesn't give me the impression *no* is an acceptable answer.

"Sure. Thank you for letting me borrow your office."

"No problem, sweetheart." For a guy named Ice, his tone's awfully warm and affectionate. "The girls are all out in the main room."

I glance at Rooster and he nods.

Off I go.

CHAPTER THIRTY-TWO

Shelby

I FOLLOW THE MUSIC BACK TO THE MAIN ROOM. SOMEONE'S CRANKED IT way up. The lights have been dimmed but Ice was right, the girls are where I left them. Anya's engaged in animated conversation with Heidi. Trinity's relocated to her husband's lap and seems quite content to stay there.

As soon as she spots me, Anya pops up and waves me over. The chair I'd been occupying earlier is taken. One stern look from Anya and the girl skedaddles like her butt's on fire.

"Where's Rooster?" Anya asks, glancing over my shoulder.

"I guess Ice needed to talk to him."

She grabs my arm, staring intently at me. "Thanks for being so cool."

I assume she's talking about what happened back there in the office. "Yeah, sure."

The music changes to something a little more in my neighborhood and I can't help tapping my feet.

"I *love* this song!" Anya screams and claps her hands together. "Do you two-step, Shelby?"

Now we're talking. "Is a frog's ass water-tight?"

She frowns and blinks at me.

"Yes." I jump up and she grabs my hand, dragging me out to the middle of the room where a few couples are dancing to their own beat that has nothing to do with the Texan twang spilling out of the speakers.

Shrill whistles rise above the music as Anya and I break into a simple Texas two-step. I think the noise is directed at us but I'm having too much fun following Anya's shuffle-steps, twirling, and just being silly in time to the music to care. At the line about the rooster having twenty gals, guys shout and more whistles split the air.

While I'm spinning I catch Rooster and Ice standing near the meeting room watching us.

Anya laughs and shakes her head. "The only gal *our* Rooster has his eye on is *you*," she shouts in my ear, referencing the lyrics.

"Ice seems to be watching you too."

Her steps falter as they stare each other down for a few seconds. She shakes it off and hooks her arm around my waist, spinning us away.

"Nah, he was best friends with my daddy. Thinks he's lookin' out for me now. That's all."

While I digest *that* bit of information, we continue to spin and twist together as if we've done this dance dozens of times.

"You're good!" I yell over the music.

She answers by wiggling her eyebrows and shaking her hips.

As the music fades someone throws on another, slower country song. Remy prowls over, panther-slow, and leans in to whisper something in Anya's ear. She nods and throws a quick glance over her shoulder before dancing away with him.

Actually, dancing isn't what I'd call their movements.

I'm not alone for long. Heidi taps my shoulder and holds out her hands. "Teach me a little?"

Bless her sweet soul, now I don't look like a dipstick out here all by myself.

I show her a few steps and she picks up the moves quickly. By the next song we're turning, spinning and twirling like crazy. Not the smoothest performance but we're having fun.

ROOSTER

By the time Ice and I return to the party, the lights have dimmed another few notches. From the look of things, brothers have already decided to start working on earning their pussy patches.

Fuck me. I should warn Shelby. After her reaction to Anya's scene, the whole pussy patch challenge might be one degenerate event too many for her to handle.

"Glad they're gettin' along," Ice shouts to me over the upbeat, fiddle-laced music.

I follow his line of sight to Shelby and Anya tearing up the dance floor. Damn, even after Anya made her so uncomfortable, Shelby's not snubbing her. She has more class and kindness than most women I've known. I haven't stopped thinking about what she said before Ice interrupted us either.

"You gonna go cut in?" I ask.

He watches the girls and seems to be considering it. The music changes and Remy, of all people, slides up to Anya and whisks her away. Ice throws them a glare that could melt a glacier. After a few seconds of watching them all but fuck standing up, he storms off.

Jigsaw wanders over with his eyebrows raised and cheeks puffed out. "Holy fuck." He whistles and shakes his head.

I'm not as amused as he seems to be. "Our support club shouldn't piss off the president of the charters we visit," I say as we watch Remy and Anya grinding away in the middle of the party room.

"How's Remy supposed to know?" Jigsaw shrugs. "She's not patched."

"Doesn't matter. He's in another club's house. He needs to learn better manners."

Jigsaw steps back and slaps my chest. "Do you think Shelby re-virginized you or something?" He squeezes his eyes shut and taps the side of his head. "I think…no I'm positive I remember *you* doing something similar when you were a prospect."

I groan and smack his hand off my chest. "That was different."

"It was *worse*."

Even if I don't want to admit it, he's right. "Thank fuck Hopper retired. Z wants me to stop by Washington eventually. Hopper would probably shoot me on sight."

Jiggy—asshole that he is—doubles over laughing. "You dodged a bullet."

"Several of them," I grumble.

"No, seriously. I hear his daughter has like four kids now."

"Yeah? Hopper shoot their daddy?"

"Probably." He clasps his hands under his chin. "Please, let me come with you when you show your face in Washington."

"I'm really not that worried about it." I honestly try not to dwell on that time in my life unless Jigsaw brings it up. Maybe Shelby *has* scrambled my brain. Sometimes it feels like nothing else existed before we met. Her presence in my life creates a glow that chases all the shadows of my past into the holes where they belong.

Murphy ambles over with a wide-eyed face and tilts his head toward Anya and Remy. "Is this going to be a problem?"

"Probably. Why don't you go collect your boy?" I suggest.

"He's not *my* boy," Murphy growls.

"Forget Anya." Jiggy slaps both of us on the shoulder and lifts his chin in Shelby and Heidi's direction. "Everyone's staring at *your* ol' ladies anyway."

Murphy rams an elbow in Jiggy's side. "Quit being a creep. They're having fun."

Creep or not, Jiggy's not wrong. The girls are playfully performing an innocent country-type dance together. Or rather, Shelby's patiently showing Heidi some steps. There's more giggling and twirling going on than dancing. A damn welcome sight after the last few days. Still, they're drawing a lot of attention. Heidi's patched, so no worries there. Everyone's seen me with Shelby and knows who she is, so I'm not too stressed about the attention they're receiving. Yet.

I bump Murphy with my shoulder. "Thanks for bringing Heidi with you. I think Shelby's really liked having the girls here."

He cocks his head, studying me for a minute, like maybe I'm trying to bust his nuts instead of sincerely thanking him. "Anytime, brother."

My gaze lands on one of the local brothers who's now eying Shelby too close for my comfort. While keeping his gaze on Shelby, he leans in toward another brother and says something they both share a laugh over. The easy smile slides off my face. Imagining whatever filthy comments they're trading nudges me forward. As I step into the crowd, Jigsaw's rumbling laughter follows me.

Shelby's moving fast. Her body brushes mine and I catch her mid-twirl, wrapping my arm around her waist and yanking her closer.

I lean down, inhaling her soft, powdery scent and kiss her bared shoulder. "You're a beautiful blur out here."

She tips her head back, staring up at me. Wide eyes, pink cheeks, sweat misting her skin, and a happy glow curving her lips. "Hey, there."

In front of us, Murphy has Heidi in a similar hold. She laughs and teases him about teaching him to dance.

Shelby turns, looping her arms around my neck and swaying her hips from side to side. "I've lost *two* dancing partners. Now, you have to dance with me."

I rest my hands on her hips. "I'm not much of a dancer."

"I happen to know you have *excellent* rhythm."

"That's different." I lean down and press my forehead to hers.

"How was your meetin'? You're not in trouble with Ice, are ya?"

"Not at all." The opposite, actually. Ice wanted to cut me in for a percentage of Anya's profits from the site. After all he's done—loaning me vehicles, putting Jackson on Shelby's case right away, personally helping me search for her, offering to monitor Suggs as he moves through the justice system—I told him I couldn't accept. He left me with the impression he might go to Z and offer to kick that percentage up to my charter, which is fine. I got no control over whatever arrangement the two presidents decide.

Murphy—*that big, ginger fucker*—disappears with Heidi, leaving the Remy situation to implode. I scan the room for Dex, who might be able to talk some sense into Remy, or Wrath, who might be able to beat it into the kid. Can't find either of them.

I lead Shelby over to a quieter corner of the room, claim a chair and pull her into my lap.

"Were you okay earlier? Out here with them, I mean." I lift my chin toward Remy who's still slow-grinding with Anya in front of everyone. Griff's too absorbed in whatever he's doing on his phone to pay attention to the girls who keep approaching him or notice the ass-kicking his buddy's about to receive.

"Oh yes." Her lips pull up. "Trinity's one badass bitch. She doesn't take shit from anyone."

My blood simmers. "Who hassled her?" Not that Trin can't handle herself, but I don't want anyone harassing my brothers' women.

"No one." Shelby waves her hand in the air between us. "Remy had some questions and she told him the appropriate place to find that information."

I sense she's not giving me the whole story but if it's important, I'm sure Trinity will relay it to Wrath and he'll handle it.

"You're okay, though?"

"I'm fine. Remy asked about their patches." She ducks her head. "Why I don't have one."

No wonder Trinity took exception. That's not a question a biker should ask. And definitely not something he should talk about to my ol' lady. *Little fucker.*

I wasn't ready to talk about this with her. Buy an RV to tour the country? Sure. Take a chance she'll balk at wearing something that proclaims her my property? Not so much.

"Does it bother you?" I purposely leave the question vague, waiting to see how she interprets it.

"No," she answers quickly. "You told me that for your club it was equivalent to an engagement ring." She squeezes my arm. "I'm not expecting…that's a big step." She tilts her head toward the front door. "You just bought me a freakin' house."

"It's hardly a house."

"You know what I mean." She drops her gaze to her lap. "I love you. I know you're committed. That *we're* committed. I don't need a ring or some leather to tell me how you feel about me."

I pull her closer and kiss the top of her head.

Truthfully, if I want my brothers to take a vote, I'm not sure when I'll be able to patch her. The few days here and there she's spent around my club won't be enough for them to decide if they trust her or not. The fact that she's a public person who has a lot of eyes on her and will continue to do so in the future won't exactly count in her favor for a club that prefers to stay under the radar. Lots of old ladies get real wrapped up in whether or not they get a patch.

Maybe it's a blessing that Shelby doesn't seem to care.

CHAPTER THIRTY-THREE

Shelby

THIS IS THE MOST RELAXED I'VE BEEN IN DAYS. IN FACT, I WANT TO TAKE this moment and tuck it in my pocket to remember the next time I'm stressed out. Sitting on Rooster's lap, the way he can't stop touching me, the possessive way he keeps one big hand clasped on my thigh like some sort of warning to every other man—and woman—in the room is a jolt of queen energy straight to my head.

I snuggle my head against his shoulder, stopping to kiss his cheek. He crooks his neck to peer down at me. "You all right?"

"Perfectly content." I stroke my hand over his beard and he dips closer to kiss the inside of my wrist. Laughter trills out of me. "That tickles."

He kisses his way up my arm and I twine my fingers in his hair, pulling him closer until our lips crash together in a hot, wet mashing of lips.

The heat from before we were interrupted in Ice's office returns with a vengeance. We're tucked into the corner, Rooster's arm trapped between my back and the chair's cushions. Doesn't slow him down. He slides his free hand from my thigh to my hip and up my side. I'm panting and really close to throwing the rest of my fucks away and begging him to relieve the pressure between my thighs here and now by any means necessary.

He pulls away and studies me for a second. "Let's go to our room."

In my eagerness to scoot off his lap and sprint down the hallway, I elbow him in the chin. "Shoot! I'm sorry."

"I'm fine." He grabs my hips and sets me upright on his thighs. I slide back against his hardness and slowly twitch my hips from side to side.

"Careful." He groans against my ear and slides his hand over my shoulders to grip my chin and turn my face toward him for another kiss. We're not making it to our room. Nope. I loop my arms around his neck and arch my back, twisting to get better access to his mouth. He slides his hands over my ribs and gently cups my breasts. "You don't want to do this here, chickadee," he whispers.

I drag my eyelids open. What we're doing is pretty innocent compared to the surrounding activity. At least four girls are laid out on the pool table with brothers' heads nestled between their thighs. Across from us, a girl's kneeling on the back of the couch straddling another brother's face while he clutches her ass cheeks, pulling her closer to his greedy mouth.

"Uh, your brothers sure are in a *giving* mood tonight." I mean, fair is fair. Last time, it was mostly girls on their knees servicing the guys or straight up screwin' on every piece of furniture. Who knew equality could be found in a biker clubhouse?

Rooster groans, but not in the sexy way he did earlier.

Shonda bounces over to us in nothing but a fabulous red satin bra and panty set with her hand outstretched. "Here, Shelby! I have a feeling you'll need one of these!" She thrusts what looks like a small metal clamp with pink rubber grips in my hand. "Rooster, you get your card from Boots?"

"No. It's—"

"Be right back!" she shouts over her shoulder, disappearing into the crowd again.

I inspect the object in my hand. "Why am I holding a," I peer closer, not sure I'm seeing correctly in the weak lighting, "heart-shaped hole puncher?"

"Fuck." He scrubs his hands over his face. The movement jostles me forward. I stand and turn to face him.

"What's wrong?"

He crooks a finger. "Come here."

I shuffle closer and he clamps a hand around my thigh, dragging me into his lap again.

"Here ya go!" Shonda thrusts what looks like a pink index card with a calendar printed on one side into Rooster's hands.

Pussy Patch 30 Day Challenge is printed above the calendar.

"Good luck," Shonda coos in a knowing way, patting me on the shoulder before taking off again.

"What…what is that?"

"Nothing." He folds the card and tucks it in his pocket.

"What's a pussy patch?"

He briefly closes his eyes. "Something stupid they came up with in church."

I cross my arms over my chest, waiting for some details. Around us, more shrieks, moans, and orgasm roars explode.

"Fuck," he groans. "Can we talk about this upstairs?"

ROOSTER

I could strangle Boots and T-Bone for this whole stupid pussy patch bullshit.

My cock's harder than a hammer, painfully confined by my jeans. I should be upstairs making love to my girl, not explaining my club's deviance.

Thank fuck she's wearing jeans. The way she's straddling my lap, if she was wearing one of her cute little dresses, I would've impaled her by now and had her riding my cock in front of everyone.

I grip her ass cheeks and yank her closer. Christ, the heat from her center sears me through two layers of denim. Holding her tight, I stand and encourage her to wrap her legs around my waist.

"Ooo." She loops her arms around my neck. "It's such a dang turn on that you can pick me up without breakin' a sweat."

I bounce her in my arms and she squeals, holding on tighter.

"You can't carry me all the way upstairs," she protests as we move through the crowded room.

"Like fuck I can't. I lift heavier weights than you all the time."

"Really?"

I flex my biceps. "These don't grow on their own, baby."

She laughs at my cockiness and leans in to brush a kiss on my cheek.

"Actually, I've been slacking off. Figure once we're on the road, I'll set up a regular routine. Wrath's supposed to help me do that."

I stop at our door, shifting her in my arms to open it. Her lips whisper over my earlobe sending a shock wave straight to my groin. "Careful, I don't want to drop you."

"Mmm." She flicks her tongue against my neck.

I kick the door closed and press her against it. She rests her head against the door and stares up at me. "That was hot." With her accent, it sounds more like *hawt*, cranking me up even more.

"You're hot." Not my smoothest compliment but with all my blood rushing south, it's the best I can do. I lean in and kiss her, sweeping my tongue over her bottom lip until she opens for me.

She curls her fingers into my cut, pulling me closer. Somehow, I manage to tug her shirt off, tossing it over my shoulder. Her bra's too complicated for my primitive brain to handle right now—especially when she starts tugging at my belt.

"Want something?"

"So, so bad," she whispers in between kisses and fiddling with my jeans.

The heel of one of her boots digs into my ass. After some wriggling and frustrated huffs, a boot thuds to the floor. She unwinds her legs, and hopping on one foot, tugs off the other boot.

"Eager?" I tease while getting to work undoing my pants.

She flicks a serious glare with a healthy dose of sexy at me. "You best buckle up. I'm about to ride you like a bull at the rodeo."

"Come and get it." I shove my jeans down and put on a show of stroking my cock for her.

She quickly sheds her jeans and panties.

"Bra too."

She flashes an amused smirk and reaches behind her to unfasten it.

As always, I'm struck stupid by her beauty. Breasts that fill my big hands perfectly. Flared hips I love grabbing onto. Strong legs that wrap around me just right. Plush thighs I want to wear as earmuffs.

I'm so lost in admiring every inch, I don't process that she's checking me out just the same.

"Damn," she draws out the word all low and sex-kittenish, "you put those poor porno boys to shame with that monster cock." She tilts her head. "Why aren't *you* starring in those films?"

Another reason I regret she had to sit through that scene. I don't want her exposed to any other cocks. Ever again. I can't help laughing, though. "This monster's for your eyes only, chickadee. Now get your hot little ass over here."

She doesn't waste time. It seems we're in sync. She places her hand on my shoulder and hikes one leg against my hip. I take over from there, slipping my arms under her thighs, palming her ass, and lifting her.

"Hang on."

She grips my shoulders and leans in to kiss me. The kiss goes nuclear fast. Digging my fingers into her ass, I pull her closer. She moans and rubs herself against me. Not quite where I need her to go. Finally, I guide her onto my cock, taking it slow and easy. Flexing my hips and slowly sliding home. She's warm and wet and fucking her bare is the best damn thing ever.

"How's that monster treatin' you?" I whisper.

She rolls her hips, adjusting to having every inch of me buried to the hilt. "Pretty dang good."

Damn, she's funny. I'm half grinning like an idiot and half ready to explode while she uses her grip on my shoulders for leverage to work herself up and down my cock. I bite my lip and hang onto my control by a thread.

Her blissed-out moans and cries increase. She stops moving, her body tightening all over, pussy squeezing me tight. My balls are ready to explode.

She arches her back, really grinding herself against me now. I admire the hot pink flush staining her skin from chest to cheeks. My tongue's half-wagging out of my mouth, desperate to taste her hard, plump nipples. As much as this position is satisfying all my caveman urges to show off my strength for her, it's limiting my ability to get my hands and mouth all over her body.

I search for something she can brace herself against. Door's no good. I'm afraid I'll hurt her back when I finally let loose.

Desk. I shuffle over awkwardly. "Behind you. Arch backwards and brace yourself on the desk."

Still clinging to me, she turns and after a second or two gets the gist of the instructions. She bends backward, releasing my neck to reach for the smooth surface.

"Oh, fuck yeah," I growl. "Lock those legs around me. I got you."

"This is some serious Tantric bridge pose," she huffs between panting little breaths.

I've never appreciated all the yoga she does more.

I let my hands roam over her thighs, the curves of her hips and up her sides, stopping to cup her breasts. "Needed to get my hands on more of you."

"Mmm."

"You all right?" I use my thumb against her clit in a steady rhythm. Her hips punch up even higher and I lock my arms around her thighs. Her legs kick straight out, doing that crazy shaking thing they do when I get her good. With her head tipped back I can't see her face. Dumb move on my part. I love watching her eyes roll back when she totally loses it. She's gripping me so tight, I see stars. Or maybe it's the orgasm that I can't hold back another second.

I fuck her furiously fast, thumping into her over and over. Her arms tremble the smallest bit. I lift her higher and move closer to the desk, laying her down.

"Phew." She gives me a relaxed, dreamy smile. "Worried I was gonna bop my head there for a minute."

I grit my teeth, my hips pistoning harder and harder. "Fuck."

Every muscle in my body straining, I throw my head back, groaning and shouting loud enough to rattle the ceiling. It's the roar of a lion-fucking-his-mate loud.

I come so hard, my knees buckle. I have to release my grip on her hips and brace myself over her, arms planted on the desk. She wraps herself around my body, pulling me closer. Our lips fuse together. It's like for a few seconds our souls merge with the universe or something. Shelby does stuff to my brain and body I can't comprehend.

How is it possible that every single time with her ends up being the best sex I've ever had in my life?

CHAPTER THIRTY-FOUR

Shelby

We're both dripping with sweat and plum worn out but Rooster still takes his time lovingly soaping me up in the shower. After a quick scrub-a-dub, we spend a lot of time playfully drying each other off. Really, more like groping and exploring each other if I'm honest.

I squeeze the rock-solid muscles of his arm. "I think you made up for any missed workouts."

He lets out a low, satisfied growl.

I'm still tingling all over. I turn toward the sink, intent on brushing my teeth. Rooster presses his big, warm body against my back and wraps on arm around me, resting his hand on my stomach. He stretches forward to clear the fog off the mirror and I can't help staring at our reflection. In the mirror, he meets my eyes.

"You look so tiny next to me." He strokes his knuckles over my cheek then hugs me tight, pressing a kiss to my temple. "But you're so damn strong."

"I'm little but mighty," I quip.

"Yes. You are," he says in a more serious tone than I expected.

I wiggle my butt against the towel wrapped around his lower half. "And I can take one hell of a pounding."

He rumbles with laughter. "Yes, you can."

I lean over and start brushing my teeth. Rooster stays close, tracing his fingers along my spine, like he's too fascinated with me to look away.

"I'm not sure how I feel about ya watchin' me brush my teeth," I mumble around a mouth full of minty foam.

"To be fair, I'm staring at your juicy peach of an ass."

I wrinkle my nose at him in the mirror. His serious expression lifts. He reaches for the heavy rings he usually wears that are resting on the counter. One-by-one, he slips them on his fingers. I turn, and clasp his right hand, bringing it closer to kiss his scarred knuckles. Drawing away, I study the heavy bands of silver encircling his ring and index fingers.

He taps his fists together in front of him. "They serve as biker brass knuckles. Legal in all fifty states."

"They're certainly heavy enough." I stroke my fingers over one ring, studying the intricate detail of the two crossed pistols in front. One side of the thick band depicts a skull and on the other side the metal has been blackened to spell out the word *outlaw* in tattoo-like lettering.

"A lot of meaning there," I say.

He glances at it as if noticing it for the first time in a long time. "The gentleman outlaw's guide to justice." His lips quirk into a smile full of fond memories. "My uncle left it to me."

"Was he in the club too?"

"No, but he was friends with lots of different bikers." He shrugs. "Spent a lot of time around them."

I move to the one on his index finger. A crowned skull engraved into the flat front. On one side, an hourglass, on the other what looks like an artist's representation of wind. I tap the skull. "Club ring, right?" That's what I've always assumed.

"Sort of. Jigsaw and I bought them when we patched-in."

"Aw, like those half-a-heart best friends necklaces?"

He huffs out a quick laugh. "I guess." He traces his fingers from the skull to the wind. "Brothers to the end." He taps the hourglass. "Life is finite."

"Oh," I breathe out, feeling a little dumb for making a joke about it now. "No wonder you can interpret my tarot cards better than I can."

The faint smile on his face flattens. "I wouldn't say that. You haven't touched them since…leaving the hospital. You want me to get them for you?"

While I appreciate the offer, a foolish feeling invades my chest at the thought. "I think I'm done doing readings. They couldn't help me figure out someone was after me, so obviously it's stupid."

He strokes his thumb over my cheek. "That's not true. You couldn't have known. Don't let this ruin something you like."

I shrug and look away.

"Maybe do a reading for the girls if you don't want to do one for yourself. Trinity would probably be into it."

"Maybe." Uncomfortable talking about it anymore, I grab his left hand to inspect his final ring. A large oval turquoise set in an elaborate band of woven silver. "Turquoise is supposed to be the protective talisman for kings and warriors. Some people thought it could protect riders from falls. I see why a biker would want that."

He stares at it with a blank expression as if it's the first time he's heard any of that. "Shit, an old girlfriend gave it to me."

Well, doesn't *that* suck all the oxygen out of the room.

I don't want to be the girl who gets annoyed about stuff like that, but *hoo-boy*, the fact that he regularly wears a ring some ex gave him is *not* landing well.

"Fuck." He tugs the ring off. "I just like the design. I totally forgot where it came from." He stalks into the bedroom, opens the nightstand drawer, and drops the ring inside. It lands with a harsh clink. He slides the drawer closed.

Huh.

I didn't even have to ask.

I'm not even sure I would have.

"You don't have to," I protest as he returns to the bathroom. "It's just a piece of jewelry."

He cups the back of my head and drags me closer for a quick kiss. "Nah, it's fine."

Thank you doesn't seem quite right but I'm so stunned, I'm not sure what else to say.

I give him another quick peck on the lips and scurry into the bedroom. After finding a clean tank top and pair of panties to sleep in, I pick up our scattered clothes. I set everything on the desk and stop to touch Rooster's cut that he left draped over the chair before we took our shower.

Besides the three-piece patch on the back, his vice president patch, and his Lost Kings MC patch, he has a few others. A worn "Route 66" patch that I'm a little jealous of. I've always wanted to drive Route 66 and the few times we were close on the tour, there was no time for detours. *Blood Makes You Related, Loyalty Makes You Family.* I've seen similar phrases on the patches worn by other Lost Kings. I'm pretty sure Jigsaw has one exactly like it. A couple pairs of angel wings, ΜΟΛΩΝ ΛΑΒΕ—ah, the classic slogan of defiance, not really a surprise there—a rooster with a crown, a rising phoenix, a broken heart, an hourglass with a skull and scythe, and a few others.

"Why aren't you naked?" Rooster's low, smoldering question interrupts my inspection.

"I've never really studied all your patches before." I peer at him over my shoulder. "Am I allowed to ask about them?"

One corner of his mouth curls up. "Ask away, chickadee. I'll answer what I can."

That's not ominous or anything.

I notice a pink square on the floor and bend down to grab it.

Pussy Patch 30 Day Challenge. Right. We were supposed to talk about this before getting carried away.

I hold up the card. "You were going to tell me about this?"

He sighs, runs his fingers through his hair, then levels me with one of his panty-melting smiles. "Come naked-cuddle with me and I'll give you all the details."

Twenty minutes later, I'm howling with laughter and clutching my stomach. "Your club's giving out cunnilingus achievement awards?"

Rooster grumble-laughs along with me. "Not *my* club. This charter of my club." He stops for a second. "Ah, shit. Sway probably did something similar when he was president. Christ, I hope Z doesn't get any bright ideas when he hears about it."

"So," I tap the card with my finger, "I take it you're allowed to participate since they gave you a scoreboard."

"Yup." He lets out a devious chuckle. "I'm not ashamed to admit, I encouraged Murphy to partake in the challenge just because I know it'll annoy the shit out of Heidi's brother every time he sees that patch."

"You're terrible."

"I know." He grins. "I'm okay with it."

I grab the card and study it again. "The calendar runs for thirty-*five* days not thirty."

I swear he almost blushes. "There was some lengthy debate about adding five free days, uh, for the monogamous brothers…just in case."

After a second or two, his meaning sinks in and now *my* cheeks warm. "Oh, well, my time of the month is usually light and short thanks to the IUD. My cranky days and food-cravings not so much—like I warned you about earlier."

He chuckles. "Is *that* what you were trying to get at with the steak and ice cream thing?"

"Yes," I huff. Why is this so weird and embarrassing to talk about when the man's inspected me inside and out every which way?

While I might be embarrassed, Rooster's clearly aroused by the discussion. He shoves the sheet away from my body and slides his hand over my ribs, down into the dip of my waist and over the curve of my hip and back. The whole time staring at my body like he's the big, bad wolf about to gobble me up.

After a few seconds, he meets my eyes. "That wasn't why I said what I did in Ice's office. Just so you know."

While I mentally replay all the things we talked about earlier, he wedges his hands between my thighs and strokes his middle finger through my slit.

At his touch, my heart flutters and my thoughts scatter. "W—what was that?"

"That I wanted to lay you out on the desk—"

"Oh, right."

He strokes harder, using more pressure each time he nears my clit.

His voice is low and hypnotic as he continues. "I wouldn't use you like that…disrespect you by not telling you if I was trying to earn that patch."

That honest admission drags me from the lust fog I'm slowly spiraling into. The club is so important to him, such a big part of his life and identity. And from other bikers I've known, not many put the comfort or opinions of women above the club. Not even the women they've exchanged vows with.

I don't know what to say.

Me, the queen of lyrics and words. Speechless.

So, I cup his cheek and say the only words I can think of. "I love you."

ROOSTER

Love that soft look in Shelby's eyes and the reverent way she touches my face. I press a kiss to her wrist, so fuckin' happy she's not thoroughly disgusted by the club's patch challenge.

I'm still lazily stroking her pussy, enjoying the way she's struggling to keep her eyes open. I shift closer, twisting my wrist, and slowly push my middle finger inside. She's so warm and wet. Tight and hot. I rest my forehead on her chest. "Lie on your back for me."

She turns, shifting closer to me, and I use the opportunity to slip my other arm under her body. "That's it." I pump my finger in and out, eventually adding another one and use the heel of my hand to keep pressure on her clit.

"L-Logan, I'm close. So close," she whispers.

"I know." I kiss her cheek. "I can tell. I *want* you to come." I stare into her dazed eyes. "Can you do that for me?"

"Oh God. Right there." Her hips jerk up, chasing my hand. I stop teasing and use my fingers to fuck her with hard, firm strokes. She trembles, squeezes, and shudders through her orgasm.

"I hope you're not done because I need to taste you now," I warn as I slide down her body.

She curls her fingers in my hair, which I take as a sign she wants me to continue. She's still fired up, writhing and twisting under me, so I waste no time shoving my face against her, licking and sucking, wiggling my tongue against her clit until she lifts her hips, mashing my face against her pussy. I groan with approval. There are no other sounds in the room besides her heavy breathing, cries of happiness, and lots of delicious, wet sucking. Her thighs tremble as she explodes with pleasure. I bring her down slowly with soft kisses and petting until she finally opens her eyes.

"Dear God," she whispers. She lifts up on her elbows and stares at me. "You are *so* earning that patch."

I rumble with laughter and kiss my way up her body.

"You know I'd do that every day, multiple times a day, patch or no patch, right?" I settle myself between her legs, pushing my cock inside her slippery heat.

She lifts her legs, locking them around me. "I think so."

I thump into her with more force. "You think?"

"Yes. Oh my. Do that again."

I nail her with short, hard strokes and she still can't seem to get enough. Lifting her hips, grinding against me just as eager as I am. I grab a pillow and try to stuff it under her without losing my rhythm. She notices and whimpers. "Don't stop. Please."

"Not gonna happen."

We both come hard and loud. "Fuck," I groan as I keep pumping into her. I could happily die right this second without a single regret.

My arms give out and I land on the mattress next to her.

She reaches over and curls her fingers around mine and whispers, "Forget stars. You make me see galaxies."

That's a beat-on-my chest statement if ever I've heard one.

I turn my head—the only body part I'm capable of moving at the moment. "Good, 'cause you're my whole universe."

She squeezes my hand.

After a few seconds, my heart rate's back to normal. I thought she'd drifted off to sleep, but she pops up, eager gaze bouncing around the room.

"Where's that hole punch?" She scampers to the end of the bed while I tuck my arms behind my head and enjoy the view of her naked ass while she searches through our pile of clothes.

She holds the little silver device up in triumph and saunters back to bed. "Gimmie that card."

Amused, I turn over and search for it. Somehow it ended up under our sweaty bodies and it's a little mashed and wrinkled. Biting her bottom lip, she happily punches a hole in the first box.

The smile on her face falters as she hands the card back. She stops halfway.

"One thing." Her gaze flicks toward my cut. "Uh, none of those patches are from sexcapades you've had with other girls, right? 'Cause, I'd rather you wear that ring," she wiggles her fingers toward the nightstand where I'd dropped the ring an ex had given me about a million years ago, "than some patch on your cut proclaiming you ate some random girl's pussy for a month straight."

The idea's so absurd to me that I end up roaring with laughter for a solid minute. "No. None of them are pussy patches."

Maybe that was too specific of an answer. She frowns. "No blow job patches? No doggy style—"

"No carnal patches of any kind on my cut," I assure her. "Each one has some meaning behind it but not like that. You can ask Jiggy to confirm tomorrow, if you want."

That finally seems to erase the concern lingering in her eyes.

She hands me the card.

"No need. I trust you."

CHAPTER THIRTY-FIVE

Rooster

Before we can get back on the road, Dawson invites us to join his new security team for a presentation, meeting, workshop, class, whatever you want to call it. Selling it to Jigsaw isn't easy. He hated school and isn't exactly eager to return to anything resembling being told what to do.

Shelby's coming with us so she can work on some songs with her band.

Feels good to have her on the back of my bike again.

She squeezes me tight and I'm thrown back to the first time she took that spot. The Texas heat. Her soaked sundress. I reach back and run my hand over her jeans-covered legs. Definitely more appropriate riding gear than that first ride.

"You all right?" I shout.

"Wonderful!"

Feels good to hear that. Every day since she left the hospital, she seems a little more like herself.

At the hotel, I walk her downstairs to where her band's rehearsing.

"I'll be right upstairs if you need me." I take both of Shelby's hands in mine. "If you want to leave early or something comes up, just send me a text."

She leans on tiptoes and kisses my cheek. "I'll be fine. Thank you for doing this." She reaches out and touches Jiggy's arm. "You too. You didn't have to—"

"No worries, songbird."

After one more kiss, I reluctantly let Shelby go, waiting until she meets up with Trent before searching for the stairs.

"I hate you," Jigsaw mutters.

"What happened to 'no worries'?"

He jerks his shoulders up and down a few times. "I didn't want to make Shelby feel bad."

I hold in my laughter and slap him on the back. "I appreciate you being here. Don't think I could do this on my own without punching someone."

He growls a few choice words and impatiently motions for me to hurry up the stairs.

The next floor's crawling with guys in dress pants, tucked-in shirts and sports coats that are probably concealing weapons in holsters.

"Stop." One meathead holds his hands out in front of him.

"We're Dawson's guests." I barely manage to hide my irritation.

"Sure. Yeah." He wiggles his fingers at me. "Hands up."

Jigsaw and I reluctantly put our hands in the air. Another guy joins our party to feel up Jiggy. This situation feels a little too similar to the night Shelby was kidnapped. I guess I should be happy Dawson's hired halfway competent people, but I'd kinda rather punch these guys instead.

"Easy, fucker," I growl when he explores my crotch for too long.

"Cut it out! What the fuck?" Dawson shouts, jogging toward us. The two molesters pause.

The guy who stopped us glances over his shoulder. "Everyone gets searched, Mr. Roads."

Dawson holds his hands out. "Not these two, okay? They're with Shelby. They're here for the training. My guests. They're cool." Poor Dawson must be afraid I'm gonna hold him responsible for being molested.

The security guys glance at each other and shrug.

"Sorry," Dawson says, motioning us forward.

"Thanks for the inappropriate touching." Jigsaw salutes the guy who'd felt him up. "It was delightful." He grins and I swear the bodyguard shivers. "I'll repay the favor later."

"They're here to watch everything. Learn the ropes before we go back out on the road. My fault," Dawson explains, walking us inside a smaller room. "I want everyone who comes backstage searched from now on. I thought I'd get to introduce you before—"

"It's fine." I wave my hand in front of me. "After what happened, I'd rather be safe."

"I'm cool," Jigsaw adds in an impossibly helpful tone. "Don't sweat it. I'm totally fine with a dude I don't know fondling my balls. Should I tip him or you, Dawson?"

I elbow Jigsaw and he grins at me. "Dawson knows I'm joking."

"Didn't even piss my pants," Dawson agrees.

"Aw, I must be losing my touch." Jigsaw slaps Dawson's shoulder and nudges him forward.

The day can only improve, right?

SHELBY

The club hosts a big breakfast for us the morning we're leaving to meet up with the rest of the tour.

We're finally ready to roll out of Virginia.

The guys work out the formation they're going to ride in out in the parking lot. Rooster and I will be in the truck following behind. I'm a little excited and a little nervous about adding the pack of bikers to my entourage. Rooster said the meeting with Dawson and his security team had gone well.

I'm waiting off to the side for Rooster to finish talking to the guys. My phone buzzes and I check the texts Trent sent me—a few goofy pictures of him on the van. He's more than eager to hit the road too.

"Hey, Shelby."

Ice's smooth, deep voice pulls my attention away from my phone and I stuff it in my pocket. "Mornin'."

"You gonna be all right out there?"

"I think so." I wave my hand toward the guys. "Thank you for loaning Pants to us." A more sobering thought hits me. From what I've gathered,

Ice was there when the guys found me in Martin's house. He'd helped Rooster locate me in that damn...*box*. A shiver races over my skin. "Thank you for helping Rooster...find me. I don't know—"

"It's okay, sweetheart. I'm just thankful we found you in time." He strokes his fingers over his chin in a thoughtful way. "I already told Rooster but I want you to know, anytime you need to come back to Virginia, you always have a place to stay here."

I have the feeling this isn't an invitation extended to everyone who passes through. "Thank you. I really appreciate that. Thank you for giving me a safe place to...recover," I finish awkwardly, not sure he wants to hear any of the emotional stuff bubbling up inside me.

"It was nice having you around." A few more beats of silence pass between us. "Thanks for being a friend to Anya." He lifts his chin toward the clubhouse. "Not all the ol' ladies are always nice to her. Club girls either."

Yeah, I guess it might be intimidating to hang out with a porn star. But Anya's so sweet, I can't imagine acting nasty toward her for no damn reason. "She's a sweetheart. I'm gonna miss her."

"Thank you. She's important to me...to the club. You didn't know that but you still showed her respect. That's serious 'round here."

"Well, my momma would tan my hide otherwise," I say lightly. What kind of women do the brothers usually bring around? Nothing I did was *that* out of the ordinary.

"Prez, thank you for everything." Rooster walks over with his hand outstretched. Ice pulls him in and pats his back a few times.

"Thank you, brother. I was just telling Shelby she's welcome here anytime you guys are passing through."

"Appreciate that. We'll definitely be back at some point."

"Good deal." He points a finger at Rooster. "Don't forget what I said about Mississippi. She'll do fine with Priest. No worries."

Rooster's face slips into a neutral expression. "Thank you."

"All right." Ice slaps Rooster's shoulder and gives me a quick handshake. "Shiny side up!" he shouts to everyone.

That seems to be the cue for the guys to fire up their bikes. The deafening rumble fills the parking lot. Heidi whoops and waves to us from her spot on the back of Murphy's bike. Trinity also turns to wave.

Murphy and Steer ended up at the front of the pack, followed by Wrath and Pants, Dex and Jigsaw, and finally Griff and Remy. The guys had teased Griff and Remy about making them ride behind the RV but ultimately decided that wouldn't be safe and allowed them to ride in the last position of the pack. I assume the choice of formation has to do with their positions in the club but don't ask for details.

"Ready?" Rooster asks.

"Heck, yeah." I hurry over to my side but Rooster's right behind me to open my door and give me a boost into the cab of the truck.

As I gaze out the window, taking in the peacefulness of the mountains behind the clubhouse, I feel like a newborn baby bird leaving my nest of safety. Older, wiser, and more jaded than when I started the tour. But the few days I spent here holed up at the clubhouse helped me regain some of my confidence.

Look out world, Shelby Morgan's back, surrounded by bikers, and taking no shit!

CHAPTER THIRTY-SIX

Shelby

WE'VE MISSED SO MANY DATES—MOST OF THE SOUTHEASTERN COAST LEG of the tour, to be exact—but Dawson was able to reschedule the one in Atlanta, so that's where my triumphant return to the stage ends up.

It's a sultry night. Everyone's excited. Backstage is bursting with people—new security people, Dawson's regular road crew, Rooster's club brothers.

Still, I'm shaking in my boots when the time comes to make my entrance.

Deep breath.

Walk out with your head held high.

Trent nods as I pass him and my lips quiver into something that I doubt looked all that reassuring.

I should be excited to be back on stage, right?

All my armor's in place—makeup, hair, dress, boots, microphone—but as I stare out into the crowd, I can't open my mouth. What if another wacko is out there waiting to attack?

I open my mouth but can't follow through.

The band keeps playing even though I've missed my cue.

My mouth opens.

No sound comes out.

This is bad.

I'm better than this. The urge to stamp my foot in frustration sizzles down my leg. Instead, I beam at the crowd. My smile falters, some people are startin' to look at me a lil' funny.

I glance over my shoulder. Rooster's waiting, blocking the entrance to the stage. Murphy's inconspicuously tucked into a corner—well, as inconspicuously as someone his size can be—his black leather cut almost blending into the stacks of equipment, light glinting off his dark red hair. My gaze pings to the right. Wrath and Pants are stationed on the opposite side of the stage. Wrath's heavily muscled and tattooed arms are crossed over his broad chest, his gaze scanning the crowd while Pants' bulky frame blocks the entrance to the stage.

I turn to Rooster. He flashes a confident smile, nods, and gives me a thumbs up. "*You've got this,*" he mouths.

I glance at the space below the stage reserved for photographers and other show workers. Trinity's crouched with her camera, aimed and ready. Heidi stands behind her, weighed down with two bags of equipment, alert and waiting, cheeks pink with excitement.

An awful lot of people here to watch me choke.

So much for my victorious return to the stage after my "horrible ordeal," as Miranda keeps calling it.

The more I worry about embarrassing myself, the harder it gets to open my mouth.

Finally, I close my eyes and take a deep breath.

"Sometimes your white knight rides a Harley,
Sometimes he saves you from drowning
When you're only in three feet of water...
I've had a lot of dreams come true,
But none as sweet as your rescue
Hello, stranger,
Am I in danger?
Only of losing my heart,
I knew it from the start
Soon I'll be singing in different towns,
And you'll give some other girl your crown
I knew I was in danger,

Of losing my heart to a stranger..."

As the last words leave my lips, I stand in the middle of the stage, head bowed, absorbing the crowd's appreciation. The realization of how much my life has changed since I wrote "White Knight" washes over me.

I haven't *lost* my heart. I've given it freely and willingly to a man who supports me without reservation.

In fact, there's a damn good chance I wouldn't be on this stage tonight if it wasn't for Rooster.

I tip my head to the side and find him still standing in the same spot. Now he's clapping and cheering as loudly as any member of the audience.

"I love you," I mouth the words slowly so he can catch each one.

"Love you too!" he shouts.

Laughing, I turn back to the crowd and raise my arms over my head. "Thank you so much! How y'all doing tonight?!"

I pull the microphone from its stand and pace a few steps to the left. "Phew! It feels good to be here!"

A wave of shrill whistles and screams from the audience enthusiastically agrees.

After I banter a little more with the crowd, the band launches into "Big Lies."

This time, I don't miss my cue.

We run through my short set list and by the end, my cheeks ache from smiling so much.

I'm okay. I did it! I survived.

Waving to the crowd, I run off the stage, right into Rooster's waiting arms.

"You were amazing!" he shouts.

"I almost choked." I bury my face against his chest.

He wraps his arms around me and rests his chin on the top of my head. "Couldn't tell. Just sounded like you were giving the band an extra-long intro for the song."

I pull back and stare at the hard line of his jaw. Teasingly, I jab my finger in his stomach to lighten him up. "So you *could* tell."

His serious expression doesn't shift. "Only because I *know* you and I've watched you perform the song. No one in the crowd noticed. And if they did, fuck 'em. I'd like to see any of 'em get back on stage so soon after what you just went through."

"Good show." Murphy walks over to us and gently pats my back. "Atlanta loves you." He points toward the sliver of the crowd visible from back here to a group of people holding up a huge sign proclaiming, "Atlanta's got Shelby Morgan's back."

Between the bright lights and the anxiety over screwing up the show, I'd been blinded to everything in the crowd. Now, I'm able to stop and observe the little details I missed. "That's so sweet." I duck my head, heat stinging my cheeks. My gaze swings between Murphy and Rooster.

"Thanks for sticking around. I felt so much better knowing you guys were here." *Working for free,* I add to myself. But Rooster's said over and over, it's a non-issue, so I won't bring it up again.

Wrath ambles up to our small group, holding Trinity's hand. Heidi runs up to Murphy, excitedly sharing her experience in the "pit."

Rooster checks his phone. "I need to go check out the meet-and-greet room." He glances up at Wrath and then Murphy. "Stick with her?"

They agree. Rooster gives me a quick kiss on the cheek before taking off with Jigsaw and Dex.

"Can I ask you something, Shelby?" Wrath rumbles. I crane my neck and study his serious expression. Depending on the situation, I've noticed he's either full of humor or so terrifying, I want to pee my pants and run away when he settles his scary eyes on me. Tonight, he seems more thoughtful than fearsome.

"Sure. Shoot."

"*Empty Room*. You write that?"

I swallow hard and drop my gaze. That song is so intertwined in the deepest parts of my soul. I should probably stop playing it live. Every time, it drags me back to losing Hayley and leaves me raw. I don't think I can stand to have one of Rooster's brothers ridicule something so personal. "Yes," I answer carefully, bracing myself.

"What's it about?"

My expression hardens as I tip my head back and meet his questioning eyes. "My little sister. Why?"

"It's hard to get all the words with everything going on." He tugs on his earlobe. "But I thought it was something like that."

"I probably shouldn't even play it. It's too personal." My way of warning him not to give me any snarky feedback.

A flash of sympathy creases his brow. "No, you should." He taps his chest. "It's honest. And it probably helps people more than you realize."

"Oh." I blink and glance away. *Honest.* I like that. "Thank you."

"Must be hard for you to play night after night."

"Yes and no."

"Shelby! Oh my God, I love you!" A shrill voice screams, interrupting our conversation.

Moving quick for someone of his size, Wrath turns, blocking me from view. Trinity squeezes in behind him, flanking my other side.

"Shelby will be signing down there in a few minutes," Murphy says, smoothly pointing her down the hall.

"But I don't have passes for that," she whines.

I tap Wrath's arm and he peers at me over his shoulder. "I can sign something for her."

He nods and nudges Murphy aside. The two of them provide a narrow passageway for me to say hello, sign a T-shirt, and take a quick selfie.

"Thank you so much, Shelby." She flashes some serious stink-eye at Murphy before taking off.

"Sorry. Rooster didn't tell us what he wanted to do if that happened," Murphy says.

"It's fine. We'll get the hang of it."

Wrath grumbles something I can't quite catch.

Rooster returns, holding out his hand to me. I curl my fingers around his gratefully and he pulls me into the middle of a circle of protection. I doubt anyone can even see me but people sure move out of the way.

Inside the room, Rooster stops to give the guys some instructions. Trinity nudges me. "I have a sign up. If people give me their email, I'll send a picture to them." She holds up her camera.

"You don't have to do that. That's a lot of extra work."

She shrugs. "That or I can set up a page where they can download their picture. Newsletter. Something."

"Thank you."

"You were amazing!" Greg slides by Trinity and wraps his arms around me. "I'm so proud of you," he says in a low voice. "How do you feel?"

"Good. Better than I expected. I was a little freaked out at first."

"But you blew them away." His expression shifts, something more concerned replacing the pride. "Now, are you ready for this interview tomorrow? It's early. They have a table reserved at the hotel restaurant."

"I'm going to be way too nervous to eat."

"Well, the meal's on them, so order big and take it with you." He grins. "Logan has the info but I sent it to your email too." He casts a suspicious look at Wrath and Murphy and sighs. "I assume Logan will be attending the interview with you but do *all* the bodyguards need to be there? It's really not the message I want to send—"

"They'll be nearby but it'll just be me at the interview, Greg," Rooster says.

"Well, I'll be there too," Greg huffs and tugs at the collar of his shirt. "They want to interview Trent and the guys as well. I've already spoken with them. They're supposed to stick to the tour and how much they love touring with you. Nothing more."

I can't imagine the guys saying anything bad about me. But who knows? Maybe they're pissed that we lost a bunch of tour dates and got grounded in Virginia for so long. While I was recovering at the clubhouse, they were stranded at the hotel. Then again, they were stranded with Dawson and his crew, so they should've had plenty of time to do some networking or line up other gigs.

I'm probably lucky I still have a band at all.

CHAPTER THIRTY-SEVEN

Shelby

The trees. I have to make it to the trees.

I'm running, running, running. Rough, uneven ground grabs and twists at my boots, tugging and pulling. I'm going to fall. He'll catch me the moment I hit the ground.

Breathing hard, panting, working my arms and legs so fast they burn. No matter how fast I run, I can't seem to get away. Did he already drug me? Why won't my legs move? The trees are just out of reach.

Something catches my hair. Tugs. My body flails, falling backwards into a wild abyss of nothing but fear.

He caught me.

I scream and scream but no sound comes out of my mouth.

"Shelby! It's okay. Shelby. Wake up, baby."

I blink and slowly the inside of the RV comes into focus. Rooster's strong arms anchor me. I rub my fingers over the soft sheets, faintly picking up the cheerful flamingo print in the murky darkness.

"You okay?" Rooster rasps, reaching for the light switch.

I squeeze my eyes shut. "I think so."

"Who are we killing?" another voice asks.

A short scream tears out of my throat. My body jumps, poised to run into the night.

Warm, golden light fills the area around Rooster's side, illuminating Jigsaw standing next to the bed with a baseball bat in his hands.

"The fuck, man?" Rooster grumbles.

"I heard Shelby screaming." Jigsaw's gaze lands on me. "You all right?"

Heat stings my cheeks. It's bad enough being weak in front of Rooster, but now Jigsaw's witnessed me having a panic attack *and* heard me screaming in my sleep like a little girl.

My tongue's too twisted with embarrassment to answer. But my gaze lands on his shirtless torso. Before I can stop myself, I'm staring at his overstuffed boxer briefs and muscular thighs.

Jigsaw clears his throat.

I lift my gaze and Jigsaw pins me with mischievous eyes. "See anything you like?" He props the bat against the floor and lifts his arm, showing off the rest of his physique.

"Could you put on some damn pants?" Rooster growls, slapping Jiggy with a pillow. "No one needs to see *that* in the middle of the night."

"Wrong." Jigsaw wags his finger in Rooster's face. "Many females would kill for—"

"Sorry I woke you," I whisper, thoroughly embarrassed.

Jiggy drops the playful attitude. "It's okay, songbird. I was just worried."

"Thank you."

He turns away and my gaze lands on the crisscross pattern of scars lining his back. Even covered in ink, they're noticeable. I slap my hand over my mouth to muffle my gasp of surprise. I turn my questioning eyes on Rooster but he shakes his head at me. His eyes seem to plead with me to not ask any questions.

"Sorry," I whisper.

"It's all right." Rooster holds out his arms. "Come here."

I snuggle closer and he reaches out to snap the light off. "You want to talk about your nightmare?" he asks.

"Not really." The awful feeling of being chased won't go away. "I think maybe I'm worried about the interview. I don't want to rehash all the stuff that happened to me. If they ask for details—"

"Hey," he says in a soothing voice, "Miranda said she gave them clear guidelines on what they could ask and what was off-limits. If they step out of line, I'll be right there to yank 'em into place. They keep it up, we'll walk out. End of story."

I wrap my arms around him, hugging him tight. "Thank you."

He kisses the top of my head. "You're totally safe, Shelby. I promise. Get some sleep."

I'm already drifting. At least this time, a sense of calm follows. Who knows how long it will last.

ROOSTER

Haven't made it to the bathroom to brush my teeth yet, but Jiggy's already in my face. I blink my bleary eyes. "What?"

"She okay?" Jigsaw asks.

I glance over my shoulder. "She's still sleeping."

He's waiting for me when I come out of the bathroom. "You're like a really annoying jack-in-the-box this morning," I grumble.

One corner of his mouth turns down ever-so-slightly. A sure sign I touched a nerve.

"Sorry," I mutter.

"She scared the shit out of me last night."

Even though I can guess the reasons why Shelby screaming in her sleep got under his skin, if I coddle him, he'll just get pissy with me. "Well, I guess you should've chosen to sleep at the hotel or outside with the others, then." I point to his shirtless torso. "She might ask you about your back if you keep parading around like that."

A sly smile replaces his grim expression. He slides his hands over his abs and pats his stomach. "Jealous? Worried she'll get an eyeful of all this perfection?"

"No. Since your annoying personality is attached, I don't have anything to worry about." I point the coffee pot in his direction. "Did you hear what I said?"

He shrugs and glances over his shoulder. "Tell her. I don't care."

That's a first. "Not my story," I mutter.

He retreats to the back of the RV and returns with a shirt. "Happy now?" he asks, slipping it on.

"Just trying to look out for you, bro." *You know, like I've been doing since we were kids.*

I glance at the clock. "Shit. She needs to be there in like an hour. Finish this for me?"

"Sure." He snatches the bag of coffee and the scoop out of my hand. "Go have glorious morning snugglefucks with your hot, famous girlfriend. I'll stay out here and play houseboy."

"Jesus Christ," I grumble, walking away and yawning. "You're too old to be so passive-aggressive."

I'm pretty sure he flips me off but don't bother turning around to confirm. Instead, I stop by the side of the bed and stare at Shelby for a few seconds. Hate like hell to wake her after she worked so hard last night. First, fighting her fears and getting back on stage, and then signing autographs and talking to fans until her voice went hoarse and I had to shut things down. Then her nightmare last night. She needs her rest. But if she blows this interview, it'll fuck up a lot of shit she's worked hard for.

"Shelby." I sit on the edge of the bed and gently run my hand over her back. "Baby, it's time to get up."

"Hmmm?" She burrows under her pillow.

"Come on." I glance at Jigsaw who finally has the coffee brewing. "You've got the interview."

"Shoot," she murmurs and flips onto her back, slowly stretching her arms over her head. "Ouch. I hurt everywhere."

I check the time again. "You have a few minutes for some yoga. I'll kick Jiggy outside."

"Hey!" Jigsaw yells.

She laughs softly and sits up, kissing my cheek. Her gaze slides to the clock "Crap. I don't have time for yoga. I barely have time for makeup."

"You don't need makeup. They said they were bringing someone, remember?"

"Yeah, I don't trust them." She reaches for an elastic and pulls her hair into a messy half-knot, half-ponytail. "What if they take one of those 'celebrities who look like ghouls without their makeup' gotcha photos?"

"Then I'll hunt them down and beat them senseless."

"Amen!" Jigsaw shouts.

Shelby chuckles and tosses back the covers to scoot by me. Tucking her elbows tight to her sides, she covers her face and runs by Jiggy. "Don't look, don't look!" she yells, slamming the bathroom door behind her.

I sigh and join him in the kitchen. "I didn't really consider how close quarters this would be. For her, I mean."

"You're used to me in your face every waking hour." He grins and pops half a muffin in his mouth.

"You have no sense of decency or shame."

"True story."

"Or boundaries," I add.

"One hundred percent," he agrees.

"Dick."

He shrugs and finishes the other half of the muffin. "You want me to go outside?"

"Gee, would ya?"

He ruffles my hair, grabs a cup of coffee and marches outside.

I knock on the bathroom door. "Place is clear."

"Okay." A few seconds later, she pops out of the bathroom. "You didn't have to kick him outside."

"You seemed uncomfortable."

She shrugs as she pulls clothes out of her drawers. "I imagine eventually it'll feel like having a big brother around." She pauses and seems to reconsider. "Except one that might notice and comment that I'm not wearing a bra in the morning."

"He will *not* notice or comment on that if he wants to keep breathing." Now I can't help dropping my gaze to her tits. "You look fantastic braless by the way."

She pulls her arms out of her sleeves and shimmies a bra under her shirt. "Thanks."

"What are you doing?" Like magic, she finishes fastening her bra, then slips off her nightshirt, quickly trading it for a tank top. "No one can see you."

She glances at the windows—covered by shades. "I know. I just need time to get used to everything."

A thought I'm not too happy about pushes its way into my caveman brain. "What did you do in the van?" I have to force out the next words. "With the guys?"

"Sleep in my bra." She shrugs. "Change under my blanket."

Fuck. For the first time, I kinda hate myself for saying goodbye to her in Texas. Knew damn well, even back then, that what we had was more than a hook-up, that she was special and I wanted her in my life long-term.

CHAPTER THIRTY-EIGHT

Rooster

Shelby's Mysterious White Knight

"What the actual fuck?" I pick up the magazine someone helpfully shoved under our door sometime either late last night or early this morning.

"No." I stare at the picture of us on the front of Glow. A national fucking magazine. My arm's around her shoulders. I'm staring down at her. She's staring up at me. It's sweet and sappy as fuck. My face is in profile but still recognizable.

I jam my fingers through my hair. This can't be happening.

Fuck.

I flip through the magazine, searching for the article.

There it is.

Full-page spread of Shelby on the roof of the hotel in the sunshine. No more pictures of my face, thank God. The one on the cover is bad enough.

At only twenty-two years old, Shelby Morgan possesses a rare Zen-like calm. She smiles warmly and takes dainty sips of her sparkling water. Every now and then her gaze strays to the enigmatic man watching her from across the room.

You'd never know that she was recently held captive by a mad man.

If this leads you to think the beautiful, up-and-coming country music star is all sugar and no spice, please reconsider.

"I'd rather call out the bullshit than smile my way through it. I did enough of that on Redneck Roadhouse."

It's the first time she's hinted that her experience on the show that launched her career was anything less than perfect. But that's old news. Today, she's still healing from being the object of a stalker's obsession.

"It was the most terrifying event of my life. I thought I was gonna die."

The article moves on to discussing the kidnapping. What details they couldn't pull from Shelby, the writer must have tried to gather by interviewing other people. Dawson's mentioned but he must not have been cooperative because there's nothing useful there. Whoever the author contacted at the FBI had "no comment on an ongoing investigation." So-called "anonymous sources" add details about the fire on Dawson's bus and the fact that Shelby was carried out in her trunk. I assume those "sources" can only be Bane or someone from Dawson's road crew. Shelby's band was interviewed but Trent assured me they spoke about the tour more than Shelby's kidnapping. Doesn't really matter, I guess. Still hate that all these people are gossiping about Shelby like she's an amusing tale to joke about over beers and not a human fucking being.

My phone buzzes and I check the message.

Z: I'm swooning over here!

A picture shows up. Z's big mouth making a ridiculous kissy face at a copy of the same magazine I'm holding in my hands.

Me: Why do you even know the word swoon?

Z: My wife says I make her swoon all the time.

Me: Are you sure she didn't say suffer?

Z: Definitely swoon.

Me: Since when do you read Glow?

Z: Since my VP made the cover.

Fuck. Great. Just what I need.

"What's wrong?" Shelby's voice trembles. "What's it say?" She reaches for the magazine.

There's no way to hide this from her, so I hand it over with an apology.

"Oh my God." Her eyes bug out as she studies the cover. "Logan, I'm so sorry."

"Why?"

"The club…I thought you didn't want to bring attention like this to yourself…"

I show her the photo Z sent me. "My president doesn't seem to have a problem with it. What I'm sorry about is that it took the attention off *you* and made it about *us* instead of your music."

"I never expected them to give a fig about my music. *Glow* is basically a big ol' gossip rag these days. They were only interested in a juicy story. Since I couldn't give them tons of details about the kidnapping, I guess they went another way." She shrugs. "The check cleared. As long as you're not mad at me, I'm not worried about it."

"I'd never be mad at you about something like this."

She stares at the cover again. "Did I ever tell you Dolly Parton was my hero growing up?"

I huff a laugh and tuck her hair behind her ear. "No, but I can picture that. She's pretty cool."

"She's a national *treasure,* Logan. Anyway, it always impressed me that she's been married for more than fifty *years*. Can you imagine?"

Before Shelby? No, I couldn't picture wanting to be with the same person that long. My father set the worst example possible in that department.

"They've always kept their relationship extremely private. Not a lot of photos or interviews. Her husband never wanted a piece of the spotlight. He never went to industry events or award shows with her. He's a quiet man and she wanted to protect him because she knew if he got the attention of the media, they'd never leave him alone."

"Don't know if that's possible these days. Everyone with a cell phone camera and a social media account thinks they're a fuckin' reporter now."

"That's true. Anyway, somehow they've made their marriage work all these years. I guess I thought that could still be a thing. I'm sorry."

She sounds so broken up, I don't know what to do but reassure her. "Shelby, I've known this was a possibility." I glance at the cover again, hating it so much. Wondering which skeletons from my past might see it. "Okay, maybe not my face plastered on the cover of a national magazine possibility, but everything will be fine."

I really hope that's true.

SHELBY

After reassuring Rooster I'm not mad about the article, it's time to call my momma. Lord knows, she'll have an opinion or ten to share with me and I want to get it over with early, so I can get ready for tonight's show in peace.

She answers after one ring. "Guess what I'm holdin' in my hand?"

Well, she sounds happy—a good sign. "*Glow* magazine?"

"With my baby girl on the cover!" she gushes.

"I never thought this would happen."

"How'd Rooster feel about them puttin' his face on the cover too?"

"Not that great, honestly."

She hums a noise I can't decipher.

"He's not keen on being public," I add.

"I imagine his club don't appreciate it too much either."

"So far, it's okay. His president seemed more amused than annoyed."

"Well, that's good." She lets out a long, slow sigh. "You knew they were going to want some juicy details about *something*. I'm glad you didn't give them much about your ordeal. You don't need the whole world salivating over those details or, Lord have mercy, some other nutter getting ideas."

"My thoughts too. Plus, I spoke to a lawyer friend of Rooster's and she advised me not to say much. And the FBI agent had already warned me not to give details to the press while the case is ongoing."

"Back up. Rooster's lawyer friend?"

"Uh, one of his brother's wives."

"Huh."

"He's done a lot for me, Momma." I hate the tentative note in my voice. "A friend of his set me up with the public relations person who cinched the interview for me. She's working on maybe having me attend the *Small Screen Music Awards*."

"Oh, honey. That would be so great. I would love to watch you walkin' as many red carpets as possible."

"Thanks."

"How's Trent?"

"All right. We haven't had a lot of time for chit-chat."

"Why not?"

"Uh, well. I'm ridin' with Rooster."

"Shelby." Her voice's thick with disapproval. Exactly the reason I haven't told her yet. "You're a star, you can't be riding on the back of his bike like some wild child. What if you get hurt?"

"I'm not a *star*. Not yet, anyway. And I'm not." I grit my teeth. If she says something nasty about the sweetest damn thing anyone's ever done for me, I swear I'm hangin' up the phone and never speakin' to her again. "Rooster bought…he bought one of those tow-behind RVs and a truck. You know, like the set-up you and Daddy always talked about when I used to sing at the fairs and stuff."

Silence.

"He surprised me with it before we left Virginia," I add.

"Well now," she breathes out. "Okay then. That's quite. Uh, that's quite a—"

"Commitment?"

"Yeah, I reckon so."

"It's really nice. I'll send you pictures later. He found the cutest little strands of flamingo lights and strung them all over my yoga space for me. It's real soothing. And it's been nice to have, you know, my own place to go after shows where I'm comfortable with all my stuff around me."

More silence.

"You there, Momma?"

"I'm here." I swear she sniffles. "Can I talk to him for a second?"

"He's meetin' with Dawson's crew right now. Why?"

"Why's he hanging out with Dawson's guys?"

"Security stuff. Dawson hired a whole bunch of security experts. Dawson invited Rooster and Jigsaw to take the class the company offers. All his roadies and crew are taking it too."

"Sounds like Dawson must've taken a shine to him, then?"

"I guess so. They seem to get along." I pause for a second, trying to come up with a way to broach my next topic. "You doin' all right, Momma? With the house and bills and everything?"

Before I left for the tour, I was contributing to the household. Since I haven't seen much in the way of funds from the tour yet, I haven't been able to help out. Now with that money from *Glow*, I can.

"I'm fine, honey. Picked up some extra shifts here and there. Without you home using up all the hot water, it evens out," she teases.

The familiar joke lightens my heart a bit. "*Glow* ended up paying for that interview." I laugh softly because I'm findin' out I'm woefully uneducated when it comes to financial matters. "You know I always wanted to buy you a house—"

"Shelby."

I keep right on going. "After taxes and everyone took their cut, there ain't enough for a house. But I want to cover the mortgage for the rest of the year, so you're not working all those extra hours."

"No. I'm your momma. That's my job."

"I'm twenty-two—"

"And you've been working and helpin' out 'round here since you were fourteen, something I hated having you do."

"I never minded."

"I know you didn't, baby. And it means a lot to me. But I want you to save that money."

"Momma, buying you a house has always been my goal and you know it. We used to talk about it all the time."

"And one day you will, Shelby. I have no doubt."

"But if I helped out, maybe you could work fewer shifts and come see some of the shows when we're in Texas at least."

She laughs softly. "Now, you're just playin' dirty."

"Is it working?"

"We'll talk about it when the time gets closer."

That's my momma, stubborn as all git out. Guess that's where I get it from.

CHAPTER THIRTY-NINE

Shelby

RUMBLING MOTORCYCLES YANK ME FROM A WARM, COMFORTABLE SLEEP. A few seconds later, my phone beeps.

I reach for it blindly and flick it on.

Trinity: Yoga time!

Isn't she chipper at ass-crack-of-dawn-o'clock?

I pat the bed but come up with nothing but cold, empty sheets. Huh. Rooster's up before me. No surprise. He seems to be an early riser. I make a mental note to ask if that's how he got his road name.

After splashing some water on my face, brushing my teeth and jumping into a pair of yoga shorts and a tank top, I pull out my mat, pop on my sunglasses and head outside.

The park we stopped at last night is fairly secluded. The guys had arranged to rent a back corner where we'd have some privacy. At the moment, Wrath and Murphy are moving two heavy picnic benches closer together.

Trinity bounces over with a colorful woven blanket draped over her arm. "Wrath sent the guys to the store for breakfast. Should give us forty minutes of private yoga time."

I chuckle at their ingenuity.

Two big strong arms wrap around my waist, yanking me in the air.

Rooster's beard tickles my skin as he peppers my cheek with kisses. "Morning, chickadee. Got a space all set up for you with no prying eyes."

The few mornings the girls and I had tried to get together for yoga attracted more attention than Rooster cared for. Honestly, it made me jittery too. I turn and loop my arms around his neck. "Thank you."

"We're all set!" Heidi jogs over waving her iPad in the air. "Swan's about to start class."

"I'm going to vomit if you keep moving the screen around!" Swan shouts. "Morning, Trinity! Morning, Shelby!"

"Oops. Sorry." Heidi slows her steps. "Where are we setting up?"

Rooster points to the truck that he's pulled tight to the curb. The grass is especially thick in that area and the truck blocks anyone in the parking lot from spying on us. "You can set the tablet up on the truck bed or on the ground. Whatever works better."

Trinity has the tablet now and she's busy talking to whoever else Swan has with her. "Is Lilly there too? I don't believe it," she says.

"I'm here," the dark-haired beauty who I remember is Z's wife waves at us. "Hope lied to get me to the clubhouse this early."

"If it makes you feel better, we're an hour behind you." Trinity points to the sky.

"No." Lilly laughs. "No that doesn't make me feel better."

"Where's my lil' buddy?" Trin asks.

"Rock and Z have the little ones," Hope answers. "They're 'helping' in the garage."

Trinity chuckles. "I want to say hi before we hang up, but let's get our yoga on."

"How are we doing this?" Swan's pretty face fills the screen again.

"Maybe set your camera back a bit so we can get an idea of what you're doing?" Heidi suggests.

"If I was doing this from Furious I'd have better equipment set up. Sorry, girls."

"It's fine," Trinity assures her. "I'm just happy to see your faces."

"I'm excited to practice with other people," I add. "I can follow along from your cues, Swan."

We make some adjustments, find our places, and settle down. Swan starts us off with five minutes of easy pose and meditation. I have trouble settling my mind and have to focus hard to anchor my breath.

ROOSTER

"That shit's harder than it looks." I lift my chin toward the girls who are quickly moving from a straight plank, down to their stomachs, then back to plank and into downward dog. Trinity and Shelby seem to be at about the same level. Although Trinity's longer legs seem to help her transition easier. Heidi struggles with a few advanced poses but never quits. "I don't know how they make it look so graceful."

"Damn right," Wrath agrees. "Takes a lot of upper body strength." He slaps Murphy's back. "I gave him a hard time about adding yoga classes but it's one of the best things we've done at Furious."

Murphy whistles "Holy shit. Never thought I'd hear you admit it."

"You have a good idea once in a while." He pokes the side of Murphy's head.

I shift my gaze to Wrath. "You must be *such* a joy to work for."

He grins at my sarcasm.

"Dex hasn't stopped bitching about how we stole his best dancer." Murphy takes a quick look around as if he's waiting for Dex to pop out from behind a tree at the mention of his name.

"Come on. Swan had to have been at Crystal Ball for years." Shit, she's been around as long as I've been in New York. "Strippers don't usually last that long."

"No shit," Wrath agrees. "She's a hard worker, so I get why he's so bent. Everyone loves her. The other dancers were so upset about her leaving, they're all coming to Furious to take classes now." He rubs his money-making hands together. "Helped pull us out of our slump. All the college boys are coming in to gawk at the strippers now."

While Wrath and I discuss gym business, Murphy keeps an eye on the girls. They're on their backs in something Shelby's called 'dead pigeon' when Murphy undoes his belt.

"The fuck you doing?" I ask, slapping his arm.

He scowls at me, doesn't answer, walks over and drops the belt down next to Heidi. She smiles up at him and scoops it up, wrapping it in her hands and using it around her foot for leverage.

"You better hope your pants don't fall down, bro," Wrath's voice booms halfway across the parking lot. "Ain't nobody here wantin' to see that pasty ass."

Murphy flips Wrath off and shrugs at me. "She doesn't have a strap with her. Trying to improvise."

Wrath rolls his eyes my way. "They *improvise* a lot." He adds air quotes around improvise in case I can't grasp his meaning.

I slap Murphy's chest. "Can't you control yourself, ya fuck beast?"

Wrath's not finished busting on Murphy this morning. "Do you have any idea how much Jack Daniels it takes to erase the vision of a Ginger Yeti violating the innocent little girl you've known since she was a toddler?"

"I'm not that innocent, Uncle Wrath!" Heidi shouts.

"We're all aware, Heidi-girl."

Murphy punches his arm and Wrath laughs harder.

"I feel like I'm missing out on all the fun being downstate," I joke.

They stop fucking around and stare at me.

"What? I'm not thinking of leaving Z or anything. Just saying." I paint a circle in the air with my fingers. "You guys are all tight. Even the girls."

"Where *are* you planning to land when she's off tour?" Murphy asks.

"Don't know yet. She's open to spending time in New York." I shrug, uncomfortable since I've been trying to avoid thinking about this too much.

Murphy slaps my chest. "You want me to drive your rig today so you can ride with Shelby? We got a good five hours ahead of us."

"You sure you don't mind?"

"Not at all." He waves his hand somewhere in the direction of north. "We got a long ride ahead of us when we head home. It'll give Heidi and me some time to talk."

"Yeah, brother. Thanks. I appreciate that."

SHELBY

As we're finishing in corpse pose, what sounds like hundreds of bikes thunder into the parking lot. Heidi jumps up to grab her tablet. She points toward their tent. "I'm going to talk to Alexa for a minute."

Trinity watches her for a few seconds before turning her attention on me. "How do you feel?"

"So good." I drop my gaze to the ground. "I'm a little sad you guys are headed home soon, though."

"Aww." She pulls me in for a hug. "I'm gonna miss you too." In a lower voice, she asks, "You're not worried about all the alone time with Rooster, are you? You two seem to get along well."

"Oh. No." The corners of my mouth twitch. "At first, I was concerned. But we mesh well." Heat stings my cheeks. "I really never get tired of being around him. Is that weird?"

"No," she answers, quickly glancing over her shoulder at her husband. "I feel the same way about Wyatt. We each have our own things going on, but at the end of the day he's the only person I want to share my space with. We always have something to talk about or I just enjoy, you know, the quiet with him."

"Yeah, I've never felt that easy silence with someone before. It's soothing." I glance over my shoulder in the direction Heidi went but she's already on her way back.

She hands over the tablet to Trinity. "Hope wants to talk to you for a minute."

"Okay."

"Everything okay?" I ask. Heidi seems sort of down instead of invigorated from our practice.

Her lips form a wobbly smile. "I've been having fun out on the road with you. Thank you for letting me come along."

"Oh my gosh, of course." I pull her in for a quick hug. "I love having you guys with me. I feel a little selfish though. I know you have lots to do at home."

She nods and swipes at her eyes. "I miss my daughter. She's totally fine." A more genuine smile flashes over her face. "She's having the *best time* with her aunties and uncles as she just told me."

"Aww. That's good, though."

"It is," she agrees quickly. "I appreciate them so much. I wouldn't have been able to finish school or accomplish any of the stuff I've done the last couple years if I didn't have Rock, Hope, and my brother helping us out. I know how lucky I am. My friend Dawn's a single mom and I see how rough it is on her."

"It's nice to have people you trust looking after her."

"Sorry." She swipes under her eyes again and pastes on a smile. "I know you're not a kid person. You don't want to hear all this."

I can't help hugging her again. "Maybe. But I'm a Heidi person, so I don't mind listening at all. I'd have trouble leaving that bundle of cuteness too."

"Thanks, Shelby." She squeezes me once more before letting go. After a few laugh-sniffles, she wipes her hands over her cheeks. "This is why Murphy says we need to add to our family sooner than later. So we'll still be young enough to do all the traveling we want once they're out of the house."

I burst out laughing. "I guess he's got a point."

"Yeah, when we go on any big club trips, Carter drives one of the vehicles, so the kids can come along. We have a big family party while the guys are all doing club stuff."

"Which one is Carter?"

"Oh, sorry. He's my soon-to-be-sister-in-law's little brother. Phew! That's a mouthful!"

I laugh with her, thinking over what she's told me. "Y'all have a very 'takes a village' approach to child-raising, huh?"

She squinches her nose. "Yeah, I guess we do. It's nice." Her expression shifts to something almost melancholy. "I went to live with my grandmother when I was little and it was pretty lonely. None of my kids will ever have to deal with that."

"Ugh, I woulda ended up dead if Grandma Morgan had raised me." I shudder at the thought.

"Yeah, mine was no picnic either," she mutters.

The guys have all returned and seem awfully disappointed we're done with yoga. No one dares say it, since Wrath's wearing what I'd call an I-dare-you-to-open-your-mouth scowl.

"Let's get everyone fed." Trinity claps her hands together and hands out tasks for everyone.

They work out a system on the grills scattered around the campground and in no time we're sitting down to plates of bacon, sausage, and piles of scrambled eggs.

Rooster nudges me and leans in. "Murphy volunteered to drive the truck for a bit. Feel like ridin' with me today?"

"Yes." I flick my gaze across the table at Murphy. "Thank you. That was very thoughtful."

"I would've offered too," Jigsaw says with a pout.

"And yet, you didn't," Dex says.

"I'm really going to miss you guys." I reach over and tap Murphy's hand.

"I'm not going anywhere, songbird," Jigsaw reassures me.

A faint smile ghosts my lips. "I know, Jiggy. I'm glad. I definitely feel safe with you on board."

He lifts his chin, giving Rooster a smug smile.

"I'm sticking around too," Dex announces.

"You are?" My eyebrows shoot up. "Oh, that's great, Dex. Thank you."

"I'm staying too, Shelby!" Pants shouts from the next table.

"Same!" Steer raises his hand.

"They're not being noble, Shelby," Hustler yells. "They just can't find any ass at home."

"Fuck off," Rooster growls.

"You guys are terrible." And Lordy, I hope that's not the only reason why they're sticking around.

My phone buzzes and I pick it up, quickly glancing at the message that pops up. "Oh look!" I nudge Rooster and show him Miranda's text.

Miranda: You've been nominated for best video of the year at the Small Screen Music Awards.

"What is it?" Heidi asks.

Heat stings my cheeks. I don't know why I feel embarrassed talking about this. It's not like everyone hasn't watched me up on stage night after night. "I've been nominated for a *Small Screen Music Award.*"

All the guys cheer and whistle, startling the birds and squirrels gathered around our tables.

"Nice job, Shelby!" someone yells.

"I remember watching those when I was a kid," Steer says. "That's cool as hell, Shelby."

"Thanks," I mutter, glancing down at my lap.

"Congratulations." Rooster ducks down and brushes a kiss over my lips. "Proud of you."

"Not sure it's anything to be proud of. She made it sound like it was a handshake kind of thing."

"The whole world is a handshake thing," Jigsaw says. "Be proud, Shelby. You put in the hard work."

That helps me find my smile again. "Thanks, Jiggy."

"Awww, Jiggy." Someone makes kissy noises at him. "Such a philosopher."

Jigsaw rolls his eyes and throws his middle finger in the air. Rooster shakes with laughter and high-fives Jiggy over the table.

My phone buzzes again.

Dawson: Congrats, Shelby. Just heard the news.

"More good news?" Trinity asks.

"Dawson congratulating me."

Heidi presses her hand to her chest. "She has Dawson Roads texting her like it's no big deal."

"You lettin' that guy text your woman, Rooster?" Hustler asks.

"You need us to fuck him up, bro?" Steer throws a few fake punches in the air.

My eyes widen in terror. "God no."

"They're just messin' with me," Rooster says.

"We're civilized," Steer assures me with a maniacal grin.

"Not really," Dex mutters.

Everyone pitches in to clean up, leaving the grounds neater than when we found them.

"Leave no trace behind," Pants explains when I mention how tidy everything looks.

Rooster checks his phone and quickly taps out a message. "All right! Listen up. We need to be there by three, so we're moving at a fast clip. Greg says roads are clear. We shouldn't have any issues."

"Let's roll!" someone shouts.

"You need to get your riding gear on," Rooster says, placing his hands on my hips and steering me toward the RV.

"So do you."

"No funny business," Jigsaw warns. "We're rolling out in ten."

"Keep your pants on," Rooster grumbles.

"No, that's what I'm asking *you* to do."

"Har. Har." Rooster shakes his head but the rest of the guys laugh.

Inside the RV, I race around, searching for something to wear.

"I've got what you need here," Rooster calls out.

"That right?" I stop and blink at the two shiny bags with Harley Davidson logos on the front he has laid out on our bed.

"Meant to give this to you sooner but since we weren't on the bike…"

"What…what is it?"

"Just some thicker jeans meant for riding, leather jacket, gloves, stuff I should've bought for you sooner."

"But I'm okay."

"We're traveling a longer distance and these roads are faster. I'd rather you be safe and a little sweaty, than roadkill."

"Yikes. When you put it that way." I shake out the jeans and study them. "How'd you know my size?"

He shrugs. "I pay attention?" He hooks his fingers in the waistband of my shorts and tugs, peering into the gap. "I can read a tag?"

Laughing, I push him away and hurry out of my shorts and into the jeans. They're a stiff, sturdy denim. A little snug in the hips and thighs, but I'm guessing that's the lack of spandex.

Rooster sits on the bed and pulls a box out of one of the bags. "Riding boots. Your cowgirl boots are cute but not quite what you need."

"When did you do all this?"

"A while ago." He motions for me to move forward and rest my foot on his leg. "You were being weird about me buying stuff for you so I figured I'd wait until you needed 'em."

"Logan," I whisper. "It's not that I don't appreciate—"

"I know." He pats his leg. "Stay still." He takes his time, carefully lacing the boots tight and secure.

"Thank you," I say when he's finished.

He dumps the rest of the stuff out. "Gloves. Jacket. You might want to tie that bandanna around your forehead under your helmet too." Everything's black leather except the bandanna which is flamingo pink.

"All right. Let me throw my hair in some braids first."

I shamelessly let out a low whistle and squeeze his buns while he's changing. He peers at me over his shoulder. "Don't start something you don't have time to finish."

With all his brothers right outside our door we don't have the time *or* privacy. "Thanks for giving us yoga time this morning."

"No problem. Wrath figured sending the guys out for breakfast supplies would give you three enough space."

"Perfect timing. And Murphy was so sweet bringing over his belt for Heidi to use as a strap. They're just the cutest."

"Cute." He chuckles softly. "Yeah, they're good together. I got a lotta respect for Heidi. She always has Murphy's back. And she loves the club as much as any brother I've ever known."

Is that a hint that Rooster wants *me* more involved with the club? How would that work when I'm on the road so much? And when I'm not on the road, I live in Texas?

Although, if I were going to pull up roots and move for anyone, it'd be Rooster. Not that he's asked me to.

I like being around his brothers. They've definitely made the tour a whole lot more fun. And I've loved hanging out with Trinity and Heidi. For once I feel like I have true girlfriends who aren't waiting to stab me in the back.

I'm not sure how to respond, so I shift the subject. "Poor Heidi was a lil' weepy about missin' her daughter and I felt so bad."

"Yeah, I bet." He finishes lacing up his boots and glances at me. "You talk it out with her?"

"A little. She seemed uncomfortable because she said I'm not a 'kid person' but that doesn't mean I don't wanna listen to a friend's troubles, ya know?"

"I'm sure that meant a lot to her."

"I hope so." I bite my lip and glance at the door. "Can I tell you somethin'?" I whisper.

"Always," he whispers back with a teasing smile.

"Talkin' about it just reinforced me *not* wantin' kids. I'd hate having to make those decisions." I cock my head. "You think that makes me selfish?"

"Nope. I think that makes you smart." He stands and drops a kiss on my forehead. "Nothing wrong with a woman who knows what she wants and isn't afraid to go after it."

"Who said I'm not scared?"

"Are you?"

"Every dang night when I go on stage. But I still love it."

"Good. Then keep on doing it until that changes. Then we'll figure out where to go next."

We'll figure out. Damn, I like how that sounds. I tilt my head, staring up at him. "Are *you* happy? Is this what you want?"

His lips curve into a slow smile. "Riding the open road with my woman? Moving from place to place. A new adventure every day? Life doesn't get any better than that."

CHAPTER FORTY

Rooster

Life doesn't get any better than that.

Shoot, as soon as those words were out of my mouth, the weight of how right they felt settled into my bones.

I gave Murphy some quick pointers about the truck. He assured me he'd be fine. We rolled my bike out of the back and loaded his in. Things took longer than I expected so we're on the road later than I wanted but we're moving at a good clip.

Jigsaw's on my left. Shelby's at my back, arms squeezed tight around my middle. Every now and then I catch a few lyrics on the wind. Nothing I recognize, so she must be trying to work out new material.

The thought forces a smile on my face. Shelby's never hinted that she *doesn't* like to ride but she never seems particularly enthusiastic either. I'd love if she got the same thrill and peace from it that I do.

The highway's smooth—there's something to be said for roads that aren't battered by ice and salt all winter long. We move as a seamless unit. In the rear view, I catch the truck every now and then. Murphy seems to be handling it fine. I keep my eye on Remy and Griff too. They've settled into riding with a pack quicker than I expected—keeping pace and not getting in anyone's way.

Shelby's arms tighten around me.

A few words in her sultry voice swirl around us. "Diamond in the dust…about to combust." She grumbles and tries again. I can't help laughing to myself. One day in the not-too-far future, I bet I'll be listening to whatever she's working out on the radio.

As soon as we pull into the arena parking lot, Shelby hops off the bike, shaking herself out of her jacket. "Oh my Lord, I'm so hot!"

"Are you about to combust?" I tease.

Her jaw goes slack. Maybe I shouldn't tease her about her lyrics.

"You could hear me?"

"Bits and pieces. Liked everything I heard."

If it's possible, her cheeks turn even redder. I reach for her with one arm and turn the ignition off with my free hand.

"Ugh, I'm all sweaty."

"I know. I like it." I drag her in for a kiss. "Love having you back there."

Her stiff posture softens as she melts into me. "I like being there." She kisses my cheek and leans in to whisper in my ear, "It's hot the way you handle this big machine."

"Shelby!" Greg's voice intrudes from somewhere behind us.

She groans and squeezes her eyes shut.

"Hold that thought." I kiss her once more.

"Thank God you're here. I was starting to worry." Greg grabs her by the shoulders and gives her a weird, stiff-armed hug. "You need a shower."

"No kiddin'?" Shelby drawls, clearly annoyed.

"Sorry, sorry." Greg holds up his hands. "Congratulations. I talked to Miranda earlier. Dawson got a nod too so at least there will be a familiar face there."

"Oh why didn't he say so?" Shelby slaps her thigh. "Dang it. He texted to congratulate me. But I didn't know he got nominated too."

"You can talk about it later." Greg's gaze lands on me. "How'd it go?"

"Good. Thanks for the alternate route suggestion."

Greg nods and stops to talk to everyone for a second. He sure has loosened up about having all these bikers in his face night after night. Not that we gave him a choice.

"Oh, before I forget. I set up a visit through *Dream Makers*. Little girl. Ten, I think. She'll be at the meet-and-greet. I'll try to have her come in last so you can spend extra time with her."

"Thank you. What's her name?

Greg screws his face up. "Laura? Lorna? Something with an L."

"Can you send it to me, so I can get it right?" Shelby says, barely hiding her irritation.

"Yes. Yes." He flicks his gaze at me, but he's not gettin' any sympathy from me on this one. He knows how important those visits are to Shelby. "Can I have my star?" he asks me with a fraction of his old sarcasm before returning his attention to Shelby. "The dressing room here is probably the nicest one you've had on the tour."

"Go ahead, Shelby," I lift my chin toward the back entrance. "I'll bring your stuff in." As much as I hate letting her out of my sight, I'm the only one who knows what Shelby likes to have with her before a show. Murphy, Wrath, and the girls follow behind Shelby and Greg. No one will mess with Shelby as long as they're watching out for her.

Jigsaw walks over, stretching out his back.

"You all right?"

"Just tweaked. I shouldn't have teased Shelby about all the yoga. Now she probably won't teach me anything, will she?"

"You're smart. Look it up."

He follows me into the van. The other guys mill around outside, rehashing the ride here and going over their plan for the night.

"Logan! Glad you're here," Dawson calls out as I'm stepping out of the RV.

He jogs over the pavement to meet us, nodding hello to all my brothers.

"Congrats, heard you got a nod too," I say when he stops in front of me.

"Oh yeah." He waves it away. "It's good for Shelby. She can use the exposure."

I nod and keep moving.

"The big, big one, Wrath? He said half your crew is headin' home tomorrow?"

I nod to Remy, Griff, and Hustler. "Yeah, they gotta get back. I'll still have some guys with me, though."

"Good, good. Look, I got a buddy with a ranch about ten miles outta the city. We're parking there after tonight's show. Probably camp out at his place for a day or two." He motions toward the truck. "You're more than welcome to park there too and hang with us." He glances at the guys. "Everyone's invited. I already cleared it with him. We always do a big bonfire. There'll be beer, music, and barbecue. It's usually a fun time." He glances at the parking lot. "Some ladies from the show usually find their way out there with the crew..."

That gets the attention and approval of my more degenerate brothers, naturally.

"Thanks, Dawson." I squeeze his shoulder. "Appreciate it. Yeah, we'll do that tonight." I glance at Jigsaw. "We're heading to our mother charter in Mississippi tomorrow. Not sure if we're staying for the whole four days off, though."

"Don't matter. Come and go as you please." He glances over his shoulder again. "I gotta run. I'll text you the directions later."

"Thanks."

Once he's gone, the guys circle around me. "That sound all right to everyone?"

"Fuck yeah." Pants pulls a wrinkled, filthy pink card out of his pocket. I groan when I recognize it. "I gotta catch up or I'm gonna miss my patch."

"Jesus Christ," I groan.

"Oh, like you haven't been gettin' your card punched every night," he says.

"I'm gonna punch your *face* if you don't knock it off."

Jigsaw remains mercifully silent.

Pants scans the crowd already gathering at the front entrance. We're too far away to make out many details but that doesn't stop him from searching.

"Please, stop eyeballin' my girlfriend's fans like they're your own personal meat market," I warn.

As if I hadn't said a word, Pants continues. He slaps Jiggy's arm and leans in close. "Let's be selective with who we bring with us. Some of these girls are too loose." He makes a squeezing gesture with his hand. "I need a real tight pussy, you know?"

Steer groans. Jiggy rolls his eyes skyward as if this isn't the first time he's heard this complaint. Hustler laughs. Griff backs away like he wants to distance himself from the bunch of us. Remy shakes his head as if he's never heard of such a stupid problem.

Dex eyes Pants for a few seconds. "Bro, I'll be honest, that sounds like a *you* problem, not a *her* problem. Relax your fucking grip when you're jerking off."

Pants glances down at his meaty fists and laughs. "Yeah, you might have a point."

The rest of the guys crack up.

"And maybe stop watching so much porn," Griff suggests with a straight face. "It gives you brain damage."

"Not-even-a-prospect says, what?" Pants says, cupping his ear and pretending to search the area as if Griff is invisible.

Dex high-fives Griff while the rest of the guys laugh.

I'm so close to punching one of these fuckin' clowns.

I snap my fingers in front of Pants and Dex's faces. "If we're done with jack-off tips for the sad and single guy, can we get back to serious topics? Help me carry this shit inside." I jerk my chin toward Shelby's guitar case and one of her suitcases.

Even though I have no idea where we're going, I end up leading everyone into the building. It's the easiest way to get the pack moving. Backstage is chaos with roadies moving shit around and security checking everyone out. Dawson's bodyguards give us a cursory glance as we pass by. I stop and ask one of them where Shelby's dressing room is and he gives me directions.

Outside her dressing room, I nod to the guys. "Everyone has their pass, right?"

They either hold them up or dig the passes from their pockets.

"Dawson asked if I'd help his guys set up tonight. That all right with you?" Steer asks.

"That's fine."

We go over our game plan for the night and I set them free for now.

Hopefully everyone can behave tonight.

After I set Shelby's stuff inside the room, Jigsaw follows me out to the merchandise booth. We pass plenty of people. Some I recognize from the tour, some I don't.

Night after night, tons of women backstage try to get my attention.

Some seem to assume giving me a blowjob will get them access to Dawson, even though the pass around my neck clearly has Shelby's name on it. As much as I'm dying to tell them to fuck off, I don't want to be rude to Shelby's fans. Instead, I smile and politely—well, as polite as I can manage—decline.

She sends me a text, asking for tea, so after the merch booth, we head backstage again.

"Why the fuck didn't we think of going into this type of work when we were younger?" Jigsaw elbows me and not-at-all-subtly lifts his chin at a gaggle of girls in short, tight dresses who keep waving at us.

"How is this different from all the club girls you've ridden over the years?" I growl.

"I don't have the knowledge that any of them have fucked my brothers for one thing."

"No, but they've fucked every roadie and band dude who's passed through town."

"So judgmental," he scolds.

Yeah, maybe. More like, I don't need him doing anything that brings negative attention to Shelby.

"Come on, I don't want to leave her too long." I hurry to grab some hot water and honey packets. Wish I could get Shelby to eat something before she goes on stage but she always refuses.

"You know, I could've done this for you," Jigsaw says, grabbing a fistful of ketchup packets.

I smack the packets out of his hand and they scatter all over the table. He stares at them with wide cartoon-like eyes. "So. Much. Ouch. What the fuck, bro? We got no condiments in the RV."

"Shelby's allergic to tomatoes."

He glances at the scattered packets again. "Does ketchup even qualify as a tomato? It's mostly corn syrup and vinegar at this point."

"I don't want to take chances."

"On what? That I'll accidentally squirt ketchup down her throat?"

"Stop being a fucker." I grab as many sandwiches as my big hands can hold. Jigsaw snags cans of soda and we head back to Shelby.

At the door to her room, I stop him with an elbow to his gut. "Do not, and I repeat *not,* hit on Cindy tonight."

"Who me?"

I glare at him until he stops with the sad clown face.

"Fine, fine. I won't say a word."

Inside, Cindy's busy twirling sections of Shelby's hair around a hot iron. I set the tea and honey on the counter in front of Shelby and give her a quick kiss on the cheek.

I pass out sandwiches to Heidi and Trinity before taking a seat at the table to eat my own sandwich while answering some emails.

SHELBY

I'm buzzing with more energy than usual as I walk off stage. That has to be my most enthusiastic crowd yet. I don't know if people are finding me through streaming charts, word-of-mouth, the *Glow* article or something else, but Lord, please let it continue.

Rooster's waiting for me in his usual spot and I practically knock him over in my excitement to get into his arms.

"You sounded really good tonight," he says against my ear.

I pull back and stare up at him.

"You sound good every night," he adds with a flicker of amusement quirking his lips.

"Sorry I need you to tell me how awesome I am every—"

He silences me with a kiss. "Love saying it. You *are* awesome," he whispers against my lips. It's loud and noisy backstage so I feel his words more than hear them.

"Thank you." I wobble a little as he sets me down.

"Tired?"

"Nope."

Heidi and Trinity rush over to congratulate me on the show. "I got great shots tonight." Trinity tilts her camera so I can check out some of the photos.

I barely recognize myself. Must be the tiny screen. If I squint, I almost look like a younger Miranda Lambert. "Damn, you take good photos."

"It's the subject." She touches my shoulder. "That's you. Raw. No filters or retouching."

Jigsaw hands me a hot pink hand towel and I immediately press it to my face and chest. “Thank you.”

“Working hard tonight, songbird. I was exhausted just watching you.”

“Did you watch?” I always assume Jiggy’s bored and busy trying to pick up chicks during my set.

“Always.”

“Aww.” I pat his arm. “Thank you.”

“All right.” Rooster cuts in between us. “Let’s get you to your dressing room.”

I’m itching to leave or do something to burn off this extra energy, but I have a meet-and-greet to get ready for.

Inside my dressing room, I peer into the mirror and cringe at the raccoon smudges under my eyes. Cindy’s long gone for the night. I pull out my makeup bag, but Trinity takes it from me.

“Here, let me help.”

“You don’t have to.” She’s already done enough tonight.

“I don’t mind.” She finds a small container of Q-tips, dips one into some makeup remover and gently swipes under my lashes. A few dabs of concealer and a fresh stroke of black liner and I’m almost good as new.

She picks up my hair, pulling it into a ponytail and I let out a sigh. For some reason it felt especially hot and heavy on my neck tonight. “Do you want me to braid this off your face?” she asks.

“I can do a quick braid.”

“Let me try out this waterfall, fishtail braid I’ve been trying to learn.” She smirks at Heidi. “I tried to do it for Alexa but I can’t get her to sit still for me.”

Heidi shrugs. “Murphy’s the only one who can get her to sit still for braids.”

“Aw, that’s so sweet.” I let out a huge yawn. All that energy I had comin’ off stage seems to be disappearing fast. “I’m more likely to fall asleep on you.”

“Perfect.” Trinity pushes me into a chair in front of the mirror and gathers all my hair in her hands, gently combing through the sweaty bundle of sticky curls. Heidi sets a few hair elastics on the counter, then takes a seat on the couch to watch.

“You’re pretty good at this for someone who’s trying to learn,” I comment after she has about a third of my hair woven into a neat piece. Wild sprigs of hair still poke out around my ears but there's not much we can do to tame 'em.

"I can do it on myself but haven't practiced on *others* a lot yet," she murmurs, not taking her eyes off her task.

When she's finished, I hem and haw over changing out of my dress. Everything feels tight and uncomfortable. What I *really* want is to burrow into my jammy pants.

"Change if you want to, Shelby. You're the star. I don't think anyone will care," Trinity says.

"Honestly, if I was meeting my favorite singer—besides you—after a show, I'd think it was pretty cool and down to earth of them to show up more casual," Heidi adds.

All right. Can't argue with that logic. I pick out a pair of black lounging pants with rainbow stripes down the sides and the flamingo shirt Trinity gave me. In the bathroom, I sigh with relief when I slip into the pants.

"Feel better?" Rooster asks when I emerge.

"Yup."

The guys whisk me down the hall. By now everything is moving smoothly. They keep the line moving but back off when they sense I want to spend a little extra time with some of the younger fans.

A little girl wearing a *Dream Makers* T-shirt is the last in line and I move around to the front of the table to greet her. "Lorna, right?"

Her blue eyes light up. "Yes, that's me."

I squat down so we're eye-level. "How'd you like the show?"

"It was so good!" She claps her hands in front of her and executes a little spin. "I danced a lot."

"You're pretty good too."

"Thank you." She curtsies for me and my heart melts. She's the cutest darn thing.

"Ooo! I like your shirt. Pretty." She taps the flamingo on my chest.

"Thank you." I lift my chin toward Trinity who's talking to the girl's mom and showing her some of the photos she took. "My friend Trinity made it for me because she knows I love flamingos and cowgirl boots."

She tugs on the hem. "I want it."

"No, honey." Her mom hurries over to us, taking her daughter's hand. "You can't have Shelby's shirt." She gives me an apologetic laugh-smile.

"I can have one made up and send it to her," Trinity offers.

The mom protests but Trinity wins in the end, jotting down their information.

"You didn't have to do that," I say to Trinity after they say their goodbyes. "I'll pay you whatever it—"

"It's fine," Trinity cuts me off. "I was talking to her mom. They've been through so much. I wanted…" Her voice trails off for a moment. "I don't know how you do this on a regular basis."

"All right! Clear out!" one of the security guards yells. "We need to set this up for Thundersmoke."

"We're going!" I wave at the guy. "Sheesh," I mutter under my breath. "Every dang night."

Heidi's busy collecting my stuff from the table, while Trinity packs up her camera equipment. Wrath scowls at the guard who yelled at us and I tap one of his tree-trunk arms to get his attention.

He raises one blond eyebrow. "Yes?"

"You sure you guys have to go home tomorrow? Trinity and Heidi are the best damn helpers. You too, of course."

He rumbles with laughter, and thoughtfully strokes one hand over his neatly-trimmed, dark blond beard. "Murphy and Heidi have to get back. Trin and I could be persuaded to stick around for a few more days."

"Oh, yeah?"

"What's up?" Rooster asks, wrapping an arm around my shoulder.

"Nothing." Wrath winks at me. "Your girl thinks I'm a better bodyguard than you."

Rooster slowly looks him up and down. "Well, you're built like a fuckin' tank, bro."

Wrath drops his cocky smirk. "No, seriously. I was thinking, it's fuckin' stupid not to drop in and say hi to Priest if I'm this close." He jerks his head toward Pants and Steer who have joined our conversation. "Blink's been wanting to meet with Steer and me for a while. Might as well get it over with."

Pants cocks his head. "Blink never reaches out to me."

"We'll fix that while we're there." He reaches over and slaps Pants' cheek hard enough to rattle some teeth. "Can't have you feelin' left out."

I assume this is all club business stuff. But no one tells me to get lost, so I just stand there enjoying the way they all joke around and tease each other. All good-natured, well, sort of. No one gets bent out of shape. They laugh every insult off. Everyone takes it as hard as they dish it out.

"All set!" Heidi hands me a tote bag with all the supplies I brought.

"Shoot. I'm sorry. You didn't have to do that."

"It's fine."

"Party time!" Pants shouts, marching out the door with his arms raised over his head.

Heidi laughs. "One last party before we head home."

"Aw, come here." I envelop her in a hug. "I'm going to miss you so much."

She squeezes me just as tight. "Me too." She pulls back. "Hopefully you'll come through New York often." Her gaze skips over my head. "When you're not on tour."

I've been trying hard not to think about it but the worry always beats at the edge of my mind. Between recording the next album, going home to help my mom, and getting ready for the next tour, I won't have a lot of free time.

"I'll try like hell." I'm not sure who I'm trying to convince.

Truth is, I won't be puttin' down roots anytime soon. And what are the chances Rooster will be able to keep following me around the country?

CHAPTER FORTY-ONE

Rooster

"YOU'RE UP, DAWSON!"

The flickering firelight plays over Shelby's face, gleaming off her glossy lips. We're way out in the middle of nowhere on some guy's ranch. Got the truck and RV parked a good distance from the fire. My brothers are busy carrying on with the roadies, band members, and the ladies who followed us out here. At the moment, I'm sitting next to Shelby nursing a beer and watching her shuffle her Tarot cards.

"Ready?" she asks.

"Hit me!" Dawson's definitely knocked back a few bottles. I was a little surprised he agreed to a Tarot reading. Although it's not as lengthy as other ones I've seen Shelby do. She's pulling one card for what she called a "quick, focused" reading.

"You have to pull the card." Shelby cocks her head. "Try to have a clear question in mind when you do."

"That might be difficult," I mutter loud enough that Dawson hears me and grins.

"Thought bikers liked to party?" he shouts even though I'm less than three feet away from him.

"I thought rock stars liked to party?" I counter, gesturing toward the groupies at the edge of our circle who keep flashing their tits at him.

He makes a snort-chuff sound and waves his arm in the air. "Gettin' too old for that."

"Wasn't aware there's a cut-off," Wrath says.

Dawson wags his finger about two feet from Wrath's face. "You two aren't over there, either."

Somehow Trinity makes sense of his word jumble. "We're an old married couple." Trinity giggles and rests her head against Wrath's chest. "Come on, let's see what card you pull."

Shelby shuffles the deck again before setting the cards between them face down. Biting the tip of his tongue, Dawson studies the cards with the intensity of a gambling addict choosing his lucky lottery numbers.

Finally, he pulls a card and hands it to Shelby.

I catch the quick downturn of her mouth when she scans the card. To me it just looks like a man lying face down with ten swords poking out of his back. Backstabber? Well, fuck. The universe sure has a nasty sense of humor. Must by why Shelby's forehead's crinkling with apprehension.

"Well, how am I gonna die?" Dawson asks.

Given the card, I wince at his question.

"We're not predicting your death," Shelby says in a stern tone she doesn't use often. "Gosh, that's morbid." She lays the card in front of him. "Ten of Swords. It's a card of betrayal. Not death."

I swear Dawson's eyes are about to bug out of his head. Hopefully, they don't roll into the bonfire.

"Well, shit, Shelby." He whistles. "This is downright spooky. What's it mean? Give me the full story."

"What was your question?"

He flicks his gaze toward me and then Wrath briefly. "What should I work on next? That's kinda what I had in mind."

"*Kinda* could have clouded the reading." She gently runs the pad of her finger over the shiny surface of the card. "The man's been betrayed by people close to him, causing him great emotional pain."

Well, this got uncomfortable fast.

I dare to sneak a look at Wrath, praying he won't crack a joke. Shelby's livelihood for the next couple months depends on Dawson's tour.

Wrath's face is stone-cold blank. I catch movement under their blanket. Trinity's pretty focused on him. Maybe he's not listening to our conversation at all and just trying not to come in his pants.

"Like the picture suggests, he's been stabbed in the back by people he trusted."

Gotta give it to the cards on this one. Having your girlfriend cheat on you with your best friend and then participating in the kidnapping of your opening act is about as close as a man can get to having ten knives shoved in his back without feeling the bite of an actual blade.

"If that ain't on the nose," Dawson mutters.

"Sorry."

"No, go on."

"Career wise, it could mean working too hard or colleagues gossiping about you."

"No doubt about that." He takes a long pull from his bottle of beer. "What else?"

"Well." Shelby studies the card and taps her finger against her chin. "You have to accept the situation in order to move forward. Things can only improve from this point, you know?" She taps the corner of the card. "See here, the sun is rising. A new day. New chance to start over. Ten is also connected to a new life cycle so a new beginning of sorts."

Dawson's hanging on every word. I can't tell if Shelby's making stuff up on the fly to ease the sting of the card or that's really what she sees. Either way, it's entertaining as hell.

"Thank you, Shelby." Dawson grabs his beer bottle and moves closer to the fire.

"My turn?" Trinity asks, crawling out of Wrath's lap. She and Shelby stare at each other, then Dawson for a few seconds, then shrug at the same time.

"Come on over." Shelby pats the blanket in front of her and picks up her cards again. "Want to try a three-card reading?"

"Whatever you're in the mood for."

Shelby shuffles her deck slowly, careful not to let any cards escape. Finally, she lays them out and has Trinity pull three and leave them face down. One by one, Shelby turns them over. This time, she smiles as she studies the cards.

"Is it good? That one looks a little scary." Trinity taps the first one—a leaning towering inferno.

"Past." Shelby taps the card. "The Tower represents abandoning truths we've held for a long time. Discarding the old ways and taking on new beliefs." Her gaze shifts briefly to Wrath. "Major changes in the foundation of a relationship."

Trinity wrinkles her nose and turns toward her husband. "Do we still technically count as newlyweds?"

"Maybe." He sits forward, showing more interest in the reading now.

"The present." Shelby moves to the next card. "Two of Cups." Her lips curve into a serene smile. "This is nice. See how connected the two of them are? It's about the power of two people coming together. Bonding."

"Aww." Trinity reaches over and curls her fingers around Wrath's hand.

"Future." Shelby holds up the last card. "The Sun. Moving toward something great, good fortune, happiness, and success."

"That definitely sounds good."

Shelby sets the sun card back down and studies all three again. "Looking at them as a whole, I'd say you've survived major changes that shifted your world view. More than once, maybe. You've found a loving partner, and will have a happy future together."

"She's a genius." Wrath nods at Shelby. For once, I don't think he's being sarcastic.

"Phew." Shelby rolls her shoulders. "I always get nervous reading cards for other people." She flicks her gaze toward the brooding Dawson and lowers her voice. "Never know if you're going to hit a nerve or piss 'em off. Yours was a good one. A nice high note to close the readings."

"You're not going to do mine?" I ask.

"Nope. I already know what your future holds."

"Yeah? What's that?"

She beams the widest smile I've seen all night. "Me."

CHAPTER FORTY-TWO

Rooster

IT'S NOT OFTEN I ROLL INTO OUR NATIONAL HEADQUARTERS. I'VE CERTAINLY never been here without my local president. And while I met with Priest after getting voted in as VP in my charter, I haven't been in his castle since then.

I don't want Shelby to worry about any of that stuff, so I keep my expression impassive and my movements easy as I take her hand and help her out of the truck.

Hopefully Priest won't razz my ass too bad for riding in on four wheels instead of two.

Jiggy ambles over to us, rubbing his hands. "Ready, bro?"

"Yeah, you?"

Pants walks over and thumps Jiggy on the back hard enough to propel him forward. "Feels good to be here, right?"

Jiggy shoots a glare at him over his shoulder. "Easy, ya fuckin' beast."

Dex joins us, glancing over at the clubhouse every couple seconds like he's dying to get this over with. "Your show, VP. Lead the way."

"Thanks a lot," I grumble. Though, Dex has a point.

Wrath probably has the most seniority out of all of us but the fucker only smirks at me when I suggest he go in first.

Since it's the middle of the day, no one's guarding the door. I don't doubt for a second whoever's inside is already aware of our arrival. This place has more security than a damn diamond vault.

"Phew. I'm melting." Shelby pushes her damp hair off her forehead. "Mississippi heat is no joke."

"Texas heat is pretty rough," Jigsaw says.

"Ain't no heat like Mississippi heat," Pants adds.

"Great. Thanks for the weather update, everyone." Dex peers down at Shelby. "Not you, sweetheart."

As we reach the door, it swings open. A prospect hurries to step out of our way. I motion for Shelby to go ahead and follow her.

The dark, cool air of the clubhouse is a welcome relief from the outside heat.

"I'll go grab the prez," the prospect squeaks out before running away.

"Welcome!" Priest's booming voice greets, approaching from across the room. He stops to shake hands and share a few words with Dex first. Knowing Priest, he'll get to me last.

"Dang," Shelby whispers. "I never knew there were so many silver fox bikers. Or is that a Lost Kings thing?"

I squint down at her. "He's probably old enough to be your grandfather."

"Prime age for my momma, though." She grins up at me and squeezes my hand. "I've got all I can handle right here."

"He has an old lady he's pretty fond of." I return her smile. "Hopefully, you'll meet her."

She narrows her eyes. "Is she like Tawny or more like Hope and Lilly?"

Wise question. "She's nothing like Tawny." Valentina's in a category of her own, really.

"Rooster." Priest stops in front of us and squeezes my shoulders. He looks me over like a proud papa bear. "One of my youngest VPs. Glad to see you outside of National."

Well, shit. Is that a hint he thinks I should visit more often? No offense to Priest, but Mississippi isn't real high on my list of vacation spots.

Best keep that thought to myself.

He pulls me in, slapping my back a few more times. "Make yourself at home while you're here."

"Thank you, Prez."

His gaze lands on Shelby and tension runs through her body. She squeezes my hand tight and lifts her chin.

"Priest, this is my old lady, Shelby. Shelby, this is our national president."

"Welcome to Mississippi." Priest nods at her but doesn't offer to shake her hand. He's never been in the habit of touching other brother's old ladies that I can remember.

Valentina glides through the room offering hellos to the guys. Everyone—even Jigsaw—is on their best behavior. She finally stops, brushing against Priest's side.

"Shelby, I'm so happy you're here. Welcome." She holds out her arms and bundles Shelby up in an inviting hug. "I've been looking forward to meeting you."

Not sure if she's a country music fan or she just wants the opportunity to vet another Lost Kings old lady. Either way, I appreciate how welcoming she is to Shelby.

"Thank you for having me, ma'am." Shelby's Texan twang spills out thicker than usual, as I notice happens when she's nervous. My fingers twitch with the need to touch and reassure her but Priest might see that as a sign Shelby's weak, and Valentina could take it as an insult. Shelby's made of tough stuff. She'll be fine.

"Come." Valentina wraps an arm around Shelby's shoulders. "Let's get you a drink and I'll show you around."

"That would be lovely. Thank you." Shelby peers at me over her shoulder once. Her lips wobble into a smile that doesn't reassure me all that much. On their way to the kitchen, Valentina collects Trinity under her other arm. At least Shelby won't be on her own.

"She'll be fine here," Priest says, his shrewd eyes studying me intently. "That was some nasty business in Virginia."

At least he doesn't waste time. Must've heard all about it. Whether Ice gave him the heads-up or someone else is hard to tell, and I don't dare disrespect our national president by asking.

"It was."

He curls an arm around my shoulders and steers me toward the club's chapel. From the corner of my eye, I catch Jiggy giving me a farewell salute. God, I'd love to flip him off.

The mother charter's chapel is a lot fancier than ours. Brand new, shiny furniture. Sparkling hardwood floors. Leather couch and chairs. Nice to see Priest putting all that money we kick up to good use. He heads straight for a small wet bar, pouring two glasses of whiskey neat.

Priest hands me one of the glasses and before I can even take a sip, he levels his stern gaze on me. "Dating someone in the public eye. Must be difficult."

Somehow I don't think he's all that concerned about my dating problems. "I'm doing as much as I can to not bring unwanted attention to the organization."

You know, if we just forget that whole magazine cover thing. For the thousandth time, I thank fuck they didn't name my club.

His jaw shifts and his unrelenting stare doesn't ease up. "You've never been a showy, braggart type, Rooster."

"No," I answer carefully, not sure where he's going with that statement.

"Good. You have a lot of potential. Z made a good call giving you that VP patch."

Why do I feel like a third-grader about to receive a report card?

"You're smart enough to know the difference between causing a problem by throwing your weight around," He leans in and taps my Lost Kings MC patch, "and quietly letting the world know there are consequences to fucking with what's yours."

I take that to mean he wouldn't be upset if I publicly gutted Suggs. Good to know. "Yes, sir."

"Ice speaks highly of you as well." He takes a slow sip of his whiskey.

I don't dare blink. Just keep holding his stare. "That's good to hear. I feel like I imposed on him an awful lot while we were there."

"You're never a burden on your brothers, Rooster." He holds his arms open wide. "That's the whole point. We are our brother's keeper."

Ah, Priest's favorite saying. I was wondering how long it would take him to bust that out. My radar's pinging like crazy. He's up to something. "I know." I shrug. "Like you said, I prefer to help my brothers quietly."

"How did you find the hospitality in Virginia?"

What the fuck's he looking for? A status report about the clubhouse? The porn business? Ice's FBI connections? All of that and more?

"Above and beyond. Ice's FBI friend helped smooth over some rough patches when we needed it."

"Good to hear Jackson's earning his keep. He's an expensive little pet." For a brief second, Priest drops the kindly dad mask and the ruthless biker who's been the national president as long as I can remember grins at me.

Trying to navigate through a conversation with Priest is draining as fuck. Every word out of his mouth can be taken several ways.

He sighs. "More porn, huh? That's Ice's big plan? Skin flicks will be our entire reputation."

I mean, it's not as if any outlaw motorcycle club will ever have a sterling rep, so I don't get why he's so bothered by the porn. "It's profitable. Legal. Ice has a clever set-up. His girl seems smart and loyal."

He raises an eyebrow, but one corner of his mouth twists, as if he's disappointed in me.

"Not like that, Prez. I was only assisting with the technical side." I nod toward the clubhouse. "Got all I can handle with my girl."

"Yes, but what's his relationship like with this 'star' who we're putting so much money behind?"

Ah, that makes more sense.

"We didn't really have time to sit around and chat about our hopes and dreams for the future, Prez." I'm not trying to be disrespectful. More like, if I sound too eager to chat about brothers and their personal business, it doesn't look good. Priest may be angling for me to act as his spy but he won't respect me if I give up the dirt too easily. It's a razor-thin edge I'm walking.

He cocks his head and stares, waiting for more information.

"Shelby hung out with her a little bit."

"Really?" I get his disbelief. Old ladies aren't usually fond of spending time with unattached women associated with the club.

"Yeah, they got along well. From everything I saw, she's respectful to the old ladies. Doesn't start drama." Priest seems to want some sort of reassurance. "I don't exactly know what their personal relationship is, but I got the impression they have history. Shelby kinda confirmed that. Ice was friends with her dad or something."

A flash of recognition seems to cross his face. He nods slowly. "I think I know who you're talking about now."

Great, because I'd really love to stop squealing on my brothers now.

"Every club's certainly free to earn how they want as long as it's not bringing us *all* down. Like you said, it's legal." He shrugs. "Your operation in New York is still profitable as well, right?"

"It's not *my* operation, Priest. But yes. Things are running smoothly and as expected."

"And you trust this gal?"

"I don't trust anyone but from what I saw, she's extremely loyal to Ice and the club." That's the last thing I want to say about Ice and his personal life.

"Think you'll have a night to spare to visit your brothers in Tennessee?"

Ah, there it is.

The quick switch in conversation doesn't throw me as much as Priest probably wanted it to. He's praised me, reminded me of my obligations to the club, pumped me for information—now here comes the real point of this conversation.

"Sure. Any reason in particular?"

"Our situation there is a bit rocky. The relationship with Black Venom MC has deteriorated a lot over the last couple of months."

I wrack my brain trying to remember any details about the smaller southern MC. "We've run into them at events in Florida and never had any issues."

"Yeah, well, the Bunnville president's trying to make a name for himself. Stirring up trouble where there doesn't need to be any."

I've been in the northeast for so long, it takes me a second to picture the territory outlines. "They're located near the Georgia border. Why are they even near Deadbranch?"

The corners of his mouth curl up, as if he's pleased with my ability to grasp geography on the fly. "Expansion? Seeing how much they can get away with? Why does any MC encroach?"

"That's suicide when our mother charter's a five-hour ride away." I stop for a beat. "Unless they think they have the backing of another club."

"That's my concern."

"So, what's Digger doing about it?" As small as our upstate NY charter is, the second Rock has a whiff of another MC sniffing around their territory, he puts an end to it. Even Sway, for all his—*many*—faults was always aware of who was trying to invade our territory when he was president. Still, having Z in charge is far better.

"Nothing," Priest spits. "Claims he's keeping tabs on the situation. But he's too busy running their whorehouse-saloon to instill much confidence."

It's not really a secret that Priest isn't fond of all the wink-of-the-pink businesses our clubs run. What exactly he expects a bunch of bikers to dabble in, and still stay semi-legal, I have no idea. Lost Kings have never touched human trafficking and never will. Priest frowns on trafficking heavy narcotics, and weapons. The few charters that defy him on the drugs and guns better make serious bank and stay out of trouble, otherwise, they land on his shit-list fast. After those big three, there aren't a whole lot of profitable areas for outlaws to earn big.

"I'll be near Nashville after the tour. Shelby's recording her album there. But we have the next few days off. I can take a detour if you feel the situation is more urgent."

"I knew I could count on you." he says with a sly eyebrow raise.

Spying on another charter for Priest is a good way to get a reputation as National's bitch. Not a title I've ever aspired to own.

But it's not like saying no to Priest is an option either.

"I'm always happy to stop in and say hello." I consider who I'm traveling with. Dawson and his crew would provide excellent coverage for a spy mission. We left them at Dawson's friend's ranch but some of the roadies weren't thrilled about staying put for the next couple days. They've been itching to have "fun." A field trip to the Royal Dolls Gentlemen's Club could be a nice bonding activity for everyone. "I'll see if we can get some of the guys from the tour to go with us. Make it seem like a casual visit."

His eyes gleam with approval. "Your woman going to be okay with you visiting there?"

Jesus, yeah, that's all I need to tell Priest. *My girlfriend won't let me go to a strip club.* "She'll be fine."

"Bring her," he suggests. "The more casual the visit seems, the better."

Thanks, Priest. Wasn't planning to go without her.

"It's not urgent, so whenever works for you."

I'm going to take Priest at his word on that for now. This could be a test, though.

"Let me know how the visit goes."

Yup, can't wait.

Not that I want to be a little bitch, but the conversation I had with Priest feels like something I need to talk to Z about.

Valentina hands me a room key and points me in the direction of where we'll stay tonight. The club has several small cabins behind the main clubhouse. From what I've been told it used to be a resort area in the Eighties. Lots of acreage and privacy.

Even though it's hotter than fucking balls, everything surrounding the clubhouse is lush and green. Trimmed and landscaped better than some state parks too.

"Must take a lot of prospects to maintain this property," Shelby says in a low voice.

I huff out a laugh. "I was thinking the same thing."

"Please tell me this cabin has a/c?"

"Yeah, probably a window unit, but it'll have it."

"Thank gawd." She pulls her tank top away from her misty skin and flaps the material around enough to give me a glimpse of her breasts.

"I want to lick the sweat from between your breasts once we're inside."

Her shocked side-eye melts into a sassier expression. "Well, there's plenty of it."

Fuck, I love her.

Inside the cabin is neater than I expected. Smells cleaner than I thought it would too. Shelby's quick to flick on the air conditioner. She lifts her hair and lets the air blow on her neck for a few seconds.

"You mind if I make a few phone calls?" I ask.

"Nope." She grabs her bag and pulls out her travel case. "I'm taking a shower."

I push my face into a disapproving pout.

"I know." She reaches up and pats my cheek. "I'll sweat more. Don't worry."

I wait until I hear the shower start to call Z. He answers on the second ring. After I explain the situation, the motherfucker has the nerve to laugh for a solid minute.

"You done, Prez?" I grumble.

"Let me think on it." A beat of silence. "Yeah, I'm finished."

"Fucking hilarious. Really."

"Aw, you fell for the old scare—compliment—favor routine. He's done it to all of us. Just means he thinks you're management material." Z laughs even harder.

"Fantastic."

"Look," he says a little more seriously, "This sounds like a win-win all around. Show Dawson and his guys a good time at one of our clubs. Gather information for Priest, make him happy—which by the way will make *me* happy—then be on your merry way to the next destination."

"You make it sound so simple."

"Because it is."

He should know better than anyone.

Nothing is ever simple in our world.

CHAPTER FORTY-THREE

Rooster

Big surprise—everyone's eager to check out the Royal Dolls Gentlemen's Club. Dawson, his crew, Shelby's band, my brothers. I think the only person who didn't share the enthusiasm was Wrath. Oh, and Greg. He didn't even answer my text. Even Dex, who so far has mostly kept to himself on this adventure, is eager to check out their operation.

"Maybe they have some ideas I can bring back to Crystal Ball," he explains.

I believe him. Dex takes everything he does for the club seriously.

"Such a diligent manager." Pants slaps Dex on the back a few times.

Before we leave, I stop to see Priest and let him know where we're headed. He seems pleasantly surprised. I knew that easy-going "stop in whenever you want" line of his was bullshit.

I also call ahead and let Digger know we're coming. Basic brother-to-brother courtesy. When I let him know I'm bringing a rather large party, I can practically hear the cash register sounds going off in his head.

"You're sure you're okay with this?" I ask Shelby. First porn, then the pussy patch, now a goddamn pussy palace. "Dating me is getting to be a tour in degeneracy isn't it?"

She palms my cheek and reaches up on tiptoes to kiss me. "You said it was important. A favor to your president and your national president, right?"

"Yeah." I'd had to at least tell her that much.

She cocks her head. "Would you want to go to strip clubs otherwise?"

"Want?" I consider carefully before answering. When I was eighteen, hell yeah. Couldn't wait to get my horny ass inside a strip joint. "Working at different ones the club owns across the country kinda killed all my natural curiosity."

She holds my gaze, parts her lips, then hesitates.

"What?" I ask.

"Hypothetically speaking, if you were having a bachelor party, would you want it at a strip club? Or is that where you'd want to go for a 'night out with the boys'?"

"I don't deal in hypotheticals, Shelby. Ask me what you want to ask."

"I just did."

"No." A genuine shudder of revulsion washes over me. Have a bunch of sweaty, glittered-up girls grind all over me for dollar bills to celebrate marrying my little chickadee? No fucking way. And why the fuck would I spend time at one instead of with my girl? "No," I say again.

"Why?"

"Well, for one thing, I'm sensing that it would bother you."

Her face remains neutral.

"For another, I meant what I said. I got it out of my system years ago. You know that saying about seeing how sausage is made makes you never want to eat sausage?"

"I think so."

"It's kinda like that."

"Ew. Don't compare women to sausages."

"I'm not. I mean the whole environment. You'll see what I'm talking about."

SHELBY

I can't believe I'm in an honest-to-God strip club. My band thought it was hilarious that I tagged along. Dawson seemed nervous or maybe embarrassed. Not sure why he cares what I think. He and Dex seem to be getting along, which is good since he's continuing on the tour with us until the end.

Trent's nervous big brother eyes keep darting my way. *No need to look out for me, buddy. I'm fine.* Or maybe he doesn't want me to see how many lap dances he plans to splurge on. Either way, he better knock it off before Rooster notices.

As we're led through the back entrance—a long, dark hallway with faint yellow lighting—I dare to peek at my surroundings. Posters of girls on the walls. Both regular dancers and special guests.

Lord, I hope no one assumes I'm a 'special guest.' My momma would freak if I told her about this outing.

We enter the main floor of the club. A large, mirrored stage with two shiny poles takes up the center of the room. Two smaller round stages take up the corners but those don't seem to be occupied.

If I had to label the rest of the decor, I guess I'd call it western-bondage-bordello themed. I've never seen anything like it. My mind's spinning as I take in the jewel-toned curtains and black leather furniture. Even the walls have what looks like some sort of sapphire colored wallpaper flocked with ornate designs. Mirrored panels strategically placed on the walls give the room the appearance of being larger than it actually is.

"Except for the stage, I feel like we traveled back in time," Trinity whispers to me.

"To a kinky Wild West?"

"Yup."

"I kinda dig it. If I ever headline my own show, I think I'd do sets and costumes exactly like this."

She laughs, instantly putting me at ease. "I can see it. A little more western flair, though."

Because we're such a large group, the manager escorts us to a space they've set up in the back. Several tables have been pushed together surrounding two large, circular booths. I glance from the booths to the chairs.

Trinity seems to be as indecisive as I am.

"Where would you rather sit?" Rooster asks me.

"Which one's less likely to have cum stains crusted on the upholstery?"

Rooster chokes on a laugh and just stares at me.

I pat the back pocket of my fancy new jeans. "I wore my Diamond Tough Denim tonight." Miranda had come through with the sponsorship deal. We'd done a quick photoshoot before one of the shows and I have another one scheduled. A stack of brand new jeans too and a fat paycheck to boot.

He steps away, speaking to one of the girls dressed in the bedroom version of a saloon girl's outfit. She quickly wipes down the booth and smiles at me.

Ugh, why'd I have to complain? I used to be a waitress. I know how hard it is to keep up on everything. "You didn't tell her what I said, did you?" I ask Rooster.

"No." He curls his arm around my waist, tucking me against his side. "Relax."

A big, burly guy with a long, scraggly black and gray beard sidles up to us, holding out his ham-sized hand to Rooster.

"Digger, how you been, brother?" Rooster engages in one of those intricate, manly secret handshakes with the older biker. He hugs me to his side. "This is my old lady, Shelby. Shelby, Digger's the president of our charter here in Deadbranch. Royal Dolls is his place."

His gaze roams over my body in a long, slow slide. The icky sensation is too much like spiders crawling over my skin. Or maybe it's the environment giving me a skeezy feeling.

Finally, Digger opens his mouth. "You're the singer. The one that got nabbed near Ice's place?"

Huh. Maybe it's because I recovered at Ice's clubhouse, so I feel more loyal to him, but I don't like the way this guy seems to be subtly implying Ice is somehow at fault for my abduction.

He turns to Rooster. "Hell, brother. You shoulda warned me. I woulda called in extra security."

"I thought I mentioned it," Rooster says in the special way he has that borders between respectful and 'fuck off.' "I think we've got it covered. Thanks."

"Shit, bro. You brought three SAAs in my joint. I should put 'em to work."

Rooster glances over his shoulder. "You can give it a try."

Digger slaps Rooster's shoulder. "First round is on the house. For you and all your guests."

"You don't have to do that—"

"I insist. First hour in the champagne room's on me too. For the whole party. Just make sure they tip the girls."

"All right."

Maybe we arrived early and the night hasn't really started yet. The club's half full. Men at different tables. All laser focused on the stage in the middle of the room. The smaller side stages appear empty for now.

Suddenly the lights dim and the music zooms up to a punishing throb. At least eight girls of varying shades of blond and tan slide onto the stage.

"Not a whole lot of variety in their look, huh?"

He quirks an eyebrow at me and tugs on one of my braids.

"Yeah, yeah." I swat his hand away. "You know what I meant."

"The night's still young."

We approach our tables and Rooster relays the information about the free drinks and bump-n-grinds to everyone. A round of tequila is ordered and a few minutes later a shot glass is handed to me.

"I can't remember the last time I drank tequila. I don't think it ended well."

Rooster clinks his glass against mine. "I'm having this and one beer, so drink whatever you want." He cocks his head and seems to reconsider. "Just not so much you're gonna fall off the bike."

"Very funny."

"*Holler and swaller*!" Trent shouts his favorite toast.

The liquid burns all the way down and I squeeze my eyes shut to tolerate the sting. Maybe that wasn't the best thing for my throat. When I open my eyes, Rooster's holding a wedge of lime in front of my face. I take my sweet time sucking the fruit from his fingers. The spark in his eyes shifts from playful to hungry.

The tart lime does little to chase away the burn of the tequila. Rooster plucks the wedge from my lips and leans in to kiss me. The earthy, mild sweetness of the tequila lingers on his breath. He doesn't seem to care that we're in the middle of a loud, busy strip club or that we're surrounded by people. Not my man. Ignoring everything around us, he pulls me closer. I part my lips and gently brush my tongue against his. I feel his rumbling growl of approval where my hand's pressed against his chest. My head spins. From the tequila or Logan's kisses? My money's on the second one.

"Get a room!" That sounds like Jigsaw.

We ignore him and keep right on kissing.

A rush of bodies whoosh by, knocking into us hard enough to break our kiss. I blink up at Rooster. He smiles at me. Not ten feet away, there are eight gorgeous, half naked dancers shaking it for all they're worth and my man can't take his eyes off *me*.

Pants intrudes on our moment by wrapping his arms around Rooster's neck and tugging him backwards. "You *have* to come get a lap dance. It's on the house."

"Thanks, I'm good."

Pants smirks at me. "You don't mind, right, Shelby? You'll let your man party, right?" He jerks his head toward our table. "Wrath, Trin, and Dex are over there. You can hang with them—"

"I'm fine." Rooster clamps his hand around Pants' wrist hard enough to make his face pale and release his hold on Rooster.

"Later." Pants jogs toward a different darkened corridor than the one we entered the building from. A guard at the entrance to the hallway waves him through.

"You can go," I offer, wanting to be an 'understanding' girlfriend who doesn't spoil her boyfriend's fun, but the words feel sour in my mouth.

Rooster takes my chin between his thumb and index finger. "I don't *want* to."

I open my mouth again—probably to stick my boot in it—but Rooster presses one finger against my lips.

At our table, Dawson and his bodyguard are still hanging out with Dex, Wrath, and Trinity.

"You didn't go with everyone else, Dawson?" I ask.

He frowns at the question. "Last thing I need is pictures of me getting a lap dance all over the damn place." He holds up his hand to Rooster. "No offense. I know this is your club's place—"

"None taken. I don't blame you," Rooster says.

Dawson gestures toward the stage. "I have a perfectly good view of all the action right here."

Actually, thanks to the mirrors, I have a decent view too, even though I'm sitting with my back to the stage.

"I can't believe I finally get out of Crystal Ball duty and now I'm fifteen hundred miles from New York in *another* strip club." Wrath shoots a glare Rooster's way.

"Hey!" Dex leans over the table and punches Wrath's arm. "Stop talking shit about CB."

"All the pretty naked ladies make you grumpy, Wrath?" I ask sweetly. "Or grumpi*er*, I mean?"

Trinity covers her mouth and laughs.

"Careful, Shelby." He wags a finger at me. "We're not quite there yet."

"Uh, Shelby?" a soft feminine voice says next to my ear. A tall, busty brunette with a hesitant smile and breasts about to spill out of her corset sets a tall glass of a pinkish-orange drink on the table in front of me. "Paloma on the house, Miss Shelby. We heard they're your favorite." She points toward the bar and the girl behind it waves at me.

"Oh my gosh. That's so sweet. Thank you!"

"We're both big fans. Already have tickets to your show in Nashville."

My mind blanks. *Say something!* "Thank you. I'm looking forward to it."

Well, that was dumb.

It's just...Dawson Roads is sittin' right over there and she's talking to *me*? It doesn't compute.

Her gaze shifts to Rooster. "You're her White Knight, right?" She presses her hand to her chest and meets my eyes again. "It's so romantic. I *love* that song."

More heat races over my cheeks and down my chest. "Based on a true story." I lean into Rooster and he slips his arm behind me, resting his hand on my hip.

"Well, if you need anything at all, I'm Erica. Digger asked me to personally cover your table. VIP service all the way."

"Thank you."

Rooster asks for a beer, then she moves to Dawson's side. "What can I get for you, Mr. Roads?"

So she *does* know who he is.

Rooster squeezes my hip. "You all right?"

"That was wild. I'm still processing."

He chuckles softly. "You're more famous than you realize."

I sip my drink, savoring the tartness of the grapefruit and lime. Erica returns with the rest of our order and sets another paloma in front of me and I thank her.

Trinity slides closer to me. "You're popular here."

"Yeah, that was so weird. I didn't know what to say."

"People don't recognize you out in the wild?"

"A couple of times." I shrug.

"I think you better get used to it," she says with a smile.

CHAPTER FORTY-FOUR

Rooster

Not that it's a contest, but I'm amused that our waitress fawned all over Shelby while treating Dawson like just another customer. Shelby's so damn sweet, the attention left her tongue-tied.

At least Dawson's not some insecure prick who gets offended. If anything, he seems relieved the girls don't make too much of a fuss over him.

I search the club. Busy but not as busy as I'd expected. The place seems well-run. This shouldn't be taking up so much of Digger's time that he doesn't know what's going on in his territory.

Across the table, I catch Dex's eye and jerk my head to the side.

I lean into Shelby. "You mind if I talk to Digger for a minute?"

"Not at all. I knew this was a work outing." She grins at me and sips her drink. Her cheeks and nose are already bright pink from the alcohol.

"Go easy on those." I kiss her temple and slide out of the booth. Dex follows me to the bar. On the way over, I send Jiggy a text.

Me: Hey, chucklefuck. If you're done gettin' your dick rubbed, could you look after Shelby?

Jigsaw: My pleasure, cock-knocker.

The bartender bounces over to us right away. "Hi, Rooster. Hi, Dex."

Her gaze drops to my VP patch, then Dex's spiffy new road captain patch. "Those look new."

Do I know this chick?

"Is Digger still around?" I ask.

"Yup. Want me to text him?"

"Please."

She moves to the end of the bar and I turn toward Dex. "What's your professional opinion?"

"Nice place. Clean. Girls don't look coked out of their skulls. I'd expect it to be busier." He shrugs. "But I think a lot of clubs are on a downward trend."

"Is CB?"

"Little bit. What's the point of going to a club to watch naked girls they can't touch, when they could just watch porn at home?" The corners of his mouth tip into a smirk. "*Your* business is literally killing mine."

I burst out laughing. "Maybe the club's just evolving."

"Maybe. I think the point was always to have a good cover to launder money from *other* activities. Can't do that with online porn."

"That's why downstate has the laundromats."

He scoffs. "Sway was so literal."

"What's up, Rooster," Digger says. "Everyone treating you okay?"

"Definitely. Erica's been great."

"Careful, I think she's got a little crush on your girl." He nudges me with his elbow and gives me a dirty old man smirk.

Yeah, not happening.

Since I'm not here to start shit, I humor him with a quick nod I hope doesn't look too dismissive.

Priest sent me here with a goal in mind, not to take in the nightlife and kick back free drinks. Still, I need to use caution. Club brother or not, I can't walk into another charter's territory and start prying into their business.

I lean on the bar and take a sip of the fresh beer the bartender left in front of me.

"How are things?" I ask Digger. "Haven't been down this way in a while. The area seems more built up."

"Had a lot of growth in the last few years." Digger glances around the bar. "Unfortunately, it's not translating to more traffic *here*. We're not as busy as we used to be."

"Seems to be an on-going decline throughout the industry," Dex says.

"Yeah? Same for your place?"

"We've had a bit of an extended slump." Dex nods to one of the dancers who strokes her hand over his shoulder as she struts by. "Maybe we can start up an exchange program with the girls. Rotate in new talent," he suggests to Digger.

Crystal Ball has always prided itself on pulling talent from all over the country. It's one of the reasons upstate has kept their place as successful as it has for so long. So this isn't exactly a new and novel concept Dex is suggesting. More like, he's trying to help me lull Digger into a broader conversation.

While they discuss logistics, I scan the room, searching for Shelby. Wrath and Trinity are in the booth alone. He jerks his head to the right when he notices me.

Oh, Shelby. What the hell are you up to?

I knew I'd let her drink too much. Haven't seen her touch a drop of alcohol the whole time I've been on the road with her. Should've known she'd be a lightweight.

It'll be fine.

The whole point for her tonight was to cut loose and have a little harmless fun, right?

CHAPTER FORTY-FIVE

Shelby

AFTER THEIR TURN ON THE STAGE, EACH DANCER WALKS THROUGH THE room, sitting in customers' laps, talking them into buying drinks, accepting tips, and trying to hustle them in the back for private dances.

The men are gross. Constantly copping feels and staring at the girls' tits. Not much different from waitressing, I suppose.

For the tenth time tonight, I'm thanking Jesus I never accepted any of the invitations I received over the years to "try out" at any of the local strip clubs back home.

Three dancers approach Dawson at once. Two in his lap and one standing behind him to rub his shoulders and whisper in his ear.

The evil bitch in me kinda wants to snap a picture and send it to Glenna Wilson. I'd caption it, "Looks like he's doing fine without you, bitch."

But I could never do that. My phone stays in my pocket.

Dawson must've reconsidered the private dance because he lets the girls lead him backstage.

"And then there were three," Trinity sighs. Wrath just shakes his head.

I sip my drink while watching Rooster and Dex at the bar.

"Shelby!" Erica and another girl approach my side of the booth. Together the two of them look like the angel and devil come to taunt me with bad choices. Erica in her blood-red and black corset and the new girl in what looks like the bridal lingerie of a 1960's virgin, complete with marabou feathered pumps.

The new girl introduces herself as Vanity and holds out her hands to me. "Please, come dance with us."

"What? Me?" I glance at the stage. "I can't do any of that." I play a little air guitar solo for them. "Guitar and singin' are my only talents."

Vanity twirls a long lock of ice-blond hair around one finger and pouts. "Please. I'll show you some moves."

Why the hell not? How often do you get offered dance lessons from a professional stripper?

Vanity leans over the table toward Trinity, "How about you?"

"I'm good." Trinity's amber eyes settle on me. "You sure about this?"

I shrug and finish my paloma, slamming it on the table with a thud. "I think I have just enough tequila in me to give it a try."

"Yay!" Vanity claps. The sleeves of the filmy white robe she's wearing slide down her arms. Erica reaches for me, curling her hands around mine and dragging me out of the booth.

"Do you dance too?" I ask her.

"I want to. The money's better. But I haven't worked up the courage to take it all off, yet."

"Oh." I giggle and stumble, bumping into her. "Yeah, I could never."

"Why?" Vanity fluffs my hair and studies my body likes she's measuring me for a new bra. "You definitely have the figure for it."

Erica pushes her friend. "Don't you dare talk my favorite singer into another line of work."

A nervous chuckle spills out of me. "No plans to switch careers."

"Okay." Vanity spreads her hands in front of her like she's about to sell me on the latest multi-level-marketing scheme. "Main stage, you enter from the back. These smaller ones, you gotta haul yourself up onto them and still make it look graceful."

Of course, I end up scrabbling my way onto the raised platform about as gracefully as a drunk monkey wearing a girdle.

Once I'm on the stage, I stare at the shiny silver pole in front of me. "Can you teach me how to spin around that thing?"

"Easy, breezy," Vanity says.

She demonstrates the different grips used for tricks, climbing, and spins. I'll never remember each hand positioning but I nod along, eager to get through the lessons and give it a whirl. So to speak.

"It might be easier with bare feet," Erica points out.

I plop down on the stage and tug my boots and socks off, setting them to the side.

The two girls share a look. "Let's start you with the attitude spin. That's a good beginner one," Vanity says. "Okay, first you start with the half-bracket grip I showed you." She demonstrates by curling her hands around the pole with one above her head and the other about chest-level. "Keep your core tight and shoulders back."

"Lemme see you do it," I say.

She executes the moves in a slow, fluid motion, then stops to explain. "Step forward with your inside leg." She pats her thigh. "Swing your outside leg in a wide circle around your body, hooking the back of your ankle onto the pole—"

"You lost me."

Her mask of patience slips for a second.

Hey, no one told you to offer the drunk girl dancin' lessons.

"Let me show you again."

My eyes follow her movements—grip, grip, step, twirl. She does it a few more times but it still looks like a graceful blur of motion.

"Okay, you try."

Grip, grip—

"No, grip lower." Vanity repositions my bottom hand.

Step, jump, nothing.

My body doesn't magically twirl around the pole.

I try a few more times and finally get my leg high enough.

"Good, good!" Erica encourages. "You're so flexible. Took me forever to get my leg to bend like that."

"Yoga, baby." I slap the backs of my thighs a few times.

Vanity smirks at Erica. "Told ya."

I try the spin again and end up sliding down the pole, dragging my feet on the floor.

"Slightly better," Vanity says. "Here, move those hips a little when you come down." She places her hands on me and shimmies from side to side, encouraging me to do the same.

The music seamlessly shifts as a new group of dancers takes the main stage. An Eighties rock song, *Candy Jar,* blasts through the speakers. Kinda cliché for a strip club, so not unexpected. I bust out some dance moves with the girls, tossing my hair around like a proper Eighties video queen.

"Nice, Shelby!" Erica laughs. "Try the spin again."

Grip, grip, step, jump, spin. I almost get all the way around the pole, but my heel slips and I land painfully on my hands and knees.

"Ouch." I giggle and dust off my hands, jumping up to try again.

"I think your jeans are causing you to slip when they make contact with the pole," Vanity points out.

I may be slightly tipsy but there isn't enough alcohol in the world to convince me to strip off my pants in a public place. An uneasy feeling settles in my gut. Maybe trying to spin my body around a pole with all the tequila sloshing through my tummy wasn't the best idea.

"That's enough of that, songbird," a gruff voice says behind me. Strong arms wrap around my waist, lifting me into the air and off the stage.

"Stop! I'm gonna puke."

"A little puke doesn't scare me." Jigsaw doesn't break his stride. Customers barely blink as he carries me to our table, they're so focused on the main stage.

At our booth, Jiggy gently stands me on the bench, leaving me with a bird's-eye view of the whole club. "Where'd your boots go?" he asks.

I point to the stage.

"Don't move," he warns.

I almost topple over and lean one arm on the back of the booth.

When my vision stops swimming, I search the bar again. No sign of Logan. Where'd he go?

Jigsaw returns with a grim expression. He holds my boots up in front of my face. "Sit."

I slide into the booth, landing on my rump.

He squats in front of me, shoving my pants leg up while working one sock onto my foot and slipping on my boot. He repeats the process with my other foot, then smooths my jeans into place.

From the corner of my eye, I catch an older man wearing a business suit taking a photo of us.

Oh, that's not good.

"Jiggy," I whisper urgently.

"You gonna be sick?" he asks, concern darkening his eyes.

"No…well maybe…but that guy over there is taking pictures."

He whips around and zeroes in on the wanna-be photographer right away. Leaping into action, he lunges for the phone.

The man jumps out of his seat so fast, his chair clatters to the ground. Instead of running toward the safety of the front door, he tries to dodge Jigsaw and run deeper into the club.

Jiggy sticks his arm out, clotheslining the guy right in the neck. *Boom.* The man hits the floor with a *splat*.

Two bouncers who'd been manning the front door come running. Before they reach the guy, Jigsaw grabs his phone, flicking his fingers over the screen, hopefully deleting the photos.

The man struggles as the bouncers drag him away.

"That was close," Trinity says. "Are you okay?"

"I think so."

ROOSTER

Digger waves his hand over his shoulder. "Follow me back to my office so we can talk about this without all the noise." He follows my line of sight. "She'll be fine. The girls will take care of her."

I nod as if I'm not worried but as soon as he turns around, I pull out my phone and send Jiggy another text.

Me: Eyes on Shelby. Now.

We're already in the hallway leading to Digger's office when Jiggy responds with a thumb's up emoji.

Wrath's out there. He won't let anything happen to Shelby. But I also know if anything goes down, Trinity will be his first priority.

Dancers scatter out of Digger's way. Some try to stop and talk to Dex and me. I snarl at a few who put their hands on me or grab my arm.

A young woman dressed in street clothes, carrying a large duffle bag, is waiting outside Digger's office door. Even though she's in jeans and a sweatshirt, her teased halo of hair and heavy makeup say she's finishing a shift.

"What's wrong, Jenny?" he asks.

"Can you walk me to my car? That guy..." her bottom lip trembles.

Digger sighs. "I'm in the middle of something." He turns and claps me on the back. "Rooster will walk you out."

Startled, I don't say anything right away, which Digger seems to take for acceptance.

"Thank you, Rooster," Jenny gushes.

Dex shrugs as he follows Digger into the office.

Fuck.

Jenny scans my cut. "You're visiting from New York, right?"

"Yeah."

"Cool. I want to get up there for Christmas this year."

"Well, I think that's what Dex and Digger are talking about if you're interested in taking a few shifts at our upstate New York club."

She quickens her steps to keep up with me. "Oh, yes. That would be perfect."

I push the back door open but ask her to wait, scanning the parking lot behind the building. All the vehicles appear to be empty. No pedo-vans lurking. I motion for her to follow me outside.

"Which one's yours?" I ask.

She points to a small, red hatchback. "So, should I ask for you if I want to schedule something?"

"Huh? Oh. No. Dex runs Crystal Ball."

She lets out a throaty laugh. "Will I see you at all if I visit New York?"

Hell fucking no.

"No. I'll be on the road with my girlfriend."

"Oh." Her heavily glossed lips push into a pout.

We stop at her car and she hits the unlock button. The alarm chirps and the lights flash. I lean in and open the driver's door.

"Thank you so much." She tosses her bag into the backseat. "I had this customer who wouldn't take no for an answer and he started waiting in the parking lot for me..." her voice trails off. "Scared the hell out of me a few times."

I scowl and glance at the club. The few times I've helped out at Crystal

Ball, hell, any of the strip clubs Lost Kings own, we've always walked the girls to their cars at night. Too many guys fell "in love" with the girls and acted like dropping their weekly paycheck on lap dances entitled them to *more* after hours.

"Digger doesn't walk you guys out?"

"No, he does. Or he has someone do it. We're short on bouncers lately, though. Squiggy's usually careful about that stuff but Digger said he's on a run or something."

I search my memory for a face to match with the name. Lost Kings isn't the largest MC out there but we're not small enough that I can remember every single patch-holder's name in a flash either. "Big, bald-headed guy?" I tap the side of my neck. "Octopus tat?"

Her smile brightens. "That's our Squiggy."

"Yeah, he's a good dude. Where'd he go?"

She shrugs. "I don't ask questions. I thought Digger said Everhart but I'm not sure."

Funny, I just came from there and didn't run into him. Granted, he could've arrived after we left. And it's not like Ice is obligated to tell me who's visiting his clubhouse and when.

"I'm working tomorrow." She steps closer and rests her hand over my VP patch. "Will I see you again?"

Not only is it rude as fuck to touch a biker's cut or patches without asking—which she should know since she works for a bunch of bikers—I don't want some strange woman's hand on me.

Gripping her wrist firm enough to send a message but not hurt her, I remove her hand. "No."

She pouts again. Guess that usually works for her. "Well, all right then..."

I open her door wider. "Go on. I'm gonna watch you drive out. Make sure no one's following you."

That must've sent the wrong signal. Her eager smile returns. "Oh. Okay."

I move to close her door but a flash of movement near the dumpster on the other side of the parking lot catches my eye. While my attention's focused over there, she pushes the door open again. "Give me your number. I'll let you know I got home okay."

Christ, she's persistent. Slowly tearing my gaze away from the dumpster, I open my mouth to say no. Then I reconsider and recite Jigsaw's number. He likes the tenacious ones.

Finally, I get her door closed and she starts the car. She wiggles her fingers at me and reverses out of the spot. I jam my hands in my pockets and walk toward the club, keeping my eye on her car. No other cars start up or follow her out of the parking lot. She turns left onto a side street and I figure my job here is done.

Inside the club, Digger's door is closed. I should probably stop in and finish the conversation we were having but I need to check on Shelby first.

The flashing lights and pounding music stab my skull as I enter the main room. My gaze shoots to the booth we'd been occupying. Most of our group's returned to the table. Shelby's nestled in the booth between Jigsaw and Trinity.

Confident she's in good hands, I return to Digger's office, knocking twice before turning the knob and pushing it open.

Digger stands as I enter the room, bracing his hands on his desk. "My girl get off okay?"

"Didn't see anyone."

"Good." He drops into his chair and motions for me to take one of the empty chairs on the opposite side. I pick the one next to the desk, pulling it a few extra inches away.

"We were just discussing the business," Dex says.

"Did you say you're light on security?" I ask Digger.

He hesitates, his gaze shifting to the left. "At the moment."

"You have a lot of issues?"

He taps a large screen sitting on his desk and turns it slightly our way. "I keep an eye on things here."

The screen is divided into eight squares, each showing a different section of the club. I quickly visualize the club and can count several places not covered on that screen.

"How's Squiggy been?" I ask. "Haven't seen that guy in forever."

Again, Digger shifts his eyes to the left. Is that his tell for when he's about to lie his ass off?

"Sent him on a mission with one of our prospects."

If it was club business, that would explain why Squiggy might've said he was headed to Everhart. Even though we're all part of the same organization, it's just bad manners to ask too many nosy questions.

Fuckin' Priest sending me here to gather intel. Digger will know where any information I pass along to Priest came from.

Time to try another approach. I ease back in the chair, casually resting my right ankle over my knee. "Think you're heading to the Florida rally this year?" He'll have to come pretty close to Black Venom's territory to hit that rally. Maybe thinking about it will loosen his lips a little.

His blank expression turns sour. "Only if National's gonna ride with us. Otherwise it's too much headache dealing with Black Venom MC's bullshit."

Finally.

"I thought we were cool with them?"

"We were. Then they opened a titty bar of their own right on the border."

"You think that's causing the slowdown in your business? It should still be far enough away."

"They poached our girls."

Dex sits forward. "Lured them away or *took* them?" he asks in a sharp tone.

Leave it to Dex to stop fucking around and get straight to the point. If we've got a rival MC kidnapping women associated with our club, I've stepped into a way more serious situation than I realized. And I need to get Shelby away from here as soon as possible. Also means Digger's hiding too much information from Priest. Ruthless national president or not, there's no way Priest would've encouraged me to bring my girl and a whole bunch of civilians here if that sort of trouble was brewing.

"Don't know yet. That's why I sent Squiggy to investigate."

"You think he might've kidnapped your women and you only sent *one* brother and a prospect to check it out?" Dex's sharp tone slices through the pretense of this being a casual conversation.

Digger ain't havin' any of it either. He slams his fists against the desk and stands, leaning over as far as he can to get in Dex's face. "I don't know they kidnapped anyone. These bitches are flaky as fuck sometimes. You oughta know that. What'd you want me to do, send a fuckin' army in and then find out I'm wrong? Tuck my balls back up my ass crack and ride home? Start a war and have Priest come down on my ass? Squiggy knows what he's doin'."

"All right. Easy." I hold out a hand toward Digger and one toward Dex. "No one's judging you."

Dex side-eyes me and I pray to fuck he doesn't open his mouth to contradict what I just said.

Digger drops into his seat. "If I don't hear from him by the weekend, I'll personally be lookin' for him. I'll call Blink to come in and back me up."

Yeah, our national SAA would be the right person to call since they're technically the closest charter.

Now I have to decide if I'm gonna rat a brother out to Priest or give Digger a couple days to do the right thing. Not a position I enjoy being in.

I knew nothing about this trip would be "simple."

CHAPTER FORTY-SIX

Rooster

FINALLY, I'M DONE WITH CLUB BULLSHIT AND RETURN TO THE PARTY TO collect my girl. Shelby's half-asleep with her head on Jiggy's shoulder. Wrath's gaze keeps scanning the bar like a caged lion trying to plan an escape from the zoo. Taking a second look around the joint, I can't say that's an unfair comparison.

Every chair around the stage has an ass in the seat. Men in business suits, men in jeans and work boots, a few cowboys in ten-gallon hats, and boys sporting college sweatshirts. All types stop in to give their hard-earned cash away.

"Guess they pick up as the night goes on," Dex says.

"Guess so." I slap his shoulder. "What was that, back there? Were you itching to get into a fight with him?"

"No, brother. Trying to play a little bad cop to your good."

"Bullshit."

He shrugs. "It pisses me off that he's acting so casual about the girls he makes money off of."

"I feel you." I glance behind us to make sure no one's within earshot. "Are you also concerned he's taking such a slow approach?"

"Fuck yeah. Unless he really doesn't think Black Venom is that big of a threat. Maybe we're just twitchy because we've dealt with shit from the Vipers and know how bad it can get."

"Maybe." I'm still pondering whether or not to give Priest all the details of our visit. I'm not asking Dex for his opinion on that. I've involved him enough. No reason to stick him in an even more awkward position. That's what Jiggy's for.

"You guys ready to bail?" I stop in front of our table and meet my brothers' eyes. Steer and Pants are wasted. Trent's still flirting with one of the dancers—gonna take a guess that his wallet's empty.

I check the table again. "Where's Dawson?"

"Still back there." One of his roadies points toward the champagne rooms.

Fuck. I lift my chin at Jiggy and slide out of the booth.

"Wrath? Watch Shelby for me?"

He nods.

Steer stumbles out of his chair. "You need me?"

"We'll see. Hang tight."

The guy working the entrance to the back area isn't a brother. At least he's not wearing our colors. He holds out his hand as if he's expecting something. "Need a credit card to get back there."

"Like fuck I do. Where's the guy who's with our party?"

"He's busy."

His smirky attitude works my last nerve and I snap, grabbing him by his shirt and jamming him against the wall. "Do you really want to fuck with me? You work for my club."

"Spit it out, needle-dick," Jigsaw growls.

"Room four."

I release him and he brushes off his shirt. "I'm calling Digger."

"Be my guest." Unless he's ready to retire from this Earth, there's no way Digger's gonna side with an employee over one of his brothers.

I push open the door to room four and stop to absorb what's in front of me.

Three girls in lingerie. Two of them are laughing, talking, and sipping champagne. The other one's tucked in the corner with her knees up to her chin and arms wrapped around her legs, looking miserable as hell. Dawson's unconscious on the couch.

Fucking great.

I recognize the scam they're running. Can't believe Digger lets this shit go on in his club. Half a dozen strip clubs on the East Coast have been raided by the FBI and shut down after pulling this stunt. Digger has to know this is exactly the kind of attention Priest doesn't want. Unless he really has no idea what goes on in his house. Can't decide which is worse.

Doesn't matter.

The girls jump up and try to run out of the room but Jiggy blocks their escape, backing them into the corner. "Sit your asses down," he orders.

I squat down next to Dawson and slap his cheek. "Hey, buddy. Time to wake up." Can't tell if he's drunk or drugged unconscious. His wallet's half sticking out of his back pocket. I pull it out and thumb through it. Empty. Looks like at least one credit card is missing.

"What'd you give him?" I yell at the girls.

"Nothing!" The tall, dark-haired one shouts. "He just passed out."

"Sure he did." I nod to Jiggy. "They emptied his wallet."

"Hell no, we didn't," the short blonde screeches. "He tipped us nicely."

"Shut up," the third girl whines.

Jiggy stares the three of them down. "Don't make me search you. It won't be pleasant," he warns.

The blonde backs up to a small black velvet ottoman that's hard to even make out in the dark.

"Don't," the brunette warns.

"Bitch, I will turn you over to the cops so fast your fake fuckin' titties will leak out your nipples." Jiggy stalks even closer until they're pressed up to the wall. "Stop playin'."

I shake my head and return my attention to Dawson, figuring Jiggy can handle the girls. "Dawson? Come on, buddy." I haul him upright and he groans. Thank fuck. Last thing I want to do is call an ambulance and bring *more* fucking attention to the situation.

"Here!" the other brunette yells. "I didn't wanna do it in the first place. They made me!" She flings the top of the ottoman open and reaches inside.

"You bitch!" the blonde screeches, attacking the other girl.

Jiggy watches them fight for a few seconds too long before separating them. The tall girl tries to run but I jump up, blocking her escape.

"What the fuck, Rooster? What are you doing?" Digger shouts, rushing into the room.

I shove the brunette into his chest. "Your girls here tried to scam my buddy. I brought my friends into your establishment thinking you'd treat my guests with respect, brother. This ain't right."

"I…I…," he sputters.

I point at the door. "Your bouncer's in on it too."

Steer pops into the room, his wide eyes bouncing around the room. "The fuck is going on, bro?"

"Digger's got a big fucking problem in his house."

Digger shoots a glare at me and I glare right back. The situation's deteriorating rapidly.

"Logan?" Dawson groans.

Thank fuck. "You all right?"

He leans over and pukes, narrowly missing my boots.

I reach down and slap his back a few times. "Better?"

"I think so," he groans.

"Here," a soft voice says next to me. I glance over and find our waitress, Erica, holding a bottle of water and a towel.

"Bitch," one of the girls Jigsaw's corralling hisses.

Erica's scared eyes meet mine for a second before she scurries away.

"What the fuck happened?" Digger demands.

"Nothing!" the tall dancer stomps her foot. "We don't know what he took before he came here. All these musicians are druggies and junkies."

Dawson's resting his elbows on his knees, head down, rubbing his temples. "Sweetheart, I ain't had anything harder than whiskey in ten years," he mumbles. "Try again."

"Nothing happened," the short blonde whines. "He bought a bottle of champagne, we started dancing for him, and he passed out."

"And you conveniently kept charging his credit card." I sneer.

She shrugs.

"Rooster, I'm sorry," Digger says. *Ouch* that had to hurt his pride to apologize in front of everyone.

I shake my head, indicating we can discuss it in private. Gotta leave the man his dignity if I want to get this sorted.

The brunette who cracked first really loses it. She screams and slides down the wall until her ass hits the floor. "I didn't wanna do any of it," she wails. "They made me. And Josh threatened me."

"Shut up, you sniveling little bitch." The taller brunette kicks her in the thigh and the girl on the floor starts wailing even louder.

"Jesus fuck," Steer groans, covering his ears.

Jigsaw grabs the tall one and yanks her away from the other girls.

"Steer, Jigsaw," Digger throws them a pleading look. "Would you mind helping me escort them into my office and keep them there, please? I need to have a word with Josh."

"That the guy out front?" I ask Digger. I wouldn't mind punching that asshole a few times before we leave.

He nods once and takes out his cell phone. "Let me ask one of my guys to hold him somewhere for me."

Jigsaw yanks the tall girl out by her wrists while Steer drags the other two by the arms.

"Wait." I stop them at the door. "Leave her." I nod to the one who gave up the truth first. Normally, I'm not a fan of snitches but in this case, I'm glad she broke as fast as she did.

She trembles like a kitten in a rainstorm as I nod for her to return to the corner of the room. Doubt she'll try to make a run for it and we might need more info from her.

Now that it's a little quieter, Digger shuts the door and pulls out a revolver.

Well, fuck. That escalated fast.

At least he doesn't point it at any of us.

Dawson hasn't looked up, so I don't even think he's noticed the rising tension in the room.

"Presley," Digger says in a low, ominous tone. "I took you in. Gave you a home. Gave you a job. Why would you disrespect me like this?"

She bursts into tears.

Dear God, can I just leave?

Click. Digger opens the revolver and slides a bullet in the chamber. "I'm waiting, Presley."

He still doesn't point the gun at her, but the threat's clear.

Her chin trembles as she tries to contain her sobbing. Finally, she opens her mouth. "Josh and Michelle set it up. I think Vanity's usually in on it with them but she was busy tonight. Skyla seemed to be in on it too but Michelle was definitely in charge. I didn't know what they were going to do until he passed out. When I tried to leave, she threatened me." She shrugs and looks down at the carpet. "They wouldn't let me leave. Josh said he'd come to my apartment and hurt me if I told anyone."

And this right here is why I wasn't lying when I told Shelby I'm not interested in going to strip clubs. Way too many girls end up so bitter and jaded after the shitty treatment they get from customers and the owners of the clubs that they see nothing wrong with robbing a guy blind. Or in this case drugging him until he passes out and stealing everything he's got.

For your regular married guy, who doesn't want his wife to know, it's bad enough.

For a celebrity like Dawson, it could probably end his career. Even if he gets the girls locked up, the damage will be done.

In *this* case it's even more complicated because this is my fault. I brought him into my club's place, thinking they'd respect that he was my guest.

"What was the fucking plan?" I ask just to be clear.

"Michelle said he'd wake up in a little while with a headache and fuzzy memory. We'd tell him he must've had too much to drink, give him a lap dance, make sure he signed his credit card tab, and send him on his way."

"Shit. Fuck." Digger pulls me aside. "I got a call from one of the credit card companies earlier this week. Several customers disputed their bills in the last few months. Figured it was just clients who had buyer's remorse and were trying to get out of paying."

I lift my chin at Presley. "How long they been running this scam?"

"I don't know." Her pleading eyes land on Digger but he won't look at her. "I haven't worked here that long. Michelle and Josh have always been tight though. The girls all gossip about it. Said they were probably fucking."

Digger nods. "She's new."

"Where's his stuff?" I ask Presley.

"In here." She reaches into the black ottoman that she'd opened earlier, pulling out a thick wad of cash, a cell phone, and some rings.

Digger glares at her and she hurries over to Dawson so fast she almost slips in the pile of puke on the floor. He lifts his head and stares at her.

"I'm sorry, Mr. Roads." She holds out her hands overflowing with the shit they jacked off him.

He plucks the rings out of her hands first and slips them on. "That's not mine," he says, tapping the bracelet.

"Jesus Christ," Digger mutters.

Dawson checks the cell phone before stuffing it in his pocket. He takes the cash and counts it quickly, pulling off a couple hundreds and handing them to Presley.

"I reckon that'll cover the part of the evening I *did* enjoy," he says to her with a smile.

All things considered, it's a classy move. Can't say I'd do the same in his boots.

Digger tucks his revolver away. "Go home, Presley, and wait for me to stop by. You try running, and I will hunt you the fuck down. You hear me?"

"Yes, sir."

He stops her at the door. "Do not talk to anyone else in this club. Go to the dressing room, collect your shit, and go home. Understood?"

"Wait, let me have Pants walk her out." I send him a quick text. "Go over to our table and ask for Pants," I tell her. "He knows you're coming. He'll walk you out so no one bothers you."

"All right."

After she leaves, Digger cocks his head.

"You don't know for sure some of the other girls aren't involved."

"Good point. Thanks, brother." He slaps my shoulder.

Dawson groans as he stands. "I'm gonna take my sorry ass back to our table and let you gentlemen speak."

"Mr. Roads, I apologize profusely," Digger says, groveling a little harder than I expected. Good. "This isn't how I run my establishment."

"Shit happens. Ain't easy to find good help these days. I know that better than anyone." Dawson flips his wallet open. "I *am* still missing a black AmEx card, though. Your guy, Josh, took it before he allowed me back here."

"I'll get it," Digger promises. "I'll make sure all the charges are reversed too."

"Appreciate it." He nods to me. "Rooster."

"Dawson." Fuck me. If Shelby's gonna stay on this tour, I see a whole lot of groveling in *my* future.

CHAPTER FORTY-SEVEN

Rooster

Now that we're alone, I feel free to lay into Digger.

"Brother, you've got a serious problem here. If the credit card companies are already onto this, it's only a matter of time before the FBI is knocking on your door. And you know how Priest's gonna react to that."

"I need to get ahead of it."

"No shit. This Josh, how much does he know about stuff that goes on here?"

"Rooster," he says in a mildly impatient tone. "I realize this fiasco might give the impression that I'm sloppy, but I don't share club business with civilians. Ever."

"Easy, I wasn't saying you did." Not quite, anyway. "Listen, I think if you want to keep the club out of it, you're gonna have to turn one of them over and let them hang for the theft charges. Whoever you think won't have anything to rat to the cops about."

"Skyler. She hasn't worked here that long."

Neither of us say it, but Josh and Michelle probably have dirt naps in their future. But that's Digger's problem, not mine.

"Now, I gotta deal with this fuckin' mess and hope my old lady doesn't get kicked off her tour." I pin him with a hard stare. "I brought my friends here thinking since *my* club owned the place, they'd be safe."

"Fuck, brother. I'm sorry. You know I'd never disrespect you like that. I don't know what to say. What can I do?"

"Nothing more than you've already done. Just make sure whatever got charged to his card tonight is reversed. Wipe their phones for any photos they might've taken too." Fuck, why didn't I think of that before?

"They're not allowed to have phones with 'em on the floor."

I stare at him.

"Yeah, yeah. I see your point."

"Look, Jenny mentioned she had some guy stalking her. You might want to see if she's in on this little drug and steal operation. Maybe the guy was after her because they drained his bank account. And if he's just a run-of-the-mill stalker, then you need better protection for your girls."

A flash of annoyance wrinkles his forehead. Maybe he doesn't like having a younger, lesser patch from a different charter telling him what to do. But too fucking bad. "I'll see what I can find out."

I slap his shoulder and dial down my anger. "You got a lot on your plate, brother."

"After all this, I hate asking, but you're traveling with a few brothers. You think any of them would mind sticking around for a couple of days to help me sort this?"

When we left Virginia after the kidnapping, the large entourage made sense. Now, it's a bit much. And I'm getting the sense some of the guys are bored. Wrath and Hustler were planning to head back to New York from here. Pants and Dex had been talking about visiting another club we're friendly with in Arizona. Honestly, Dex would be the best one to leave here since he has experience running a strip club and is frankly far better at it than Digger.

"I might be able to spare a few guys. Let me talk to them."

"I'd appreciate that." He hesitates again. "Where y'all staying tonight?"

"Hadn't decided yet."

"Let me call in a favor at a local place. I'll cover the rooms to make it up to you."

It's gonna take more than a night at some cheap motel to make up for this fuckery but I'm not about to spit in his face when he's doing what he can to make this right.

CHAPTER FORTY-EIGHT

Shelby

SOMEONE'S BEATIN' ON A BASS DRUM INSIDE MY SKULL.

My mouth tastes like cotton balls and sweaty socks.

Heavy. My body's too heavy to turn over.

"You okay?" Rooster's low rumbling voice reassures me I'm still alive.

"Blargh," I mumble.

Something cool and smooth presses against my hand. "Here, drink this."

I peel my eyes open and stare at the short, stubby glass of water Rooster's holding out to me. "Where are we?" I whisper.

"Hotel. Come on. Drink."

I take the cool glass and sip the water slowly. Flashes from last night return. *Did I try to pole dance?*

When I'm finished, I hand him the glass and he sits on the bed next to me. "Better?"

"A little," I whisper.

My phone's on the nightstand and I reach for it, turning it on. About a dozen messages pop up one after the other.

Miranda: You need to call me.

Greg: Where are you?

Miranda: Call me right now!

Trent: Shit! What did U do last night?

I blink and stare at the screen.

"What's wrong?" Rooster asks, reaching for my phone.

"I don't know." I show him the messages.

Since Greg and Miranda seem in a yellin' mood and my head's pounding, I ask Trent what's up.

Trent: How'd I miss this last night?

There's a link attached.

Shelby Morgan off the rails!

Exclusive footage of her stripper pole escapades.

Has Shelby Morgan gone from country music's sweetheart to bad girl? Shelby seems to have gone off the rails since her kidnapping ordeal. Keen-eyed readers spotted her at the Royal Dolls Saloon, an upscale gentlemen's club rumored to be owned by associates of the new cowboy in her life.

In the one performance she probably hoped no one would ever see, Sippin' on Secrets *has obtained an eye-popping video of the country music darling taking lessons on how to ride a stripper pole from scantily-clad dancers and more!*

While the night started off as a fun time off from a rigorous touring schedule, it was Shelby's sultry performance that left tongues wagging.

According to insiders, Shelby arrived at the club around 11 p.m. surrounded by four men, an unidentified woman, and members of her band. Dawson Roads, accompanied by his bodyguard and his band, arrived shortly after.

The group was there to let loose, ordering expensive drinks and getting rowdy.

The Royal Dolls Saloon is no stranger to X-rated romps. Their advertising claims customers are given the royal treatment and a sensual experience from the most beautiful women in the country. Private dances start at $100, according to regulars, making Shelby's freebie performance a bargain.

Was this a once-in-a-lifetime lapse in judgment or has Shelby Morgan found a new career gyrating on a stripper pole and collecting dollar bills?

Oh, it's all coming back to me now. I rub my forehead and scan the article again.

"Are you fucking kiddin' me?" I toss the phone on the bed and fall back against my pillows.

My head throbs. This is why I don't drink often.

Rooster sucks in a sharp breath.

I open my eyes and find him holding my phone in a white-knuckled grip. His jaw's set in a tight line as he reads the article.

"Don't bother," I mutter.

After a few tense minutes of silence, he sets the phone down. "I'm sorry. I never would've taken you there if I thought that would happen. It shouldn't have. They usually keep things under wraps. But last night was nothing but nonstop fuckery. I'm really sorry."

"I don't care. I'm a grown-ass woman who can go wherever the hell I dang well please. I wasn't naked or even topless. Notice it's all about judging *me* being there. Barely a mention about Dawson who got a freakin' lap dance from three girls."

He winces at the mention of Dawson's name but I don't bother to stop my tirade and ask why.

"Like, it's perfectly acceptable for him to be in a strip club but God forbid I have fun one night. Fuck them. I hate the double-standard more than anything."

The corner of his mouth twitches. "I love your spirit but it's still not the kind of bullshit you need right now. And that's my fault for gettin' you mixed up in my club's business."

I reach out and rub my hand over his thigh. "I woulda been plenty pissed if you'd gone without me. I saw those girls eyein' my man and didn't like it one bit."

His mouth stretches into a pained smile. "Nothing interested me there. Trust me."

"Where'd you go, anyway? When Jiggy tore me off the pole, you were gone. Shoot, I barely remember you carrying me out of there and the ride here."

He groans and scrubs his hands over his face. "I told you I needed to talk to Digger, right?"

"Yup."

"Well, he asked me to walk one of the girls out to her car. Some guy had been harassing her and he was short on people."

"Aw, that was sweet of you."

He peers down at me. "That was like five minutes, max. But she kinda hinted at something related to what I was there to talk to Digger about so I stopped in his office. Had *that* talk."

"Get what you needed?"

"Yes and no. When I came out you were sort of out of it. I realized Dawson was missing. Guys said he was still gettin' a lap dance." He goes on to explain what's probably a sanitized version of what went down when he found Dawson.

By the end, I'm sitting upright with my hands covering my mouth. "Oh. My. Lord. I'm dead. I'm so dead. He's gonna kick me off the tour, isn't he?"

"No." He pries one of my hands away from my face. "I talked to him last night. And I'll talk to him again later today. I won't let that happen."

"Is he okay?"

"I think so."

"Shoot, I remember those girls." I squeeze my eyes shut trying to recall some details. "They made a beeline straight for him. I even wanted to take a picture and send it to Glenna just to be a bitch."

He snorts. "Well, you're not supposed to take pictures inside the club." He taps my phone. "But obviously that's bullshit."

"Oh, yeah! Some guy was taking pictures of me. Jiggy went after him and took his phone. They kicked the guy out." I reconsider the order of events last night. "It was after I was up on the pole, though. So maybe someone else took the pictures sent to the blog."

"The whole place is sketchy as fuck and I'm fuckin' pissed I brought you there."

Since Rooster can be so hard on himself, I inch closer to wrap myself around him and let him know I'm not mad. "It's *not* your fault. Besides Dawson, I think everyone else had an awesome time. I even had fun until I thought I was gonna puke." I glance at my phone. "I look pretty hot in those pics, so I don't care. Maybe I'll tell them I was trying out for a part in a movie, generate some Hollywood buzz for myself." I squeeze his arm. "That might be fun."

He grunts and noncommittal noise.

My phone buzzes and I finally pick it up.

Miranda: We need to talk about this.

Another message from her pops up with a link to the same article.

Me: Already read it.

Someone knocks on our door. Rooster slips on his jeans before answering.

"You see this?" Dawson rasps.

"Come on in." Rooster steps aside.

I glance down, not even sure what I'm wearing. One of Rooster's T-shirts. Still, I pull the sheet up around me and put my back against the headboard. "Mornin'."

"Mornin', Shelby. Sorry to intrude."

His flat tone's hard to interpret. Fear flutters through my belly. Is he here to fire me from the tour?

"You all right?" He drops into a chair a couple feet from the bed.

Rooster sits next to me, resting his hand on the sheet over my leg. It's a simple, lovey-dovey gesture. He always touches and connects with me in little ways. But for some reason, with Dawson here in our room, it feels possessive and primal. So, so sexy.

This isn't the time to get hot and bothered, you nympho.

I realize they're both staring at me, waiting for an answer.

"What? Oh, yes. I'm okay. Are *you*?"

Dawson shifts his gaze to Rooster. "Guess you told her?"

"Just the highlights."

Dawson's cheeks turn a bit pink. "Not my finest moment."

"I'm sorry I suggested we go there," Rooster says. "That's all on me."

"Logan, I'm a grown-ass man. I had one of my security guys with me—who, by the way, I'm gonna fire."

"Shit," Rooster mutters.

"Don't feel bad for him," he says in a much harsher voice than I've probably ever heard Dawson use. "You're the only one who bothered to look for me. That's what *he* was gettin' paid to do."

Rooster doesn't say anything.

"If you hadn't been there, that coulda been a real disaster."

"If it weren't for *me*, you wouldn't have been there *at all*," Rooster counters.

Could we please stop reminding him of that fact?

Dawson slaps his thigh. "Shit, you think that's the first titty bar I been to in my life, Logan?"

The two of them share a laugh.

"Here's the thing," Dawson leans forward, resting his elbows on his knees. "The security experts were fine. We all learned some stuff from 'em, yada, yada. But you and your guys are street-smart and you pay fuckin' attention."

Rooster glances at me and I see the guilt flashing in his eyes. Dammit. He's still blamin' himself for Suggs gettin' his grubby hands on me. I just know it. I can't say anything to contradict whatever bullshit's in his head right now. Not in front of Dawson. So, I curl my fingers around his and squeeze tight.

"Here's what I'm proposing," Dawson continues. "Any more side trips or adventures like that, I want to hire one of y'all to be my guard."

"You don't have to pay any of us to be your friend, Dawson. The guys like you fine."

He chuckles. "I get that. Other things might not be as entertaining, though."

"You need one of us to hold your hand at the dentist or something?"

"Yeah, maybe." He sits back in the chair, resting his elbows on the arms. "I'm guessing Wrath's only looking out for his lady. Besides, he mentioned they're headin' home."

"Probably today, actually."

"I like Dex. He seems trustworthy."

"He is, absolutely."

"I get the impression you and Jigsaw are a package deal."

Rooster pats my leg. "Yeah, plus, he doesn't like lettin' Shelby too far out of his sight."

"Aww," I sigh.

"Can't you tell?" He raises an eyebrow. "You see him handin' out cute lil' nicknames to anyone else? Or rushing in with a baseball bat if he thinks someone's after them?"

Now that he mentions it, *no*.

"Y'all must be havin' a time on that RV," Dawson says.

"Not like that," Rooster growls.

"Easy, I'm kiddin'. Now, Steer—that dude looks like he could put a hurtin' on someone. And he's already been helping out during my set and at my meet-n-greets, so I know he pays attention to details."

"He's our SAA for a reason," Rooster agrees.

"Will you let me make them the offer?"

"I don't have to *let you* do anything. They're free to do what they want."

"But they're here because of *you*. I'd be steppin' on your toes if I asked them without talkin' to you." He stares at me for a few seconds. "To be honest, I'd rather put the four of you on my payroll."

Rooster's quick to shake that off. "No offense, but I'm here for Shelby, Dawson. If it's a choice between her or you, I'm picking her every time, no matter how much you're paying."

"As you should. Wouldn't respect ya otherwise. But it looks like her record company ain't coming through. And to be honest, it's *my* tour. My name's on everything. It don't look too good when stuff happens to my opening act." Dawson smiles wide enough for little crinkles to form at the corners of his eyes. "Don't know if anyone's gonna accept a slot opening for me next summer. You might be stuck with me again, Shelby."

My heart thumps. Is this his way of asking if I'll tour with him again? "I'd do it in a heartbeat."

"Yeah? Even knowin' my ex might still be stewing?"

"Fuck her," I blurt out. "Sorry."

"Nope. I like your spirit, Shelby." His expression turns more serious. "I'm not talking opening for the opener here, either. You've paid your dues. You're never late. Always accept the soundcheck when I run over my time. Never run over your set. You do a hell of a job promoting the tour with your fans and stuff. It'd be an honor to have you go on stage right before me."

I'm under no illusions that I'll be ready to headline a tour on my own by next summer, so this is definitely the next best thing. "Thank you. Yes, of course I will."

"We'll talk to Greg and get that sorted. Still got plenty of dates left on this tour to worry about." He turns to Rooster again. "Now, about that payroll. How 'bout you set up something official and I'll get that over to my accountant. That way I'm not feelin' like a schmuck when your guys are helpin' me out and stuff."

My phone vibrates, drawing all of our attention.

"You plannin' to answer that?" Dawson asks me.

"No, it's Greg calling to yell at me."

"He better not yell at you." Rooster snaps up the phone and hits accept.

"Why are you doing this to me, Shelby?" Greg moans. Guess he and Miranda aren't planning to give me some leeway on this one.

"You got Logan."

"And Dawson." He leans forward and shouts at the phone. "Don't be yellin' at the lady, Greg."

"Where's Shelby?" Greg asks.

I lean closer to the phone. "I'm right here. And I didn't do anything *to* you, Greg. I went out with my friends."

"Can I talk to you privately?" Greg asks.

"Sure, sure." I grab the phone from Rooster and scoot to the other side of the bed, scurrying into the bathroom.

I need to pee and since Greg's kinda pissed me off this morning, I feel it's acceptable to do it while he's still ranting. I mute my end of the conversation, though. I'm a lady after all.

"Greg," I cut in when I'm finished but he's still rip-roarin' mad.

"Did you see the pictures of you smiling and twirling around the pole like a…like a…"

"Like a girl having a good time? You know pole dancing is actually a sport, right? Maybe I was trying to get in shape since all these magazines keep insinuating I've got too much junk in my trunk."

"No one takes pole dancing lessons from half-naked strippers in what looks like a damn whorehouse, Shelby. You know better."

"Dawson was there too." Damn, I hate that whiny tone to my voice. "Why isn't anyone bent about that?"

"He's a man. I thought you'd come to terms with how this business works?" He blows out an annoyed breath. "Why are we having this conversation? You want to win that CMA award, this isn't the way to do it, Shelby."

Shoot. The double-standard burns my ass, but he's right. I still have to work within the confines of the industry if I want to reach my goals. "I didn't think it was that big of a deal."

Rooster pushes the door open and snatches the phone out of my hand, flipping the speaker on again. I don't even bother to protest.

"It's my fault," he rumbles. "No one should've been taking photos there."

"The video and photos are shit," Greg concedes. "So it must've been a customer or something sneaking the shot." His voice gets distant likes he's looking at something on his screen while he's talking to us. "Hardly even looks like Shelby. If it wasn't for the clear shot of you in the parking lot, I'd go with a 'that's not even her' defense."

Oh, hell no. I can already see the tracks Greg's thought train is barreling down. "I won't lie or apologize for going out and having fun with my friends."

"Shelby—"

"No."

"Where's Dawson? He still there?"

"No," Rooster answers. "He had to run."

Greg grumbles. "This might kill your chances at the CMAs. Hell, you might not win that Small Screen award either, Shelby. That show's coming up soon."

"Well, I guess we'll have to wait and see." I take a deep breath. "But I'm not apologizing."

CHAPTER FORTY-NINE

Rooster

AFTER SUCH AN EVENTFUL MORNING, IT'S ALMOST ANTI-CLIMACTIC WHEN we finally roll into National's parking lot.

Shelby's so happy to see the RV she runs inside of it to change and I follow.

"Babe, I'm gonna run inside. I need to talk to Priest."

She emerges from the bathroom in shorts and a tank, her face damp and hair in a ponytail. "I might take a nap. Is that okay?" She eyes the bed longingly.

"You want to use the cabin? I still have the key for it."

"I kinda wanna sleep in my own bed. But I also want to take a bath."

I turn on the fan. "Why don't you nap here. I'll come get you when I'm done. We're not leaving until tomorrow morning. Plenty of time to bathe you." In fact, I'm looking forward to it.

"All right." She yawns and pads over to the bed. I pull back the covers and tuck her in, stopping to kiss her cheek.

"Better?"

"Mmm."

Chuckling, I step outside, closing and locking the door.

"Is she okay?" Jigsaw asks.

"Shit. Why you sneaking up on me?"

"Everyone else went inside," he says, ignoring my question. "You need me to talk to Priest with you?"

I appreciate the offer but I'm not dragging Jiggy into this conversation. "Nah, that's all right."

"You planning to tell him everything?"

I'd gone back and forth about it the whole ride here. Ultimately, Priest ranks higher than Digger in the hierarchy of who I owe my loyalty. Plus, I'm still fuckin' pissed that Dawson got drugged and almost robbed blind. And I'm absolutely furious someone took pictures of Shelby *and* leaked them to that stupid blog.

"Digger's a fuckup ten different ways," Jigsaw says. "You're not throwing him under the bus. You're protecting the whole club."

"My guilt vanished the second I saw that damn blog this morning."

Jiggy wanted to go back to Digger's and interrogate everyone to find out where the pictures came from. But it wasn't worth the extra time. I wanted to get as far away from that place as possible before anything else happened.

Inside the clubhouse, Jiggy and I part ways. I travel the long corridor to Priest's office and knock on the door.

"Come in," he calls.

Valentina's on his desk with her back to the door but turns and smiles when she sees me. "How was your trip?"

"Eventful."

She slides off the desk, stopping to give Priest a lingering kiss. Nice to know they're still into each other after decades together.

Shit. That's what I want. I want that with Shelby.

It hits me so hard, I almost run back to the RV.

Relax. Get this over with first.

Valentina stops in front of me. "Glad you're back, Rooster."

"Thank you."

She closes the door behind her and Priest offers me the seat in front of his desk.

"Well, how'd it go?"

I tell him the whole story. From Squiggy's possible disappearance, Dawson's adventure in fuck-up-land, and the photos of Shelby. I make sure to throw in a few compliments about how nice the place looks. I'm not a total dick.

Priest blinks and sits back in his chair, lacing his fingers together over his chest. "Are you fuckin' kidding me?" he finally says.

"Wish I was."

"Did that fuck things up for your old lady? This guy's basically like her boss right now, isn't he?"

I don't usually think of their arrangement in those terms, but yeah I guess so. Dawson holds the power to hire and fire. Somehow, even after that messed up night, he hired both of us. I still haven't sorted all that out.

"I'm impressed with the way you handled the situation," Priest says, pulling me away from my thoughts. "You kept a level head. Didn't let things escalate or get out of control. That's how a good leader handles a complicated situation."

I don't think I did anything that special. Nothing any one of my brother's wouldn't have done. "Z's been a good mentor."

His mouth quirks and he stifles a laugh. "That's interesting."

"How's that, Prez?"

"*Sway* was your president for years. Z's been your president for a few months. Yet, you seem to have more loyalty to Z."

Well, shit. I didn't even think about the words before they came out of my mouth. "No disrespect to Sway was intended. I've—"

"You don't have to explain it to me, Rooster. It's obvious I should've replaced Sway years ago. I always figured with Rock nearby, I didn't need to look at New York too closely."

Fuck me. Fuck me. Fuck me.

A bolt of unease ties my stomach in a knot. Saying the wrong thing here could bring unwanted attention from National down on Z's head. Rock's too.

"You made the right call, Prez. Z's brought a lot of good changes to our charter. We're in good hands now." *Please don't visit us more often.*

"I know. I was impressed when I visited. Hopefully, we'll be able to drop in again soon."

Z and Rock are gonna kill me.

"He still mad about leaving upstate?" Priest asks.

"I don't think Z was ever *mad*. Disappointed, maybe. I don't want to speak for him. It's brought both clubs together. We never realized how much Sway did to fuel the animosity between our clubs. He never wanted us to trust Rock and his crew. So we all kinda kept our distance."

Priest grunts and waves his hand in the air. "That was ancient bullshit that Sway should've gotten over years ago. I'm glad Rock never indulged him in that petty crap."

"Yeah, that's before my time, so I can't speak on that."

He nods and sits back. "I like that about you, Rooster. You don't talk to hear your own voice."

"Thanks, I guess."

"They say it's the quiet ones you're supposed to look out for." Priest's evil grin should be enough to make me shit my pants but I don't move a muscle. I have nothing to hide or worry about. I've never betrayed my club in any way.

When I don't react, he nods. "Instead of *Rooster,* your road name should've been *Hawk.* Quietly observing. Waiting to swoop in and make the kill."

He's got me all wrong. I run my hand over my beard slowly. "What's on your mind, Priest?"

"You think Digger's gettin' too old for the job? Too soft?"

"I can't make that call. I spent less than twenty-four hours there."

"Sometimes your caution is frustrating."

I can't win today, can I?

"That's not my intention." I blow out a breath and recall the savage look on Digger's face when he was making the decision of who to turn over to the cops. "Soft? No. He handled the situation with the girls like a boss."

"But?"

"I don't know if it has anything to do with *age.*"

He smirks. "Speak freely, Rooster. You're not gonna hurt my feelings."

"It might be that he's got too much on his plate. He had a call from the credit card company but didn't investigate. His SAA's missing but he's not concerned. He might have reasons I'm not aware of, though. But if it were me, I would've checked on him sooner."

"So would I."

"That's your call, Priest." Just leave me the fuck out of it.

If I had to guess, Blink and at least one other brother will be on the road to Deadbranch by tonight.

"How long you plannin' to be on the road?" he asks.

Shelby's tour is all sorts of fucked up thanks to the delays but I don't want to get into specifics with Priest. "At least another month or two. Then she'll be recording her album."

"You got any control over those dates?"

"Not really." I shrug. "She's the opening act."

"But some of those dates bring you close to our charters, right?"

Wouldn't surprise me one bit if he'd already looked up every date on the schedule. "Yes, sir. Of course, I'll stop by and pay my respects."

"I don't doubt you will." He pauses and studies me for a moment. "What you did in Deadbranch probably saved this club a lot of fucking trouble. You understand that, don't you?"

"Uh, I guess."

"I realize it cost you personally, and I'm sorry."

Damn. I highly doubt Priest apologizes often. "Club comes first, Priest. I know that."

"It does. But our brothers' happiness is important too." His gaze shifts to the door. "And ain't *no* brother happy if his old lady ain't happy."

I laugh with him. "She handled it okay. Her manager's still not pleased about the exposure, but he'll get over it."

"Still, if there's a way to make amends, I want you to tell me." He holds up his hand. "Think on it. I don't need an answer right now. I owe you one, though."

"Okay." Priest owing anyone a favor probably happens about as often as a total solar eclipse. "I will."

"One last thing, what's our relationship with the other clubs in New York looking like?

At least I don't have to hesitate. "Good. Wolf Knights are still moving out of Slater County."

"What about the Devil Demons MC?"

"Solid." I gesture toward the door. "Actually ran into their prez at one of Shelby's shows. He called to offer some help during her...what happened."

He sits back and crosses his arms over his chest. "Chaser? That right?"

"Yes." I have no idea how much of Chaser's background Priest is aware of. "He has some entertainment connections. Hooked me up with someone who could help Shelby. Also said he'd introduce me to some Demon brothers if I need a hand with security at any of her shows."

"Very nice." His wide eyes and thoughtful nod say he's impressed and not annoyed that I'm cozy with the president of what's technically a rival MC. "That might come in handy on the West Coast where the two clubs' relationships haven't always been as...*harmonious,* shall we say, as they have on the East Coast."

"Sure."

He narrows his eyes. "And I assume any work you have would be offered to Lost Kings."

"Absolutely."

"Washington's your home charter, right?"

Technically, I grew up in Northern California and then Oregon. Spent very little time in Washington. I shift in my seat, uncomfortable with the turn our conversation just took. "Yeah."

"You know we've had issues there. Any chance you can stop in. Just observe, the way you did in Deadbranch."

Yeah, because that worked out so well for me. This time, I'm not taking an entourage.

"Absolutely, I was planning to stop there. Shelby's got dates in Spokane and Tacoma." There isn't a whole lot of wiggle room in the schedule around those dates, but I've got time to figure it out. Obviously, this visit isn't optional.

"Good. Bring her with you. Introduce her so they get to know your old lady."

I hesitate, not sure I should even mention this. "Unfortunately, sometimes it draws attention to *me*. Being photographed with her."

He searches through a stack of papers and uncovers the damn copy of *Glow* with Shelby and me on the front.

Are you fucking kidding me?

"Who's the largest one-percenter club in the country?" he asks. "Fuck, the whole world?"

I'm not sure what that has to do with the magazine but the answer rolls off my tongue easily. "The club we never name."

"Right. You notice how pervasive they are these days? They're everywhere. Insidious. In the Nineties they started treating the club as a business entity. Now, they've wormed their way into all facets of pop-culture. Built up a 'mystique' around the outlaw life."

Exactly the kind of shit most true bikers hate. "Yeah, and it encourages every fool who buys a Harley to LARP around at being a biker."

He raises an eyebrow.

"Live action role play," I explain.

"Heh. I like that." He grins. "Exactly, they're even on those stupid reality shows. People treat them like celebrities. And yet, they've never gotten out of guns, extortion, and a host of other shit. They just do it in plain sight now."

"Yeah, until the government goes after their colors."

"Government *lost* that battle, don't forget." He sets the magazine down. "Why do you think that is?"

"Like you said, they treat their club like a business."

"Right. But there's something else. They've infiltrated government agencies in some way at every level. Their women work in courthouses. Family members in law enforcement. Bribing people. Forming relationships. Maintaining those relationships over years."

I don't know if I'd call bribing elected officials with tapes of them in bed with young women who aren't their wives "maintaining relationships" but, whatever.

"Ice has made significant progress with a few agencies," Priest says.

He sure has. And here I was worried Ice's ties to ATF and the FBI were a *bad* thing, when all along, it sounds like Priest's been encouraging it.

"That'll benefit all of us."

"Or get us all sent to prison." Shit, I can't believe I said that out loud.

"I understand your concern and it's not without merit."

"What's any of this have to do with me?"

"This." He taps the magazine cover. Christ, I want to hunt down every copy and toss them in a bonfire. "Doesn't bother me. It normalizes us. Puts people at ease. She has a lovely wholesome image."

Why do those words sound creepy as fuck coming out of Priest's mouth?

"It's not a negative to be seen with her. Makes the big, bad bikers seem less scary."

I think I liked Priest better when he threatened us to keep a low profile and didn't want us to draw attention to ourselves.

"I thought the whole point was to fuck everyone's opinion and live outside the bounds of society?"

"Times change, Rooster. We can adapt to the world around us. Or rot in prison."

Adapt it is.

CHAPTER FIFTY

Rooster

After we leave Priest's compound we head to the ranch where Dawson and his guys are hanging out.

Along the way, our caravan pulls into a rest stop to say goodbye to Wrath, Trinity, and Hustler. They're headin' home from here.

Shelby and Trinity share a teary goodbye.

"You're going to come visit us for Christmas, right?" Trinity asks.

Thank you, Trinity.

Shelby takes my hand, pulling me closer. "Sooner, I hope."

I definitely like the sound of that.

They hug and promise to get together for online yoga practice at least once a week.

"Be fabulous, flamingo," Trinity says, pulling away.

Wrath even wraps her up in a hug that almost swallows her whole. "Don't take any shit, kid." He glances at me and smirks. "Not even from Rooster."

Shelby sniffle-giggles as she pulls away. "I won't. Promise."

Hustler shakes her hand and wishes her luck.

After another round of hugs and goodbyes, we're back on the road and arrive at the ranch before sunset.

It's a party again. Music's pumping. Bonfire's roaring. Drinks flowing. Shelby stares at the scene in front of us and yawns.

"Not in a celebrating mood tonight?" I ask.

"Honestly, no."

Still, we do a lap around the party. She checks in with her band. I talk to some of the roadies. Then we head to the RV for the night.

"I need to give Z a call, you all right?"

She holds up her ear buds and her lyric notebook. "Trent sent me some files. I'm gonna give 'em a listen."

"You remember to write down that 'diamond in the dust, I'm about to combust' line?"

She throws a pillow at me. "Hush your mouth, Logan Randall."

Laughing, I take a seat at the dinette and call Z.

"My hero!" Z says so loud, I can picture his big ol' dimpled grin. "What the fuck you been up to, motherclucker? Priest had all sorts of glowing compliments for you *and* me."

I'm not feelin' like much of a hero. "Jesus, brother. That visit to Digger's was a clusterfuck of epic fuckery."

I relay a sanitized version of what went down. Never know who might be listening in on our calls. But I'm able to give Z the general gist of things.

"I didn't want to say anything, but I saw the hit piece on Shelby," he says when I finish. "You think it's gonna hurt her?"

"Don't know. Her manager seems to think so." I glance over at Shelby but she's absorbed in whatever she's listening to and scribbling furiously in her notebook. "I didn't get to tell you the best part. Priest's fine with the exposure. He'd now like us to follow in the footsteps of the Eighty-Sixers."

"I'm sorry. What?"

Again, I give him a general outline.

"Has he lost his mind?" Z yells. "That reality TV shit is half the reason they're at war with every MC in the country."

"I didn't want to question him too much, Z."

"No. You did fine." He cackles. "I can't wait to tell Rock this little gem."

"Glad I could amuse you."

"Well, I guess it's a relief."

"Trust me, I still plan to lay as low as possible." I have my own reasons for not wanting my face in magazines that have nothing to do with the club.

Finally, we hang up. Shelby's still awake, so I ask her to come outside with me.

We stop at the truck where I pull a blanket out of the back seat.

The guys have settled down somewhat but the bonfire's still roaring. We walk away from it toward the open field.

"Where are we going?"

I stop and stare at the sky. This should be a good spot. I spread the blanket out and drop down, holding my hand out to her.

"We have a perfectly good bed in the RV, you know."

I roll onto my back, pulling her with me. "I know, sassy pants. But I wanted you to see this."

Together, we stare up at the stars. So many of them.

"Ohh," she breathes out. "It's beautiful. Thousands of tiny diamonds and cosmic dust on inky satin."

Who else would describe a simple night sky so poetically? "I know I was teasing you before. But your line about diamonds made me think of this."

She rolls to her side, so she's facing me. "Really?"

"I used to like sleeping under the stars sometimes when I was a kid." I turn to her. "I know that's not your thing so we won't stay long."

"With you, it could be my thing." Her velvety voice caresses my very soul. "The whole world seems less scary when I'm with you."

"The stars scare you?"

"Not the stars. The things that lurk in the darkness." She rolls onto her back and slips her hand in mine, softly running her thumb over the back of my hand. "The universe is so big, I feel like it could swallow me whole sometimes."

"I'd never let that happen."

CHAPTER FIFTY-ONE

Shelby

By the time we pull into Baton Rouge a few days later, Greg seems to be over the stripper pole fiasco, as I've named the incident.

Sippin' on Secrets had the nerve to DM me on Instagram for a comment. I may or may not have answered with an unladylike middle-finger emoji.

No regrets.

Tonight, I'm pacing around my dressing room humming my scales when Greg busts in.

"Knock much, Greg?" Rooster growls. "That's a good way to walk in on something you don't wanna see."

I snicker into my hand. "He ain't lyin'."

"Neither of you are funny," he grumbles.

"Hey, Shelby." Cindy breezes into the room, bumping Greg out of her way. "How're we feeling tonight?"

"Nervous."

"Oh, hush, honey. You're gonna be great as always." She pats the chair. "Come on now."

Rooster continues working, ignoring Greg's presence as much as one can in such a small room.

After seeing all the work he did for Anya's website, I'd asked him to update mine. Between the photos Trinity took and other content we added, it's looking a lot more professional. It'd probably be less annoying if Rooster didn't have to run all of it by Greg. But so far, they haven't murdered each other.

"You want me to add the pages for each of the guys, right?" Rooster asks me.

"Yup. Trent should've sent you pics and bios."

"I got 'em."

Trinity and I have been going back and forth on more flamingo pun ideas and illustrations. Rooster's planning to add a merch shop on my website to sell the stuff once we figure out the designs. We added a few flocking fabulous tank tops to my merch booth and so far, they're selling well.

"What do you think about putting your hair up tonight?" Cindy asks. "It's so hot out there."

"Sure."

While she works on me, I stick my ear buds in and listen to the pieces Trent and I recorded together earlier on my phone. The quality's crap. But it's good enough to get the general feel and make some notes.

"You're wearing the purple dress tonight, right?" Cindy asks.

"Can we do big, glam eyes with that metallic gold and purple combo we did in Atlanta?"

"Sure."

When she's finished, I scoot into the bathroom to change into my dress. I strip down to my bra and panties. I kinda miss the days when we didn't have so many people in and out of my dressing room before a show so Rooster and I could fool around.

Laughing to myself, I pick up my phone and send him a quick text.

Me: I miss pre-show orgasms.

Five seconds later, he knocks on the door and opens it.

"You rang?" His mouth twists into my favorite cocky smirk as he swaggers into the room and closes the door behind him.

Nervous laughter bubbles out of me. "Is Greg still out there?"

"No, I told him to get lost." He flips the lock on the door.

"You did not."

He stalks closer, backing me up against the sink. "I absolutely did." He runs his gaze over me from head to toe. "Why didn't you ask earlier? I don't want to mess up your makeup and stuff before you go on stage."

"We were busy." I shrug, feeling a little silly now. "I wasn't serious. I don't expect you to deliver orgasms on demand."

He meets my eyes. "Oh, I plan to deliver."

That damn confident, cocky statement makes my knees wobble. The dull ache between my thighs intensifies.

"Hmm." He slides his hands over my shoulders and down my arms. "Slide your panties off," he says in that low, hypnotizing voice that melts me like butter. My panties hit the ground faster than a shooting star across the sky.

"Nice," he praises.

He runs his hand over his chin and strokes his beard as his gaze roams over my body. "How are we gonna make this work?" The question's low and more like he's asking himself the question.

"You look like you're doing mental sex physics in your head or something," I tease.

"I am." He cups my hips and lifts me onto the sink, then kneels in front of me.

"What are you doing?" I ask, raking my nails through his hair.

"Well, I'm not here to paint your toes, chickadee." He picks up one foot and kisses the top. "Put your legs over my shoulders." His voice dips to a slow, seductive note.

Excitement thrums through my veins. While I had a stab of guilt about treating him as my own personal orgasm delivery service, his enthusiasm erases my doubt.

With the tight space and awkward angle, it takes some effort to do as he asks and there's nothing graceful about the process. He pulls me to the edge of the sink and crams his head between my thighs.

"Oh!" My body jolts as his tongue sweeps over my flesh. None of the usual soft kisses and nibbles along my thighs tonight. Logan's getting right down to business. I brace myself with one hand behind me and the other on his head, my fingers curling into his hair.

Even though he's laser focused, he's gentle as he sucks my clit into his mouth and strokes with the tip of his tongue.

"Holy moly. You are so fucking amazing at that."

He answers with a dirty, rumbling laugh.

I'm throbbing with need. He strokes with the perfect cadence to set me off.

"Right there." My fingers curl in his hair. "Oh!" I yelp as my body convulses with release. My thighs quiver as the sensation explodes through my body.

He kisses the inside of my thigh. "That was quick. You *did* need me."

I realize how tight my fingers are curled in his hair and release him, stopping to touch myself.

He groans. "Fuck, that's beautiful."

"What?"

"Your fingers on your pussy."

"Like this?" I tease, dragging one finger through my wetness.

"Shelby," he groans, not taking his eyes off me.

"Fuck me, Logan," I whisper.

He slips my legs off his shoulders and rises from the floor like a warrior about to conquer and claim his territory. I meet his eyes and shudder with excitement as he unbuckles his belt.

"Take your shirt off."

With a playful slowness, he eases the shirt up over his head, leaning over to drape it over a hook on the wall. "Better?"

I run my hand over his stomach, over his rippling abs. Our eyes meet again. "I could do our laundry on your abs."

He laughs, his muscles tightening and flexing. Continuing my exploration, I flatten my palm over his chest. He's broad and thick with muscle. I trace my fingers over lines of ink. His eyelids lower like a content lion as I curl my hand around his neck and draw him closer.

He hurries to finish undoing his jeans, freeing himself. His hips jerk as I work my hand up and down his cock in a steady rhythm. He lets out a tortured groan.

"Come closer," I whisper.

My invitation snaps him out of his trance. His hands are on my hips, pulling me to the edge of the sink, but it's not quite the right height. He lifts me, shuffling to the side, bracing me between his hard chest and the wall. His cock presses against me and I wrap my legs around his hips. He drives in inch by inch, staring into my eyes the whole time, backing off if I flinch, waiting until I'm ready to accept all of him.

"How's that?" he asks.

"Really good." I brace my arms on his shoulders and roll my hips. He digs his fingers into my skin, holding me tight while matching my slow tempo. Another orgasm slowly builds. He drives into me harder. Faster. I'm climbing higher and higher but not *quite* there. What I need seems out of reach.

"Logan, I can't," I whisper breathlessly.

"Am I hurting you?" He loosens his grip on my hips.

"No, no. Don't stop."

"I'm not. I got you." He reaches between us to stroke my clit.

I squeeze my eyes shut, concentrating on his touch. "That's good."

His thrusting slows and I open my eyes to find him focused on the counter. "What?"

He holds out his hand. "Give me that thing."

"What thing?" My eyes land on what he's pointing to. "No, that's for my face!"

He digs the little egg-shaped silicone facial brush out of my makeup bag. "Not anymore."

With a wicked grin, he flicks it to the highest setting, then presses the flat, smooth side against my clit.

My body jolts. "Shit!"

"Fuck," he groans. "I feel it vibrating down my dick."

"I've never used it that high. It'd probably rattle my teeth out of my skull."

He laughs and leans in to kiss me. "Hold it there."

I take my poor, violated face brush and slide it to a spot that feels good. Rooster's big hands roam over my body as he pounds into me harder.

"You okay?" he asks.

"I'm fully understanding what it means to be *nailed*."

His thrusting slows. "Is that good?"

"Oh, yeah."

He mashes his lips against mine—there goes my lipstick. I tighten my arm around his neck and keep moving my hips, trying to match his frantic pace, shifting the vibrating brush a little lower.

My back bows.

"Yes," Rooster's deep raspy voice fills me with pride. "Fuck yes."

"Uh." I can't form any words. My legs shake and I stretch them straight out, allowing Rooster to take my full weight.

"That's it. Keep coming. Fuck," he groans.

Suddenly, it's too much. My body jerks. I toss the vibrator toward the sink and wrap my legs around Rooster again.

"That's my girl." He kisses my forehead. "That was fucking beautiful."

"Still feels so good," I whisper.

I can't even begrudge the cocky smile that returns to his face. The man deserves *all* the praise.

"Shelby," he whispers urgently. "I want to come on your tits."

I reach behind me and somehow wiggle my bra clasp loose, strip it off and toss it toward the sink. "Please don't shoot in my hair."

"I'm aiming for those pretty pink nipples baby, trust me."

He pulls out and sets me on my feet. I lean against the wall, arching my back to give him an easy target.

He lets out a long primal groan. Warmth hits my stomach and between my breasts.

A few seconds later, he braces himself with an arm against the wall and touches my cheek, tipping my head back. Our lips meet. A soft, sliding kiss. "Don't move," he whispers.

I stay like that, eyes closed, lips pursed, until he returns. He swipes something damp over my chest and belly. "Mmm, I feel so *claimed*," I murmur, opening my eyes.

He kisses my lips again. "You are." A dirty gleam flashes in his eyes. "Also, I didn't think you'd want my cum running down your leg during your show."

"Aren't you a gentleman," I drawl in a light, teasing tone.

"Did I deliver?" he asks.

"You need to ask? I can barely stand up."

He chuckles as he leans over the sink to wash up. He soaps his hands and cleans my face brush under the running water.

"You might as well toss that, I'm not using it on my face again."

"Nah, let's keep it for emergencies. I'll buy you another one for your face."

Now that the sex-high is fading, I'm worried about my hair and makeup. Also, the time.

"Shoot. How long were we in here?" I hurry over to the mirror and breathe a sigh of relief. "Not too bad. I can fix the lipstick."

"I tried to be careful," he says, rearranging a few stray bits of my hair.

I pull a lipstick that's close to the color Cindy used out of my bag. Thankfully, since we went with bold eyes, she used a mild color on my lips and I'm able to touch it up easily.

Rooster keeps his hands on me the whole time I'm in front of the mirror, running his fingers down my spine, spanning my waist with his hands, skimming his palms over my butt and thighs.

I wiggle my hips. "Wishing you'd chosen a different target?"

"No," he scoffs. "I just like touching you."

Swoon. How does he always say the sweetest things? "I like touching you too."

He leans in and kisses my shoulder. "Good."

I hurry into my underwear and bra, then take my dress off its hanger. "Will you help me?"

"Of course."

We get the dress in place and I check myself in the mirror one last time. "My shoes are out there."

Someone's knocking at the door in the other room. "Come in!" I yell.

"It's locked," Rooster says, striding out of the bathroom with his shirt in his hands. He flings the door open and a red-faced Greg's waiting on the other side.

"The walls are thin here," Gregg huffs. "Just thought I'd mention that."

My cheeks heat up but I toss off the embarrassment quickly. Someone's *always* having sex backstage somewhere. It's not like I'm the first.

"Your flamingo tanks are sold out," Greg says. "I thought you'd want to know."

"Oh, wow!" I grab my phone to text Trinity and give her the news.

Greg's phone beeps. Groaning, he flicks the screen on. "What now?"

His already red face slides toward an even deeper scarlet. "Oh, this is bad," he mutters.

"What?"

He bites his lip and hesitates.

"What?" I ask again, marching toward him and reaching for his phone.

He shoots a glare at Rooster. "What *else* went on in the strip club the other night?"

I stop and frown at his hostile tone. "Nothing, why?"

"Because *this* is bad."

Greg turns the screen toward me. My heart stops as I read the headline.

'White Knight? Or Cheating Bastard? We Have the Inside Scoop!'

CHAPTER FIFTY-TWO

Shelby

"SHELBY, NOTHING HAPPENED." ROOSTER STARES AT THE PHONE, SLOWLY scanning the article. "Greg, give us a minute," he says without looking away from the screen.

"We really need to—"

"Get out, Greg!" I snap, not in the mood for more of his crap.

While I'm waiting for him to leave, I find my own phone and pull up the article.

White Knight—the super-sappy with a side of corniness and cheese love song by sassy country singer Shelby Morgan has been burning up the streaming charts for weeks. In an interview with Glow magazine, she claimed it was written about her current boyfriend. But is it all a lie?

After breaking the story about Shelby's wild night out at the Royal Dolls Gentlemen's Club, Sippin' on Secrets *has obtained more exclusive photos of the wild shenanigans that transpired.*

A hawk-eyed reader spotted Shelby's main squeeze in a compromising situation with a stripper. Talk about a downgrade!

Was her boyfriend's cheating what prompted Shelby Morgan's wild meltdown?

Can we expect a new angst-ridden cheese-fest of a song to commemorate the breakup?

Only time will tell. But we'll have the scoop, so check back often for more updates on this continuing drama! Tell us in the comments, is Shelby's knight in shining armor really a cheater in tin foil?

I don't have time for this nonsense. I have to be on stage soon.

The happy buzz from our little romantic interlude fades, and irritation moves into its place.

I scroll through the pictures, which show nothing more than Rooster standing in a parking lot with a woman. In one of the photos, she's touching him and standing within kissing distance. From Logan's stiff posture and the snarly expression on his face, it doesn't look like he's enjoying the attention.

The final picture is of Logan staring off into the distance with the caption, *"Worried about getting caught?"*

"This is so stupid," I mutter.

Logan's quiet. I glance up from my phone and find him standing closer than I expected.

"Nothing happened, Shelby. I walked her out. That's it. I talked to her about the club."

"She's touching you here." I show him the photo.

"Yeah, and I wish they'd published the next photo which was me removing her hand."

I squint at him. "From *her* body or yours?"

He blinks in confusion. "What?"

"You said you removed her hand. Did ya like, chop it off or something?"

"Are you making a joke?" He taps the phone. "About this?"

"What else am I gonna do?" I scroll through the pictures. "You honestly think I'd believe these nitwits over you?"

"Thank you." The tension in his shoulders relaxes. He gestures to my phone. "Whatever they write means nothing. I don't care what strangers think of me. It's what *you* think that matters."

"Well, I think you're the best man I've ever known." I lean up and kiss his cheek.

"Let's set this aside." His loving eyes burn with determination. "You need to clear your head and focus on the show. We can figure this out later."

And that's how I know I'm right. A cheater or a selfish man would be more worried about defending *himself* than my show. A confident man with nothing to hide would focus on what's important.

AFTER MY SET, GREG AMBUSHES US IN MY DRESSING ROOM.

"Miranda has time." He bustles through my door red-faced and out of breath. "We need to sit down and have a video conference to figure this out."

"Greg, I'm tired. My throat's scratchy. Can't we do this tomorrow?"

"No." He sets his tablet on my table and connects with Miranda.

Her someone-pissed-in-my-cornflakes scowl doesn't inspire confidence.

Reluctantly I take the chair next to Greg. Rooster sits opposite of me.

"This isn't good," Miranda says instead of hello. "The stripper pole was bad enough but it might've died down. Now, this?"

"Hold your horses. Logan didn't do anything," I say with as much patience as possible. "He walked the woman out to her car so she didn't get mugged, for God's sake. This is ridiculous."

"It's the optics of the situation, Shelby."

"I don't give shiitake mushroom about optics!"

"Shelby," Miranda says in her let's-be-reasonable tone. "This could end your endorsement deals."

"Give me a break. I was wearing the jeans in those stupid stripper pole photos. My ass looked fan-flocking-tastic. They oughtta be thanking me for all the free publicity."

Logan cough-laughs and I glance at him.

"Love you," he mouths.

"Who's there?" Miranda snaps. "Is that Logan?"

He stands and walks around to my side, leaning over the table. "Yup, it's me."

"Greg, can you—"

"No, Miranda," I cut her off. She's not talking Greg into kicking Logan out of the room. "Logan didn't do anything wrong. This is bullshit."

"Shelby, I'm trying hard here. And you're fighting me at every step. I know what I'm doing," Miranda says.

I take a breath and try to calm myself. "I appreciate that, Miranda. I do. But this is *my* personal life. These guys are attacking someone I love." I choke back a sob. "It's not right."

"Okay," Miranda says in a softer tone. "I understand." She pauses. "Look, since you're not willing to leave, Logan, you're just gonna have to sit through what I need to say to my client."

"Say whatever you need to say, Miranda. I know the truth, so you're not hurting my feelings."

She gives him a curt nod before returning her attention to me. "Shelby, honey, you're *really* young. I know it doesn't feel that way. But, I've been through this before. Many, many times. I've seen talented women throw away promising careers for a cheating boyfriend. Really ask yourself if the pain is worth it."

"Jesus Christ," Rooster mutters.

"Miranda," I say as calmly as I can. "I appreciate you're trying to look out for me. I understand your concern. However, in this situation, that is *not* what's happening." There. That sounded professional and not too emotional, I hope.

"Greg?" Miranda turns his way.

I grit my teeth.

He clears his throat and sits forward. "I understand your perspective. But keep in mind, you haven't met Logan yet. I've been on the road with them for weeks. He's devoted to her, Miranda. I have trouble believing there's any truth to the story."

Clearly, that's not the answer Miranda wanted or expected.

Honestly, the way Greg busted in here, I didn't expect it either.

I swallow over the lump in my throat and whisper, "Thank you, Greg."

Miranda takes a deep breath. "Okay. All right. I will issue a statement that the piece is all lies and you two are on solid ground."

I blow out a long sigh of relief. Finally, someone's listening to me. "Thank you."

"But."

Dammit. I knew there'd be a catch.

"What?" I ask warily.

"I'd like Logan to sit out the Small Screen awards."

"What?" I gasp. "No!"

"I want you to go with Dawson," she says, ignoring my objection. "You're already on tour together. It'll help keep the focus on your music and the tour."

My gaze goes to Rooster, searching his face for an answer.

But his expression's blank.

"If Logan attends," Miranda continues, "the spotlight's going to be on this story instead of *you*."

"But they'll move on by then," I protest.

"We don't know that. They're way too interested in your love life. Look how the *Glow* article got hijacked. Now this. They're going to keep coming for Logan and digging into his life. Is that what you want for him, Shelby?"

Son of a biscuit!

She's got me there. Logan never wanted any of this publicity in his life. Every time one of these stupid articles is published with his picture attached, he risks exposing his club. Sure, up until now, they've found it amusing, but how much longer will that last? What if they name his club next time? Will his president find that as funny?

Logan reaches for me, curling his hand around mine. "It's fine, Shelby. I have some business up in Washington I need to handle. I'll take care of that while you're in Irving for the show and meet up with you when you're done."

"But..." He's giving me an easy out. Maybe he really doesn't *want* to go. Logan's already done so much for me. Uprooting his life to drive me all over the country, buying the RV, having all his time consumed with my tour, my music, and the shows. Every day he's focused on making me happy. And how does he get repaid? Some idiots on the Internet calling him a cheater.

He's probably dying for a break. He didn't choose to be in the spotlight. At least I sort of knew what I was in for way back when I agreed to be on *Redneck Roadhouse*. But Logan never asked to have every move he makes scrutinized.

It's not fair for me to expect him to attend an awards show where he'll be miserable.

In their whole fifty years of marriage, Dolly Parton only had her husband escort her to one event. And yet, they're still together. They make it work. We can do this. It'll be okay.

"All right," I say.

"Good. Glad that's settled." Miranda claps her hands like she's dusting this mess off. "I'll get a press release out."

Rooster leans in and kisses my cheek. "It's the right choice, chickadee. I want you to enjoy your night without worrying about all this other stuff."

I answer with a weak smile.

If it's the right choice, why does it feel so dang *wrong*?

CHAPTER FIFTY-THREE

Rooster

Little Rock.

Tulsa

St. Louis.

I might be missing a few stops. Touring the country when it's your job isn't the same as riding the wind for fun. Half the time, there's no room in the schedule to take Shelby anywhere fun.

After the fucked-up "cheating scandal" I had a call with Digger where I expressed my *extreme* displeasure about the photos taken in *his* parking lot after *he* insisted I walk one of his dancers out. He apologized profusely. Either he's a good liar or he didn't set me up and really has no fucking clue what's going on.

He promises me he'll look into the situation and get me some answers.

I'm not holding my breath.

I didn't call Priest because that would feel too much like whining to dad. I'm sure he's aware, though. Z had been outraged on my behalf, and I have a feeling he called Priest to air out his grievances.

Sippin' on Secrets must be bored because they keep reposting different variations of the two non-stories. Gossip about Shelby must be bringing in more traffic than their pathetic site usually sees.

All that means is Shelby's popularity is growing.

In my free time, I work on tracing who's behind the celebrity blog. More and more, I suspect it's some kid working out of his mom's basement. Little shit's in for a surprise soon.

I'm also building Shelby's website and social media in a way that suppresses the gossipy stories as much as possible. I spend time scrubbing my own social media, so no one connects me to Anya, Stella, or any other porn girls associated with the club. I also pray like fuck none of the club girls I've been involved with in the past decide they'd like to sell a story.

Finished mapping out a plan for this afternoon, I close my laptop and glance over at Shelby. "You all right?"

She's been quieter and quieter since the "scandal." Never wants to go anywhere. Just from the RV to the venue and back. Can't even talk her into a few nights at a hotel.

The guys have been hanging out with Dawson and his crew more and more. Which is fine. He's paying for the privilege now. And it gives us more alone time.

That we spend not talking or doing much.

"Hey," I call out when she doesn't answer. I stand and approach the bed slowly.

She has her ear buds in and her notebook on her lap. She glances up as I approach and smiles.

Relief bursts in my chest. She hasn't been smiling enough lately.

"What?" she tugs the ear buds out and sets her notebook to the side.

"You all right?"

Another faint smile. "Trying to work out a song." She pats the bed next to her and I drop down, resting my hand on her leg.

"Have you tried going over it with Trent?" Supposedly they've always written their songs together, but other than sending each other files, and playing on stage together every night, they don't hang out.

"That's all I need," she grumbles. "Someone taking a photo of Trent and me together and saying I'm sleepin' with him too."

Fuck. I knew that's what was bothering her. "Hey, put that shit out of your head. You're not going to live in fear of those assholes."

"I'm not *afraid*. I'm tired of it."

I've been questioning whether I made the right call by agreeing not to go to the awards show with her. At the time, it seemed reasonable. Now, I'm not so sure.

"You pick a dress for the small screen thing?"

She grabs her phone and flicks through a few screens, finally stopping to show me a puffy-looking baby blue ball gown. She taps the screen and another similar dress in bright yellow fills the screen.

"They're both pretty."

"I'm not sure blond and yellow go together too well." She tugs on her ponytail. "They said they'll hold both and I can pick the one I want after I try 'em on."

"Good."

She bites her lip. Hesitates. "I'm nervous as all get-out."

"Don't be. You'll be great."

The corner of her mouth turns down. "At least I'm not performing. Show up. Collect my award—or not. Then skedaddle back to my hotel." She forces a smile. "Easy peasy."

"Right. And I'll be back the day after to take you to San Fran."

She moves closer. "Logan, you're not some chauffeur to me. You know that, right?"

I stroke my knuckles over her cheek. "I know."

"Good."

"Come here." I hold out my arms and she crawls into my lap, wrapping herself around me.

"I love you," she murmurs.

I run my hands over her back and hold her tight. "Love you too."

We stay like that for a few minutes, our worlds shifting into alignment. "Hey, you wanna go for a ride with me? That always clears my head. Maybe you can throw some lyrics out on the wind and see what comes back to you."

"Oh." She pulls away, interest sparkling in her eyes. "I like that. Let me write it down." She reaches for her notebook.

While she's writing, I push her hair off her shoulder and kiss her neck. "There's a piece of historic Route 66 not too far from here. Ever wanted to take a photo in front of a sixty-foot tall lit up soda bottle?"

She shakes with laughter. Best damn sound in the world.

"No, I can't say that I have. But I'm game."

'Let's do it."

Now she's more animated. She eagerly scoots out of my lap and rushes to her closet, searching for her riding clothes.

At least I've fixed things for now.

CHAPTER FIFTY-FOUR

Shelby

"SHELBY," ROOSTER RASPS AGAINST MY EAR. HIS BEARD TICKLES MY shoulder and my arm twitches.

"Sleeping." I'm plum tuckered out after our adventures along Route 66.

Rough fingers hook under the strap of my tank top, slowly dragging it down my arm. Warm lips, and the softest, sucking kisses follow.

A delightful shiver of pleasure stretches my body out, pulling me a little more from slumber.

Rooster kisses my shoulder again.

"Mmm, that's nice."

"I had the best dream." His hand skims my hip, slides over my stomach and dips under my shorts.

Automatically, my body rolls to give him access. "What?" I ask.

"I had my face buried right here." He presses his hand between my legs. "Licking your beautiful pussy like it was my last fuckin' meal." Every growly word stirs the desire swirling in my belly faster.

"Oh." I'm fully awake now. I wriggle until I'm on my back.

Rooster slowly slides his hand over my ribs and cups my breast, gently teasing his thumb over my nipple. "Would you like that?"

"Yes." I reach down, gripping his fully-hard cock through his shorts.

"No. No." He attempts to shift away. "Not yet."

I squeeze a little harder and he groans. "Bad girl."

"Very, very bad," I agree.

He shoves my shirt out of his way. I sit up enough to take it off, tucking it under my pillow.

"Good girl." He slides his hot, wet tongue over one nipple, stopping to suck it into his mouth.

"Oh," I gasp. My hips jerk.

"Shhh," Rooster whispers in my ear. "Can you be quiet for me?"

"I'm trying."

We both listen for a few seconds, staring in the direction of Jiggy's section. No sounds or movement.

Rooster tucks the sheet around me before dropping kisses along my jaw and over my chest. Slowly, he eases his big body down the bed, under the sheet, stopping to suck and kiss each nipple. He moves lower, tickling my belly with his beard. A giggle bursts out of me.

I clap one hand over my mouth. Good thing. More laughter bubbles up as he dips his tongue in my belly button before moving lower.

I grip the sheet, tenting it enough to peer into the darkness. "You're going to suffocate under there," I whisper.

Instead of answering, he pushes my thighs apart and nuzzles my center. He kisses and nips my inner thigh.

All the tickling, shivery sensations swirling together leave me breathless with anticipation.

He slides his fingers over the thin strip of cotton still covering me. Up and down, slowly increasing the pressure with each pass. Part of me wants to scream at him to rip off my panties and touch me. The rest of me is enjoying this way too much to make demands. He stops the maddening strokes and concentrates all his attention on using two fingers to trace circles over my clit.

I'm on the verge of begging when he finally pushes the material aside and brushes his knuckles against my slick flesh.

My hips jerk from the contact. A low, growling noise of approval rumbles against my thigh. I'm so worked up, so on the edge.

I want to sob with relief when he hooks his fingers in my underwear and drags them down my legs, tossing them somewhere. I don't even care where they end up.

One big, warm hand parts my lips. An exquisite exploratory lick.

I sigh and relax into the pillow.

He drags his tongue over my flesh again and again. Harder, more intentional licks. Sensation sizzles through my belly. My back bows.

"Oh shit!" I gasp.

"Shhh," he reminds me.

I bite one fist. My other hand curls into his hair, pushing his head back in place. He laughs softly before diving in again. Feasting. No hesitation. All I can do is hold on tight while he drives me into a frenzy of desire.

A warbled moan passes my lips when he flattens his tongue against my clit, licking and teasing until I'm thrashing on the bed. My fists curl tight, twisting the sheets.

He drives a finger deep, stopping to rub the sensitive spot inside me.

I let out a low moan.

He spreads his free hand over my lower stomach, pressing down with firm but gentle pressure. Desperately, I reach for him and tug on his hair.

"I can't." My whisper fades to an urgent moan.

He responds by sucking harder, then easing off. Shamelessly, I grab his hair, grinding against his face. He lets out a hungry noise, the sound vibrating against my core.

So good. Right there, there, there...

Little sparks explode into big fireworks. All my muscles clench tight. My toes curl. Back arching, my body writhing and bucking.

I'm still shaking as he kisses his way up my stomach, pulling the sheet around us as he wedges himself between my legs.

He kisses along my jaw, stopping to whisper in my ear, "Can you take more?"

While I'm remembering how to form words, he slowly slides his cock through my wetness. My body jerks when he grazes my oversensitive clit.

Trembling and still seeing stars, I finally answer. "Yes, please. Stop teasing me. Hurry."

Eager and greedy, that's me.

Still, he takes his sweet time, wrapping me up in his arms, whispering loving words against my throat. He drives into me in one long, slow thrust.

A thousand tiny, perfect bursts of pleasure light my insides.

"Yes." I dig my heels into the mattress, arching my back. He hitches one of my legs up. No longer cognizant of anything else around us, I wrap my legs around his waist, kicking off the sheet. "Fuck. Right there. Harder."

He slams his mouth over mine, kissing deep, swallowing my words. I wrap my arms around him, holding on tight. Kissing him back just as hard. Binding us together. Solid. Unbreakable. A heavenly harmony—where I end, he begins and everything in between.

Pleasure racing, I lift my legs higher, my body pulsing around him. "Come with me," I beg. "Please."

Muscles straining, hips snapping into me, he keeps going. Faster. Harder. Crushing me against his body.

"Yes. Fuck, that's so good." I nip his earlobe. "Right there."

It feels like my orgasm will never end.

"Ten-star performance, guys!" Jigsaw's voice booms through the darkness.

Our sensual spell shatters into a million pieces.

Rooster's body freezes mid-thrust.

Whoops. That's right. We're not alone. And I wasn't even attempting to be quiet anymore. I bite my lip—to stop myself from screaming, laughing, or crying, I'm not sure.

A frustrated growl bursts out of Rooster. "Motherfucker! I'm gonna kill you," he shouts over his shoulder.

I'm teetering somewhere between embarrassed that Jigsaw overheard such an intimate moment and still-tingling-with-so-much-pleasure-I-don't-care if he made a video for instant replays.

Giggling, I reach up and press my hand to Rooster's cheek, turning him to face me again.

"Kiss me before you kill him," I whisper.

He leans down and brushes a distracted kiss over my lips.

"Wait. Did you?" I wriggle my hips. He's still harder than a baseball bat inside me.

"No." He groans and drops his forehead to mine. "No, I did *not*."

"Poor timing? Oopsie." Jiggy cackles in the darkness. "Well, at least I waited for Shelby to finish."

"Shut. Up," Rooster snarls.

I press my fist to my mouth, biting down to stop myself from laughing any harder at our absurd situation.

"I should've known better," Rooster grumbles.

"Ignore him." I squeeze my inner muscles tight and he groans. "Focus on me."

"I can't." He pushes away but I dig my fingers into his arm to stop him. In the shadows, his eyes glitter as he stares down at me. "You really want to keep going knowing he's listening?"

I run my fingers through his hair, hoping to calm him down and bring him back to me. "The damage is done."

"Got that right," he mutters, glancing down to where we're still joined. "This actually fucking hurts."

"I'll step out so you can get yours, buddy," Jigsaw yells. A second later the back door opens and closes.

"Thank fuck." Rooster shakes his head and tucks his arms around me. "You sure you still want—"

I hook my arm around his neck and raise myself enough to kiss his question away. "I need you to come inside me," I whisper in his ear. "You made me feel *so* good. I want to return the favor."

He slides his hands down my side, cupping my ass and rolling us. "Get on top of me," he urges.

I yelp and grab for the sheet, not trusting that Jiggy went for a walk.

"He's an asshole but he knows I'll slice out his eyes if he tries lookin' at you," Rooster assures me. Even so, he pulls the sheet up and over both of us, creating a grown-up blanket fort of privacy.

"Give me a second." As much as I want to make him feel good too, I'm a little out of sorts.

It's so dark I can barely make out his outline. There's a soft, wet popping sound and a second later, Rooster shoves his hand between my thighs, stopping to swirl his finger around my clit. "Oh," I moan and throw my head back. "That helps. That helps a *lot*."

The familiar fiery sensation returns, singing through my blood. I slowly rock my hips back and forth.

"That's good. Perfect. Just like that," Rooster groans, slipping into a sensual groove again. "Keep going. Yes. Harder."

Since we're hopefully alone now, I ignore all the little squeaks and noises the bed makes. Rooster clamps down on my hips, thrusting up so hard, I lose my balance and brace myself against his chest.

Breathing fast and harsh, he lets out a primal groan of pure male satisfaction. I fall against his sweaty chest, molding myself to his body. He wraps strong arms around me, binding us together. One of his big hands palms my ass, squeezing. I turn my head, kissing and sucking the sensitive spot below his ear. He groans even louder into my hair as his orgasm thoroughly sweeps him under.

"Come here." He rolls to the side and leans closer to kiss my forehead. We're both breathing hard, sweaty foreheads pressed together, free hands softly traveling over each other. "Thank you."

"That's my boy!" Jigsaw cheers from outside. A loud round of clapping follows.

I burst out laughing, drawing away.

"That's it," Rooster growls. "He's dead."

Laughing even harder, I slide down the mattress, covering my face with the sheet. The bed shifts as Rooster stands. I poke my head out and slide my gaze over his body. The weak moonlight from the window highlights every marvelous line and angle as he jerks a pair of shorts over his hips.

"Damn, you're a gorgeous man, Logan," I whisper.

His severe expression softens and his shoulders drop. He leans over and kisses my cheek. "I'll be right back."

I grab his arm. "Don't go. Stay here with me."

A moment of indecision flashes across his face but then he climbs into bed, holding out his arm so I can snuggle up against him.

He tucks his other arm behind his head and peers down at me. "Sorry I woke you," he says in that charmingly cocky way that doesn't hold a note of regret.

"No you're not."

"I couldn't help it. One minute, I was dreaming about you. The next I was awake and your hot, soft little body was curled next to me." He squeezes his eyes shut and smiles. "I *needed* to taste you."

"I'm not complaining. You can wake me up for that anytime you want."

"Not gonna lie." He reaches underneath the sheet. "I panicked for a second there. Thought my balls were going to explode when Jiggy interrupted my flow."

I snort-giggle against his side.

"You saved me from a deadly case of blue balls, chickadee." He tickles his fingers over my ribs and I laugh even harder.

"Anytime." I trace my finger over his bottom lip. "Feel free to wiggle that wicked tongue around my clit whenever you want."

He sucks my finger into his mouth and stares into my eyes.

"Careful, I'll take you up on that." He kisses my fingertips and curls his hand around mine. We're quiet for a few minutes.

"Should we tell Jiggy it's safe to return?" I ask.

"No. He can sleep outside tonight."

CHAPTER FIFTY-FIVE

Rooster

WHAT A NIGHT.

I glance over at Shelby.

Still asleep.

We don't have to leave for a few hours so I'm not waking her. Already interrupted her sleep enough last night.

As I pad through the darkened RV, my gaze lands on Jiggy's sleeping form, prone on his mattress. My foot twitches with the urge to kick him awake just for the hell of it.

I slip my phone in my pocket and go outside to check on a few things instead.

Maybe twenty minutes into tidying up the inside of the truck, my phone buzzes.

Lynn.

Great, what does Shelby's mom want to bust my balls about now?

"Morning, Lynn," I answer. "You're up early."

"Logan, I need to talk to you." The anxiety rattling in her voice can't be missed.

Pulling myself out of the truck cab, I stand and pace a few steps away. "What's wrong?"

"Where's Shelby? Is she okay?"

'I fucked your daughter into oblivion and she's still unconscious' probably isn't what a mother wants to hear. "She's sleeping. What's going on?"

"Where are you?"

"I'm outside. Why? What's the matter?"

In the background, there's a rattling sound and her voice is barely above a whisper when she finally responds. "That *monster*…Martin Suggs…sent me a letter."

Molten rage explodes in my chest. "What?" I snap. "When?"

"It must have come yesterday but I didn't open it until now."

"Did you read it?"

"Y-yes," she answers in a shaky voice. "Logan, I'm really scared. This man, he's...crazier than an outhouse rat."

"No lie," I grumble. After the shit we did to him—Jigsaw cut off one of the man's fingers for fuck's sake—you'd think he'd work harder to scrub Shelby from his twisted brain. "Don't throw the letter away."

"I didn't. It's here."

"Can you read it to me?"

"Jesus, Logan. I don't know if I want to look at it again…oh my."

I feel like shit for making her do this, but I need to know what I'm dealing with. I should've ended Suggs when I had the chance.

"Okay. Ready? 'Dear Mrs. Morgan. I can't reach Shelby, so I am reaching out to you. By now, I assume you are aware of my relationship with your daughter. During the time we spent together, I observed some issues that I must discuss with you.

Number one, you have raised a wanton and disrespectful young lady. You should have been much more concerned with what sort of messages you exposed her to during her formative years. She is headstrong and willing to cavort with men beneath her and is utterly unrepentant. This is a direct result of your lax parenting. You seem to approve of this appalling behavior.'"

"Holy fuck," I breathe out.

"There's more," she says.

I squeeze my eyes shut and press the spot between my eyes where a headache's forming. "Go on."

"'When Shelby and I are finally reunited, you will submit to me and be disciplined in order to better serve your daughter's needs. This is not negotiable. I am older than you. My knowledge is superior in this area and will only benefit Shelby as well as the children she will bear for me—your grandbabies. As her mother, you should want what is best for her growth. You should desire that she reach her fullest potential, even if you failed yourself.'"

She hesitates and there's a soft sob on the other end.

"Fuck, Lynn." I swallow hard, trying to control my fury. "He's certifiably nuts."

"Let me finish." She blows out a breath. "'Please speak with your daughter as soon as possible, so that these false charges against me can be dropped and that I may be reunited with my little rabbit as soon as possible. Sincerely, Martin Suggs.'"

"Can you send me a photo of the letter and the envelope? And I know you've already opened it—"

"Once I realized who it was from, I tried to be careful and not touch it too much."

"Good. Put it in a plastic bag. Jackson will probably want it. He'll probably want to talk to you too."

"That's fine. This guy...he's twisted. Just tell me my baby girl is okay."

"She's fine, Lynn. I'm literally standing outside the RV. No one's getting near her."

"Please, don't tell her about this. She has a show tonight. And the awards coming up. She doesn't need this."

"I can't make any promises, Lynn." I don't want to stress Shelby out either, but I also don't want to lie to her.

"Have her call me, please? I need to hear her voice."

"Sure. I'll have her call as soon as she wakes up."

We talk for a few more minutes. When we disconnect our call, I move closer to the RV, listening for any sounds Shelby's awake.

Quiet.

Moving slowly, I creep inside and go straight to the hidden panel over the dinette. I pull out one of the burner phones inside. It seems to have enough juice for a short phone call.

Enough is enough. It's time to end this. Do what I should've done when I found that piece of shit. He's not going to continue terrorizing Shelby and her mom for years to come.

For this phone call, I enclose myself in the cab of the truck.

Ice answers on the third ring.

CHAPTER FIFTY-SIX

Shelby

STILL MILDLY EMBARRASSED ABOUT LAST NIGHT, I CAN'T QUITE MEET Jigsaw's eyes as I hand him a cup of coffee.

He unleashes one hell of an exaggerated yawn before taking a sip. "Thank you, songbird." His eyes glitter with amusement as he peers at me over the rim of his mug. "I'm *exhausted*. I had such a *hard* time sleeping last night."

Another big yawn, this time he adds a long, slow stretch, his fingers touching the ceiling and shirt lifting.

"Har, har." I boost myself up on the counter and sip my own coffee.

His playful smile falters. "I'm sorry you were a bystander in the teasing. Really, I just like fuckin' with Rooster." He pats his chest. "It's like breathing. I'm not really aware I'm doing it."

I blink and meet his semi-serious stare. I haven't gotten the impression Jigsaw apologizes often. So I'm touched to a certain extent. But do we really need to discuss this? "I've noticed."

"If it makes you feel better, I didn't hear anything until—"

I hold up one hand, cutting him off. "Please. Don't. Can we pretend nothing happened?"

His lips twist in and out of a smirk. "Sure."

After a few quiet sips, he sets his mug on the counter with a *thunk*.

"You make him happy, you know?" He waves his hand between us. "Besides the obvious, I mean."

Heat creeps over my cheeks. I'm never going to live last night down am I? Then my embarrassment clears, and his words sink in. "You two are close."

"I've always got my brother's back." He tilts his head. "That means I've got yours too."

What he confessed about Suggs comes back to me. In many ways, their loyalty to each other seems to rise above their ties to the club. "How long have you two known each other?"

He scrunches his face and lifts his gaze to the ceiling, as if it's hard to dig so far back into his memory. "Shit, forever? Feels that way."

"Did you know his parents?" I've never asked Rooster for more information about his family and I'm suddenly feelin' all kinds of guilty about that.

"For a while," he answers carefully.

I'm not sure how to take that answer. "Rooster said they passed away? How old was he?"

Jigsaw backs up a step. "That's really not a thread you should be tugging at behind Rooster's back."

Behind Rooster's back? He makes it sound so underhanded. "I was just wondering."

"If and when he wants to tell you the story, he will."

"Okay. Sorry." My cheeks heat with shame. It was stupid to ask Jigsaw instead of Rooster. I sure am a selfish girlfriend. Always spilling my troubles to Rooster but never asking him about his past pain. Take, take, take, and never giving.

"Don't apologize." His fists clench at his sides. "I didn't mean to snap at you."

"No, you're right."

A few more tense seconds of silence pass between us.

"He really loves you, Shelby. I've never seen him like this over anyone." He waves his hand around, indicating the RV.

My cheeks warm even more and I look away. "I love him too." Shoot, does Jiggy think I'm taking advantage of Rooster? "I didn't ask him to do this, you know. I want to pay him back. If I ever can."

"He ain't taking money from you. Anyway, I'm not talking about money." He waves that concern away. "I mean everything. Just...no matter what happens, don't forget that."

No matter what happens? What does that even mean? "Wait, do you think I'm going to get famous and drop him for someone else?"

The puzzled expression he gives me kinda stings. Maybe that sounded haughty of me.

"I don't think you're that type of girl, Shelby."

The door swings open and Rooster steps inside, ending our conversation. His gaze slides over Jigsaw, then me. "What's going on?"

"Nothing." Jigsaw takes his mug and retreats to the dinette table.

"Morning." Rooster runs his hand up my thigh and leans in to kiss my forehead. "He behaving?" he whispers in my ear.

"Yes."

"I've been a perfect gentleman," Jigsaw says.

Rooster growls at him over his shoulder.

"*Gentleman* is probably stretching the truth." I wink at Jigsaw. "But we're good. Where've you been?"

"Taking care of some issues." He picks up my coffee and sips it slowly. His face screws into a scowl. "You don't use sugar, do you?"

"I'm sweet enough." I take my cup out of his hands.

"That's true."

I slide off the counter and pour coffee into the big rooster mug I found for him on our last shopping trip and hand it over.

"Aww, you two are domestic bliss." Jigsaw lets out a dramatic sigh. "You warm my dark and blackened soul."

"Don't start with me today," Rooster warns.

"Why you still pissed? You got to bust a nut, didn't ya?"

I choke and gag on my coffee.

"Asshole." Rooster looms over the table, close to punching Jigsaw.

Jigsaw holds his hands in the air but doesn't seem all that concerned that Rooster wants to clean his clock. "What? I apologized to Shelby."

Rooster turns and raises an eyebrow at me.

"He sure did," I confirm. "But he didn't have to."

He shoots a glare at Jigsaw but steps away, returning to my side. "Yes. He did."

A smile tugs at the corners of my mouth. "Now, Logan, you have to admit we weren't being respectful of our guest last night."

Jigsaw ducks his head and snickers into his hand.

"I'm not admitting shit," Rooster grumbles. The sweet way he reaches out and curls his arm around my shoulders negates the harsh statement. "Hey, I need to talk to you about something, okay?"

Dread curls in my stomach. "What's wrong?"

"I talked to your mom this morning."

"Really? Is she okay?"

"Suggs sent her a letter."

"What?" I stagger into the counter, sloshing coffee all over my thumb and wrist. Rooster pries the mug from my hand, setting it on the counter, and thrusts my arm under the faucet. Cold water blasts my warm skin. "I don't think it was hot enough to burn," I mumble.

Instead of answering, he shuts off the water and dries me with a small kitchen towel, carefully inspecting my skin for injuries.

"What do you mean he sent my mother a letter?" I ask when he's finished. "What did it say?"

"Same crazy sort of crap as before. Nothing you need in your head. She didn't even want me to tell you."

"Like hell."

"Yeah, I figured. I spoke to Jackson. He's sending a field agent to collect the letter from your mom. He's supposed to check with the jail too. Suggs shouldn't have been able to get that letter out in the first place."

"Great," I grumble. Just what my momma needs. Feds knocking on her door.

"He's not getting out, Shelby. If anything, this will strengthen the case *against* granting bail."

"I hope so."

"She really wants to talk to you. Why don't you hop in the truck so you have some privacy and give her a call?"

"Okay." I grab my phone and a hoodie, slipping it on and pulling the hood over my head.

ROOSTER

I walk Shelby outside, boost her into the truck and then return to the RV to talk to Jigsaw.

"First things first." He wiggles his eyebrows at me. "Your balls feel better today?"

"Wait until the next time some poor, unfortunate soul wants to hop in your bed. Karma's a bitch."

The devilish expression slides off his face and he takes a quick glance out the window before crowding into my space. "Have you ever talked to her about your past?"

"What? No. Why?"

"Before you dropped the news about Suggs, she asked about your parents. I wasn't sure what to say, so I told her to talk to you."

"Fuck." I run my hands through my hair. "Yeah, because that worked out for me so well last time."

"I get it, bro. But Shelby's *nothing* like Ashley."

"Don't even mention that fucking name." My gaze scans the immediate area as if my ex might pop up like a nightmare returning from the abyss. "I don't want it tainting my space with Shelby."

Jiggy snort-laughs. "You're starting to sound like your girl. Should I go find some sage to burn?"

"Fuck off."

"She would've crawled out of her shallow pit by now if she recognized you after your brooding, lovesick face was plastered all over the country on that stupid rag."

"Who knows if she reads that shit anymore. I really couldn't give a fuck less."

"Why not just tell Shelby before she finds out on her own? It's not that big a fucking deal." He winces and stares down at his hand, curling into a fist on the counter. "Shit. I'm sorry."

"I know what you meant." I pat his shoulder. "After the tour."

"Sure." He rolls his eyes.

I gesture toward the truck. "I think I've got bigger problems right now."

"Is Lynn okay?"

The question throws me for a second. "No, she was freaked the fuck out. This letter was even creepier than the originals. Jail hasn't taught him any lessons."

He stares at me.

"I called Ice. He's gonna get it done."

"Good. Told you we should've wasted him when we had the chance."

"I agree." My fists curl at my sides. "Especially since Jackson seems to be dragging his feet doing anything about Glenna's involvement."

"Never happening, bro. Let's just help Shelby take over the whole country music universe and push that bitch into oblivion."

Those words coming out of Jiggy's mouth ease my black mood. Always a surprise with him. Guess that's how we ended up best friends for so damn long. "What do you wanna do? Become the mafia boss of country music?"

He shrugs and flashes a maniacal grin. "Stranger things have happened."

CHAPTER FIFTY-SEVEN

Shelby

"End of the road. For now, anyway." Rooster shifts the truck into park.

Tears fill my eyes and I turn toward the window.

"Shelby?"

I swallow down the pain and paste on a smile before facing him. "Are you sure the RV will be okay here?"

It had been a devil of a time maneuvering it into the hotel's parking garage. He and Jigsaw had to talk to one of the attendants for a special spot. Every minute of uncertainty had jacked up my anxiety over this situation even more.

He flashes the hotel ticket and places it on the dash. "We're fine. You've got your set of keys, so if you need anything you can come out and get it. Just…don't walk out here by yourself. Have Trent or someone come with you."

"I don't plan on leaving my hotel room."

Nope, I'm gonna drown my sorrows in some ice cream and delightful romance novels.

"All right. Let's grab your stuff."

The guys had already stopped to unload Rooster's bike. The small bag he'd need for the short trip was already packed. We can't prolong this goodbye.

Rooster hefts my suitcases out of the backseat with ease, setting them down on the concrete. "Anything else?"

I search the cab of the truck and grab my cell phone charger. Otherwise, I've got it all.

"Nope. All set." I use my sunniest voice.

But a cloud of doom still follows us inside.

ROOSTER

The demons of every mistake I've ever made follow me north. Lurking at my back no matter how hard I twist the throttle. Back then I had nothing to lose.

Now, I have everything.

Stupid.

I should've insisted on going to the awards show with Shelby. Leaving her in L.A. had hurt like hell.

Obligations. Responsibilities to my club. I can't forget them. I promised Priest I'd check this out. First time I've been on the West coast in years, and I'll admit I've missed it.

Dex, Steer, and Pants had backtracked to San Diego to hang out with friends. They weren't interested in attending a red carpet show no matter how much Dawson was paying. For an event like that, the professionals he worked with were the better choice.

Shelby will be busy with interviews, photo shoots, dress-fittings and other crap Miranda set up for her. Someone will be with her every time she leaves her hotel room. She'll be safe.

Doesn't make me feel any better about the situation.

About six hours into our trip, Jigsaw and I stop outside Santa Rosa for dinner.

After we place our order, he leans over the table. "As your road captain, I feel obligated to warn you this trip's a suicide mission."

"Why's that, genius?" I can't meet his eyes because on a gut level, I know he's right.

"We still have at least another ten hours on the road ahead of us. That's why. Then you're gonna do what? Assess the situation in a day and ride the sixteen hours back?"

I sip my beer and stare at the television over the bar. "Didn't need more than a day to see Digger's situation was a mess."

"Bro, Washington's got way more issues. We both know it. We shouldn't even be going in there without Dex, Steer, and Pants for backup."

"There won't be enough time to stop in when we pass through Washington at the end of the month either."

"Sure there will." He presses his finger into the table. "She's got one night in Portland." He taps another finger a few inches away. "And a night off before Tacoma. They're an hour from Portland. It's an easy stop."

"Then straight to Spokane. So same problem."

"Yeah, but at least you won't be exhausted from so many hours on the road."

"We did plenty of longer runs when we were younger."

"We did lots of stupid shit when we were younger. You really wanna play that game?"

Even though he's right, I don't feel like admitting it.

The waitress drops off our burgers. "Eat your dinner and stop annoying me."

He rolls his eyes and grabs a bottle of ketchup, making a big production of splattering it over everything on his plate.

"You're such a dick," I mutter.

We're both quiet while we demolish our food.

When we're finished, he pulls out a map and spreads it out on the table.

"We're not far from the old stomping grounds. We could always visit." He taps a spot on the map that represents the hellscape of my childhood.

My stomach clenches tight. "Why? You wanna try to find your family?" I say casually.

Anger flashes in his eyes.

Remorse twists me up for making the dick suggestion. But he started it.

"No, asshole," he says with murderous calm. "I thought maybe you'd like to leave some flowers on your mom's grave."

Ouch. Low blow. "Why? She's not there."

"What about Aunt Em? We're gonna go right by there. You won't pay your respects to her either? Your uncle?"

Now he's just kicking all my soft spots. I sit back and blow out a long breath. "You really wanna stop in Bent Rock?"

"It's mostly good memories."

"Easy for you to say."

"Is it?" he snaps.

Yup, another dick comment. I glance at my half-empty bottle of beer. Can't even blame the alcohol for the shit coming out of my mouth.

"Is Warren still runnin' your uncle's place?" he asks after we've cooled off.

"Fuckin' Warren." I laugh. "Yeah, he sends me updates."

"He even turning a profit or just running the place into the ground?"

"Nah, I think he knows if he doesn't make any money, I'll kick him out."

"You ever think about moving back? You have the house. The bar. There's a charter not that far away. Hopper's not the president anymore, so you'd be welcomed back."

Don't have to give that answer a lot of thought. "No. You?"

"I go where you go. Really doesn't matter to me."

And now I feel even worse for being a dick.

"I like what we have in New York. Especially with Z running things. It feels more like a family now. Here, it always felt like a bunch of drunk bikers committing crimes as a hobby."

He snorts. "Good description. Maybe it's changed."

"Doesn't sound like it."

"Maybe *you* can change it."

"I'm not here to change anything."

Not even myself.

CHAPTER FIFTY-EIGHT

Shelby

My palms won't stop sweating but I don't dare wipe them on my dress. I went with the yellow and sweaty palm stains will definitely show up.

"You look like Belle from Beauty and the Beast," Cindy says.

"That's what the dress reminded me of too." I twirl around, watching the long skirt flair out around my legs.

"Careful." She steps closer to tighten the glittering rose clip in my hair. "I'm so worried that thing's gonna fall out."

"It'll be fine." I pick up my small, beaded purse. "Can you take a picture?" I ask, handing over my phone. "I want to send it to Logan."

"Sure. Go over by the window where the light's better."

She snaps a bunch of photos. I'll post a few to social media *after* I leave L.A. I don't want some freak figuring out what hotel room I'm in by the landmarks in the background or something.

"Are you sad Logan's not here?" she asks after handing me my phone.

"Yeah," I answer quietly. "I couldn't make him do it, though. Not after all he's done for me. I hate people who don't even know him writing such shitty things. I can't keep asking him to subject himself to that. It's not fair."

"Oh, honey." She carefully curls her arms around me for a loose hug that won't crush my dress. "Logan's a strong man. I don't see him gettin' too bothered about that stuff."

"I know. He didn't *say* he was upset."

"Of course not."

Someone knocks on the door. Cindy runs to answer and gasps in surprise. "Dawson!"

"Evening. Is our girl ready?"

"I'm ready." I rush over, holding my dress up so I don't trip over it.

"I'm heading out," Cindy says, grabbing her gear.

I air kiss her cheek and promise to give her all the details later.

"You look lovely," Dawson says, briefly sweeping his gaze over me. "I think this will match, too."

He hands over a wide black velvet box.

"What is it?"

"Open it."

Inside, a glittering choker of what I assume are diamonds sparkle up at me. "Whoa," I breathe out.

I glance up, meeting his eyes. "I can't accept this from you, Dawson."

His lips quirk. "It's a loaner, darlin'."

My cheeks warm. Duh, of course he's not giving me jewelry that probably costs more money than I can count.

"Well, I promised your man I'd keep you safe tonight, and this came free with the necklace." Dawson jerks his thumb over his shoulder and I finally notice the stiff, muscular guy in a suit standing behind Dawson. "To make sure we don't steal the diamonds," Dawson whispers in a voice loud enough to carry into the corridor.

The guard doesn't move a muscle.

"He's like one of those guards at Buckingham Palace. Never smiles." Dawson winks at me. "Or speaks."

"Be nice." I swat at him.

"Come on." Dawson snaps his fingers. "Help her put it on, James."

"Hi, James," I say as he approaches.

"Evening, Shelby."

"So, you *do* speak!" Dawson says.

James rolls his eyes as he takes the box out of my hands. Seems

Dawson's the problem, not James' sense of humor. This should be a fun night.

I turn around and he slips the necklace around my throat, snapping the clasp tight. "Tell me, James, if someone tries to kidnap me, are you gonna go after *me* or the necklace?"

I turn around and face him.

"You," he answers.

"What a relief."

"As long as you're still attached to the necklace, of course."

I burst into giggles, releasing the tension that's built up all afternoon. "Great. That's perfect."

In the limo, James returns to his silent robot act. I consider asking if he plans to follow me into the bathroom tonight, but, afraid I might not like the answer, I keep my mouth shut.

"You nervous, sweetheart?" Dawson asks, passing me a glass of champagne.

I hold the glass, studying the golden bubbles. "Last time I drank, it didn't go so well."

He scoffs. "Tell me about it."

"Thanks for not…holding *that* against Logan."

His eyes widen. "Ain't Logan's fault. Meant what I said the mornin' after."

"Well, thank you. And thanks for agreeing to this tonight. I know Miranda forced—"

"Shelby, Miranda didn't force anything on me."

"I'm sure you had someone else you'd rather have on your arm."

He stares out the window. "Not really."

The limo rolls to a stop, mercifully ending our awkward conversation.

"You ready, darlin'?" Dawson asks.

"I don't think so." My mouth trembles into a shaky smile.

He steps out first and offers his hand to help me down. "Thank you."

"Dawson! Dawson!" photographers shout from different directions.

"How do you wanna do this?" Dawson asks.

My nervous eyes meet his calm ones. "Don't leave me." I want to kick myself for saying something so ridiculous but I'm suddenly terrified. Of the crowd. Of the photographers. Interviewers. Random fans. All of it overwhelms me at once.

He presses his hand to my back and steps onto the red carpet, pushing me along, yet somehow keeping his distance. We stop and smile for a few photos.

He leans down. "Can't lie, I'd rather not have any photos taken of us with my hands on you. Your boyfriend's fully capable of chopping them off and beating me to death with 'em."

That finally cracks me up, chasing away my nerves.

"I ain't kiddin', darlin'."

"Dawson! Dawson! Are you and Shelby dating?"

"No, sir. Shelby's a good friend," Dawson answers smoothly. "That's all."

"Shelby! Are you sleeping with Dawson?" someone else shouts.

Why do I get the rude questions?

"Don't answer that asshole," Dawson growls, turning us away from the cameras so we can continue to the next stop.

A short woman in a tight, shiny ice-blue gown stops short in front of me. I bang into her before I can catch myself.

"Oh! I'm sorry."

Next to me, Dawson mutters, "Motherfucker," under his breath.

It's the only warning I have before Glenna Wilson turns around. Her eyes widen and she lets out a startled gasp.

Too stunned to feel anything I just blink and stare at my sworn enemy.

She recovers from her shock quickly, easing into a haughty pose of indifference.

"Dawson," she greets.

When he doesn't bother to answer, she settles her gaze on me. Her big blue eyes examine me for so long, sweat drips down my back.

"You plannin' to etch my portrait?" I finally ask, irritated that I'm stuck here. I wouldn't be shocked if someone planned this so they'd have a juicy story to write.

Dawson's body twitches but he doesn't laugh or say anything.

Glenna's eyes flit toward him then back to me.

"Let me be honest," she drawls.

Lord save me. In my experience, people who say that are only seeking permission to be openly cruel.

I raise an eyebrow, trying not to look massively annoyed, lest someone snap a photo and caption it "Shelby and Glenna showdown over Dawson Roads." Or something equally inane.

"You're an awfully poor substitute for me," she says. "Don't expect to keep him long."

I curl my arm around Dawson's and lean into him. Rooster will understand when I explain why. "Oh, honey," I say in my most syrupy voice. "You mad you threw away a diamond and picked up a rock?"

Dawson peers down at me with an amused expression.

"So much for nothing going on," she says to Dawson.

"We may not be together, but I know a good man when I see one," I say. "I have a boyfriend."

She taps one of her long, red fingernails against her chin. "Yes, I think I read something about him somewhere recently."

"All lies," Dawson says. "A concept *you* should understand since lies are your mother tongue."

"Dawson! Smile for us!" someone calls out. "Shelby, Glenna! Oh, what a great shot!"

Hell no. I don't want to be in a picture with this bitch. I back away, turning around.

Enjoy a photo of my round, rosy butt, jerks.

"Come on, Shelby," Dawson says, taking my arm.

"Wait," Glenna says. "I'm sorry about what all happened to you." She flashes a demure smile that probably hardens cocks all over the country and flutters her lashes at Dawson. "But I want you to know I had nothin' to do with it."

What an odd thing for an innocent person to blurt out for no reason.

"Come off it, Glenna," Dawson snaps. "You all but admitted it to me."

"I did no such thing."

"It don't matter. This ain't the time or place." Dawson takes my elbow and steers me toward the door. "Let's go, Shelby."

"Shelby, wait." Glenna's voice ricochets through the crowd.

"Are you nuts?" I whirl around. Enough is enough. "You know, I grew up admiring you. But you're not only a nasty piece of work, you're dumb as hell."

Her eyes widen. No one's probably told her off in years.

"*Nothing* has ever happened with Dawson and me." Damn, I'm fired up now. "So, you wound up that sicko and unleashed him on me for no reason."

Her face pales. Maybe she finally gets the depth of what she participated in.

"He stuffed me in a friggin' box," I fume. "I could've *died*. Do you get that?"

"I didn't know." Her voice strikes the correct contrite note this time.

"What'd you think he wanted to do with me? Bake cookies and doodle in some coloring books?"

"You have to believe me, Shelby."

"You're about as trustworthy as a drunk raccoon in a chicken coop. I don't believe a word you say. You should be sittin' in a jail cell right next to Martin Suggs, but for some reason you're here annoying me."

I whirl around so fast, I almost trip over my stupid heels. Dawson catches my arm and guides me away from Glenna.

"Damn, girl," he says in a low voice. "That was spectacular. Bet ya someone caught that on camera too."

"Shoot." My face burns.

"Nah, it's probably a good thing. She all but admitted it. Maybe we can use it to finally have her arrested."

Do I even care anymore?

Somehow we manage to avoid Glenna while we're mingling in the lobby.

Dawson's sweet as pie, stopping to introduce me to important people as he ushers me to our assigned seats.

But he's not Rooster.

Through it all, I keep the same fake smile plastered on my face.

Even when they call my name for *Best Female Video,* no joy enters my heart. Sure, I smile and act surprised. I walk on stage and accept my little trophy. I strike the right notes of gratitude for the microphone.

But inside I'm in tatters.

My heart and mind are waging a secret battle. I can't ask Rooster to attend one of these shows with me. But I don't know if I can do another event like this without him.

CHAPTER FIFTY-NINE

Rooster

"YOU'RE AN IDIOT," JIGSAW GRUMBLES.

Our hotel outside Bent Rock has a large screen television for us to watch Shelby and Dawson walk down the red carpet together. They're not holding hands for the cameras, so I guess that's something.

"Thanks for the diagnosis, you little shit goblin."

"Seriously." He gestures to the screen. "At least he's not an asshole. But I still wouldn't trust him around my woman. The dude has a higher body count than a fuckin' redwood tree."

"You've never had a woman in your life, so your advice lacks teeth."

"I wouldn't let another man borrow my Harley for a photo op. That toothy enough for ya, dick?"

A host of second thoughts crowd my mind as I stare at the screen. I'd bowed out way too easily when Miranda suggested Shelby and Dawson should attend this thing together.

"She looks like a fairytale princess." I gesture toward the screen. "You think having a big, glowering biker next to her was gonna be helpful? Especially after that mess in Tennessee?"

"What? The tin foil cheater thing?" He waves it off. "Everyone knows Shelby's got your balls in a mason jar."

"I'm not talking about my *balls*, you clown."

He points his beer bottle at the screen again. "You could've shrugged on that velvet sport coat, arranged your big ol' balls into a thousand-dollar pair of jeans, shoved your stinky feet into some alligator boots that cost more than your first bike, and walked your woman down that red carpet instead of lettin' Dawson do it." He shudders. "Not like anyone expected you to wear a tux to this vapid shindig."

"Somehow I don't think any of those designers were in a rush to loan me alligator boots."

"Don't be dense. You know what I mean."

"I can't keep bringing all that negative attention to Shelby. It's taking the focus off her music."

"*Duh.* That's why it would've made more sense for you to show your face there as a united front. Now everyone will be gossiping about her fuckin' Dawson. Or did that *not* occur to you?"

"I thought about that." Like, every second I've been away. "I needed to come up here. It made sense to do it now."

His eyes widen and he reels back. "Whoa. I should've brought my hip boots to wade through this bullshit. Are you fucking kidding me? You had *zero* plans to stop here until I told you to."

"Yeah, because I was *supposed* to be in Washington."

He stops and sighs.

Aw fuck. I know that sigh. Recognize that expression slipping over his face too.

Shit's about to get real and I'm not in the mood for it tonight. Not when he dragged me to a place I both love and hate. Where I gained and lost everything.

I'm missin' Shelby so bad it aches down to my bones.

"There's no way anyone's gonna recognize you from back then if that's what you're worried about," he finally says.

Okay, that's in the neighborhood of the conversation I expected but not quite where I thought he'd start.

"That's *not* what I'm worried about." Not exactly. "But yeah, since you went there, that's not a story she needs surrounding her right now." Or *ever*.

"Logan, she's not Ashley."

The sting of my ex's betrayal isn't as sharp as it used to be. Still hate hearing that fucking name.

"Fuck, even *I* can see how much Shelby loves you," he continues. "It's written all over that girl's face every time she looks at your dopey ass."

"Thanks, I'm touched."

"I mean, personally, I don't get it." He wrinkles his nose and gives me a disdainful once-over. "I suppose she's entranced by your big, dumb beard or something."

"Yeah, that's probably it."

"You look nothing like that kid. No one's gonna uncover all that shit and attach it to you today." He pauses and dread fills my gut anticipating whatever he's going to say next. "And even if someone did, Shelby wouldn't care. She's not stupid or shallow."

"A story that ugly..." I shake my head. I almost think it would be better to let Shelby go than to put her through that circus.

Except, letting her go would be the same as cutting out my heart.

"It's not your fault." He takes a long, serious swallow of his beer. "Besides it doesn't matter anymore. Those skeletons are buried deep."

Maybe. But fuck knows no matter how much dirt you throw on top of them, skeletons always have a way of crawling out of the darkest holes.

CHAPTER SIXTY

Shelby

My head throbs.

No, wait. That's someone knocking on my door.

My eyes open. I stare at the shadowy ceiling, waiting to see if whoever it is knocks again.

Thud. Thud. Thud.

I flick a glance at the clock. Who the heck would be waking me up this early?

Groaning, I sit up and blink a few times. I hadn't had a drop of alcohol last night, yet I still feel like I got run over by a herd of angry hogs.

The knocks come a little quicker, followed by a muffled voice calling my name.

Rooster?

No, he's supposed to be up north somewhere.

I hurry to the door, but check the peephole quickly to confirm it's him.

"Rooster!" I twist and yank on the knob, so eager to see him, I can't get the door to open.

"Shelby?"

"Give me a minute!" I stop my frantic tugging on the handle and realize the deadbolt's engaged. I twist it and fling the door open. "What are you doing here?" I slam into his chest, loop my arms around his neck and jump up to kiss his cheek.

He wraps his arms around me tight, lifting me up. "Missed you too much." His lips slam into mine. Something rustles against my behind but I'm too busy trying to get closer to him to figure out what it is.

He pushes into the room, kicking the door shut behind him.

"I missed you," I whisper between kisses. "A lot. Really a *lot*." I don't even know what I'm saying, I just need him to know how happy I am that he's actually here.

"Missed you too." He sets me on my feet and thrusts a bouquet of peach roses at me. "Congratulations. So proud of you."

Pleasure warms me all over. He stopped somewhere to buy roses? I grab the flowers and promptly stick my nose in them, inhaling their sweet scent.

"You watched?"

"Hell yeah. I wasn't going to miss it." He brushes his knuckles over my cheek. "You looked really pretty."

Tell him how badly you wanted him there with you.

But I can't seem to force out the words. Rooster already does so much for me. Has given up the last few months of his life to travel with me. I can't guilt him into doing something I know he'll hate just because I'm too insecure to go without him.

"Jiggy gave me shit all night," he says in a low voice.

"You made him watch too?"

"Made him," he scoffs. "Like anyone can make that asshole do anything."

I search the room for something to put the roses in, finally landing on the ice bucket. "Why'd he give you a hard time?" I ask over my shoulder.

The warm wall of Rooster's big body closes in behind me. He runs his finger over my shoulder. "For not going with you."

"What?" The metal bucket slips from my fingers, clattering onto the desk.

He grips my shoulders and turns me to face him. "I should've been there with you."

"No." I shake my head, willing the quiver in my voice to vanish. "I can't ask you...you hate that kind of stuff. It's a lot. I understand why you—"

"Shelby." His serious tone draws my attention to his face. "I knew those kinds of events were part of the deal. What Miranda said got to me. I don't ever want to bring you bad attention. That shit that went down in Tennessee was fucking awful and that was my fault—"

"No, it wasn't. I wanted to go. It's—"

"I should've been watching *everyone* in that place a hell of a lot closer."

"Logan, you're not responsible for everything."

He hesitates.

Tell him.

"I missed having you there, though," I whisper. "I'm sorry. I'm not trying to guilt you into going with me next time or anything." I shrug, helpless to come up with an explanation. "It felt like a piece of me was missing. And I wanted to tell you all this little stuff. Share the whole experience with you. I'm sorry. I know you don't care about those things and you'd hate it."

He moves in closer, backs me up against the desk and curls his arms around me. "I'll be with you at the next one."

"The next one is *the* big one. The one that really counts. It'll make last night look like a toddler's birthday party."

He snorts. "I don't care. I'll blend into the background. As long as I'm with you."

"I'd really, really like that," I whisper.

"You mean that?"

"Yes." I can't help it, I have to ask. "But what about you? They're going to keep writing crap. Eventually your club might get brought into it."

"I have a feeling *Sippin' on Secrets* won't be around much longer.' He shrugs. "The rest of it we'll handle as it comes up."

My selfish little heart is so happy he's here, I don't bother to ask what he means.

CHAPTER SIXTY-ONE

Rooster

SHELBY'S HALF-ASLEEP, USING MY ARM AS A PILLOW. AT FIRST IT WAS SWEET but now my arm's falling asleep. Slowly, so I don't wake her, I roll to the side. My phone dings and I pick it up off the nightstand.

Ice: Done.

There's only one thing that could mean.

Me: Thank you.

Martin Suggs won't be sending another letter.

Should I tell Shelby?

The decision's made for me when my phone rings.

Jackson.

"Yeah?" I answer as quietly as possible. Shelby still moans and rolls over.

"I figured you'd want to hear this right away," Jackson says without any other introduction.

"What? Don't you dare tell me Suggs made bail." I should at least try to act like I don't know what he's about to tell me.

He pauses. Good, maybe he bought the innocent act.

"No. Martin Suggs was found dead in his cell this morning. Hanging from his bedsheets."

Way too easy for him. I should've specified to Ice it needed to be bloodier.

"Holy shit. Are you sure?"

"Oh, I'm sure. I can send you photos if you want."

"That's all right."

"Tell Shelby I'm sorry. He took the coward's way out. Then again, I wouldn't expect anything less from him. But she deserved to see justice done."

I'd argue justice *was* done and Shelby's been spared having to relive this over and over for the next few years. "Do you need to talk to her?"

"No, you can give her the news. Have her call me if she has any questions or if she needs anything." Almost as an aside, he casually asks, "Where are you now?"

"On the other side of the country." Damn good alibi if you ask me.

"That's *not* why I was asking. The media will be all over the story. She might want to lay low."

"I'll handle it. Thanks, Jackson."

"You're welcome. Take care."

Shelby's sitting with the sheet wrapped around her. Her bottom lip trembles with fear as she watches me set the phone down. "What's wrong? What happened?"

No point in sugarcoating it. "Suggs is dead."

She closes her eyes and releases a slow breath. A single tear slips down her cheek.

"Don't cry for him." I swipe the tear away with my thumb.

"It's not for him. It's for *me*. I've been trying not to think about it but it's always there in the back of my mind. That fucking creep. I've wished him dead a thousand times. Then, he sent my mom a letter—" She stops abruptly and tilts her head. "Rooster, you didn't have anything to do with his..."

Danger. Shelby's way too fucking smart.

I pull her down next to me, wrapping my arm around her. "Now, how would I have done that, chickadee? I'm on the other side of the country."

She presses her palm against my chest and sits up again. "I don't know. I'm sure your club has friends in low places."

"Nice song reference." I bop the tip of her nose and she swats my hand away.

"I'm serious." She rests her hand over my heart. "I don't want something so dark staining your soul. He's not worth it."

"Trust me, I've done worse and my soul is content with my choices." Maybe that means I don't have a soul, but that can't be true. Not when everything inside me wants to wrap around this woman and protect her until I die.

"Logan," she whispers.

"It's done, Shelby. Jackson said Suggs hung himself." My voice takes on a harsher edge. Because I'm annoyed she's accusing me of murder or because she's right?

"Damn. He couldn't even get shanked in prison?"

"And you're worried about *my* soul?" I give her a wry smile.

"I'm worried about my own soul too," she says. "Sometimes I don't like the person that experience turned me into."

How is that possible? "What—strong and brave?"

"Mean. Bitter. Scared."

"I don't see any of that."

"That's because *you* make me better."

"Like medicine?" I try again for a light tone but she doesn't smile.

"Kinda." Her nose wrinkles and she glances away. "I acted ugly last night."

"How?"

"We ran into Glenna Wilson outside the auditorium. I kinda told her off."

"Good. She deserves it."

"That's what Dawson said."

"How was he?"

"Nice. He made sure I was comfortable but he said he was afraid to touch me because he didn't want you to beat him to death." She fixes her pissy little stink eye on me. "Did you threaten him?"

I wink at her. "That's between me and Dawson."

CHAPTER SIXTY-TWO

Shelby

"*On the road again...*" I can't help singing the same few lines over and over while I finish my shower. The awards show was fun and I've enjoyed all the primping and pampering that went along with it. The hotel is lovely, but damn I'm eager to settle into my RV and get back to the tour.

"Rolling out in thirty!" Rooster shouts.

"I'm almost done!"

"I'm teasing." His voice sounds a little closer now. "Take as long as you need. Want me to run downstairs and grab some coffee?"

"Nope." I shut the shower off and slide the door open. Rooster's waiting for me with a towel in each hand. I wrap my hair first, then dry off with the other one. "I would love it if you'd help me dry my hair, though."

"You've got it."

My heart thumps. I reach for him, skimming my fingers over his shoulder. "You make me swoon, Logan Randall, you know that?"

He touches my cheek and smiles faintly. "I always want you to feel that way."

"You never told me how the heck you made it back here so fast." I watch his reflection while I drag a comb through my wet hair.

"Jiggy and I didn't make it to Washington."

That's weird. I thought it was important to pay them a visit. "Where'd you go?"

He fiddles with the blow dryer. "Just a small town on the border."

Border of where?

But he flicks on the dryer and I don't have a chance to ask.

By the time we're finished, I've forgotten the question.

DOWNSTAIRS, WE FIND A SMALL CAFE ON THE FIRST FLOOR OF THE HOTEL. The lobby's bustling with people. No one seems to be paying attention to anyone, though. The inconspicuous hotel security guards stationed at each entrance definitely reassure me.

I slip on my big sunglasses but leave my hair down. In a town full of real celebrities, no one should care enough to recognize lil' ol' Shelby Morgan.

"What else do you want?" Rooster asks as we approach the counter. "Besides coffee."

"One of those little egg-white thingies."

"They're like two bites. You sure you only want one?"

"Maybe two."

The corner of his mouth curls up. "Two spinach and cheese egg-bites and a large coffee."

Could I love this man any more than I already do? "Have I mentioned how happy I am that you're here?"

"Yeah, but I don't mind hearing it again." He curls his arm around my waist. "Jiggy should be here soon. Then we'll get on the road. Stop and see some beaches."

"I feel bad you made him ride all by himself."

Rooster laughs. "Don't. He badgered the hell out of me for not going to the show with you."

"Aww. You know I'm not mad about it, right?"

"Yeah, chickadee. I know. Still, won't happen again. Promise."

As we approach the counter, he releases me to pull out his wallet. I unzip my purse but the stern side-eye he gives me has my fingers zipping it shut. "Go grab us a table," he suggests.

I glance at the small, cluttered seating area. Except for one lone woman wearing an enormous sun hat, the space is empty. Everyone seems to be taking their orders to go.

I snake my way through the tables and chairs, finally deciding on a spot in front of the floor-to-ceiling window.

The heat from outside's already beating against the glass. Glad I'm wearing shorts. Maybe I can get a little color on my legs later.

Rooster's gaze constantly searches the surrounding area as he waits for our order. Every so often, his eyes land on me and he smiles.

My gaze wanders, stopping on the girl in the hat who seems to be gawking at my man.

Hands off, lady.

Can't blame her, though. Rooster's one exquisitely-sculpted man. I spend a few moments enjoying the way he stands, confident and calm. Hands in his pockets. Wide shoulders back, chest lifted. He likes wearin' his jeans a lil' on the baggy side, which suits me fine. No one else needs to know about the firm rear end he's hiding under that denim.

Finally, the clerk hands him his order. Rooster catches me eyeballin' him as he turns and heads my way. He lifts his eyebrows, a playful expression rippling over his face.

"Whatcha lookin' at, chickadee?" he says as he sets the small green tray in front of me.

I bat my lashes and answer in a slow drawl, "How sexy you look in those jeans."

"That right?" His gaze drops to my crossed legs peekin' out from under the table. "Did I tell you how much I'm looking forward to staring at those sleek legs of yours on our drive to San Francisco?"

"Yes, but you can tell me again."

"Can't wait." He leans down and kisses my cheek. "I'm gonna run to our room and grab the rest of our stuff, load up the truck, and move it around front so we're ready to go when Jiggy arrives."

"Do you want me to help?"

"Nope." He takes another quick look around. "You'll be all right here." He nods to one of the security guards. "No one should bother you."

"Logan Randall, I'm not a little kid. I'll be okay." I search the area again. "Best believe I'll scream my head off if someone tries stuffin' me in a box."

The playful smile on his lips fades. "Not funny."

"I'm fine." I pick up my phone. "Got plenty of comments to go through on my social media and some photos to post."

"I shouldn't be long."

Content in the sunlight, I munch on my egg-bites and sip my coffee while I post some photos from the other night. Comments pop up almost instantly. I respond to the nice ones and delete the nasty ones without comment—because *fuck mean people*. I'm sick of 'em.

"Shelby, right? I wanted to speak to you." A husky female voice interrupts my scrolling.

Big hat girl.

My inner warning bells start clanging.

Why'd she wait so long to approach me? No, correction, why'd she wait until Logan left the area to approach me?

If she's a fan, she would've said something right away, wouldn't she?

"You *are* Shelby Morgan, right?" she asks again. "The singer?"

"Yes," I answer carefully, slowly running my gaze over her to see if she's reaching for a weapon or something. Can't be too careful after what happened in Virginia.

I scan the room, searching for Rooster. Or hell, anyone at all. The security guard by the elevators is staring straight ahead toward the front door. The clerks behind the counter are busy cleaning out the coffee pots.

At least people are around if I need to start screaming.

Wait a second.

I take another gander at this gal. Can't be more than a buck twenty soaking wet. She's got some height on me, but I'm pretty darn spunky when I wanna be.

She's beautiful. Perfectly shaped oval face and smooth, clear skin. Neatly put together in a dainty polka-dotted dress paired with a slim belt. Long, sleekly blown-out caramel-colored hair. A shade of blond I don't think is found in nature often. Must spend a fortune at the salon. Lightly tanned skin, like she perfectly times her sun exposure down to the second.

A rich, spoiled mean-girl vibe I'm all too familiar with rolls off her in waves. I grew up around girls like this. Went to school with lots of 'em. Got bullied, insulted, and pushed around by entitled brats plenty of times.

But I'm not poor little Shelby Morgan anymore. I'm making my own damn money off my own god-given talent, not livin' off my parents or some trust fund. I'm not about to take guff from anyone.

I stand, forcing her to scuttle away a few steps. Pulling my shoulders back, I straighten to my full height, which is unfortunately still about two inches shorter than this haughty gal.

"What can I help you with?" I ask in my own imperious tone.

"I read the *Glow* article. About what happened to you."

Oh. Okay. Maybe I should calm my tits. That scene with Glenna the other night might've rattled me more than I realized.

Is this chick a reporter? Or shoot, maybe she's another victim of Martin Suggs? Or a therapist trying to drum up business?

I look her over again. Nah, she doesn't look old enough. I peg her to be a couple years older than me. Besides, that has to be an unethical way to round up clients.

"And?" I prompt.

"I want to talk to you about that man you're with."

Over her shoulder I spot a blur of black leather. *Jigsaw*. Thank God. He seems to be searching the lobby.

Not caring if I seem rude or not, I raise my hand and wave. "Jiggy! Over here!"

The girl reaches out and wraps her fingers around my arm, forcing me to meet her intense eyes. "Shelby, you need to listen to me."

"Get your hand off me." I jerk out of her grasp.

She glances behind her and mutters, "Son of a bitch." Whirling back to me, she reaches for my hand again. "Listen, the man you're with. He's not who he says he is."

"What in the Sam Hill are you talking about?"

"Shelby! You all right?" Jigsaw calls out. He comes to a dead stop about two feet from the woman. His eyes bug as recognition sets in.

Rage twists his features. "Ashley, what the fuck are you doing here?"

Clearly they know each other.

How?

I look her over again. She doesn't look like a club girl or porn star. How does she know Logan? Or Jigsaw?

Where the heck did they go if they didn't go to Washington?

"Jensen." She gives him a look that could freeze hot lava. "I should've figured *you'd* be around here somewhere."

"Come on, Shelby." Jiggy muscles between us and curls his arm around my shoulder. "You need to fuck off back to wherever you came from, Ashley." Jigsaw's threatening voice should send her screaming from the hotel, but she defiantly lifts her chin.

"Still coveting his girls, I see." Ashley sneers. "Careful, Shelby, or you'll end up as his sloppy seconds."

Jigsaw growls and coils tight.

Now this bitch has really pissed me off. I shrug out of Jiggy's grasp. "I don't know you and I'm not interested in whatever trouble you're trying to cook up. You hear me?"

"Shelby!" Logan's voice echoes through the lobby.

Jigsaw tugs on my hand. "Come on. Let's go."

Ashley reaches for me again. "I'm trying to help you out here. You don't know the full story."

Taking a wild stab in the dark, I figure this is Logan's ex from high school. The one Jigsaw supposedly lost his virginity to a few weeks after she and Logan broke up. "I'm not interested in petty high school bullshit, sweetheart. You need to get over it and move on."

"No, honey." Her lips curl into a cruel smirk. "You're the one who doesn't understand."

"Ashley?" The shock and devastation in Rooster's voice tears me away from the girl.

Eyes wide and jaw slack, Logan stares at the girl, slowing his steps. He slides his tongue over his lip. A nervous gesture I've never seen him do before.

That slight movement unnerves me more than anything else about this encounter.

Something about her has him rattled.

The man who handles seven hundred pounds of machinery with ease.

He's waded into rivers to save me.

He's gone toe-to-toe with FBI agents.

He's jumped into bar fights to rescue me.

He's utterly fearless.

The man who wears his motorcycle club's cut with pride and doesn't give a fuck what anyone thinks of him.

I shift my gaze to the girl again.

This hundred-and-twenty-pound bag of hair worries him.

Why?

Rooster stops next to me, strong and steady. His calm mask has slipped into place. Almost as if I imagined the glimmer of fear.

"What the fuck are you doing here?" he rumbles, low and ferocious.

As if he hadn't even spoken, Ashley doesn't take her eyes off me. "This guy. Your *white knight*," she rolls her eyes, "is lying to you."

"Horse feathers." My whole body's shaking. With fear or anger, I can't tell. "You don't know the first damn thing about us."

"Well, I know one thing." She finally slides her gaze to Rooster. A bitter smile twists her pretty face. "His name isn't Logan *Randall*."

Rooster and Shelby's story will conclude in Diamond in the Dust (Lost Kings MC #18)

THE LOST KINGS MC® WORLD

By Autumn Jones Lake

Suggested Chronological Reading Order

1. Kickstart My Heart (Hollywood Demons #1)
2. Blow My Fuse (Hollywood Demons #2)
3. Wheels of Fire (Hollywood Demons #3)
4. Cards of Love: Knight of Swords
5. Slow Burn (Lost Kings MC #1)
6. Corrupting Cinderella (Lost Kings MC #2)
7. Three Kings, One Night (Lost Kings MC #2.5)
8. Strength From Loyalty (Lost Kings MC #3)
9. Tattered on My Sleeve (Lost Kings MC #4)
10. White Heat (Lost Kings MC #5)
11. Between Embers (Lost Kings MC #5.5)
12. Bullets & Bonfires (Standalone in the Lost Kings MC world)
13. More Than Miles (Lost Kings MC #6)
14. Warnings & Wildfires (Standalone in the Lost Kings MC world)
15. White Knuckles (Lost Kings MC #7)
16. Beyond Reckless (Lost Kings MC #8)
17. Beyond Reason (Lost Kings MC #9)
18. One Empire Night (Lost Kings MC #9.5)

19. After Burn (Lost Kings MC #10)
20. After Glow (Lost Kings MC #11)
21. Zero Hour (Lost Kings MC #11.5)
22. Zero Tolerance (Lost Kings MC #12)
23. Zero Regret (Lost Kings MC #13)
24. Zero Apologies (Lost Kings MC #14)
25. Swagger and Sass (Lost Kings MC #14.5)
26. White Lies (Lost Kings MC #15)
27. Rhythm of the Road (Lost Kings MC #16)
28. Lyrics on the Wind (Lost Kings MC #17)
29. Diamond in the Dust (Lost Kings MC #18)
30. Crown of Ghosts (Lost Kings MC #19)

ABOUT THE AUTHOR

Autumn Jones Lake is the *USA Today* and *Wall Street Journal* bestselling author of over twenty novels, including the popular Lost Kings MC series. She believes true love stories never end.

Her past lives include baking cookies, bagging groceries, selling cheap shoes, and practicing law. Playing with her imaginary friends all day is by far her favorite job yet!

Autumn lives in upstate New York with her own alpha hero.

www.autumnjoneslake.com

facebook.com/autumnjoneslake
goodreads.com/autumnjoneslake
pinterest.com/autumnjoneslake

Flocking
Fabulous

www.ingramcontent.com/pod-product-compliance
Lightning Source LLC
LaVergne TN
LVHW020039110826
845155LV00029B/558

* 9 7 8 1 9 4 3 9 5 0 6 6 9 *